B000 000 007 6597
ABERDEEN LIBRARIES

The Best of Daughters

Also by Dilly Court

Mermaids Singing

Born into poverty and living under the roof of her violent and abusive brother-in-law, young Kitty Cox dreams of working in a women's dress shop in the West End.

The Dollmaker's Daughters

For Ruby and Rosetta Capretti, life in the slums of the East End holds little promise. Despite their humble background, Rosetta is determined to work under the bright lights of the music hall and Ruby longs to train as a nurse.

Tilly True

Dismissed from her position as housemaid under a cloud of misunderstanding, Tilly True is forced to return home.

The Best of Sisters

Twelve-year-old Eliza Bragg has known little in life but the cold, comfortless banks of the Thames, her only comfort the love and protection of her older brother, Bart.

The Cockney Sparrow

Gifted with a beautiful soprano voice, young Clemency Skinner is forced to work as a pickpocket in order to support her crippled brother, Jack.

A Mother's Courage

When Eloise Cribb receives the news that her husband's ship has been lost at sea she wonders how she and her children are ever going to manage.

The Constant Heart

Despite living by the side of the Thames, eighteen-year-old Rosina May has wanted for little in life. Until her father's feud with a fellow bargeman threatens to destroy everything.

A Mother's Promise

When Hetty Huggins made a promise to her dying mother that she would look after her younger sister and brothers, little did she know how difficult this would be.

The Cockney Angel

Eighteen-year-old Irene Angel lives with her parents in a tiny room above the shop where her mother ekes out a living selling pickles and sauces, whilst her father gambles away what little money they do manage to earn.

A Mother's Wish

Since the untimely death of her husband, young mother Effie Grey has been forced to live on a narrowboat owned by her tyrannical father-in-law Jacob.

The Ragged Heiress

On a bitter winter's day, an unnamed girl lies dangerously ill in hospital. When two coarse, rough-speaking individuals come to claim her, she can remember nothing.

A Mother's Secret

When seventeen-year-old Belinda Phillips discovers that she is pregnant, she has no option other than to accept an arranged marriage, and give up her child forever.

Cinderella Sister

With their father dead and their mother a stranger to them, Lily Larkin must stay at home and keep house whilst her brothers and sisters go out to work.

A Mother's Trust

When her feckless mother falls dangerously ill, Phoebe Giamatti is forced to turn to the man she holds responsible for all her family's troubles.

The Lady's Maid

Despite the differences in their circumstances, Kate and Josie have been friends since childhood. But their past binds them together in ways they must never know.

Dilly Court

The Best of Daughters

arrow books

Published by Arrow Books 2012

2 4 6 8 10 9 7 5 3 1

First published in Great Britain in 2012 by
Arrow Books
Random House, 20 Vauxhall Bridge Road,
London SW1V 2SA

www.randomhouse.co.uk

Addresses for companies within The Random House Group Limited can be found at:
www.randomhouse.co.uk/offices.htm

The Random House Group Limited Reg. No. 954009

A CIP catalogue record for this book
is available from the British Library

ISBN 9780099562573

The Random House Group Limited supports The Forest Stewardship Council (FSC®), the leading international forest certification organisation. Our books carrying the FSC label are printed on FSC® certified paper. FSC is the only forest certification scheme endorsed by the leading environmental organisations, including Greenpeace. Our paper procurement policy can be found at
www.randomhouse.co.uk/environment

Typeset in Palatino by Palimpsest Book Production Limited,
Falkirk, Stirlingshire
Printed and bound by CPI Group (UK) Ltd, Croydon, CR0 4YY

In fondest memory of Archie, faithful friend.

Beauty without Vanity,
Strength without Insolence,
Courage without Ferocity,
And all the Virtues of Man without his Vices.

'Epitaph to a Dog', Lord Byron

Acknowledgements

Until I read Janet Lee's excellent book *War Girl: The First Aid Nursing Yeomanry in the First World War*, published by Manchester University Press, I knew nothing about the FANYs and their selfless courage and feats of bravery.

The amount of research that this author has done is incredible, and she tells the heroic story of these brave women in such an interesting manner that it captures the imagination from start to finish.

The characters in my story are, of course, fictional, but the details of the FANYs selfless work are as accurate as I could make them, and I hope I have done them justice.

Chapter One

Warwick Square, Pimlico, London 1912

In her frantic dash to escape the police Daisy had lost her hat and broken a heel off one of her shoes. She crept into the house, tucking her purple, white and green suffragette sash into her handbag. Closing the door quietly behind her, she tiptoed across the marble-tiled entrance hall. She paused for a moment to check her appearance in one of the many gilt-framed mirrors that were to be found throughout the house. These splendid examples of the rococo style were a testament to her father's love of light and space and her mother's innate vanity. She made a futile attempt to tidy her long dark hair, but she had lost most of the pins in the headlong flight from the scene of the crime, which had been both frantic and undignified.

She had only narrowly escaped being arrested by the police, who had appeared in force as her fellow suffragettes hurled stones and bricks through shop windows in Oxford Street. She herself had thrown several but to little effect. How Teddy would laugh. Her brother had always teased her about her pathetic attempts at overarm bowling when they played cricket in the garden of Rainbow's End, their holiday retreat in rural Essex. But Teddy would not be amused by her efforts today. Like most men of her acquaintance he had no sympathy with the movement, and her father was even more entrenched in his attitude.

She turned with a start at the sound of footsteps on the stairs but she breathed a sigh of relief when she saw that it was her younger sister. It would have been a different matter if Mother had come upon her in such a sorry state.

'Good heavens, Daisy. You look as though you've been dragged through a hedge backwards.' Beatrice paused with one hand on the curved mahogany banister rail. 'What on earth have you been doing?'

Daisy put her finger to her lips. 'Not so loud. I don't want anyone to see me like this.'

'Then you'd better go upstairs and change. Mother is entertaining some of her cronies in the drawing room, and she wanted you to join them ages ago.'

'Oh, no. You didn't tell her where I'd gone, did you?'

'I couldn't very well, because I didn't know.' Beatrice jumped the last two steps. 'I love doing that,' she said, chuckling. 'Nanny Harris used to tell me off if she caught me doing anything so inelegant.'

Momentarily forgetting that she was a wanted woman Daisy smiled. 'You'll never grow up to be a young lady, Beatrice,' she said in a fair imitation of their former nanny's voice. 'You're fifteen, not five.'

'And you won't get anywhere by changing the subject.' Beatrice angled her head. 'You've torn your skirt and broken the heel off your shoe. Have you been in a fight?'

Daisy hurried past her, heading for the stairs. 'I'm going to my room.'

'You've been with them, haven't you?' Beatrice followed, tugging at her sleeve. 'Don't run away from me, because I'm not giving up until you tell me everything.'

As she reached the first floor landing, Daisy glanced anxiously over her shoulder. Any minute now their mother would emerge from the drawing room to investigate. Mother had ears like a bat, and a nose for trouble. 'All right,' she said in a low voice. 'Come to my room, but for heaven's sake keep your voice down.' She ascended the next flight of stairs, limping slightly as she compensated for the lost heel on her right shoe.

On the second floor, in the sanctity of her blue and white bedroom, Daisy tossed her handbag onto the button-back chair upholstered in toile de Jouy, a theme repeated in the matching wallpaper and curtains. She slipped off her navy-blue linen coat, noting with a frown that several of the buttons were missing, which must have happened when a burly police officer made a grab for her. It would be difficult to explain that away if it came to her mother's notice.

'Well, I'm waiting.' Beatrice flung herself down on the bed, folding her arms across her chest as if prepared to remain there until her sister broke down and confessed all.

Daisy took her shoes off and examined the broken heel. 'I hope the cobbler can fix it. This was a new pair and ridiculously expensive.'

'Never mind the silly old shoe. Tell me what happened.'

'We were demonstrating in Oxford Street, if you must know. Then the police arrived and some of the women were arrested, but I managed to make a dash for it and jumped on a bus.'

'Looks like you had a tussle with someone. Was he handsome?'

'Don't be silly, Bea. I'll be in terrible trouble if Father finds out.'

'It'll be all over the front pages of the newspapers by morning,' Beatrice said, grinning. 'I wonder if there'll be photos too.'

'Oh, God! I hope not.' Daisy shivered as she stripped off her cream shantung afternoon gown. The hem was torn where she had snagged it with her heel as she leapt onto the bus. It would need some skill to make a repair invisible to Mother's eagle eye, and the dress was almost new. Daisy sighed. She had spent almost all her clothes allowance and she dare not ask Father for more.

'You'll be infamous,' Beatrice said smugly. 'The Honourable Rupert won't pop the question if he finds out that you're a suffragette.'

Daisy opened the wardrobe and took out the first gown that came to hand. It was a shade of reseda that she did not particularly like, but it complemented her green eyes, or so she had been told on numerous occasions by ardent admirers. She slipped the cool silk over her head. 'Do me up, please, Bea.'

Obligingly Beatrice jumped up and tugged the material together. 'Breathe in.'

'Ouch. You pinched me.'

'You're such a sissy. How would you get on if you had to go to prison and be force-fed?'

'I'm not that brave. I support the cause with all my heart, but I'm a dreadful coward when it comes to violence of any sort.'

'I think I'd be terribly courageous,' Beatrice said dreamily. 'I'd be a real heroine, if only I believed in all that stuff, which I don't.'

Daisy twisted her head round to stare at her in amazement. 'Don't you want women to get the vote?'

'I don't really care one way or the other. Politics is boring, and politicians are ugly old men with beards and dull voices.' She gave Daisy a gentle push. 'There you are, all done up. Perhaps you'd better go and see what Mother wants. It's probably something to do with your birthday party.'

Daisy hurried to the dressing table and picked up a hairbrush. 'I'm heartily sick of the whole thing. I'd much rather have a quiet family dinner than a big do for my twenty-first.' She began brushing her hair, wincing as the bristles became caught in the thick tangle of dark curls.

Beatrice moved swiftly to take the brush from her. 'Let me do it. You're all fingers and thumbs. Perhaps it's the shock of coming so close to being arrested. What would Father say if he had to go to a police station and bail you out?'

'Don't,' Daisy groaned. 'I can't bear to think of it.'

'Well, dear, if you will live dangerously, you must face the consequences.' Beatrice coiled her sister's hair into an elegant chignon at the nape of her neck, fixing it with hairpins and a tortoiseshell comb. 'How's that? Aren't I a clever girl?' She snatched a silver-backed mirror from the dressing table and held it so that Daisy could see the full effect of her coiffure.

'Yes,' Daisy said, smiling. 'You would make a wonderful lady's maid.'

Beatrice replaced the mirror with a thud. 'If I were a fugitive from the law like you, I'd be careful not to annoy my sister in case she decided to turn me in.'

'You wouldn't really.' Daisy rose from the stool and gave her a hug.

'It all depends upon how I'm treated. Be nice to me, or I'll tell Mother, and that would be a thousand times more frightening than ending up in Bow Street.'

'I suppose I'd better go downstairs and face the inquisition.' Checking her appearance in the cheval mirror, Daisy frowned. 'I look a bit peaky. Do you think they'll notice?'

Beatrice shook her head. 'It doesn't matter if they do. Mother and her generation are so old-fashioned. They think that having a pale complexion is the sign of a true lady.'

Daisy squared her shoulders, taking a deep breath. 'Wish me luck, Bea.'

'Where have you been all afternoon, Daisy?' Gwendoline demanded, looking her daughter up and down with a disapproving frown.

'I went shopping, Mother.' Daisy cast a surreptitious glance at her mother's friends but they kept their eyes tactfully averted, sipping their tea or nibbling daintily on slices of seed cake.

'It's a pity that you didn't consult me first, Daisy. You

are so thoughtless.' Sunbeams slanted in through the tall windows, tinting Gwendoline's golden hair with playful highlights. She sat erect like a queen granting an audience to her subjects, or, Daisy thought ruefully, like a judge about to pronounce the death sentence. At the age of forty-five Gwendoline Lennox was still a handsome woman who had kept her figure by rigorous attention to the teachings of Dr Banting. She ruled her family with an iron hand in a chain mail glove. Outward shows of affection were alien to her nature and she did not believe in spoiling her children. She did, however, take her position as the wife of a wealthy stockbroker very seriously indeed. Patroness of several charitable institutions, Gwendoline did her duty to the poor and needy.

'I'm sorry, Mother.' Daisy shifted from one foot to the other. She could feel an undercurrent of sympathy emanating from her audience, but she would have been surprised had any one of them been brave enough to speak up for her.

'I should think so too.' Gwendoline turned to the woman seated next to her on the sofa. 'More tea, Jane?'

'No, thank you. One cup is quite sufficient.' Lady Pendleton smiled and patted the vacant space beside her. 'Did you buy anything nice, Daisy dear? Do sit down and tell us.'

Daisy sank down on the sofa, stifling a sigh of relief. Lady Pendleton was one of her mother's oldest friends and the Honourable Rupert, as Bea insisted on calling him, was her son. It was an open secret that the matriarchs were united in their ambition to arrange a match between Rupert and Daisy. The problem was that although Daisy liked him well enough, she thought of him simply as Teddy's best friend. They had played together as children but then the boys had gone away to boarding school, followed by university, and now Rupert was just about to complete his officer training at Sandhurst, while Teddy, somewhat reluctantly, was a junior clerk in their father's office in the City. She turned with a start as she realised that Lady Pendleton was speaking to her. 'Was it something to wear at your birthday party, Daisy?'

'It wasn't anything very interesting, Lady Pendleton. I needed some stockings and some embroidery silk.'

'And that took you all afternoon?' Gwendoline did not look convinced.

'I expect the dear girl was window shopping.' Mrs Harper-Colton, a plump middle-aged widow with a kindly disposition, smiled at Daisy from the sofa on the far side of the imposing Carrara marble fireplace.

Her companion, Miss Spruce, a genteelly poor spinster, nodded her head in agreement. 'I can spend hours just looking in the windows of the department stores, especially Selfridge's. And sometimes I go inside, not intending to purchase anything you understand, because I never wear rouge or anything like that, and anyway my limited means does not allow me to indulge in luxuries, but I simply love to breathe in the glorious scents in the perfume department.' She paused for breath, blushing and staring down at the cup and saucer clutched in her hands. 'I'm sorry. Once I start chattering I find it hard to stop.'

'Indeed you do, Lavinia,' Mrs Harper-Colton said

with a wry smile. 'You chatter more than all three of my girls put together.'

'You must miss them terribly now that they're all married with homes of their own,' Lady Pendleton said sympathetically.

'At least they all found suitable husbands and were off your hands before they reached their majority.' Gwendoline aimed a meaningful glance at her daughter.

Daisy sighed inwardly and remained silent. Mother would never let her forget the fact that the Harper-Colton girls, all gangly, toothy and with not a brain between them, had achieved what every ambitious matron wanted for their female progeny. Each one of them had snared a wealthy husband who could keep her in comfort for the rest of her life. It was an inescapable fact that she was expected to follow suit, and to do it before she was considered to be officially on the shelf. No one seemed to give her credit for being able to think for herself, and both her parents would be utterly horrified if they knew that she supported the Women's Social and Political Union. Even now she could hear the screams and cries of protest from the women as the police descended upon them with truncheons at the ready. There had been no quarter given and probably none had been expected by the seasoned suffragettes. It was the first time that Daisy had been subjected to the violence of such a demonstration, and she was still shocked and shaken by the scenes she had witnessed.

'Pay attention, Daisy,' Gwendoline said crossly. 'It's your party that we're discussing. You might pretend to be interested.'

Jolted back to the present, Daisy attempted a smile. 'I'm sorry, Mother. I was miles away.'

'That was quite obvious. Perhaps you'd better leave us to make the final arrangements, since you don't seem to care one way or the other.'

Everyone was looking at her and Daisy felt the blood rushing to her cheeks. 'I do care, Mother. I'm sorry, what were you saying?'

'I was simply enquiring if you had any preference as to the floral arrangements on our tables in the private dining room at the Hotel Cecil. I have to give the final decision by tomorrow morning at the latest so that the florist can order the appropriate blooms and foliage. Jane and I have decided on gardenias, freesias and roses with sprays of stephanotis and a mist of gypsophila.'

'That sounds lovely.'

Gwendoline sighed heavily. 'You'd say the same if I suggested dandelions and buttercups. You should think you're very fortunate to have a father who is prepared to indulge you in this way.'

'I do, Mother. I am grateful, and I appreciate all the trouble that everyone is going to on my behalf.' Daisy paused, glancing from one face to the other. She could see doubt and scepticism on each one, except for Miss Spruce who merely looked confused.

Lady Pendleton placed her arm around Daisy's shoulders and gave her a hug. 'I expect it's all a bit overwhelming for a self-effacing girl like you, my dear. But rest assured, Rupert will be there to make sure you have a wonderful time. He's such a dear boy, and he's very fond of you. I'm sure he already thinks of himself as one of the family.'

'I'm certain that my daughter feels the same way.' Gwendoline paused, as if waiting for Daisy to agree, but when no response was forthcoming her smile faded. 'What do you say, Daisy?'

She could stand it no longer. Daisy rose to her feet. 'Actually I have an awful headache. Would you mind if I went to my room, Mother?'

'Poor dear.' Lady Pendleton smiled up at her. 'Too much excitement is bad for one. You should lie down and rest.'

Mrs Harper-Colton nodded wisely. 'And a cold compress is always efficacious.'

'A cup of camomile tea always helps to soothe my nerves,' Miss Spruce added eagerly. 'Especially when taken at bedtime.'

'Go then,' Gwendoline said with a dismissive wave of her hand. 'Do what you always do and leave me to make all the arrangements.'

Daisy did not try to defend herself. By this time her head really had started to ache miserably, and she was certain that she had an enormous bruise on her shin where someone had accidentally kicked her during their rush to escape arrest. She hurried from the room and went upstairs to lie on her bed until the dinner gong sounded.

She was half asleep when it summoned the family to dinner. She roused herself with difficulty and rose from her bed. She was stiff and sore, but at least her head had stopped aching. She filled the willow-pattern bowl on the washstand and splashed her face with cold water. Feeling slightly more alert, she changed her dress for the third time that day before taking a seat at the dressing table. She tidied her hair and added a dab of face powder and just a hint of rouge to complete her toilette. Satisfied that she looked reasonably presentable she stood up, shaking out the creases in her blue crêpe de Chine dinner gown.

She made her way downstairs, but just as she was about to enter the dining room she was startled by the jangling of the doorbell. She hesitated, waiting for Betsy to come rushing up from the basement kitchen, but the bell rang again and there was no sign of the maid. Thinking that it was probably Teddy, who was always losing his key, Daisy went to open the door. But it was not her brother who stood on the step; it was one of the suffragettes, a young girl from south of the river. Daisy had met her when they had been put in charge of the tea urn at one of the Women's Social and Political Union meetings, and she had seen her earlier that day in Oxford Street. 'Hello, Ruby. What can I do for you?'

'I come to ask you a favour, miss.'

'You came all this way to see me? It must be something very important.' Daisy glanced over her shoulder as she heard footsteps behind her, but it was only the parlour maid, who had come to a halt outside the dining room with a large soup tureen clutched in her hands.

'Sorry, Miss Daisy. I couldn't see to the door and fetch the soup at the same time.'

'It's all right,' Daisy said calmly. 'I'll deal with this, Betsy.' She turned back to Ruby. 'What do you want?

I'm afraid I can't ask you in. As you can see, we're about to dine.'

'I can see that, miss. It's just that I got instructions to do something.' She winked and tapped the side of her nose. 'It's top secret, but after what happened today I don't feel as how I can face it on me own. They're going to do something really shocking. We might get locked up in the Tower for it.'

Daisy stared at her, trying to decide whether this was some elaborate joke, but then the suffragists were always deadly serious, and she could see that Ruby was in earnest. 'Why me, Ruby?'

'Because you've got a kind face, miss. You talk to me like I was your equal. Some of them what demand equality with men don't seem to think it applies to us poor working girls.'

'I'm sure that's not true,' Daisy said, although she knew that it was. The class system was rigid, even in a movement dedicated to women's rights. 'What is it that we have to do?'

Ruby glanced round nervously as if expecting to see a policeman on every street corner. 'Meet me outside Buckingham Palace tomorrow midday. There'll be others present but I'd feel so much better if you was at my side, miss.'

Daisy was trying to think of a suitable response when a hansom cab pulled up at the kerb and Teddy leapt out. 'All right, Ruby,' she said hastily. 'I'll be there, but you must go now.'

A wide grin almost split Ruby's snub-nosed features in half. She took Daisy's hand and shook it vigorously.

'Ta, miss. You're a toff. I knew you wouldn't let me down. If we get arrested I know you'll take care of me.' She bounded down the steps, almost cannoning into Teddy who stood aside, staring at her in astonishment.

He took the steps two at a time. 'Who on earth was that funny little creature, Daisy? What did she want?'

'Nothing. She was just asking the way. She was lost.'

'I'll say she was. Lucky for her that Mother didn't see her. She'd have sent her away with a flea in her ear. She wouldn't want the neighbours to think that we associate with that class of person.' He pulled a face, kissed her on the cheek and breezed into the house, tossing his bowler hat onto the hallstand. 'I hope I'm not late for dinner. I'm absolutely famished.'

'You're late, Teddy.' Victor Lennox glared at his son over the top of his gold-rimmed pince-nez. 'And you too, Daisy. Whatever happened to manners?'

'Sorry, Father.' Teddy took his seat at table. 'Had to stay behind at the last minute. Wretched fellow on the telephone went on and on. I thought he'd never stop gassing.'

Victor frowned. 'That's no way to speak about a client, Teddy. I hope you treated him with due respect.'

'I'll say I did,' Teddy said, making a quick recovery. 'I'm always the soul of tact and diplomacy.'

'That's enough, Teddy.' Gwendoline placed her soup spoon at a precise right angle on her empty plate. 'No business talk at the table, please.' She focused her attention on Daisy. 'And what is your excuse for being late? Another sick headache?'

Daisy had been trying to make herself as inconspicuous as possible, which was difficult as Beatrice was pulling faces at her behind her starched linen table napkin, but now all eyes turned in her direction. She crumbled a piece of bread roll between her fingers, playing for time while she thought up a convincing reply. 'The doorbell rang, Mother. The servants were busy serving dinner and so I answered it myself.'

Gwendoline uttered an exasperated sigh. 'You ought to know better, Daisy. What would people think if they had seen you? Why do you think we employ servants?'

'They cost us enough in wages,' Victor said drily.

Ignoring her husband's caustic remark Gwendoline glared at her daughter. 'And who, may I ask, was calling at such an inconvenient hour?'

'It was just a young person asking for directions.' Daisy popped a piece of bread into her mouth, hoping that this was the end of the interrogation.

'That's true,' Teddy said earnestly. 'Dashed pretty little thing, but no dress sense. She looked as though she'd bought her outfit at a jumble sale.'

'Trust you to notice what she was wearing.' Beatrice giggled. 'But she took your fancy all the same. You're turning into quite a ladies' man.'

Gwendoline glowered at her. 'That's enough. Eat your meal, Beatrice.'

'That's an interesting point, Mother,' Beatrice said innocently. 'Technically do you eat soup, or drink it?'

'Don't be silly.' Gwendoline turned her attention once again to her elder daughter. 'Don't forget to pick up your gown for the party tomorrow. I'd do it myself but you'll need to have a final fitting, just to make sure it's perfect. I don't want to give Emily Harper-Colton the chance to gloat because her girls have all found rich husbands, and you're still unmarried at twenty-one and perilously close to ending up an old maid.'

Victor cleared his throat. 'I say, hold on, old girl. That was uncalled for. Daisy is taking her time. She doesn't want to accept the first chap who offers for her.'

'She's waiting for Rupert to come up to scratch and then she'll turn him down,' Beatrice said slyly.

'That's not true. There's nothing remotely romantic between Rupert and me.' Daisy raised her chin, meeting her mother's cold gaze stare for stare. 'And I'm afraid I can't go to the dressmaker's tomorrow morning. I have a prior engagement.'

'Then you will break it, Daisy. I won't have my arrangements upset because you are a stubborn and ungrateful daughter. You will collect your gown and it will be perfect or I'll want to know the reason why. This party is costing your father a great deal of money, and everything will be just so.'

'A great deal of money,' Victor repeated, nodding his head. 'Your mother is pinning all her hopes on this event, Daisy. If you don't end the evening engaged to at least two eligible young men she'll think that the whole colossally expensive affair has been a fiasco.'

The fitting seemed to be taking forever. Daisy had put the wretched gown on several times and suffered the dressmaker's assistant sticking pins into her tender flesh without protest, but the hands on the clock moved slowly but inexorably towards midday. 'Is this going to take much longer?' she enquired, trying hard not to sound too impatient as the dressmaker returned, her arms filled with beaded chiffon. 'You see I have a luncheon appointment at twelve.'

'I'm afraid I've had to take the garment in at least half an inch, Miss Lennox, but it's finished now. Would you like to try it on again just to make certain?'

Daisy shook her head. 'No. I'm sure it will be absolutely fine. Thank you.'

Minutes later she was outside on the pavement hailing a taxicab. 'Buckingham Palace, please.'

The cabby grinned. 'Going to lunch with royalty, miss?'

She smiled, shaking her head. 'Not today.' She opened the door and climbed in, placing the box and her parasol on the seat beside her, but the cabby did not seem in a hurry to pull away.

He turned his head, eyeing her curiously. 'You ain't planning on joining them mad women, are you, miss?'

'I don't know what you're talking about,' she said, staring straight ahead. 'Drive on, please. I'm late as it is.'

'I've already taken a few of them there. You don't look like the kind of young lady who ought to be associating with that sort of person.' He waited for a few seconds and when she chose to ignore his comments he drove off, muttering something unintelligible beneath his breath.

A large crowd had gathered outside the palace, and Daisy's stomach lurched as she saw a contingent of mounted officers controlling the onlookers while policemen on foot were attempting to deal with the women who had chained themselves to the railings. She was almost deafened by the noise as she stepped out of the cab with her parasol clutched tightly in her hand. Men were shouting and women were screaming insults at them or chanting their slogan *Deeds Not Words*. The clattering of horses' hooves and the rumble of traffic only added to the general din and confusion.

The cabby leaned out of the window. 'Ain't you got a home to go to, young lady? I've a daughter about your age and I wouldn't want her to be mixed up with this lot.'

She hesitated, torn between the desire to retreat into the comforting anonymity of the cab and the urgent need to support the cause. Her heart was pounding against the confines of her stays, and her knees threatened to give way beneath her. If only she were not such a coward. At this moment she hated herself.

'Make your mind up, love. I got a living to make.' The cabby's lined face creased into even deeper furrows as he fixed her with a hard stare. 'You'll end up in the clink if you ain't careful, ducks.'

She took a deep breath. She must not let the brave suffragettes down. She thrust a half-crown into his hand, and at that moment she spotted Ruby being hauled from the railings by a burly police constable. Even at a distance, Daisy could see the girl's mouth opened in a scream as he hit her with his truncheon. Forgetting everything, she raced to her aid.

Chapter Two

Handcuffed to a young police constable, Daisy came face to face with the law in Bow Street police station. The sergeant seated behind the desk wore an expression of barely controlled irritation. He was assisted by an equally harassed-looking junior officer as they took the names and addresses of the women who had been arrested outside the palace. Ruby was protesting loudly but some of the younger suffragettes were visibly upset and openly weeping. Daisy was too stunned to say anything. After a bone-rattling ride to Bow Street in the confines of the horse-drawn Black Maria, she had tried to recall the precise course of events that had led to her arrest, but all she could remember was hitting the constable with her tightly furled parasol and knocking his helmet off. She had known then that she was in deep trouble.

'Next.'

She was not dreaming: this was a living nightmare. She was standing in front of the desk, looking up into the face of a man who quite obviously had little sympathy for women's suffrage.

'Name?' He glared at her, pen poised.

The full impact of what she had done hit her with the force of a tidal wave. What would her parents say when they discovered that their elder daughter was a common criminal? She wished that she could faint away like the young woman who had been standing to the left of her, but she realised now that she was made of sterner stuff. She was scared, worried and also angry. She gave her name and address in a clear, calm voice, but inwardly she was seething.

'Take her to the cells, constable.'

Daisy stared at him in disbelief. 'You're locking me up? But I haven't done anything wrong.'

'That's for the magistrate to decide, miss. Think yourself lucky that you'll be in court this afternoon and won't have to spend the night in custody.'

Custody. The word sent icy chills down her spine. She was being sent to a cell like any other felon. 'Please, sergeant. May I get word to my father?'

'This ain't the Ritz, miss. Take her away, constable.'

She opened her mouth to protest but a tug on her wrist was a painful reminder that handcuffs were made of cold steel and she had no choice other than to follow the police officer. They came to a halt at the end of a long, narrow corridor. 'Please will you do one small thing for me, constable?' she asked, clutching his sleeve. 'I'll be in terrible trouble at home when they find out what I've done.' He hesitated, but she could see a flicker of sympathy in his eyes, and she pressed on without giving him a chance to refuse. 'Please telephone my father's office and tell him where I am. This is all a dreadful mistake.'

'They all say that, miss.' He unlocked the handcuffs.

'Lennox and Carlton, stockbrokers in the City. If you would just lend me your pencil and notebook I'll write the number down.'

'It's against all the rules, miss.'

She was quick to hear a hint of hesitation in his voice and she forced her dry lips into a smile. 'Have you got a sister, constable?'

He clipped the handcuffs to his belt. 'Yes, miss.'

'Then I beg of you to think how you would feel if she were in similar circumstances.' She held his gaze, pleading silently, and was rewarded with a reluctant grin.

He handed her his notebook and pencil. 'Not a word to anyone, miss.'

She wrote the telephone number on the pad and returned it to him. 'Thank you so much. He'll see to it that you are recompensed for your trouble.'

He opened the cell door. 'In you go, miss.'

She found herself in a small, windowless room filled with angry women. Ruby pushed her way through the crowd and came to stand by her side. 'Bastards,' she shouted as the door closed and the key grated in the lock. She slipped her hand through the crook of Daisy's arm. 'Never mind, ducks. We won't let them beat us.'

Daisy rubbed her wrist where the metal had chafed her delicate skin. 'Beat us? Do you mean corporal punishment?'

'Gawd love us, don't you know nothing, miss? I mean we won't let them get us down.'

'My mother will be furious,' Daisy said, sighing. 'I

was supposed to be home hours ago.' A sudden thought made her go weak at the knees and she leaned against Ruby for support. 'Oh, my God!'

'What's up, miss? Are you sick or something?' Ruby pushed a plump, purple-clad woman out of the way. 'Shove over, love. I think she's going to pass out.'

With a supreme effort Daisy managed to regain control of her limbs. 'No, really. I'm all right, thank you.'

'Well, you've gone the colour of the walls in here and that ain't a pretty sight. What's up?'

'My ball gown. I left it in the taxicab.' Tears spilled down Daisy's cheeks. 'And they took my parasol.'

Ruby pursed her lips. 'If that's all you got to worry about, you're lucky.' Her expression softened and she patted Daisy's hand. 'Don't worry, ducks. They'll give it back to you after you've been up before the beak. That's if he lets us go.'

Momentarily forgetting her lost gown, Daisy was suddenly curious. She knew next to nothing about this tiny young person with a fiery temper and the pugnacity of a bulldog. 'How do you know all this, Ruby? Do you think we might be locked up?'

'It's a possibility, my dear.' The plump lady in the purple outfit shot her a pitying glance. 'This is obviously your first time.'

Daisy nodded dazedly. 'Yes.'

'I expect you'll get off with a slapped wrist then. I'm almost certain to be sent down as they say in the criminal underworld.'

'You've been in prison, ma'am?'

'Several times, but only for the cause. One can get used to almost anything.'

'I wish I were as brave as you,' Daisy said sincerely. 'May I ask your name?'

'Adela,' she replied, smiling. 'Adela Pankhurst.' She turned away as another woman claimed her attention.

Ruby leaned against the wall. 'Best settle down, miss. It looks like we're going to have a long wait.'

It was late afternoon before Daisy's name was called. The magistrate gave her a cursory glance as he listened to the case against her. 'What have you got to say for yourself, Miss Lennox?'

'I'm sorry, your worship.' She had not meant to sound weak and subservient but she was tired, hungry and frankly terrified. The talk in the holding cell had centred on the treatment the suffragettes received in prison, and it was enough to frighten the bravest of souls. The first-hand accounts of forced feeding and brutality had sickened her. She was sorry too. Sorry that her desire to protect Ruby had made her act in such a reckless manner. Until that moment she had never struck anyone in anger, at least not since she had reached maturity. Fights with Teddy when they were children did not count. But she did regret knocking the policeman's helmet off, and the parasol had been a Christmas gift from Rupert. Even if it was returned to her she suspected that it was beyond repair. She dragged herself back to the proceedings as the magistrate addressed himself to her, glaring as if he were speaking to a naughty child. 'You have acted wantonly and disgracefully, Miss Lennox. You are a young lady from a good family who ought to have known better. I cannot condone violence but as this is your first offence I am prepared to be lenient. Fined ten guineas and bound over to keep the peace for six months. If I see you in my court again you will incur a custodial sentence.'

She walked from the courtroom in a daze. Ten guineas was more than Betsy earned in a year.

'You're free to go, miss.' The court usher opened the door leading out into the main reception area.

'But I can't pay the fine.'

'It's been paid for you, miss.' The usher pointed to a tall young man in army uniform.

He was standing with his back to her, but she recognised him instantly. 'Rupert.' Daisy hurried towards him. 'You're the last person I expected to see.'

He turned at the sound of her voice and smiled. She heard a woman standing close to them utter a gasp of admiration, and even in her agitated state Daisy had to admit that her childhood friend had grown into a handsome man. The Honourable Rupert Pendleton with his fair hair, laughing blue eyes and classic features was every young girl's dream of a hero; particularly so in his officer's uniform. He was tall, slim and his bearing exuded confidence and authority, tempered by a charming smile and a generous curve to his lips. He was what Bea would vulgarly call a 'good catch', especially for a girl whose pedigree was inferior to his own. Any mother from the upper middle class would be overjoyed if her daughter were to marry above her station in life, especially if the man in question was the son of a viscount. There was, as far as Daisy was concerned, one drawback. She did not love him. Rupert was like a brother to her.

He enveloped her in a hug. 'Are you all right, old girl?'

'I am now, Rupert. But how did you know I was here?'

'I happened to be visiting Teddy at the office when your tame police constable put the call through.'

'Does Father know?'

'Not yet, but he will when the petty cash doesn't balance at the end of the day. Teddy doesn't carry that much money on him, so he helped himself.'

'How did he know I was going to get a fine?'

Rupert slipped his arm around her shoulders. 'Put it this way, Daisy. Both of us have been in tight spots when we were at Cambridge. We've been up before the beak enough times to have a pretty fair idea of the penalties incurred for civil disorder, but to be on the safe side Teddy put a call through to your father's solicitor. He gave us a rough idea what to expect and I came galloping up on my white charger to save a maiden in distress. Let's get out of here.'

She shook her head. 'I've got to find out what happened to Ruby.'

'Who on earth is Ruby?'

'I'll explain later, but first I must ask the desk sergeant. You don't mind waiting for a moment, do you?'

'Would it make any difference if I did?'

She met his quizzical gaze with a smile. 'Thank you, Rupert. You always were a good sport.' She was about to tackle the gloomy desk sergeant when she caught sight of Ruby edging her way through the motley crowd of people who occupied the waiting area.

'I knew you'd forget it,' Ruby said breathlessly, thrusting the battered parasol into Daisy's hand. 'I had to go and claim it for you, so I said as how I was your personal maid. I hope you don't mind, miss.'

Daisy stared at the torn silk and broken ribs of the parasol, but suddenly it did not seem to matter. 'Thank you,' she murmured. 'That was really kind of you, Ruby. I was just about to make enquiries about you.'

'Lord love you, miss. I can take care of meself.'

'I'm sure you can.' Daisy did not quite believe her, but she was not about to argue. 'What happened in court?'

'Bound over to keep the peace. The beak could see that I ain't got two pennies to rub together, but I'll cop it next time if I get nicked.'

'You won't risk it again, will you? You heard what those women said about prison.'

'We can't give up now. That's what the men in charge want. They think we're little girls who must do what their dads tell them, or else. Well, I ain't for one. I want a say in what happens to me and my children in the future.'

Daisy glanced up at Rupert, wondering how much he had heard of Ruby's impassioned speech, and she was suddenly ashamed of her inclination to hurry home and forget all about women's suffrage. He met her anxious gaze with a smile. 'We've got a warrior princess here, Daisy. Boadicea would have been proud of her.'

'Are you laughing at me, guv?' Ruby glared at him with a belligerent lift of her chin. 'I just want what's right and proper.'

'Of course you do,' Daisy said, shooting a warning glance at Rupert. 'But on a more mundane note, how are you going to get home? Have you got the bus fare?'

'I got Shanks's pony, miss.'

Rupert linked his hand through Daisy's arm. 'We're going to get a taxicab to Pimlico and you're welcome to a lift that far, Miss— Sorry, I didn't quite catch your name.'

'Ruby Flagg, mister.'

'Where do you live, Miss Flagg?'

Ruby eyed him warily and then grinned, nudging Daisy in the ribs. 'He's a proper toff, ain't he?'

'Yes, he is, and you must allow us to see you safely home. Your family will begin to worry.'

'Me mum passed away ten years ago and me dad never sobers up enough to know what time of day it is, let alone who's in or out of the house. Anyway, I live in Vauxhall. You won't get a cabby to go south of the river. You'd think it was heaving with Red Indians armed with bows and arrows.'

'We'll see about that,' Rupert said firmly. 'Come along, ladies. The desk sergeant is glaring at us. I think we've outstayed our welcome.'

Despite their combined efforts to persuade Ruby otherwise, she insisted on being dropped off close to

Vauxhall Bridge and seemed determined to walk the rest of the way. Her parting words plunged Daisy into a state of panic. 'I hope your ball gown turns up, miss.'

Her hand flew to her mouth as she watched Ruby's small figure striding out purposefully towards the bridge. She had completely forgotten the gown. Now she would have to face her mother and be condemned as guilty on all counts.

'What on earth is the matter?' Rupert asked anxiously. 'What did she mean?'

Daisy hiccuped on a sob and the explanation tumbled from her lips amidst a flood of tears. The traumatic experiences of that day, coupled with the expense that her parents had incurred due to her folly, were all too much to bear. She would have died rather than let herself down in front of Rupert, but his kindness and understanding made it all the worse. He slipped an arm around her shoulders. 'Come on now, old thing. There must be some sort of lost property office that cabbies use.' He leaned forward and tapped on the glass. 'Could you tell me what happens to items that get left in taxicabs? Is there somewhere we could go to find this lady's box?'

The cabby shook his head. 'Can't help you, I'm afraid, guv. Where to now?'

'Warwick Square.' Rupert settled back on the seat. 'Chin up, Daisy. It's not the end of the world. I'm sure you'll look absolutely splendid whatever gown you wear for your party.'

She wiped her eyes on the back of her hand, sniffing. 'If I live that long. Mother is going to kill me.'

'I'll come in with you. She's always had a soft spot for me.'

'You're a man, and one day you'll inherit a stately home and a title. You can do no wrong in her eyes.'

'I'll do what I can, Daisy.' He squeezed her fingers. 'But perhaps you ought to think carefully about joining the WSPU.' He grinned. 'Don't look so surprised. I've read all about it in the newspapers, and some of the chaps at Sandhurst have mothers, sisters and even maiden aunts who are involved in the movement. But it's dangerous and I don't want to see you suffer for a hopeless cause.'

She snatched her hand away. 'Hopeless? Is that what you really think, Rupert? I had you down for an open-minded fellow, not a misogynistic ostrich with his head in the sand.'

His lips twitched. 'That's one thing I've never been called in the past, and I do think that women should have their say in how the country is run. I just don't think that violence is the way to go about it.'

'So says the man whose profession is to kill people.'

'That unfortunately is often the outcome, but I prefer to think that I'm protecting my country and those I love most in the whole world.' He patted her hand. 'Don't let's fall out, Daisy. I'm too fond of you to want us to be on opposing sides.'

She managed a watery smile. 'You always were a charmer.'

'And you were always covering up for us when Teddy and I had done something wrong. Now perhaps I can return the favour.'

'I don't remember that, but I'm very grateful for what you've done for me today, and you were very kind to Ruby. But for her I would have found it even harder to cope when they sent us to the cells.'

'You wouldn't have been in the cell if it weren't for her. You can't save the whole world, Daisy. You must look after yourself.'

She remained silent, preparing herself to face her mother's wrath as the cab drew up outside her house.

She entered the hall, handing her damaged parasol to Betsy. 'Is my mother at home?'

'Yes, miss. She's in the drawing room.'

Daisy caught sight of herself in one of the many mirrors. She was hatless again, having lost it somewhere close to Buckingham Palace, and her hair had come loose, curling in a dark cloud around her face. This was becoming a habit and she dared not put in an appearance looking less than immaculate. She turned to Rupert. 'You might have told me that I look a complete wreck.'

He handed his peaked cap and gloves to Betsy. 'You look fine to me, Daisy Bell.'

She frowned. 'Don't call me that.'

'You used to love that song.' He hummed a few bars of the popular tune, causing Betsy to stifle a giggle.

'Thank you, Betsy,' Daisy said stiffly. 'That will be all. No, wait a moment. We'd like tea and cake in the drawing room. I'm famished. What about you, Rupert?'

'That would be just the ticket.' He flashed a smile in Betsy's direction. 'And if Cook has made one of her delicious chocolate cakes, I would be her slave forever.'

'Oh, sir.' Covering her mouth with her hand, Betsy bobbed a curtsey and hurried off in the direction of the green baize door, which kept the two worlds neatly apart.

Daisy shook her head. 'You shouldn't tease the girl, Rupert.'

'You sound like my mother, Daisy Bell.'

She knew that he was trying to make her laugh, and he almost succeeded. 'Call me that silly name if you must, but only in private. I don't want Mother to get the wrong idea.'

He took her hand in his. 'We're good friends though, aren't we? You know you can always rely on me.'

'The best of friends,' she said, standing on tiptoe to kiss his cheek. 'And thank you for rescuing me today. But now you can do something else for me. Go and charm my mother while I make myself fit to be seen. Will you, please, Rupert?'

'Of course. I'll do anything for a slice of Mrs Myers's chocolate cake; you know that, my dear.'

'Wretch.' She pushed him away, chuckling. 'You always could make me laugh. Just work your magic on Mother. I won't be long.' She headed for the staircase and ascended with as much speed as was possible in her fashionable hobble skirt, making her way to her room.

It was a full twenty minutes before she felt presentable enough to face her mother. She was inwardly quaking but making a supreme effort to appear calm she strolled into the drawing room. The speech she had been rehearsing as she tidied her hair died on her lips. The tea tray was untouched on the table and her mother was seated on the sofa, ashen-faced and clearly upset. Racked with guilt, Daisy went to sit beside her. 'Mother, it isn't such a terrible thing. It will soon be forgotten.'

Gwendoline stared at her blankly.

'Daisy,' Rupert said softly. 'Mrs Lennox has had some rather bad news. I think perhaps it would be best if she told you about it herself.'

'Mother?'

'It's nothing that should concern you, Daisy. Don't fuss.' Gwendoline folded her hands tightly in her lap, shifting her position on the sofa so that she put a space between herself and her daughter.

At the best of times she did not encourage physical contact with her children, and Daisy could see that this was not the moment for an outward demonstration of affection. 'But what is it?' She looked to Rupert but he shook his head with a slight shrug of his shoulders.

Gwendoline rose to her feet and went to stand by the window, gazing out onto the square. 'It's to do with business, Daisy. Your father will sort it out in due course, I'm certain.'

She sounded anything but certain. Daisy bit her lip. She had been expecting trouble, but nothing had prepared her for this. She had never seen her mother in such an agitated state. It was alarming and apparently had nothing to do with her recent arrest. 'Is there anything I can do, Mother?'

Gwendoline turned on her with a scornful curl of

her lip. 'What would a silly girl like you know about business matters?'

Rupert rose to his feet. 'Perhaps I'd better go.'

'Yes, perhaps that would be best.' Gwendoline managed a tight-lipped smile. 'See him out, Daisy.'

There was nothing that Daisy could do other than to obey her mother's curt command. When they were safely out of earshot she caught Rupert by the sleeve. 'What on earth is going on? Why wouldn't she tell me anything?'

His expression was unusually grave. 'Your father's partner has absconded with a great deal of money. It's not common knowledge yet, and Mr Lennox is doing everything he can to save the company.'

'You knew about this?'

'Teddy told me everything.'

'And you kept it from me?'

'You had enough to cope with, Daisy. I was hoping that your parents would break it gently, but it appears that I was wrong.'

'Poor Father. He must be in a terrible state.'

He raised her hand to his lips. 'You mustn't worry. Mr Lennox is an astute businessman. I'm sure he will get to grips with the situation before it becomes a complete disaster.'

'I'm not a child, Rupert. I don't believe in fairies or Father Christmas.'

He smiled, touching her cheek with his fingertips. 'That spell in prison has turned you into a hard woman, Miss Lennox.'

It was her turn to chuckle. 'I was expecting to have

the riot act read to me, and I deserved it too. Father will discover that I've just cost him ten guineas and I've lost my ball gown, which must have set him back a small fortune.'

'There's just a slim chance it might have been returned to the dressmaker. Did she have her name on the box?'

Daisy shook her head. 'I don't think so, but it might be on the inside of the lid. I've never really looked.'

'Then we'll go and find out.'

'Now? But I should stay with Mother.'

'My dear Daisy Bell, you never could hide your feelings or tell a convincing lie. Ten minutes in your mother's company and you'll have confessed everything and she'll be even more distraught than she is now.'

'All right, I'll come, but I haven't got the taxi fare.'

'Then it's fortunate that I have.' Rupert headed towards the staircase. 'Come along. Don't dawdle or the woman might have closed up for the night.'

Ensconced this time in a hansom cab, Daisy sat back and watched the city streets flash past. 'It seems as though I've spent the whole day racketing around London,' she said with a wry smile. 'And all the while my poor father has been striving to avert a catastrophe. I've been so wrapped up in battling for women's rights that I've neglected my family. I should have realised that something was wrong.'

'And done precisely what, Daisy? You weren't to know what was happening in the city, and there was precious little you could have done anyway.'

She turned to look him in the eyes. 'Did Teddy know?'

'He must have had an inkling but he didn't mention it until today. Perhaps your father kept it from him too, so you see you mustn't feel guilty.'

'It's awful being treated like a child. I wouldn't have agreed to this wretched party at the Cecil had I known. There are people starving and women being locked up and maltreated for their beliefs, and here am I making you race round London looking for a damned ball gown.'

He threw back his head and laughed. 'To tell you the truth, I'm enjoying myself immensely. All we need, Daisy Bell, is a bicycle made for two.'

She nudged him in the ribs. 'Stop it, Rupert. I'm baring my soul to you and all you can do is quote that ridiculous song at me.'

'But I've made you smile, my darling.'

She sighed. 'Don't call me that either. You'll only encourage our mothers to think that we're about to announce our engagement.'

'And that would never do.'

She shot him a sideways glance. 'You're teasing me again. Stop it.'

'Don't spoil my fun.' He patted her hand. 'Look, we're almost there. I'll go and make enquiries and you stay in the cab.' He had alighted before she had a chance to argue, and waited anxiously while he questioned a young female apprentice who had opened the shop door. He returned almost immediately. 'Back to Warwick Square, please, cabby.' He sat down beside her. ‘No go I’m afraid, Daisy. Nothing’s been handed in. It looks as though we’re out of luck.’

Her spirits plummeted. There was nothing for it now other than to return home and make a full confession.

Chapter Three

Daisy hardly spoke during the drive back to Pimlico. Rupert said goodbye to her at the door, squeezing her hand. 'Chin up, Daisy Bell. I don't think that a ten guinea fine or the loss of an expensive frock is going to push your father into bankruptcy.' He kissed her on the cheek. 'I'll see you at the party tomorrow night and I want the first dance with you.' He climbed back into the cab. 'Grosvenor Square, cabby.'

Daisy rang the doorbell, wishing that she had invited Rupert to stay for dinner. At this moment she needed someone on her side. She could not count on Bea, who would probably think her disgrace was a scream, and Teddy would be simply furious. He was of the same mind as their father when it came to women demanding their rights. They were both deeply entrenched in the attitudes of the last century where a woman's place was most definitely in the home.

The door opened and Daisy felt as though she was entering the Tower through Traitors' Gate. 'Is my father home yet, Betsy?'

'Not yet, miss.' Betsy stood aside to let her pass. 'There's something for you. A cabby delivered it not five minutes ago.' She jerked her head in the direction of the hall table. 'He said he'd only just finished his shift or he'd have dropped it round sooner.'

Stunned, delighted and struggling to convince herself that it was the cardboard box containing her ball gown, Daisy opened it with shaking hands. There, lying between sheets of tissue paper, was her beaded chiffon creation in the most delicate shade of eau de Nil. She turned to Betsy with a tremulous smile. 'Did he say anything else?'

'He said he hoped you'd excuse him looking inside it, but he was hoping to find the address of the young lady what lost it, or the shop where it had been bought.'

As Daisy lifted the shimmering garment from its wrappings a slip of paper floated to the floor and she bent down to pick it up. Her name and address were printed in pencil on a scrap torn from a notebook. It must have been left inside by some happy oversight on the part of the dressmaker or her apprentice. Daisy could have shouted for joy, but her attention was diverted by the sound of footsteps on the staircase. She looked over her shoulder to see her sister rounding the bend in the stairs.

'Where have you been, Daisy? There's something frightful going on and I've been here all by myself. No one tells me anything and Mother is in the foulest of moods. She shouted at me for nothing when I went into the drawing room just now.'

Daisy laid her gown back in the box and tucked it under her arm. 'Come up to my room, Bea. There's something I must tell you.'

* * *

With Beatrice ensconced on the chaise longue beneath the tall window overlooking the square, Daisy shook the creases from her ball gown and hung it in the burr-walnut wardrobe.

'What's going on?' Beatrice demanded, curling her feet beneath her. 'I've had a dreadful day and you've been out gallivanting with Rupert. I know because I saw you get out of the hansom cab and he kissed you.'

'It was just a peck on the cheek,' Daisy said casually. 'And if you'll just stop grumbling for a moment I'll tell you everything.'

'You're engaged to him. I know it. You'll announce it at the party tomorrow night and everyone will think you're wonderful, and no one will give me a second glance. It's just not fair.'

Daisy felt a pang of sympathy for her younger sister. She knew very well what it was like to be treated like an irresponsible child, but Bea was fifteen and it was time she started acting like a grown-up. 'Stop feeling sorry for yourself, and listen.' She perched on the edge of the bed and launched into a brief account of the day's events, and, for once, Beatrice heard her out in silence. 'So you see,' Daisy concluded, 'we've got to tread carefully tonight. I don't know whether to tell Mother now, or to wait until Father gets home and speak to him before dinner. What do you think?'

'I think they're both going to slaughter you, and if Father really is going out of business who knows what will happen? We might have to leave Warwick Square and move to the country. I'd really love living permanently in Rainbow's End instead of just spending the summer holidays there.'

'It won't come to that, silly.' Daisy spoke with more conviction than she was feeling.

'I'm not silly. It's the logical conclusion,' Beatrice said huffily. 'If we can't afford to live in London then we'll have to go and live in the house in Nutley Green. Maybe Mother will come off her high horse and stop trying to foist you off on poor Rupert. She'll be starting on me next and I'm definitely not the sort of girl that toffs go for.'

Momentarily diverted, Daisy chuckled. 'And how do you define a toff?'

'The Honourable Rupert, of course. He's a toff to end all toffs. You'd end up as Lady Pendleton if you got your hooks into him, and I'll be the spinster sister living in the attic at Pendleton Park.'

Daisy slid off the bed and went to sit beside Beatrice, giving her a sympathetic hug. 'I'm not going to marry Rupert, and we don't need to define ourselves by marriage. You and I are individuals, Bea. When we get the vote we'll be able to change the world, and we won't need a husband to assure our place in society.'

'And pigs might fly,' Beatrice said, sighing. 'But before all this happens you've got to convince Father that you're not an empty-headed female out to cause trouble for the establishment. Good luck, Daisy. I'm glad it's you and not me.'

* * *

Daisy entered her father's study, having decided to tell him everything and get the whole grisly business out in the open before dinner.

Victor Lennox hung the telephone receiver back on the hook, looking up with a question in his eyes. 'Daisy?'

'May I have a word, Father?'

'It's not a good time, my dear.'

'I know, but this is really urgent.'

A whimsical smile curved his lips. 'Is it about your party tomorrow night?'

'No, Father. It's something much more important.'

'Then sit down and tell me about it.' He motioned her to take a seat and she sank down on the nearest chair. Taking a deep breath she launched into much the same account of the day's happenings as told to Beatrice earlier. 'I am so sorry, Father,' she said when she came to the end. 'I know this is a bad time. Rupert told me about the trouble you're having.'

He bowed his head, resting it on his hands. 'It couldn't be worse, Daisy. I'm almost certain to lose the business and my credibility in the City will be in ruins.'

'But what about Mr Carlton? Won't the law catch up with him?'

'Possibly, but it's not very likely. Jeremiah has already left the country. I doubt if I or my clients will ever see a penny of the money he took.'

'What will you do, Father?'

He raised his head to look her in the eye. 'You're a sensible young woman, Daisy. At least you are for the most part, although heaven knows I don't approve of the women's suffrage movement. At least, I don't agree with the way they go about things. There are other methods of changing the law that don't include violence or damage to the property of others.' He raised his hand as she opened her mouth to argue. 'But that's neither here nor there. We have a family crisis on our hands, and the only solution I can think of will be to sell this house and remove to the country. At least I've invested my money wisely and I own both properties. I may be able to start off again in a small way, but we will have to live more simply and I'm afraid we won't be able to keep the servants on.'

'I'm so sorry that I've added to your problems, Father. The fracas outside the palace is certain to be in the newspapers tomorrow morning, if not tonight.' She rose to her feet. 'Anyway, I quite understand that you must cancel my party.'

Victor shook his head. 'On the contrary, my dear. We will carry on as usual. The party is paid for and to cancel would serve no useful purpose. You will enjoy your twenty-first birthday as planned.' He picked up the telephone receiver. 'Now, if you'll excuse me, Daisy, I have some urgent calls to make before dinner.'

She left the study, almost bumping into Beatrice who had been hovering outside the door. 'Were you eaves-dropping again, Bea?'

'No, of course not.' Beatrice caught her by the hand. 'What did he say? Are we going to live in the country? Is the party on or off?'

'Let me go. I must speak to Mother before Teddy lets the cat out of the bag.'

'Too late, I'm afraid. He thought she already knew. You know what Teddy's like for putting his foot in it. But you haven't told me what Father said.'

'Later, Bea.' Daisy wrenched her hand free. 'I'm going to face Mother now. I should have told her everything as soon as I got home.'

'Yes, you should,' Beatrice said smugly. 'Now you're for it. Wait for me. I wouldn't want to miss this for anything.'

'Do as you please. It won't make any difference. Mother is going to hit the ceiling.'

Daisy's words had been prophetic. Gwendoline paced the floor, wringing her hands. 'You stupid, stupid girl, Daisy. I can't believe that a daughter of mine would get mixed up with those dreadful creatures who disgrace the name of womanhood.'

'Mother, please.' Daisy lifted her hand in protest but dropped it to her side as her mother turned on her with eyes blazing.

'Be silent, girl. You've brought shame upon the family. What will Myrtle and Lavinia think when they see your name in the morning papers? We'll be a laughing stock, and Jane Pendleton will never speak to me again. You've ruined your chances of marrying into the aristocracy. In fact, I doubt if any respectable man will want you now.'

'Hold on, Mother,' Teddy said, frowning. 'That's a bit strong. As I understand it, Daisy was simply trying to help a friend.'

Gwendoline turned on him like a fury. 'And you've

stood by and allowed your father's business partner to swindle their clients.'

'That's not fair,' Daisy protested angrily. 'Teddy's not to blame for what happened to Father's business, any more than I was responsible for the actions of others at the palace.'

'You are both as bad as each other.' Gwendoline sank down on the sofa. 'You were supposed to be collecting your ball gown, but you attended the rally knowing full well that those women were going to do something dreadful.'

'No, I didn't, Mother. I went at the request of a fellow suffragist, but had I known what they intended to do I too would have chained myself to the railings. We should have a say in how our country is governed. I believe in what they're doing.'

'Then you are no daughter of mine. I disown you, Daisy Maria Lennox. I rue the day I brought you into the world. There will be no celebration of your birthday tomorrow. I'm cancelling the party.'

It was all over the papers next day. The embezzlement of funds from a prominent firm of stockbrokers in the City coupled with the disappearance of one of the partners made headline news. The pictures of suffragettes chained to the railings of Buckingham Palace featured on the second page, but unfortunately the press photographer had captured the moment when Daisy had whacked the police constable with her parasol, sending his helmet flying into the air. She had had her back to the camera, but Ruby's face was clearly recognisable and both their names were printed in the caption. The article below it contained details of their court appearance together with those of the other women who had been arrested.

Having seen the newspapers, Gwendoline locked herself in her bedroom and refused to come out. The household was thrown into chaos with a constant stream of tradesmen hammering on the front door demanding to be paid. Word seemed to have gone round that the Lennox family was on the verge of bankruptcy. The telephone rang almost constantly until Daisy took the receiver off the hook and left it dangling. Her father and Teddy had gone into the office early that morning and the family home was in a virtual state of siege. The only person enjoying the drama was Beatrice, who stationed herself in the drawing room peering out from behind the curtain at the small group of reporters who had gathered in the street below.

'I thought I'd find you in here,' Daisy said with an exasperated sigh. 'Really, Bea. This isn't a peep show. Come away from the window.'

'It's exciting. Like something out of the French Revolution. I expect to see a tumbrel arriving any minute and we'll be dragged off to the guillotine.'

'Hardly,' Daisy said, suppressing a grin with difficulty. 'You have an over-active imagination, my girl.'

'Well, at least they'll take Father off to the debtors' jail. I'll be like Little Dorrit, heroically supporting my poor papa by doing fine sewing for an eccentric but rich old lady.'

'You couldn't darn a sock, and the Marshalsea prison

was demolished years ago, so I'm afraid you'll have to move to Rainbow's End with the rest of us. You can make yourself useful by packing up your things. We can't expect Mrs Myers and Betsy to do all the work, especially if Mother is going to have to let them go.'

Beatrice turned away from the window. 'No, surely not? We can't manage without them.'

'We might have to. Now come along, let's get the cabin trunks down from the attic.'

'But it's spidery and horrible up there, and Teddy says it's haunted. Can't Betsy do it instead?'

Daisy shook her head. 'Don't be such a baby. We've got to learn to stand on our own two feet now, Bea.'

But Beatrice was not listening. She had turned her attention once again to the scene in the street below. 'Someone's just thrown a stone at the window, Daisy. There's a girl waving at me.'

Daisy hurried to her side. 'It's Ruby. I wonder what she wants.'

'There's only one way to find out.' Beatrice raced from the room.

'Oh, no.' Daisy picked up her skirts and ran after her. She was just in time to see her sister sliding down the banister and landing with a flurry of starched petticoats. 'Don't open the door, Bea.' But her warning came too late. A gust of air blew in from the street bringing with it the smell of warm grass and even warmer horse dung. A man was attempting to force his way into the house but he was elbowed out of the way by Ruby, who slammed the door in his face.

'Whew!' she said, dumping a carpet bag on the floor. 'I only just made it.'

Beatrice gazed at her in open admiration. 'He was twice your size. How did you do that?'

'Sharp elbows. You got to be quick on your feet where I comes from.' She glanced at Daisy and grinned. 'We're famous, miss. I got me mug plastered all over the papers.'

Daisy glanced anxiously at Ruby's shabby piece of luggage. 'It's nice to see you again, Ruby, but why are you here?'

'I got fired from me job in the vinegar works, and I thought I'd scarper before me dad discovered that I'd been up before the beak. Very strict about that sort of thing he is. So the long and the short of it is that I come to offer me services to your family. I can cook and clean and I don't eat much.'

'Oh, Ruby, I'm sorry. But it's not a good time,' Daisy said gently. 'As a matter of fact we'll be leaving for the country at the end of the week. We won't be able to take you on.'

'We can't even afford to pay Mrs Myers and Betsy,' Beatrice said, nodding in agreement. 'We're going to have to look after ourselves and grow our own food. We're going to be really poor.'

Ruby folded her arms across her chest. 'Then I'll work for nothing, just me bed and board. I got no home, so anything is a step up from the gutter. Now where do I begin?'

Faced with such determination, Daisy was at a loss. 'Well, perhaps you could help out just for today. It's not up to me, Ruby. My mother will have something to say, and I don't hold out much hope that she'll take you on.'

'Then I'll do what you need me to do today, and tomorrow I'll start looking for another job. Where do I start?'

'She can help you get the cabin trunks down from the attic,' Beatrice said hopefully. 'She doesn't look the sort who would mind spiders and ghosts.'

'That's right, miss.' Taking her straw hat off and setting it down on top of her bag, Ruby rolled up her sleeves. 'Lead on. I ain't afraid of nothing, except me dad when he's had a drop or two over the odds.'

Daisy led the way. She was certain that her mother would object to Ruby's presence in the house, but when Gwendoline eventually emerged from her room she was too preoccupied with the forthcoming party to make any objections. She seemed to be in a state of denial and astounded Daisy by agreeing that extra help was needed. 'The girl can stay and help us with the move to the country. We need another pair of hands and I'm far too busy with last minute preparations for the party to think about anything else.' She shot a searing look at Daisy. 'Yes, young lady. As usual your father is determined to spoil you. I would cancel the party but he insists that it should go ahead as planned. Think yourself very lucky.'

Daisy could not help wishing that the party had been called off as she stood between her parents, ready to receive her guests. She smiled until her face ached but very few of the people on her mother's guest list, with the exception of Rupert, would have been her personal choice. She had lost touch with most of the friends she had made at the expensive girls' boarding school she had attended. They were either married or lived in different parts of the country too far away to consider travelling to London for a party. The young persons present were all sons and daughters of people whom her mother cultivated for their wealth and position. They were bright young things with very little thought in their heads other than the next social event. As Daisy shook their hands or kissed their cheeks, she was suddenly aware how shallow and brittle these acquaintanceships really were. She suspected that most of these so-called friends would vanish like morning mist if her father were declared bankrupt. The world that her mother had created so lovingly would burst like a soap bubble.

'Daisy, you look positively ravishing.' A genuinely friendly face beamed at her. 'Happy birthday, my dear.' Lady Pendleton squeezed her fingers gently and kissed her on both cheeks, before moving on to speak to Gwendoline.

Rupert followed in her wake. 'You do look splendid, Daisy Bell.' He raised her hand to his lips and brushed it with a kiss. 'And that must be the gown you almost lost. It's lovely and so are you.'

'Thank you,' she murmured, smiling up at him. 'The cabby delivered it to our door.'

'I hope you tipped him well.'

His infectious grin warmed her heart. 'Thank you for everything you did yesterday.'

'It was a pleasure, Miss Lennox. And I hope you've remembered to save the first dance for me.'

'Move on there, old boy.' One of Teddy's friends shuffled up behind him. 'Don't hog the gorgeous Daisy. I want to give her a birthday kiss too.'

Rupert held on to Daisy's hand. 'You'd better make certain the lady doesn't object before you take liberties, old boy.'

'Move on, Tulley, old man,' Teddy said, nudging his friend impatiently. 'Let's get the formalities over. I could do with a drink.'

Rupert winked at Daisy as he walked away. 'See you in a while, Daisy Bell.'

She shook Tulley's hand, keeping him at arm's length. 'Good evening, Bobby. Let's keep this formal, shall we?'

'You're a hard woman, Daisy Lennox. A dashed heart-breaker.'

'Except that his is made of India rubber and it bounces back every time,' Teddy said, chuckling. 'Do hurry up, Tulley. A chap can die of thirst standing here.'

When the last guest had been welcomed Daisy moved away from her parents and was immediately claimed by Rupert. His smile was replaced by a look of genuine concern. 'How goes it?'

She glanced around, making certain that no one was listening. 'It's awful. Mother is beside herself although she's putting on a good show tonight, and poor Father hasn't said much, but I know he's desperately worried. I could kill that wretched man Carlton.'

'You and several hundred others, I should think.'

'I know. It's terrible. Father is going to sell the London house in the hope of paying back at least some of the money that Carlton embezzled. We're leaving for Rainbow's End at the end of the week.'

'I've always loved that name. When I was a boy I was convinced that a crock of gold was buried in your garden.'

She smiled. 'Yes, I remember. You and Teddy decided to dig up the vegetable beds and were severely punished. At least, Teddy was, and I suppose your father was furious too.'

'I couldn't sit down for a week after the beating I received. But I still love that old house. I believe it used to be the dower house in the eighteenth century, but the dowager Lady Pendleton at that time considered it was too small and had another one built overlooking the lake.'

Daisy sighed. 'I can't imagine what it must be like to have all that family history to fall back on. As far as I know my grandfather was a tea merchant and gambled away most of his money on the horses. Mother's side of the family isn't well documented although she's convinced that they had blue blood running in their veins. She's taking this very badly.'

'If there's anything I can do? Please don't be afraid to ask.'

She met his anxious gaze with a smile. 'You're a good friend, Rupert.'

He was about to respond when Beatrice rushed up to them, clutching an over-full glass of lemonade. 'Rupert, dear Rupert. Mother won't let me have a proper drink. Will you be a darling and put a dash of gin in my glass?'

'Certainly not,' Rupert said, tweaking one of her curls. 'This is Daisy's party. We don't want you falling down drunk and disgracing the family.'

'That's rich considering the state we're in at present.' Beatrice tossed her head, scowling. 'And the cost of all this would keep us for a year in the country. We'll be living off bread and jam next week.'

'Bread only, I'm afraid.' Daisy managed to keep a straight face. 'It will always be jam tomorrow, never jam today.'

'Oh, you beast!' Beatrice flounced off in the direction of her brother and Bobby Tulley, who were chatting over drinks.

'Never mind her,' Rupert said, chuckling. 'You can always have the pick of the kitchen garden at Pendleton Park. We won't allow young Bea to starve.'

Daisy glanced over his shoulder. 'Here comes Mother. I'd better circulate.'

'Let's give her something to think about, Daisy Bell.' He took her hand and tucked it through the crook of his arm, turning to face Gwendoline with a smile. 'Wonderful party, Mrs Lennox.'

The frown lines on Gwendoline's brow were wiped away in an instant. 'How kind of you to say so, Rupert.'

'And I hear that we might soon be neighbours. Daisy tells me that you're thinking of spending more time at Rainbow's End. Mother will be delighted and so will I. It will be like old times.'

'I hadn't looked at it in quite that way, but I'm sure you're right.' Gwendoline smiled vaguely and moved away to speak to a middle-aged couple who had just arrived.

Daisy gave Rupert's arm a gentle squeeze. He always managed to say exactly the right thing when dealing with her mother. He could charm her out of a mood simply with a smile. She wished that she possessed a similar talent. 'Let's not think about tomorrow. I'd love some champagne.'

'Then champagne you shall have.' He beckoned to a waiter who was circulating with a tray laden with brimming glasses. Taking two, Rupert gave one to Daisy. 'I expect you're wondering why I haven't given you a birthday present.'

She sipped, eyeing him over the rim. 'No. Well, perhaps I did, just a little.'

'I'm not joining my regiment for a couple of weeks, so in between fittings at Hawkes, I thought I'd spend the time at Pendleton Park.'

'That will be nice.'

He grinned. 'And even nicer, I plan to give a certain young lady driving lessons.'

She stared at him, momentarily at a loss for words. 'You're going to teach me to drive?'

'I thought you'd prefer that to a bicycle made for two or a gold watch.'

'You know that I've always wanted to get behind the wheel. You are so thoughtful, Rupert. I could kiss you, but I don't want to give everyone the wrong idea.' She would at least have hugged him, but they were standing in the middle of the dance floor, and the head waiter chose that particular moment to announce that dinner was served.

Rupert proffered his arm. 'What's the betting that we're seated next to each other, Daisy Bell?'

'Odds on, I should think, and I had nothing to do with the seating plan. Mother has arranged everything.'

Beatrice almost knocked them down as she rushed towards the top table. 'I'm absolutely starving,' she muttered crossly. 'I thought the formalities would go on forever.'

As expected, Rupert had been placed next to Daisy at the top table. A covert glance from her mother confirmed her suspicion that this had been arranged with one thought in mind. She gave Rupert an apologetic smile as he held out her chair. 'I'm sorry,' she said in a low voice. 'Subtlety isn't a word in my mother's vocabulary.'

He took his seat beside her. 'Let her enjoy her moment of triumph, old thing. I fear she'll come to earth with a bump when all the excitement is over.'

Daisy glanced at Beatrice, who was seated between Teddy and Bobby. Someone had given her a glass of wine and she was imbibing with relish. Bea might suffer in the morning but maybe she had the right attitude. Perhaps money and status were, as Daisy had suspected all along, terribly overrated. A fresh start in the countryside would prove an exciting challenge for the whole family. She turned to Rupert with an eager smile. 'What make of car do you drive? Do you think I'll need many lessons?'

Chapter Four

Summer 1913

'Steady on, Daisy. The speed limit's twenty miles per hour.' Holding his hat on with one hand, Rupert clutched the side of his sports car with the other. 'You're not on the race track at Brooklands,' he added, chuckling and ruining the effect.

'Spoilsport.' She reduced speed with the greatest reluctance. 'But it's so easy to go fast in this car, and it's the best feeling in the world. Almost like flying.'

'You're doing really well, considering there's been such a long gap between your lessons, but I'll be most upset if you damage my beautiful new car.'

'Mother would have a fit if she could see me now. She thinks I've gone into town to change my library book.'

Rupert relaxed against the padded leather squabs, his smile fading. 'How is she coping? It must be almost a year since you moved to Nutley Green.'

Daisy concentrated hard as she negotiated a sharp bend in the road, stamping on the brake as she came across a herd of cows. 'Damn,' she breathed, resting her head on the wheel. 'That was a close one.'

'That's why I told you to slow down. These narrow country lanes are devilish difficult, and there's nowhere to go other than the ditch if you meet something coming the other way.' Rupert patted her on the shoulder. 'Cheer up. No harm done.'

Gaining control of her breathing as the erratic beating of her heart slowed down, Daisy straightened up. 'You were right, and I was getting carried away. Sorry, Rupert, but at least I didn't damage your beautiful red Prince Henry.'

'One of Vauxhall's finest,' he said proudly. 'And I wouldn't be sitting here calmly if you'd scraped the wing of my pride and joy, especially as I've got to report back to the barracks first thing in the morning.'

She looked straight ahead, watching the cows as they meandered on their way towards the farm gate. 'You've had such a short leave. When will you get another one?'

He grinned. 'You only love me for my motor car.'

'You won't catch me out that way. Oh, look, the cows have gone, and I've stalled the engine.'

'Yes you have. So you'd better get out and crank the starting handle.'

She pulled a face. 'That's not very gentlemanly. Besides which I can hardly walk in this silly hobble skirt.'

'Well, you girls will be slaves to fashion. I'm surprised you allow the dress designers to dictate to you in that way.'

'Don't tease. I still support the suffragists even if we do live too far away from London for me to take an active part in the movement.' She opened the car door and climbed out, moving slowly as the tight skirt made it impossible to take anything other than tiny steps. She turned the handle a couple of times without any luck and was about to lose patience when Rupert came to her aid.

'I wanted to see just how much of an independent woman you are, Daisy Bell.' He took it from her and the engine started at one turn. 'She recognises her master's touch.'

Daisy hit him with her driving glove. 'You brute.' Laughing, she returned to the driver's seat. 'Get in quickly or I'll drive on and leaving you standing.'

He vaulted in beside her. 'No chance of that, my dear Daisy Bell.'

She drove off, accelerating slowly. 'When are you going to stop calling me that ridiculous name?'

'I don't know. Perhaps when you give me your answer.'

'To what? You haven't asked the question.'

'Ah, now that's the point. If I proposed to you now you would almost certainly turn me down.'

She could never quite tell when he was teasing her and she shot him a covert glance. 'Of course I would. We're more like brother and sister. It simply wouldn't work.'

'Maybe not, but every time I hear that song it reminds me of you.' He leaned back, closing his eyes as the sun beat down on them and the summer breeze tugged at his tweed cap. 'Tomorrow I'll be back in uniform, and I'll think of this when I'm out on manoeuvres or writing reports. I'll remember the warm sun on my face and the soft breeze filled with the scent of clover and warm grass, and I'll see you with the wind in your hair and roses in your cheeks.'

She slowed the engine and turned her head to give him a searching look. 'You sound as though you're going to be away for a long time. Is there something you aren't telling me, Rupert?'

He responded with a lazy smile. 'Of course not, but there's just a chance that we might be posted abroad.'

'We're not fighting anyone at the moment, are we?'

'We live in uncertain times, Daisy. With the continuing troubles in the Balkans, and Germany mobilising more troops, you never can tell what might happen.'

'Don't spoil a lovely day with that sort of talk, and please don't mention it in front of Teddy. He's been dying to join the army ever since you got your commission. His heart was never in the business and he absolutely hates living in the country.'

'But I heard that your father is doing well now that he's started up again, albeit in a much smaller way than before.'

'I believe so, although he doesn't talk about it at home. He goes off to his office in Colchester every morning and returns again in the evening. Teddy is forced to go along with it because he has no alternative, but if war was declared he'd be one of the first to enlist, I know it.'

'Poor chap. I feel for him.'

She braked as they reached the crossroads. 'Don't tell him what I said. It wouldn't take much to make him kick over the traces and be off. It would break Mother's heart, and Father would have to manage on his own since he can't afford to take on staff. At least he's always saying he has one foot in Carey Street, and I believe him.'

'I'm sure it can't be as bad as that. Look out, there's a horse and cart to your right.'

'I saw it coming before you did. Which way now? Perhaps we ought to go home.'

'I've a better idea. Let's go into Colchester and find a tea room. I have a sudden fancy for cucumber sandwiches and fancy cakes.'

'All right, but you'd better take the wheel when we get to town. Father would have a fit if he saw me driving your motorcar. He hasn't quite forgiven me for getting myself arrested last year. I think both my parents are worried that I'll take up with the suffragette movement again.'

'Will you?'

Daisy flexed her work-worn fingers as they gripped the steering wheel. 'I really don't have the time or the wherewithal to get me to the places where they hold their meetings or demonstrations. Father refuses to have a telephone installed at home and I've lost touch with the suffragists I knew in London.' She shot him an amused glance. 'Except for Ruby, of course, but she works terribly hard at home. Mother has to admit, reluctantly because she doesn't really like her, that Ruby lives up to her name and is a treasure beyond price. She cleans the house from top to bottom and no one can beat her when it comes to doing the weekly wash.'

'Does this paragon of virtue cook as well?'

'No. That's a bit beyond Ruby's capabilities so I've taken over in the kitchen. Mother would kill me for admitting it to you, as she considers that it's a terrible comedown, but I enjoy cooking and I find I'm rather good at it. At least, I haven't poisoned anyone yet.'

'Maybe one day you'll allow me to sample your cuisine?'

She drew the car to a halt at the side of the road. 'We don't entertain any more. Mother might have some of her church-going ladies to tea occasionally, but that's as far as it goes. We have to be careful with money, Rupert. It's not like the old days.'

His brow puckered in a frown. 'I don't like to think of you living like this, Daisy. You were meant for better things.'

'Don't. You sound just like my mother.' She opened the car door. 'You'd better take over now, but thanks for the lesson. I'll have to wait ages for my next one.'

He reached across to take her hand in his. 'Marry me, Daisy. Let me give you the life you deserve.' He studied her palm, tracing the lines with his fingertips. 'You were brought up to a life of ease. You're a lady, not a drudge. Marry me and you can drive the Prince Henry every day of the week if you want.'

She stared at him in amazement. She had thought for a moment that he was joking, but looking into his eyes she realised with a shock that he was sincere. Fighting down a momentary feeling of panic, she chose her words carefully. 'That's very sweet of you, Rupert. But feeling sorry for me isn't the same as loving me. I couldn't marry you or any man unless we were both very much in love.'

'But you do care for me, don't you?'

'Of course I do, but you're just being kind and heroic, and I think the image you have of me is romantic and quite unreal.' She withdrew her hand gently and climbed out of the car. 'Thank you for asking me. It was really lovely.' She hesitated, gazing at him anxiously. 'Is the offer of tea and cake still on?'

He slid into the driving seat. 'Actually I've rather gone off the idea. Would you mind awfully if I dropped you at home? We'll do the afternoon tea thing on my next leave.'

'No, of course not. And I'm sorry if I've upset you, Rupert. I really appreciate what you were trying to do.'

'No, you're right, Daisy. It was a silly idea, especially as I haven't the faintest idea where I'll be this time next year.'

They drove home in silence, with Rupert concentrating doggedly on the road ahead and Daisy seated beside him, wondering how such a bright sunny day could suddenly seem so bleak and foreboding. Their goodbye in the road outside Rainbow's End was stiff and formal. She watched him drive off with a lump in her throat. They had seen so little of each other in the past year, but on each occasion they had picked up where they left off. Now it felt as though their childhood friendship had ended and things would never be quite the same again. She stood outside the garden gate, gazing at the dwelling which had once been the family's holiday retreat from the hurly-burly of London life, but was now their one and only home.

The former dower house snoozed in the late

afternoon sunshine like an elderly lady napping in a deckchair. Roses clambered up the mellow red-brick walls and festooned the portico over the front door. Some of the roof tiles were missing, and two of the chimney stacks leaned precariously as if bowing to each other. She hesitated with her hand on the gate, taking pleasure in the riot of colour in the herbaceous borders. Hollyhocks, larkspur and the old-fashioned granny's bonnets gave off a heady perfume, and glorious oriental poppies spilled their pink, white and scarlet petals like confetti on the crazy paving path. Bees buzzed in the spice-scented lavender and birds sang, but it was winter in Daisy's heart as she let herself in and made her way slowly round to the back of the house. She felt a terrible sense of loss but she knew that she had done the right thing. To marry Rupert simply as an escape from the life she was compelled to lead would have ended in disaster for them both.

She did not enter the house immediately, choosing instead to walk around the garden. It was quiet and peaceful and she needed a few moments to compose herself before she faced the family. The lawn spread before her like a green blanket, smooth and evenly trimmed, stretching as far as the orchard where apples ripened in the summer sun. Soon it would be time to pick them and the blackberries that festooned the hedgerows. This year Daisy intended to make jam and to experiment with chutney using the tomatoes and onions that she had cultivated in the vegetable patch. Her father had bought chickens and a rooster and they resided in the ancient hen house at the bottom of the garden. It was a ramshackle affair, patched and nailed together in a haphazard manner, but it kept them safe from the marauding foxes. They were pecking about in the run, but soon she must lock them up for the night and collect any eggs that Bea had missed that morning.

Daisy sighed, pushing thoughts of Rupert to the back of her mind and stifling a niggling feeling of regret. She could have taken the easy way out, she thought, as she walked back to the house, but that would not have been fair on either of them. Besides which, she had responsibilities now. She was no longer a lady of leisure, planning her day around social engagements. Dinner would not appear on the table as if by magic as it had in the old days. There were vegetables to prepare and lamb cutlets to cook. Her father and Teddy would be most upset if there was not a hearty pudding on the menu. She must hurry if she was to get everything done by seven o'clock when the family assembled in the oak-beamed dining room for their evening meal. She entered the house through the scullery door and was pounced upon by Ruby.

'Where've you been all afternoon, miss? Your ma's been fretting and fuming because you was supposed to make a plate of fancies for her blooming stall at the church bazaar on Saturday.'

'It's only Thursday. She ought to realise by now that my baking day is Friday.'

Ruby sniffed and wiped her hands on her apron. 'Your ma lives in a different world from the rest of us, miss.' She picked up a bucket of kitchen scraps. 'Shall I go and feed the chickens? That's one job less for you.'

'Thank you, Ruby. You are a jewel by name and a jewel by nature.'

'Ta, miss. Flattery always works with me.'

'I meant it,' Daisy said earnestly. 'And please don't call me miss. No one thinks of you as a servant. You're part of the family.'

'I'm as much a Lennox as the clock on the wall, but it don't bother me one bit. I know I'm priceless.' Ruby gave her a saucy wink, picked up the bucket and went outside with it looped over her arm.

Daisy went through the scullery to the large airy kitchen, which overlooked the back yard and the garden beyond. The late afternoon sunlight streamed through the diamond-paned windows, warming the quarry-tiled floor to wine red. She took off her hat and hung it on a peg behind the door, next to the bell board once used to summon the servants. She smiled grimly. How times had changed. She plucked a pinafore from its hook and put it on, rolling up her sleeves to begin preparations for dinner.

She had just finished peeling the potatoes when the bell labelled *Drawing room* jangled on its spring. She ignored it at first but the insistent ringing set her teeth on edge and she threw down the knife and marched out of the kitchen and along a narrow corridor to the square entrance hall. She entered the room to find her mother sitting on the sofa with an aggrieved expression on her face.

'Mother, please don't ring the bell. I'm not a servant.'

'Where's the wretched girl? You should have sent her to find out what I wanted.'

'Ruby has gone outside to feed the hens. Where is Bea, by the way? Couldn't you have asked her to do whatever it is you want? She does precious little round here.'

'Don't speak to me in that tone of voice, young lady. We may be living like paupers but I'm still your mother.'

'I'm sorry, Mother. But I am rather busy. What can I do for you?'

'Have you forgotten the fancies for the bazaar on Saturday?'

'They'll be ready on time.'

'And why didn't you ask Rupert in for tea? I saw him drop you off outside the gate.'

'He had things to do, Mother.'

'You told me that you were going to the library.'

'I bumped into Rupert in town and he offered me a lift home.' The lie tripped off her tongue so easily that she did not even feel guilty. Surely she was entitled to a life of her own? And yet, looking at her mother's set expression, she knew that having a daughter who was almost twenty-two and not engaged to be married was even worse than having a suffragette in the family. In a few years' time she would be officially on the shelf, like a jar of last year's jam that had gone mouldy, but in the meantime she was expected to behave like the perfect daughter: biddable, and compliant, never questioning her lot. 'What was it you wanted, Mother?'

'A little civility wouldn't go amiss. You've become quite surly since we moved to the country. It's far harder for me. I've had to leave my dear friends and live like a peasant, but all you've left behind are those wretched women who led you into mischief.' She glared at Daisy, looking her up and down with her lips pursed. 'You look and dress like a washerwoman. Is it a wonder that Rupert doesn't want to have anything to do with you?'

'I've got work to do.' Daisy turned on her heel and was about to leave the room when Gwendoline called her back.

'All I wanted was a cup of tea and perhaps a biscuit or two. I can't exist on the meagre diet we are forced to endure these days. I have a delicate constitution.'

'Then I'll make a pot of tea, Mother. You only had to ask.' Daisy could not keep the edge out of her voice, and she knew if she stayed a moment longer she would snap and say something she might regret. She loved her mother but there were times when her patience was stretched to the limit by her autocratic parent's demands. She left the room, relieving her feelings just a little by allowing the door to slam behind her.

She returned to the kitchen, wondering if she had done the right thing by refusing Rupert's proposal. The last thing she had wanted was to hurt him, but had she accepted his offer of marriage she would have joined the legions of women who married for security and were forced to depend on their husbands for everything. Even as the idea came into her head it was rejected. One day, she thought, I will find my own level. I'll make something of my life and if I do decide to marry, it will be for love.

She set about making tea for her mother but she could not face another nagging session, and in her present state of mind she might still say something she regretted. When Ruby returned from seeing to the chickens Daisy sent her in with the tray.

Dinner was prepared and being kept warm in the oven. Daisy glanced at the clock, wondering why her father and Teddy were so late. On a normal day they arrived at six-thirty on the dot. Father lived his life by the clock and detested unpunctuality. Every morning at eight o'clock precisely he and Teddy drove off in the Humberette, which kept breaking down with monotonous regularity, but perhaps that was not surprising as he had bought it second hand at a knock-down price. It was ten minutes to seven, and she was beginning to think that something was really wrong when Bea came running into the kitchen, flushed and breathless. 'There's been an accident,' she said excitedly. 'I was looking out of my bedroom window, wondering why they hadn't come home yet because I'm absolutely ravenous, and I saw the car swerve into the hedge. Father was driving and now he's just sitting there, doing nothing.'

'Where's Teddy?'

'He went racing down the road. I think he must have been going for help.'

Daisy peeled off her pinafore. 'Is Father hurt?' she asked anxiously.

'I don't know. He was holding his head. Perhaps he banged it on the steering wheel. They hit the bank quite hard.'

Daisy hurried through the house and out into the front garden with Beatrice following close behind. The Humberette was slewed across the road and steam was pouring from the radiator. With a cry of horror, Daisy ran to the car and wrenched the door open. She helped her father from the driver's seat. His face was deathly pale and there was a livid bruise forming on his forehead.

'Are you all right, Father?'

He shook his head, wincing. 'It's just a bump, but I need to sit down.'

'Let's get you indoors.'

'I can't leave the car here. It's blocking the road.'

He seemed dazed and disorientated. His hands were trembling, and Daisy was afraid that he might be slightly concussed. She turned to Bea. 'Take Father into the house. I'll send for the doctor.'

'No doctor,' Victor said emphatically. 'Can't afford to pay a quack just to tell me I've got a lump on my head the size of an egg. Teddy's gone for the mechanic. Just stay by the car, Daisy. I've always said that blind bend was dangerous.' He looped his arm over Beatrice's shoulders. 'I need a tot of brandy, that's all.'

Beatrice nodded. 'Yes, Father. Let's go indoors and I'll pour you a very large glass of Armagnac.'

'Not too large,' Daisy said, frowning. 'He should sit down and have a cup of sweet tea. Don't worry about the car. I'll keep watch until Teddy brings help.' She waited until they were out of sight and was about to lift the bonnet when she heard the sound of running feet and someone shouting.

'Stop. Don't do that. You'll scald yourself.'

Startled by the urgent tone of his voice she moved aside and was joined by Bowman, the odd-job man and mechanic who had fixed the car and delivered it back to the house after previous breakdowns. 'I was only going to look.'

'And you'd have had a nasty accident. You should leave this sort of thing to them that knows what they're doing, miss.' Bowman took a rag from the pocket of his grease-stained overalls and proceeded to fling the bonnet open. He stood back as a cloud of steam escaped into the atmosphere. 'I'd say the radiator's cracked. The motor must've hit the bank at some speed. Were you driving?'

'No, I was not.' Insulted, Daisy glared at him. 'If I'd been driving I wouldn't have swerved into the hedge.'

His dark eyes twinkled and his lips twitched. 'I beg your pardon, Miss Lennox.'

Somewhat unnerved by his direct gaze, Daisy looked away. 'My father was driving.'

'Swerved to miss a fox.' Teddy came to a halt at Daisy's side, breathless and panting. 'Damn thing leapt out of the hedge in front of us. I'd have run the blighter over.'

'That would be a bit hard on the fox. I hope he got away.' Bowman leaned over the engine, wiping oil away with the rag.

'Bloody thing disappeared into the hedge again,' Teddy said crossly. 'I'd have shot it if I'd had a gun.

Anyway, never mind the fox. What about the motor? Can you fix it here and now?'

Bowman shook his head. 'It'll need a tow to my workshop. I can't do a thing without the proper tools.'

Teddy took off his boater and wiped his brow on the back of his hand. 'Dashed annoying. How long do you think it will take?'

'Can't say. I'll probably have to order spare parts from the manufacturers, and that can take time.'

'Damn.' Teddy frowned. 'We need the motor to get us to the office every day.'

'I could lend you a tandem, sir. Had one in for repair and the owner couldn't afford to pay.'

Daisy stared at him suspiciously. Bowman was obviously being sarcastic but Teddy, seemingly oblivious to that fact, appeared to take his throwaway remark seriously. 'Don't be ridiculous,' he said crossly. 'My father wouldn't be seen dead on a bicycle. He's a stockbroker of some repute.'

'So I heard, sir.'

There was a wealth of meaning in Bowman's voice and Daisy felt her cheeks flame with embarrassment. Ruby, who often chose to linger in the village post office and chat to the locals, had told her ages ago that their move to Nutley Green had given the gossips a field day. They knew all about the family's misfortunes and of her involvement with the suffragettes and subsequent arrest, but what right had this common workman to judge her family based on nothing more than idle tittle-tattle? 'I'm sure that Lady Pendleton will be able to help us out when it comes to transport, Mr Bowman,' she said stiffly.

'I'll keep the tandem handy just in case, miss.' He tipped his cap.

She knew that he was laughing at her, and she was instantly ashamed of her rather juvenile attempt to put him in his place, but the wretched fellow seemed impervious to snubs. 'I hardly think that will be necessary, thank you.'

'Always ready to oblige a lady, miss.' Bowman turned to Teddy. 'Am I right in thinking that you want me to organise a tow? Farmer Hayes sometimes helps out with his shires, if he's not too busy.'

Teddy shrugged his shoulders. 'Do what you have to, Bowman. But we need the motor repaired urgently. Do you understand?' He hesitated, frowning. 'On second thoughts, I'll come with you. Hayes might be more helpful if he knows with whom he's dealing.'

Daisy felt her colour rise. She had found Bowman extremely annoying, but there was no need for Teddy to speak to him in that manner. 'I'm sure we'd be very grateful for any help you can give us, Mr Bowman,' she said hastily. 'Please do whatever is necessary.' She turned on her heel and walked back to the house.

Ruby met her in the entrance hall, her face puckered with concern. 'They're in the drawing room. Going at it hammer and tongs, they are.'

'It's all right,' Daisy said with more confidence than she was feeling. 'Will you be an angel and check the oven for me?'

'My pleasure. Us angels have to stick together.' Ruby scuttled off in the direction of the kitchen.

Taking a deep breath, Daisy entered the drawing

room. As Ruby had said, the atmosphere was strained to say the least. Beatrice had been kneeling at her father's side but she scrambled to her feet when she saw her sister. 'You can take over now,' she said in a low voice. 'I've had enough of this.' She went to sit on the window seat, turning her head to gaze out into the front garden.

'How are you feeling, Father?' Daisy asked anxiously. 'I still think I ought to send for the doctor.'

'He doesn't need a doctor,' Gwendoline said angrily. 'He needs to have his bumps read. He could have been killed driving that death trap, and what would have become of us then? Have you thought of that, Victor?'

'My dear, it was nothing. The motorcar came off worst.'

'It wouldn't have happened if you'd had a chauffeur as we did in London, or if you had bought a new motor instead of that rattletrap.' Gwendoline rose to her feet and began to pace the floor. 'Why couldn't we have moved to a smaller house in town and lived like civilised human beings, instead of being penned up like animals in this wreck of a house? The roof leaks when it rains and we're miles from anywhere. If it weren't for dear Jane Pendleton I think I would go quite mad.'

'Let me pour you a sherry, Mother,' Daisy said, moving swiftly to a side table. She picked up a cut-glass decanter and poured a small measure. 'It's good for shock.'

Snatching it from her Gwendoline tossed it down in one go. 'That's right, and I'm the one suffering from shock. I knew that this mad venture would end in disaster.'

Victor held his empty brandy glass out to Daisy. 'But I'm the one who's had the bump on the head, and this is the last of my Armagnac.'

'You don't care about us,' Gwendoline muttered, sinking down on the sofa with her empty glass clutched in her hand. 'All you care about is stocks and shares, and silly things like that.'

'It's how I earn my living, Gwendoline. It has provided us with a not inconsiderable income over the years. These last months have been a struggle, I have to admit, but it's never easy to start again.'

'I blame that dreadful man Carlton. I never liked him. His eyes were set too close together and he had crooked teeth.'

Daisy could see that her mother was working herself up into one of her states. 'I think we ought to eat soon, Mother. The chops will be ruined if they stay in the oven much longer.'

'How can you think about food at a time like—' Gwendoline broke off mid-sentence as the screech of rubber tyres on the road outside was followed by an ear-splitting crash.

Beatrice leapt to her feet with a loud shriek. 'Oh, my God! It's the Prince Henry and it looks as though Rupert was driving.'

Chapter Five

The Humberette had suffered the most and had almost concertinaed into the hedge. Rupert's cherry red Prince Henry was a sorry sight but the occupants appeared unscathed. By the time everyone reached the accident scene Rupert, Teddy and Bowman were on their feet examining the damage.

'What happened?' Daisy asked, clutching her brother's sleeve.

Teddy shook her hand off. 'How do I know, silly? One minute we were tooling along and the next moment we rounded the corner at speed and clouted the poor old Humberette.'

Rupert's face was pale beneath his tan. 'Brakes must have failed,' he said, running his hand through his fair hair. 'It's never happened before.' He turned to Bowman. 'What d'you think?'

'I'd say the wire snapped when you put your foot down, but as far as I can see the Prince Henry's come off lightly.' Bowman walked round to the front of the vehicle where the starting handle had lodged in the spokes of one of the Humberette's wheels. He shook his head. 'This one will need more than a tow. It looks like a Meccano set.'

Victor groaned. 'How much will it cost to fix my car?'

'How long is a piece of string?' Bowman shrugged his shoulders. 'It could be done, but it would take time, and money.'

'Come into the house, Victor.' Gwendoline took him by the arm. 'I never liked that motorcar anyway. Perhaps we could hire a carriage of some sort. It would be so much more genteel.' She led him unprotesting back to the house, with Beatrice trailing behind.

'Can we have dinner now,' she asked faintly. 'I'm dying of hunger.'

Ruby hurried after her. 'I'll get you some bread and cheese, miss. It'll tide you over until everyone is ready to eat.'

Daisy moved closer to Rupert. She could see that he was shaken despite his outwardly calm appearance, and she felt a twinge of remorse. If she had handled his proposal better he might have been concentrating more on his driving. 'I'm sorry about the Prince Henry,' she said softly. 'Awfully bad luck.'

'Awfully bad driving, Daisy Bell. Teddy warned me that your father's motorcar was just round the corner but I misjudged my speed. Must have had my mind on other things, but it was my fault entirely.' He turned to Bowman. 'I'll leave my machine in your capable hands, Barnaby old chap.'

'You trust him with your precious Prince Henry?' Teddy stared at him in disbelief. 'Surely you'd want a qualified Vauxhall engineer to look at it?'

Once again, Daisy felt herself blushing. She wished that Teddy would not talk about people he considered to be socially beneath him as if they were deaf and totally without feeling. She glanced at Bowman but he had his head under the bonnet as he inspected the Vauxhall's engine. He seemed intent on the task in hand but she was certain he must have heard. She nudged her brother in the ribs, jerking her head in Bowman's direction. 'He can hear you,' she whispered.

'Who cares?' Teddy took a silver cigarette case from his breast pocket and selected a cigarette. He offered the case to Rupert. 'Have a gasper. It'll calm your nerves.'

'No, thanks. My nerves are just fine.' Rupert drew Daisy to one side, lowering his voice. 'I wanted to see you to apologise for this afternoon. I shouldn't have driven off like that. It was childish and I'm ashamed of myself.'

'I'm not too proud of myself either. I could have put it better, but you took me by surprise.' She held out her hand. 'Friends?'

He took it in a warm grasp. 'Friends, of course. I'll sleep better knowing that there's no hard feeling between us.'

'Of course not.' She squeezed his fingers. 'After all, I don't want to upset my driving instructor.'

'You don't need me any longer, Daisy. You're competent enough to apply for a driving licence.'

'That will have to wait until I've saved up five shillings, and anyway I don't really need one at the moment. It looks as though the poor old Humberette will be off the road permanently.'

She must have raised her voice without realising it as Bowman straightened up and turned to face them. 'I can fix it, but it will take time.'

Teddy, who had been smoking and staring moodily into the distance, suddenly took notice. 'You can?'

'I've got a lot on at the moment, but if we can get what's left of it into your stables I could work on it in my spare time.'

'There you are,' Rupert said cheerfully. 'That sounds like a perfectly good offer, Teddy. In the meantime I'm sure that Mother will lend you one of our carriages so that you and Mr Lennox can travel to and from your place of business. You only have to ask.'

'That's very kind of you, old boy.' Teddy cocked his head on one side. 'That sounds like heavy horses. Let's hope it's Farmer Hayes coming to the rescue.'

'We don't want the shires to come to grief in that tangled metal.' Bowman sprinted to the bend in the lane, waving his arms to attract the attention of the farmer.

'That chap thinks more about animals than he does people,' Teddy said, grinding the stub of his cigarette beneath the heel of his highly polished shoe.

'But he's a first class mechanic, and they're hard to find.' Rupert held on to Daisy's hand a little longer than was strictly necessary. 'I'll say cheerio, old thing. I'm leaving early in the morning so I won't see you before I go.'

She met his intense gaze with a tremulous smile. 'We'll have those cucumber sandwiches and cakes on your next leave.'

'I'll look forward to it.' He turned away, addressing himself to Bowman. 'I'll leave the motor with you, Barnaby. Do what needs doing and send the bill to my mother at Pendleton Park. I'll see that it gets paid promptly.'

Bowman saluted with a grin. 'It'll be a pleasure to work on such a vehicle, sir.' He shot a sideways glance at Daisy. 'I'll be round some time tomorrow to take a closer look at the Humberette, Miss Lennox.'

His respectful tone was at odds with the boldness of his expression, and there was something in his smile that Daisy found unsettling. She drew herself up to her full height. 'Good evening, Mr Bowman.' Turning her back on him she stood on tiptoe to brush Rupert's cheek with a kiss. 'Goodbye. Take care of yourself, my dear.' She left them discussing how best to deal with the damaged vehicles, but she had the feeling that Bowman was watching her as she walked towards the house. The prospect of having him working on the car so close to home was making her uneasy and she decided to broach the matter with her father when he was feeling better. After all, there must be other persons who could repair motorcars just as efficiently as Bowman.

Teddy stomped into the kitchen next morning, struggling to attach a starched white collar to his shirt. 'Give me a hand, Daisy. This bloody stud keeps popping out.'

She left the pan of porridge she had been stirring and went to his aid. The offending collar stud slipped easily into place. 'What a fuss about nothing. What's the matter with you this morning? Did you get out of the wrong side of the bed?'

He snatched a slice of toast from the silver rack. 'No. It's the old man. He's insisting on walking into Colchester. If he thinks I'm trudging three miles a day to work and the same again at night, he's got another think coming.'

His pained expression made Daisy want to giggle but somehow she managed to keep a straight face. 'It'll make you very fit.'

'Rubbish. I don't believe in all that stuff that you girls suck in as though it's God's truth.' He reached for the marmalade. 'We'll spend more in shoe repairs than we would in cab fares. Now if we were on the telephone we could have ordered some form of transport for this morning.'

Daisy slapped his hand as he went to stick the butter knife into the marmalade. 'For heaven's sake, Teddy. Just because we're living in the country doesn't mean you can behave like a pig. Let me take the tray into the dining room where you can sit down and eat your breakfast like a civilised human being.'

'Can't. Father says we've got to leave early or we'll be late opening the damned office. I honestly wish I'd gone in the army like Rupert, the lucky blighter. What wouldn't I give to be in his shoes?'

'Don't talk like that. If there's a war and they introduce conscription, you'd be one of the first to be called up.'

'I can't wait.' He turned with a guilty start as their father burst into the room.

'What are you doing, Edward? I've been waiting for you.'

'Won't you stop and have some breakfast, Father?' Daisy asked anxiously. 'It's a long walk into town.'

His expression softened slightly. 'I'll get something later.' He held the door open. 'Come along, boy. We'll be late.'

Munching and muttering beneath his breath, Teddy left the kitchen followed by his irate parent. The door had barely closed before it opened again and Beatrice burst into the room. 'I was almost knocked down in the rush. What's going on?'

Daisy noted her sister's riding outfit with raised eyebrows. 'You're lucky that Father was in a hurry, Bea. You know what he thinks about women wearing jodhpurs and riding astride like men.'

'I've done with side-saddles. You've no control over your mount on one of those silly things. They may look elegant, but I'm not riding down Rotten Row.' Beatrice paused, sniffing the air. 'Is something burning?'

'Oh, no!' Daisy hurried over to the stove, seizing the bubbling pan and lifting it off the hob. 'I've burnt the porridge and it's your fault for coming down dressed like a boy.'

'Scoop the top bit off, no one will notice.' Beatrice pulled out a chair and began helping herself to toast and butter. 'Anyway, you're supposed to be the suffragist. You should encourage me to be myself and not give in to male prejudices.'

Daisy placed the saucepan on the table with an emphatic thud. 'What's the matter with everyone this morning? We've got a perfectly good dining room but you and Teddy want to eat in the kitchen.'

'I don't see why we have to pretend that we're still living in London. What's wrong with eating in here?'

'Mother wouldn't hear of it.'

'Well she doesn't get up until mid-morning, and I'm hungry. It seems a frightful waste of time setting the table and carting hot food all the way to the dining room so that it's barely warm when it gets there. Besides which, we never have bacon or kidneys these days, and I've almost forgotten what kedgeree tastes like.'

'We have to economise, Bea. We can't afford to live as we did in Warwick Square.'

'I suppose not. Give me some of that beastly goo then. It's like being back in the nursery.'

Daisy spooned a generous helping into a bowl and passed it to her. 'Don't take too much cream. Mother likes it in her coffee.'

Beatrice pulled a face. 'And we mustn't upset Mother.' She poured a liberal amount onto her porridge, adding a heaped dessertspoonful of sugar. 'Why don't we get a cow? Then we could have as much milk and cream as we like.'

'Maybe we will one day when Father's business picks up.'

'I'll be old and grey by then.'

Daisy poured tea into two cups and passed one to Beatrice. 'Where are you off to this morning?'

'I'm going to ride Pumpkin to Folly Farm and help Jimmy with the harvest.'

'You're lucky. I'll be spending the morning baking, but I wondered if I could borrow the pony this afternoon?'

'Why? You don't like riding.'

'I want to do a few errands and it would save me time, that's all.'

Beatrice eyed her curiously. 'What are you up to, Daisy Lennox?'

'Nothing very interesting. I thought I'd pay a call on Lady Pendleton, but if you're going to be out all day I'll walk.'

'Why are you going to see Rupert's mother? Are you trying to ingratiate yourself with your future mother-in-law?'

Daisy choked on a mouthful of tea. 'Certainly not. If you must know, I was going to ask if we could borrow some sort of conveyance so that Father and Teddy could drive to work. It was Rupert's idea.'

'I thought you two were getting very pally.' Beatrice dropped her spoon into her empty bowl and leapt to her feet. 'I'm off then.'

'It wouldn't hurt you to stay and help in the house.'

'You've got Ruby to do that, and you know I can't cook. But I'm very good at handling farm machinery, and the Gurneys are thinking of buying one of these new-fangled steam tractors. Wouldn't that be smashing?'

'I suppose so, but it wouldn't help Father and Teddy to get to and from work. We've got to be practical, Bea. They earn the money, we don't. The least we can do is to help all we can.'

'I can't ask Mr Gurney to pay me. What would that look like?' Beatrice said, pouting.

Daisy could see that she was getting nowhere with this conversation. She put her teacup down on its saucer with a sigh. 'Go on. Go to the Gurneys' farm and have a lovely day. We'll manage somehow.'

Beatrice gave her a hug. 'You're the best sister a girl could have.' She angled her head, grinning. 'Well, sometimes you are, and at others you're a pill, but I love you.' She danced out of the kitchen, almost bumping into Ruby as she came in from the scullery.

'Good Lord, Miss Bea. Where's the fire?'

'I'm off,' Beatrice cried gleefully. 'See you later, Ruby old chum.' She disappeared into the scullery, banging the outside door as she left the house.

'That girl will meet herself coming back one day,' Ruby said, chuckling. 'I suppose she's off to see her boyfriend at the farm.'

Daisy recoiled at the idea of her sister being romantically involved. 'Don't be silly, Ruby. She's much too young to think like that.'

Ruby snorted with laughter. 'You have lived a sheltered life. Your little sister is sixteen and she's got her eye on that Jimmy Gurney or I'm a Dutchman.' She picked up the teapot and filled a cup, adding a dash of milk before taking a mouthful. 'That's better. I was gasping for a cup of split pea.'

Daisy sat down for the first time since she had risen from her bed that morning. She buttered a slice of toast. 'Help yourself to porridge, Ruby.' She took a bite, chewed and swallowed. 'What kept you so long? I thought you were just putting the soiled shirts to soak in the washhouse.'

'I did that, and then I heard a noise in the stables so I went to look and found that mechanic fellow tinkering with the motor. I asked him what he thought he was doing there so early and he says he's got a busy day ahead, so he wanted to get an early start.'

'You've been gone for ages.'

Ruby's pale cheeks flushed to a rosy shade of pink. 'Well, we did have a bit of a chat. He's a bit of all right, if you ask me.'

Daisy considered this in silence. She would not call him handsome, but there was a certain animal magnetism about him that made him hard to ignore. And if the truth were told, she had not forgotten the humorous glint in his sloe-dark eyes, or the boldness of his gaze which bordered on the impertinent.

'I think he's really good-looking,' Ruby said eagerly. 'Wouldn't you say so?'

'Why, yes. I suppose he is,' Daisy said, trying hard to sound casual. 'I hadn't given him a second thought.'

'Shall I take him out a cup of tea and that last bit of toast, if it's going free?'

'No, you eat your breakfast.' Daisy rose from the table. 'I've finished mine, and anyway I want to speak to Mr Bowman. I need to find out how much his services are going to cost.'

'We're broke, ain't we?'

'Not exactly, Ruby. But every penny counts.' Daisy picked up the teapot. 'I'll make a fresh brew. Mine's cold anyway.'

Minutes later she was making her way around the side of the house, heading towards the stable block with a mug of tea in her hand. As with the rest of Rainbow's End, the half-timbered buildings had seen better days. The roof over the coach house looked ready to cave in at any moment, but, Daisy thought with a rueful smile, it had been in that state since she first came here as a child. Twitch grass had forced its way between the cobblestones and moss was growing on the brickwork, but somehow that just added to its rustic charm. The double doors were propped open and she hesitated on the threshold. 'Hello.'

Barnaby Bowman appeared from the dark depths of the building, holding a spanner in one hand and an oily rag in the other. His dark hair was ruffled and his overalls were open to the waist, exposing an expanse of bronzed flesh that made Daisy hastily avert her eyes. 'What can I do for you, Miss Lennox?'

She felt suddenly shy and unusually tongue-tied. It seemed rather foolish to have interrupted his work when her father had already agreed that he might start on the repairs. 'I – I just wanted to see if you'd assessed the damage,' she said lamely. 'And I thought you might like a cup of tea. I didn't know if you took sugar so I just put one in, but you can have more if you want.' She broke off, raising her eyes to his face, and found him watching her intently. For some unknown reason she found this infinitely more disturbing than his somewhat cavalier attitude towards her the previous evening.

He took the mug from her hand. 'Thank you.' He held her gaze for a moment and then turned away. 'Come and see for yourself.'

Her heart rate quickened as she followed him into the dim interior of the coach house. The smell of engine oil and petrol had all but obliterated the sour stench of damp rot and bat droppings. It took a few seconds for her eyes to become accustomed to the poor light, although a few stray sunbeams filtered through gaps in the roof where tiles were missing. She could just make out the shape of the Humberette, but it was in a sorry state. Bowman and Farmer Hayes had done a good job getting the damaged motor under cover, but she could see that to make the car roadworthy again was a considerable undertaking. 'It's a bit of a mess. Do you think it can be put right?'

He brushed the sweat from his brow with the back of his hand, leaving a streak of oil on his forehead. 'It could be fixed, but it's a big job and it won't be cheap.'

She bit her lip. She did not want to admit that her family was in straitened circumstances, but in all fairness to Bowman she did not want to let him start on a job that they could not afford. 'You'll have to speak to my father,' she said after a moment's thought. 'He'll decide if it's worth going ahead with the repairs.'

'A new motor like this would cost at least a hundred and twenty-five quid, which is more than most blokes earn in a year.'

She stiffened, sensing the underlying criticism of people who could afford such luxuries while others struggled to survive. Suddenly it had become a battle of wills between them to see who would give way first. 'So how much do you estimate that it would cost to make it roadworthy?'

'Can't say off the top of my head, but it wouldn't

be anything like that sum, and Mr Lennox would have a reliable motor at the end of it. I'm a good mechanic.'

She was not going to allow him the last word. 'Very well then, I suggest you give my father a written estimate before you start on the work. We wouldn't want to waste your valuable time.'

'Anything you say, miss.' He raised the mug to her and then downed the rapidly cooling liquid in one long, thirsty gulp. He handed it back to her. 'Thanks for that, and now if you'll excuse me, I'd better get on with the job in hand.' He turned away and she found herself dismissed like an errant schoolgirl.

Annoyed but not quite certain why she should let a man like Bowman make her feel this way, Daisy left him to get on with his work and went out into the sunshine. A gentle breeze fanned her cheeks and she took deep breaths of the sweet country air. She felt oddly unsettled, as though her world had tilted slightly on its axis and she could not quite get her bearings. There was something about Bowman that both attracted and repelled her. If Ruby's reaction to him was anything to go by he would be a disturbing influence in a household dominated by women. She hoped that his estimate would make it impossible to hire him, and she was even more determined to seek help from Lady Pendleton.

She hurried back towards the house, but she hesitated outside the scullery door and raising the mug she pressed her lips to the spot where Bowman's mouth had left its mark. She closed her eyes and felt a shiver run down her spine. Ashamed of her irrational and sentimental action, she let the mug fall to the ground where it shattered into shards. What kind of madness had this man wrought not only on her but also on level-headed, street-wise Ruby? She went indoors to fetch a dustpan and brush.

After a morning spent in the kitchen baking bread and cakes both for the family and for her mother's stall at the church bazaar, Daisy cooked lunch and served it in the dining room. Ruby ate her meal alone in the kitchen and Daisy left her to do the washing up while she went upstairs to change out of her working clothes and into something more suitable for calling on Lady Pendleton. She had not told her mother of her intention as she would have been sure to forbid such a venture and Daisy did not feel like an argument.

Dressed in a cream shantung afternoon gown trimmed with navy-blue piping, and wearing a large straw hat to protect her complexion from the sun, Daisy set off down the garden and through the orchard to a wooden gate half hidden by brambles and ivy. They had discovered it as children and found it led into the grounds of Pendleton Park. It was here that she and Teddy had first come across Rupert, who literally dropped upon them from the branches of an oak tree where he had been hiding from his tutor. Daisy smiled as she remembered those glorious days of freedom when they roamed the estate, swimming in the lake and playing hide and seek in the cool green woods. They had been enchanted summers but all too soon it was time for herself and Bea to return to London and the boys were packed off to boarding school. She could see them all in her mind's eye as she crossed the deer park to the avenue of trees which led to the great house. The impressive Jacobean mansion had been built at the beginning of the seventeenth century, and the magnificent grounds designed by Capability Brown. She had visited the house many times in the past, but she was still a little over-awed as she knocked on the oak door with its wrought-iron hinges and metal studs. She could not imagine herself as mistress of all this. She took a step backwards as the heavy door swung open to reveal the butler, Warrington, who had been with the family since he was a boy. Now he was stooped and grey but Daisy knew that he was held in great esteem by the family above stairs, and below stairs he was king.

'Good afternoon, Warrington,' she said, stifling the urge to curtsey to such an august personage. 'Is Lady Pendleton at home?'

'I'll see if her ladyship is receiving visitors, Miss Lennox.' He stood aside to let her into the great hall. The black and white marble floor tiles echoed to the sound of his footsteps as he headed for the staircase, moving slowly like a rheumaticky tortoise. Daisy was left to wait amongst the suits of armour, which stood stiffly to attention against a background of oak-panelled walls decorated with shields, halberds and crossed swords. Shafts of fragmented sunlight filtered through the mullioned windows, and the Pendleton ancestors stared down at her from gilt-framed portraits, making her feel very small and insignificant.

After what seemed like an age, Warrington reappeared and escorted her to the crimson and gold saloon on the first floor, ushering her into the room and announcing her as if she were a person of some importance. Lady Pendleton sat by an open window with her embroidery frame at her side, but she rose to her feet as Daisy entered the room and held out her hands. 'How lovely to see you, my dear. Do come and sit down.' She turned to her butler with a charming smile. 'I'm sure Miss Lennox would like some refreshment, Warrington.'

'Yes, my lady.'

Daisy was certain that she could hear his joints creaking as he bowed out of the room, closing the double doors softly behind him. Lady Pendleton did not seem to notice anything untoward and she resumed her seat, motioning Daisy to take the chair opposite. 'You look hot. Have you walked all the way from Rainbow's End?'

'It's not very far.' Daisy hesitated, not quite knowing how to raise the subject of transport. 'You heard about the accident to our motor?'

'Yes. Rupert told me all about it. He was terribly sorry. He said it was his fault entirely. Your father must allow us to foot the bill.'

Embarrassed, Daisy sank down on the edge of the spindly gilt chair. 'I didn't come to ask for money, Lady Pendleton.'

'Of course not, but all the same we must make amends. I'm well aware that your father is financially embarrassed, although I'm sure it will only be temporary.'

'I did come to beg a favour,' Daisy said, pressing home her advantage. 'I wondered if we could borrow a gig or a dog cart, just for the time being until the motor is back on the road. I know that Father wouldn't dream of asking, but he and Teddy actually walked into Colchester this morning.'

'Consider it done, my dear. When you're ready to leave I'll send for our head groom and he'll sort something out for you. I'm sure we've several vehicles that are hardly ever in use these days, and you'll need a carriage horse too. Our stables are filled with animals eating their heads off without adequate exercise. I'm certain that Donovan will find one suitable for your use.' She sat back in her chair, smiling. 'Now, tell me how you're getting on at Rainbow's End. I keep meaning to call but I have so many demands on my time that I never seem to get round to it. Of course, I see your mother in church every Sunday, but it's hardly the place for talking about personal matters.'

'We're managing very well, thank you.'

Lady Pendleton gave her a searching look. 'I'm sure you are, but I was actually asking about you, my dear. How are you finding life in the country? Everything moves at a much slower pace.'

'I don't have the time to be bored, Lady Pendleton.'

'Rupert has been teaching you to drive.'

It was a statement rather than a question and Daisy nodded her head. 'Yes, my lady.'

'He's very fond of you, and he was very upset when you turned him down.'

Daisy stared at her in dismay. 'He told you that?'

'No, my dear, but I know my son. He left home that day in such a happy mood and returned looking like a thundercloud. I knew it wasn't simply the damage to his precious motorcar that had brought him so low.'

'I'm sorry.'

'Don't be. I'm sure you had your reasons.'

'I'm terribly fond of Rupert, but I don't think that's enough. I couldn't marry a man I didn't love with all my heart.'

Lady Pendleton smiled but there was sadness in her blue eyes. 'I'm sure you know best, Daisy dear.' Her attention was diverted by someone tapping on the door. 'Enter.'

A small procession of maidservants dressed in black with starched white aprons and goffered headbands brought in trays laden with sandwiches, cakes and tea. They moved swiftly and silently like well-practised dancers performing a ballet as they set a rosewood table with an embroidered cloth and laid out plates, napkins and cutlery.

'Would you like me to pour, my lady?' The most senior housemaid bobbed a curtsey.

'No, thank you. That will be all.' Lady Pendleton reached for the silver teapot, straining the tea into a bone china cup. 'Milk and sugar?'

'Just milk, please.' Daisy eyed the plate of dainty cucumber sandwiches and she was reminded of Rupert's invitation to take tea with him. 'They're his favourite,' she murmured.

Lady Pendleton picked up the plate and offered it to her. 'They always were and he loves scones with strawberry jam and cream, but I doubt if he'll be having afternoon tea in the mess today.' She eyed Daisy thoughtfully. 'Perhaps you'll feel differently when you've had time to think about his proposal. Rupert can be impulsive but he knows his own mind. I doubt if he'll change, but you might, given time.'

'Why me, Lady Pendleton? I don't understand why you favour me when I come from such an ordinary family.'

'Has your mother never told you about my background, Daisy?'

'I know that you went to the same school. That's all.'

'My family were what one might describe as ordinary people. My grandfather was a master cabinet maker and a good businessman. He opened up a shop in Oxford Street just as the other department stores were beginning to appear. My father went into the business and made it what it is today. He could afford to buy me an expensive education and that was when your mother and I became friends. We both married for love. It's as simple as that. Rupert is very much like me and there isn't an ounce of snobbishness in his whole body. I was so happy when you two met and became friends, and if your friendship for my son blossoms into love I would be absolutely delighted.'

'I see. Thank you for telling me.' Daisy stared at the sandwich on her plate, but her appetite deserted her. She took a bite but her throat seemed to close up when she attempted to swallow. She wished with all her heart that Rupert would walk through the door and they could start again. Not that she had changed her mind about marrying him, but a soldier's life was always going to be dangerous even in peacetime, and she wished that she had sent him away in a happier state of mind.

Intuitive as ever, Lady Pendleton seemed to sense her discomfort and swiftly changed the subject. A message was duly sent to the head groom and Daisy began to relax and enjoy herself. They parted on the best of terms with Lady Pendleton promising to call at Rainbow's End as soon as her commitments allowed.

Daisy made her way to the stables, where she discovered that a governess cart had been dusted off and a sturdy Welsh cob harnessed between the shafts.

Donovan held the reins while she climbed onto the driver's seat. 'Are you used to handling horses, miss?'

'Of course,' Daisy said stiffly. She did not want to admit that the last time she had driven a horse-drawn vehicle was when she was fourteen, and then it had only been a short tool around the grounds with Rupert at her side giving her instructions. She settled herself on the seat. 'Thank you, Donovan.' She flicked the reins. 'Walk on.'

To her amazement the well-trained horse moved off at a brisk trot and headed in the right direction for which she was grateful. She would have to practise if she were to become a proficient driver, but luckily the cob seemed to need little guidance. It was not quite so easy however when she arrived at Rainbow's End, and as she climbed down from the driver's seat she realised that she had not the faintest idea how to unharness the animal or how to get the cart into the coach house. Bea might know, but Pumpkin's stall was empty and it was still only mid-afternoon.

The horse turned his head to look at her with large limpid eyes and she shrugged her shoulders. 'I'm sorry, boy. I'm afraid I'll have to leave you here until I can get help.' She hesitated. Would he stay put? There was nowhere to tether him and it would be embarrassing to say the least if the animal decided to return to the stables at Pendleton Park without a driver. She cursed her stubborn pride that had made her refuse to ask Donovan for assistance. She had no doubt that he would have accompanied her had she asked, and he would have been happy to show her what to do. She took off her straw hat, fanning herself with it as the sun beat down from an azure sky. If only Rupert would appear now and help her out of her predicament. She would not even mind a lecture.

Then, almost as if in answer to her silent prayers, she heard the sound of a motorcycle engine approaching from the direction of the village. She stepped into the lane, hoping to flag the person down and ask for help. It was hard to admit defeat, but the horse was pawing the ground and any minute might decide to wander off. She waved frantically as the rider rounded the corner but as he drew to a halt she realised that it was Bowman, and seated precariously on the crossbar in front of him was none other than Ruby. She slid off, rearranging her skirts with a sheepish grin. 'I had to go into the village to take the cakes to the village hall for Madam,' she said hastily. 'Barnaby was coming this way and he offered to bring me home.' She shuffled her feet. 'I'll go inside and put the kettle on, shall I?'

Daisy was too busy calming the horse to make any objections. 'Yes,' she said through clenched teeth. She would give Ruby a lecture on the dangers of riding on motorcycles later. She glared at Bowman as he balanced the bike on its stand. 'What do you think you were doing? She might have been killed.'

Chapter Six

'Don't worry, miss. I'm a good rider.' He took off his goggles and his eyes danced with amusement. 'She was quite safe in my hands.'

'That contraption doesn't look very safe to me. Anyway, what are you doing here? I thought I told you not to go ahead with the work until you'd given my father an estimate.' She was not prepared to admit that Lord Pendleton would be paying the bill.

He put his hand into his pocket and pulled out a crumpled sheet of paper. 'I've made a note of the parts needed with a rough guide to their cost and my charges. It might come to more if the job takes longer, or it could be less if everything goes to plan. You won't get it done cheaper elsewhere.'

She took it from him. 'Thank you. My father will be in touch.'

He did not move away, but stood staring thoughtfully at the cart and the restive animal. 'I recognise this old trap. I think I fixed it once at the big house.'

'Probably. It's on loan until my father gets the motor back on the road.'

He took the reins from her, making soothing noises to the unsettled cob. 'So are you going to see to this poor brute or are you going to leave the horse and cart parked outside like a motorcar?'

She stiffened, unwilling to admit that she did not know what to do. 'I – er . . .'

He grinned. 'Would you like me to do it for you? I don't suppose a lady like you has ever had to do anything so menial as rub down a horse or muck out a stable.'

'You're impertinent, Bowman.'

His smile faded and he released the reins, causing the horse to move restlessly in the shafts. 'I'm sorry, ma'am. You'll have to excuse a country bumpkin forgetting his manners. I'll be leaving you now.' He was about to go but she called him back.

'No, please don't leave me. You're right. I do need help.'

'And I'll be pleased to oblige a lady in distress.' There was a mocking note in his voice, and to make matters worse, he made it look so easy. He guided the horse into the coach house, and having unharnessed the animal he led it into the stables. 'There,' he said, stroking the horse's neck. 'It's not difficult when you know how.'

'Thank you,' Daisy said stiffly. 'I'm obliged to you, Mr Bowman.'

'It's Barnaby. We're going to see a lot more of each other while I'm fixing your father's motor, so we might as well start as we mean to go on.' He shut the stall door, bolting it on the outside.

She could not help noticing his sinewy, sun-tanned forearms, so different from her brother's stick-thin wrists and puny, milk-pale arms. She made an effort to keep the conversation formal. 'You're very confident. He might refuse to accept your estimate and get someone else to do the work.'

'He might, but he won't. There aren't many good mechanics in these parts. In fact there aren't that many motorcars. I'm what you might call a forerunner in the machine age. It won't be long before there are millions of motorcars on the road and petrol pumps in every village. We're at the beginning of an exciting time, Miss Lennox. You mark my words.'

His enthusiasm was catching and Daisy found herself looking at him in a new light. She had thought him an ill-mannered yokel but she realised now that she had been both wrong and foolish. She had spent too much of her life listening to her mother's prejudiced views, and had looked down on a man merely because he wore overalls and worked with his hands. She realised now that she had become a snob, and she was ashamed. 'You do make it sound quite thrilling,' she said reluctantly.

He beamed at her and this time there was no mockery in his smile. 'It is. We're coming into a modern world where fellows like this won't be needed for work.' He stroked the cob's muzzle, receiving an appreciative whicker in response. 'Anyway, I must get on. I've got a leaky tap to fix at the vicarage and a blocked gutter to clear at Major Henderson's house.'

'Of course. Don't let me keep you.' Daisy stood aside to let him pass but he paused, standing too close to her for comfort.

'Good day to you, miss. Any time you need anything

just send for Barnaby Bowman.' He grinned, exposing a row of even white teeth, and then he was gone. The scent of male musk, engine oil and Lifebuoy soap lingered in the air and she stood very still, watching his swaggering walk as he went to retrieve his motorcycle. He kick-started the engine and drove off in a cloud of dust.

It was only as she left the stables and walked towards the house that she realised she was still clutching the crumpled estimate in her hand. She quickened her pace, hoping that her father refused to sanction the work. Bowman was a disruptive influence. She made for the scullery, intending to lecture Ruby on the dangers of motorcycles.

Victor Lennox, who had never willingly done a day's exercise in his whole life, had arrived home tired and footsore. Teddy had blisters on his feet that needed urgent attention and he was convinced that he had sunstroke. He declared that he was too exhausted to think about food and all he wanted was to lie in a darkened room and mourn for the life he had once led. He left the room, limping.

Close to tears Gwendoline begged her husband to accept the Pendletons' generous offer to pay for the repairs on the Humberette, but his jaw set in a stubborn line that Daisy recognised only too well. 'I may be close to bankruptcy, Gwendoline, but I refuse to accept charity.' He turned to Daisy. 'You may tell Bowman that I'll pay him weekly for his time, plus whatever it costs to get the necessary spares.'

'Yes, Father.' She glanced nervously at her mother, hoping that they were not going to be treated to a display of histrionics.

'Do as you will, Victor,' Gwendoline said with a disapproving tut-tut. 'You always have it your way. Nobody listens to me.'

He smiled gently. 'Of course we do, my dear. But you must allow me to be the best judge of how I conduct my business.'

'You didn't do too well when it came to Jeremiah Carlton. If it hadn't been for that criminal we would still be living in Warwick Square like civilised human beings.' She spun round, catching sight of Beatrice who was creeping past the door in an attempt to reach her bedroom and change out of her breeches. 'Just look at your youngest daughter, Victor. She's running wild and mixing with peasants like a native.' She beckoned frantically to her daughter. 'Come here this minute, Beatrice, and show your father how you went out today.'

Hanging her head, Beatrice slunk into the room. 'I've been helping the Gurneys with the harvest, Father.'

Victor glanced at her jodhpurs and sighed. 'I don't know what young girls are coming to these days. But I suppose it's better that you spend your time doing something useful rather than joining those despicable suffragists or listening to jazz music and smoking cigarettes.'

'Don't put ideas into her head.' Gwendoline fanned herself vigorously with a lace handkerchief. 'Go to your room and change into something decent, Beatrice. I despair of both my daughters.' She shot a withering look at Daisy. 'Your face is quite pink. You must have been out in the sun without a hat, and you've got hands like a navvy. It's no wonder Rupert didn't come up to scratch. You'll end up on the shelf, my girl. And Beatrice will disgrace us all by marrying a farm labourer.'

'Oh, Mother!' Beatrice ran from the room and the sound of her running footsteps echoed throughout the house as she raced upstairs. Daisy took a deep breath, reminding herself that their mother had probably suffered the most from their move to the country. She met her father's worried look with a meaningful nod of her head. 'Shall we go and inspect the governess cart, Father? Lady Pendleton said we can have it as long as we like, and it's better than walking to work each day.'

'Your father goes to business, Daisy,' Gwendoline said, sighing. 'Common people go to work. Professional gentlemen go to business.'

Victor rose wearily from his chair. 'Yes, let's go and see the grand equipage that will take Teddy and me to business each day.' He winked at Daisy. 'Lead the way, my dear.'

Despite Daisy's misgivings, Bowman started work on the Humberette next day. He worked all morning on the motor and it was all she could do to prevent Ruby from taking him cups of tea at half-hourly intervals. She seemed to have been smitten by his good looks and easy charm, although she denied any attraction on her part, saying that it was just common decency to make certain that a working man was well treated. When Daisy saw the fourth mug of tea about to be taken outside she put her foot down. 'No, Ruby. This is ridiculous. We can't afford it for one thing, and for another you spend more time chatting than you do actually working. It's got to stop.'

Ruby tossed her head and made a show of drinking the tea herself. 'I was just going out for some fresh air.'

'It's raining,' Daisy said coldly. 'He'll never get the motorcar back on the road if you keep distracting him.'

Ruby's bottom lip stuck out in an ominous pout but she said nothing and returned to the onerous task of blackleading the range. An atmosphere prevailed in the kitchen for the remainder of the morning. It was the first time that Daisy and Ruby had clashed head on over anything or anyone, and by midday Daisy had had enough of Ruby's sulks. She glanced at the clock on the wall. 'Perhaps Bowman would like a cup of tea before he breaks for his lunch,' she suggested tentatively. 'Would you like to go and ask him?'

Ruby's eyebrows were drawn together in a forbidding scowl as she mopped the quarry-tiled floor. 'I wouldn't want to be accused of wasting my time or making free with the master's tea, miss.'

'I thought better of you, and there's no need to take that tone with me, Ruby Flagg.' Daisy whipped off her apron and flung it onto the nearest chair. 'You've been behaving like a two-year-old all morning.' She made for the scullery door. 'I'll go, since it's obviously too much to ask of you.' She slammed out of the kitchen. It was still raining and she regretted the fact that she had not stopped to pick up an umbrella, but she could not lose face by going back indoors. She broke into a run, arriving at the coach house dishevelled and out of breath. Shaking the raindrops from her hair, which had escaped from the chignon at the back of her neck and was curling wildly around her face, she went inside. She could smell cigarette smoke and hear the clink of metal against metal. Bowman was still working on the motor and had his back to her. She strolled over to him, controlling her erratic breathing with difficulty. 'So you're still here,' she said casually. 'I thought you would have gone by now.'

He took the hand-rolled cigarette from his lips. 'Are you checking up on me, miss? There's no need. I'm making a note of my hours.'

She was unused to tradesmen talking back. First it had been Ruby and now Bowman had challenged her authority. There seemed to be a revolution going on in Rainbow's End, and she did not know whether to stamp on it before it escalated or to join the rebels. She had listened to so many lectures on women's rights that she could not in all conscience blame Ruby for standing up for herself, but Bowman was another matter. There was something almost feral about him that was annoying and at the same time exciting. She could not imagine him submitting to anyone in authority. 'I'm not checking up on you, Mr Bowman. I came to see if you wanted another cup of tea.'

'You shouldn't be waiting on the likes of me, miss. Where's that girl of yours? She'd be more than happy to oblige, I'm sure.'

'Ruby is busy.'

He flicked the cigarette end out of the open door onto the wet cobblestones. 'What are you doing here, miss?'

She recoiled. 'I beg your pardon?'

He chuckled. 'Don't look so offended. I mean it as a compliment. What I should have said is that you're too good for Nutley Green.' He glanced at her hands, clasped tightly in front of her. 'You're a lady. You shouldn't be slaving over a hot stove all day.'

'I don't think that's any of your business, Mr Bowman.'

He sat back on his haunches, looking up at her. 'I saw your picture in the papers last year. You were one of them suffragettes and you knocked a copper's helmet off.'

She felt the ready blush rise to her cheeks and she dropped her gaze. 'I'm not proud of that. I don't believe in violence.'

'There may be a lot worse things happening soon than smacking a constable on the head with a brolly.'

His serious tone made her raise her eyes to meet his and she saw with a shock that he was in earnest. 'What do you mean?'

'It's common knowledge that the Germans are building up their army. They're always talking about it in the pub. Anyway, I don't trust the Kaiser even if he is related to the royal family.'

'I expect it's just men talking when they've had too much to drink. I'm sure there's no need to worry.'

His serious expression melted into a smile that

made her feel dizzy. He had a way of looking at her that made her pulses race, and he treated her like an equal, which was confusing. He did not seem to realise that there were social barriers designed to keep them in their respective places. 'I suppose Ruby told you about the episode outside the palace,' she said in a desperate attempt to distance herself from him without being too obvious. 'She really shouldn't gossip about family matters.'

He rose to his feet, his smile fading. 'No, she never said a word. Like I said, I read it in the papers. Anyway, it was all over the village. Everyone knows what you did and most of them think the better of you for it.'

Once again he was standing so close to her that she could feel the warmth of his body. It was so unfair. He was not playing by the rules. She took a step backwards. 'I'd better let you get on.'

'I'm done for today. I've got to order some spares from Vauxhall and I don't know how long it will take for them to come, so I won't be here for a day or two.' He turned away and began packing his tools in a canvas bag.

'All right then,' Daisy said lamely. 'I hope they'll arrive soon. I mean, it's important to get the motor back on the road as quickly as possible.'

He headed for the open doorway. 'The rain's stopped,' he said, turning to her with a smile. 'It'll be fine for the church bazaar. There's a dance afterwards in the village hall. Will you be there?'

Taken off guard she shook her head. 'I don't know. I hadn't considered it.'

'It won't be what you're used to, but you might enjoy a bit of rustic fun.'

'You really do think I'm a terrible snob, don't you, Bowman?'

'Who me, miss? Whatever gave you that idea?'

'Now you're laughing at me. It's not polite.'

'I'm sorry for being a bit of a turnip, miss. We simple country folk can't help having straw growing out of our ears.'

She followed him outside, catching hold of his sleeve. 'You don't know me and you shouldn't pigeon-hole people.'

He met her angry stare with a steady gaze. 'Ever heard of the pot calling the kettle black? It seems to me, Miss Lennox, that you're as guilty of that as anyone.'

'How dare you? You're forgetting your—'

'My place, miss? Is that what you were going to say? You and your fine ideas about equality. Does that just apply to women with a good education and a plum in their mouths?' Looping the canvas bag over the handlebar of his motorcycle he drew her roughly into his arms and kissed her on the lips. He held her for a moment, his eyes boring into hers. 'You're a woman and a damn pretty one too, if only you'd drop the airs and graces.'

'You uncouth brute.' She raised her hand to slap his face but he caught her by the wrist.

'Steady, Miss Lennox. You almost stooped to my level.'

'Don't ever do that again.' She jerked free from his

grasp, taking a step backwards and glaring at him. She was furious with him and with herself for allowing him to take such liberties.

'I'm not promising anything. You look even prettier when you're cross.' He mounted his motorcycle. 'I hope to see you at the dance tonight. It's a do to raise money to repair the church roof. You'd be doing your civic duty, Daisy.' He kick-started the engine and roared off down the lane.

Speechless and still shaking with anger, she took a couple of minutes to calm down before returning to the house. She could hear her mother's voice as she entered through the scullery, and found her in the kitchen interrogating Ruby who looked flushed and flustered.

'Where have you been?' Gwendoline demanded angrily. 'Ruby didn't know and I've been waiting for my lunch. You know that I'm supposed to help Lady Pembleton on the cake stall this afternoon, but I've got one of my heads coming on and it's all your fault.'

Ruby sent a sympathetic look in Daisy's direction. 'Sorry, miss.'

'Don't apologise to my daughter, Ruby.' Gwendoline edged her out of the way, coming to stand close to Daisy with a martial gleam in her eyes. 'You know I have to eat at regular intervals or I feel faint. Now I'll have to lie down all afternoon and you will have to stand in for me.' She paused for breath, eyeing her critically. 'You look a perfect fright, Daisy. Where were you when I needed you?'

'I was discussing the repairs to the motorcar with

Bowman, Mother. He has to send for spare parts so there will be a delay while he waits for them to arrive.'

Gwendoline raised her hand to her forehead, closing her eyes as if in pain. 'Stop. I don't want to hear about that wretched vehicle. If only we'd brought our chauffeur to the country instead of that simple girl, none of this would have happened.'

'Mother, please.' Daisy cast a worried glance at Ruby, who was pulling faces behind Gwendoline's back. Resisting the urge to giggle, Daisy steered her mother towards the doorway. 'Go and sit in the drawing room, Mother. Give me ten minutes and I'll have your lunch on the table, and then you must lie down. I'll see to everything, so don't worry.'

'Beatrice has gone to the farm again. She's running wild and it's all because your father didn't keep a close enough eye on his business affairs. This was a terrible move. You'll be gallivanting around with the peasants next.' Gwendoline tottered out of the room.

Daisy closed the door on her, leaning against it and sighing. 'I'm sorry, Ruby. Mother didn't mean it.'

'Yes, she did. Don't worry, I know exactly what Madam thinks of me and I can live with that. It's what all toffs think of people what don't speak proper and come from south of the river. I'm used to it.'

'It's not how I am,' Daisy said firmly. She went to the larder and brought out a bowl of salad and what was left of the boiled ham from last night's dinner. 'I've just had a lecture from Bowman about being snobbish. You don't think I'm like that, do you, Ruby?'

'Not always, but it's always going to be a case of

them and us. It's how the world works whether we like it or not.'

Daisy laid the food on the table and went to the dresser to select some plates. 'Are you going to the dance in the village hall tonight?'

'I might, miss. If I can have the time off. I ain't promised nothing.'

'Did Bowman ask you?'

'He mentioned it, miss. But I never said I would.'

'You and I will go together, Ruby. I'm tired of staying at home night after night. It might be fun.'

Ruby stared at her in amazement. 'Are you sure? I mean, it's not going to be what you're used to.'

'Then it's time I did something new. The world is changing, Ruby, only most people don't seem to realise it.'

Daisy spent the afternoon helping Lady Pendleton on the cake stall. It was the first time that she had taken part in any of the village activities, and she was aware that she was being closely scrutinised by the locals. She knew Mrs Cobb who ran the post office and general store and her daughter, Ada, who served behind the counter. Smith the postman was there with his wife who took in washing. Their two sons were also in attendance, both of them looking slightly bored as they huddled in a corner of the hall smoking cigarettes and eyeing the girls. Jed, the elder, was apprenticed to Boxall, the farrier, and Cyril was the butcher's boy. He was to be seen riding round the village on a rusty bicycle with a large wicker basket in the carrier filled with packages wrapped in bloodied brown paper. Both Jed and Cyril obviously had a sweet tooth as they bought most of the cakes that Daisy had baked, and Jed wanted to know if she was going to the dance. Ruby had told her that Jed was stepping out with Iris Woods, who worked as a scullery maid at Pendleton Park. Luckily Iris was not around when he approached Daisy, but she appeared later giving Daisy a very old-fashioned look. Her companion, a thin-faced girl with carroty hair who was parlour maid at the manor house, made rude comments about the madeleines that Daisy had baked. Until that moment Daisy had been undecided as to whether or not to attend the dance, but their unfriendly attitude brought out her stubborn streak.

'Don't take any notice of them,' Lady Pendleton said, having overheard the spiteful comments. 'Flossie Boxall and Iris are cousins and related to half the village. It's very hard for newcomers to be accepted in Nutley Green, but you're doing very well, Daisy.' She turned away to serve the vicar's wife, who purchased all the madeleines, explaining that they were her husband's favourite. She gave Daisy a vague smile before wandering off to inspect the bring and buy stall.

By the end of the afternoon Daisy felt that her face had set in a rictus grin and her feet were killing her. She helped Lady Pendleton pack up the stall, which did not take long as all the cakes had been sold.

'Thank you, Daisy,' Lady Pendleton said, patting her hand. 'You've been a marvellous help. I can see that you're cut out for this sort of thing.'

'I don't know about that. I seem to have got on the wrong side of some people.' Daisy piled the Pendleton Park china plates into a picnic hamper. 'I've already been told I don't belong in the country.'

'And who said that? It was very rude as well as unkind.'

Daisy shrugged her shoulders. 'It was just the mechanic who's fixing Father's motor. No one of consequence.'

'If you mean Barnaby Bowman then I should warn you that he's got quite a reputation with the ladies.'

'He won't get anywhere with me.'

'My dear, I wasn't suggesting anything of the sort. No, I meant your maid. He's broken a few hearts around here, so she'd better be wary of his charming manner.'

'I think I can keep him in his place.'

'I should hope so, Daisy.' Lady Pendleton glanced out of the window. 'Ah, here's Parkin. I told him to pick me up at five. May we give you a lift home? It's on the way.'

Daisy was about to thank her politely and say she wanted to walk, but she saw Jed striding purposefully in her direction. 'Thank you. That would be most kind, my lady.'

'I think we've known each other long enough for you to call me by my Christian name. After all I am your godmother, and maybe one day . . .' Lady Pendleton left the sentence hanging in mid-air.

Daisy felt twelve years old again and suddenly shy. 'Oh, I couldn't. I mean, it doesn't seem right somehow.'

'We've left Victorian starchiness behind, my dear. I'm a modern woman, and although I don't openly support the suffragists, I'm with them in my heart.'

'You are? I thought you would think badly of me for my involvement with the WSPU. Not that I've had a chance to do anything useful since we moved here.'

'Well, I wouldn't approve of you throwing yourself under a horse's hooves like that heroic woman, Emily Davison, but I think peaceful protest will win the day in the end.' Lady Pendleton tapped on the window and beckoned to her chauffeur. 'Parkin will carry the baskets,' she said as Daisy attempted to lift one of them. 'They're much too heavy for a girl like you.'

Parkin dropped Daisy at the garden gate. She went inside the house and was immediately accosted by her sister. 'Darling Daisy, my most favourite person in the whole world.'

Daisy hid a smile. 'What do you want, Bea?'

'Jimmy has asked me to go to the dance with him and I haven't anything to wear. Could I borrow your pink tussore with the blue satin sash and would you put my hair up for me?'

'Have you asked Mother if you can go?'

Bea's face fell. 'I was hoping you'd do it for me. She's got one of her heads.'

'I know. That's why I did the church bazaar for her. But actually I quite enjoyed helping Lady Pendleton on the cake stall. She was so sweet to me, and guess what?'

'I haven't a clue.'

'She only asked me to call her Jane. Can you imagine that?'

'Honestly? No.' Beatrice stared at her in amazement. 'I don't think Mother would approve. But never mind that. Will you put in a word for me? And if she allows me to go to the dance, may I borrow your gown? And your pink satin dancing shoes?'

'I suppose you'll pester me until I do.'

'Yes. Absolutely.'

'Then leave it to me. I can't promise anything, but I'll try.'

After dinner that evening, Daisy, Beatrice and Ruby set off for the village hall, escorted by a rather unwilling and grumpy Teddy, who had been dragooned into accompanying them by their mother. He chain-smoked all the way to the village, complaining bitterly that he was a hard-working man who wanted a bit of peace and quiet at the end of the day. 'I never used to work on Saturday afternoons when we had our offices in the City,' he said, stopping to light yet another cigarette from the stub of the old one. 'We used to leave it to Jeremiah and his minions to stay there until evening.'

'Which is probably why you lost the business,' Beatrice said, dancing on ahead. 'Hurry up and stop moaning, Teddy. You'll enjoy yourself when you get there.'

'I don't mix with the peasants,' he muttered beneath his breath. 'The village girls are probably fat and homely.'

Daisy slipped her hand through the crook of his arm.

'Don't be such a pessimist, Teddy. I saw some of the local girls today and although they weren't very friendly, they were very pretty. You might be pleasantly surprised.'

Teddy tossed his cigarette onto the gravel as they came to a halt outside the village hall. 'Here we go. It's a far, far better thing I do . . .'

'Shut up and open the door like a gentleman,' Beatrice said, hopping up and down with excitement. 'This is my first grown-up do, and if you spoil it I'll make your life hell, Edward Lennox. And I can do it, so don't glare at me like that.'

They entered the village hall, which had been transformed in a short space of time with Chinese lanterns hanging from the rafters and strategically placed swags of greenery. The vicar's wife was playing the tinny old piano accompanied by her only daughter, Cissie, on the violin. Daisy decided that Cissie could do with a few more lessons, but the music was jolly and there were several couples already on the dance floor performing something energetic.

Teddy was about to turn on his heel and leave when he caught sight of Iris and Flossie. They seemed to have been abandoned by the Smith brothers, who had joined the men at the refreshment table. Iris turned her head to give him an appraising look, and apparently liking what she saw gave him a dazzling smile. Seemingly drawn together by some invisible magnetic force, they walked slowly across the floor to meet each other.

'Good gracious,' Beatrice said in a fair imitation of

their mother's voice. 'Love at first sight.' She stood on tiptoe and waved. 'Cooee. Jimmy.' Apparently forgetting that she was supposed to be a young lady, she picked up her skirts and ran towards him, leaving Daisy and Ruby standing by the door.

'Since none of these gents are going to ask us,' Ruby said, grinning, 'can I get you something to drink, miss?'

'I'm tired of telling you that it's Daisy when my mother is out of earshot, and I'd love some fruit cup or whatever's going.'

'Right you are then, Daisy.' Ruby sashayed off, leaving Daisy on her own and feeling distinctly out of place in her elegant silk gown. The young men were clustered around the table where beer was being served from a keg, and they were eyeing her up and down in a way that made her feel like a prize heifer at a cattle market. The girls who were sitting this dance out were also staring at her with a mixture of envy and hostility written on their solemn faces. Perhaps this had been a terrible mistake. She was beginning to regret the impulse that had led her to brave the unknown. She had never been to any kind of social function without a partner or a chaperone, and she wished she had stayed at home. She moved aside instinctively as the door opened.

'So you decided to come after all, Daisy.'

Chapter Seven

'Good evening,' Daisy said coolly. She turned to face Bowman, hoping that he had not noticed the colour that suffused her cheeks, or the way her breath caught in her throat at the sight of him. Spruced up and smiling, he might have stepped from the pages of a romantic novel. She tried to convince herself that he would have been the villain of the piece, but if anything the hint of danger made him even more attractive. A tantalising glimpse of his chest was revealed by a white shirt open at the neck, and his slim hips were accentuated by tight-fitting black trousers, quite different from the baggy overalls he wore for work. His appearance was strikingly at odds with the rest of the young men, who looked slightly uncomfortable in their Sunday best suits. She swallowed hard and was about to reprimand him for the use of her Christian name when he forestalled her by proffering his arm.

'Would you like to dance?'

'I – er – not really. Ruby is fetching me a drink.'

'You did come here to enjoy yourself, didn't you?'

'I'm not sure that dancing with you would be the answer, Mr Bowman.'

'Surely you can't resist the Turkey Trot, even though it's being murdered by Mrs Sellars and young Cissie.'

His eyes twinkled mischievously, and he took her by the hand. 'Let's show them how it's done.'

More accustomed to a sedate waltz or even a one-step, Daisy experienced a feeling of panic. Everyone was looking at them and she could see Teddy glaring at her from across the hall. 'I don't know how to do it,' she murmured.

'It's easy when you get into the swing of it.'

There was no escape. If she walked off the dance floor she would make a fool of him, and if she stayed she was in danger of making a fool of herself. But when he took her in his arms she felt suddenly as light as air. Mrs Sellars, the vicar's wife, was not the best pianist in the world and her daughter Cissie occasionally missed a beat as she scraped away on her violin, but the ragtime music was infectious and soon everyone was joining in. As the floor became more crowded Daisy began to relax, and to her surprise she discovered that she was genuinely having a good time. Bowman was a natural dancer. He moved with the grace of a panther and he made her feel as though she was the only woman in the room. She was almost sorry when the music stopped and he led her over to where Ruby was standing with two glasses of fruit punch in her hands. She handed one to Daisy with a disapproving frown. 'You look as though you need this.'

Daisy took it from her with a breathless smile. 'Thank you.' She drank deeply. It was lemony and sweet with slices of apple floating on the top, but it was refreshing. There did not seem to be any alcohol content, which was just as well as Daisy could see her sister downing a glass as if it were tap water. She turned to Bowman and was about to thank him politely, but he was staring at Ruby with an appreciative gleam in his eyes. He reached out and took the glass from Ruby's hand, raising it to his lips and tossing it back in one gulp.

'I needed that.' He placed the glass on the windowsill. 'How about a dance, Ruby?'

Her face was suddenly wreathed in smiles and she walked into his arms. 'It's a waltz. I ain't too good at this one, Barnaby.'

In answer, he whirled her onto the crowded dance floor.

Daisy stood motionless, clutching her empty glass in both hands. So he had just been playing a game and flirting with her. She could not believe that she had allowed a man like Bowman to treat her as if she were a common shop girl, and now he had abandoned her to work his charms on another victim. She felt as though all eyes were upon her. Everyone must have noticed the way Bowman had used her to show off his prowess with women. How they would laugh at the posh Miss Lennox who had been passed over for someone who, to all intents and purposes, was her maidservant.

Daisy was tempted to slip out of the door and run all the way home, but pride made her stiffen her back and hold her head high. If only Rupert were here. He would look after her and treat her like a lady. Bowman had proved what he was, a philandering wretch who thought that he was God's gift to women. She spun round as someone tapped her on the arm and she came face to face with Jed Smith. He was sweating profusely in an ill-fitting black suit which must have been bought when he was younger and slimmer. His bulging biceps strained at the wool worsted and his face was flushed above the starched white shirt collar.

'Want to dance, miss?'

She tried not to wrinkle her nose as she caught a whiff of sweaty maleness, and she was about to refuse when she caught sight of Bowman and Ruby dancing cheek to cheek. 'Thank you,' she said, casting a wary glance at Iris, the young woman he was alleged to be courting. 'That would be nice, Mr Smith, but won't your lady friend mind?'

His sandy eyebrows lowered, almost meeting together above his large nose. 'It looks as if Iris has taken a fancy to your brother, miss.' He grabbed her round the waist and seized her hand. 'Seems like a fair swap.' He dragged her into the milling crowd of dancers and began pushing her round the floor, apologising profusely as he trod on her toes.

She bit her lip in order not to cry out with pain. Her cream satin dance shoes would be ruined, but she forced a smile. She would not let Bowman see that she was suffering or allow him to think that he was the only man in the hall who wanted her as a dance partner.

When the music stopped Jed mumbled his thanks and shambled off to join the men, who raised their pint mugs as if in a toast, slapping him on the back and roaring with laughter. The suspicion crossed Daisy's mind that he had only asked her to dance for a bet. She shifted from one foot to the other, wishing that she had not agreed to come. Being stuck in a prison cell crowded with angry women was a picnic compared to the humiliation she was suffering now. She wanted to tell Teddy that she was leaving, but he seemed reluctant to disentangle himself from the arms of the luscious Iris, and Ruby was still clinging to Bowman's arm, gazing up at him as if he were her hero. This evening had been a huge mistake. The air was thick with cigarette smoke, and the combined odours of cheap perfume, sweat and beer were making her feel sick and dizzy. She opened the door and made her escape.

Outside the air was cool and fresh and fragrant with the aroma of damp earth and newly mown grass. Moonlight illuminated the forecourt of the village hall and stars twinkled in the black velvet sky. The tinkling sound of a nearby stream was far sweeter music than that played by Mrs Sellars and her untalented daughter. Daisy paused for a moment, taking deep breaths in an attempt to overcome the humiliation and anger that made her want to go back inside and tell Bowman what she thought of him. Hot tears burned the backs of her eyes and her throat constricted painfully. She must not cry. She had shed no tears when they lost their home and the way of life she had been brought up to expect. She had kept the family together during the past year, taking on tasks that were alien to her without complaint. But then she had allowed herself to be taken in by a man who was completely different from anyone she had ever known. She had succumbed to the animal attraction that exuded from every pore of his body. How he must be laughing now.

She took a hanky from her pocket and blew her nose.

'What's the matter? Aren't you feeling very well?'

She stared straight ahead, tucking the hanky back in her pocket. 'I'm fine, thank you, Bowman.'

He laid his hands on her shoulders and turned her to face him, looking deeply into her eyes. 'Come inside and dance with me.'

She was acutely aware of the warmth of his body. The touch of his hands sent shivers down her spine but she brushed them off, meeting his concerned look with her head held high. 'Why? So that your friends in the village can laugh at my expense?'

'Don't take any notice of them, Daisy. They're just idiots.'

'You were right when you said that I don't belong here. I was a fool to come tonight. I should have known better.' Despite her attempts to remain calm and collected her voice broke on a sob and suddenly she was in his arms. His mouth claimed hers in a kiss that was irresistibly sweet and tender. All thoughts of punishing him and pushing away were driven from her head by the overwhelming desire to respond in kind. She slid her arms around his neck as her knees threatened to give way beneath her. Her lips parted and her pulses raced. She had never experienced anything like this. He was soothing her, exciting her and tasting her as if she were a delicious confection of everything sweet and wonderful. No man had ever pressed her against his body so that she could feel their hearts beating to the same rhythm. They fitted together perfectly, as if they were a matched pair. Nothing else mattered. Social mores were abandoned.

She was half swooning with ecstasy when suddenly they were wrenched apart.

'Take your bloody hands off my sister.'

Teddy's angry voice cut through the choir of angels that had been singing in Daisy's head. She staggered backwards as Bowman released her suddenly and grabbed Teddy by the lapels of his dinner jacket. 'Or what, pipsqueak?'

Teddy's face was pallid in the moonlight and his pale blue eyes seemed colourless, like those of a sheep. His mouth worked soundlessly as he struggled to free himself. 'Let me go or I'll call for a constable.'

Bowman released him with a scornful laugh. 'The village bobby is probably in bed with his missis at this moment. Anyway, what would you say? Would you tell him that you didn't like a bloke kissing your sister? Perhaps you'd best ask Daisy. She wasn't exactly fighting for her honour.'

His words hit her like the sudden shock of iced water. A few seconds ago they had been like lovers but once again they were miles apart. She raised her hand and slapped him across the face. 'You cad,' she cried breathlessly. 'You bounder. Consider yourself sacked, Bowman.'

Teddy straightened his tie, glancing nervously over his shoulder as people poured out of the village hall and some of the younger men stepped forward, taking off their jackets. He held up his hands in a gesture of conciliation. 'There's no need for that. Perhaps I was a bit hasty. After all, no harm done and we need him to fix the motor.'

'He just insulted me,' Daisy said icily. 'He followed me out here. I didn't invite him.'

Bowman threw back his head and laughed. 'That's right, Miss Lennox. Pretend you didn't like it, but we both know the truth.' His expression hardened and he took a step towards Teddy. 'I didn't shame your sister; you did by bringing everyone out here to gawp at her. Take her home now before Jed Smith decides to take you apart for getting off with his girl.'

Ruby broke away from the crowd and ran to Daisy's side. 'You men are all the same. Come on, miss. I'll see you safely home.' She glared at Bowman. 'You and your fancy talk, Barnaby Bowman. Think yourself lucky that Mr Teddy said you've still got your job, but you won't get no more cups of tea from me and that's a promise. You're a rotter.' She slipped her hand into Daisy's. 'Let's go.'

Teddy hesitated. 'We'll see you on Monday morning then, Bowman. You will fix the motor though, won't you? It's all been a bit of a misunderstanding.'

Bowman grinned and touched his forelock. 'As you wish, sir.'

Daisy hurried away with the sound of his mocking voice echoing in her ears.

'Don't be upset,' Ruby said earnestly. 'No man's worth that.'

'I slapped his face, Ruby. I've never stooped so low.'

'I doubt if he'll be the last bloke who'll try to take liberties with you. Not with your looks and your nice way with people, but you need a man from your class and not a common chap like Barnaby. I can handle the likes of him, but he's not your type.'

Teddy caught up with them, puffing away on a cigarette. 'That was a close one. For a moment there I thought I was going to be set upon by those louts. I could take on Bowman, but not the whole bloody lot of them.'

'Of course you could, sir,' Ruby said in a soothing tone she might have used on a fractious child. 'But it's best to put it all behind us now. I don't think that Mrs Lennox would want to hear you were both caught up in what might have ended in a brawl.'

'Good thinking, Ruby.' Teddy uttered a shaky laugh. 'I'd have done that chap some mischief if I'd had a go at him. I was boxing champion in my year at school. Did I ever tell you that, Daisy?' He strolled on ahead, leaving a trail of cigarette smoke in his wake.

'They're all little boys at heart,' Ruby said, shaking her head. She shot an anxious glance at Daisy. 'Are you all right?'

'Yes, of course. It would take more than Bowman to upset me.' It was a lie but Daisy was not going to allow anyone to see the great chasm that had opened up where her heart was once situated. His kisses had been so amazingly wonderful and tender that she was finding it hard to believe he had not cared for her just a little bit. She gave Ruby a grateful smile. 'But thanks for being concerned. We seem to be doomed to get into scrapes together, Ruby.'

'That's what it's all about, ducks. We women have

to stick together. Deeds not words is our motto. Did you know that Emily Davison has that on her tombstone? I read it in the newspaper before I used it to clean the drawing room windows.'

'Deeds not words,' Daisy agreed, squeezing Ruby's fingers. 'We have to fight on.'

Bowman turned up as usual on Monday morning, but Daisy managed to avoid seeing him. Although Ruby had vowed that she would not take him so much as a sip of water Daisy saw her sneaking out of the kitchen with a mug of tea in her hand. Her initial reaction was to give Ruby a good telling off, but she decided to keep a dignified silence. Bowman was just a man hired to do a job; nothing more. What had passed between them on Saturday evening had been a moment of madness on her part and almost definitely a cynical ploy by Bowman to keep a lucrative job. Perhaps he had heard the rumour circulating on the village grapevine that Lord Pendleton was paying for repairs to the Humberette. Daisy was beginning to realise that very little was missed by the dedicated gossips who spent their lives spreading hearsay and scandal. If this particular titbit of news had reached Bowman's ears it might have spurred him on to take advantage of her inexperience in order to ensure more work in the future, or even to secure a valuable patron like Lord Pendleton. She suspected that Bowman was ambitious and would not be content to spend his life as an odd job man, but she was not going to be a pawn in his end game.

She worked hard that morning, following the recipes

in the cookery book she had had the forethought to bring from the house in Warwick Square. She minced the remains of the lamb she had roasted for Sunday lunch and made a shepherd's pie for dinner that evening, with a treacle pudding for dessert. Mother would hate it, saying such food was only suitable for the servants' hall, but Father and Teddy would wolf it down without any arguments. Despite her mother's constant complaints that they were almost destitute and living on the breadline, Daisy was beginning to realise that they were many times better off than the average person in Nutley Green. Perhaps it was little wonder that they had been objects of ridicule to the locals when they turned up at a Saturday night dance dressed as if they were attending a function at the Hotel Cecil or the Savoy.

She was not looking forward to her next shopping trip to the village, and she was tempted to send Ruby or Bea in her stead, but she abandoned that idea very quickly. Even if she gave her a list, Ruby would be sure to exercise her own form of economy and return with something hideous like a bullock's head, which she insisted was a delicacy when boiled for several hours. Bea was even more unreliable and would probably squander the housekeeping money on chocolate and a selection of the luscious cream cakes sold at the bakery. But Bea was rarely at home these days as it was harvest time and she spent most of her time at the Gurneys' farm. It was only after they reached home on Saturday evening that Daisy had realised Bea was not with them. In their hurry to escape a fight they had left her behind. Daisy had ordered Teddy to go back and get her, but he had refused, protesting that he would not be responsible for his actions if he saw Bowman again. Daisy did not believe him but there was little she could do other than wait for her sister's return. Bea had arrived just after midnight seated on the crossbar of Jimmy Gurney's motorbike, and Daisy had been too relieved to scold her for staying out late. After all, it was her fault for not making sure that she was with them when they left the village hall, and Bea had obviously had a wonderful time with Jimmy. Her eyes were sparkling and her cheeks flushed, and it was not simply due to the chilly night air. Daisy suspected that her sixteen-year-old sister was in love with the farmer's son. She prayed that it was just a passing fancy, a schoolgirl crush, but Bea was so happy that she did not want to be the one to tell her that the romance was doomed from the start. There would be a frightful row if their parents were to find out.

Daisy glanced at the clock. Ruby had been absent for a good twenty minutes and had apparently forgotten their agreement to put Bowman in his place. It was simply not good enough. She cleared the table, stacking the utensils in the scullery sink, and was deciding whether or not to go looking for her errant maid when Ruby breezed in from the garden. Her wide grin was enough to convince Daisy that she had made up with Bowman and they were now on excellent terms. 'You can take over now, Ruby. All of this needs washing up. Mother is having lunch at Pendleton Park and Bea is out, so you can make yourself a sandwich or have some bread and cheese for lunch.' Daisy took off her apron and hung it on a peg behind the door.

Ruby stared at her wide-eyed, her smile fading. 'Are you cross with me, miss? I was only having a chat with Barnaby.' She slanted a sideways glance at her. 'He asked after you. He hoped that you wasn't too upset by what happened on Saturday night.'

'I haven't given it another thought.' Daisy tried to sound convincing, but even to her own ears it sounded like a lie. She retreated into the kitchen. 'I'm going to the village. We need some things.'

Ruby hovered in the doorway, watching her anxiously. 'Let me go. I can get whatever you want.'

'No, thank you. I could do with some fresh air anyway.' Daisy picked up her straw boater and pinned it on, checking her appearance in the fly-spotted mirror on the wall. 'And I hope you won't waste any more time chatting with Bowman, Ruby. He's charging us by the hour.'

'No, miss.'

Daisy picked up her purse and slipped it into a wicker shopping basket. 'I won't be long.' She left without a backward glance. She knew she was being mean but she simply could not help herself. Ruby had the right to choose her own friends, and if Bowman was her ideal man then she was welcome to him. She set off, hurrying past the coach house with her head down. She could hear the clink of metal on metal emanating from the open door, and the now familiar smell of the tobacco that Bowman rolled into cigarettes. She quickened her pace, walking briskly towards the village. Let them snigger behind her back; she would show them that she did not care. For good or ill her family were residents of Nutley Green just the same as the Boxalls and the Smiths.

By the time she reached the outskirts of the village she was beginning to have second thoughts. Perhaps she should have entrusted the errand to Ruby.

'Afternoon, miss.'

Daisy came back to earth with a start as Reg Smith, the postman, whizzed past her on his bicycle. With a cheery wave of his hand he continued on towards the village. She responded in kind even though he could not see her, but his friendly greeting had given her the courage she needed to continue on her way. Even so, she was aware of covert glances as she walked along the main street, but she forced herself to ignore them. She came to a halt outside the butcher's, averting her eyes from the dead game birds and rabbits that festooned the shop front. She opened the door and went in, but the smell of blood and sawdust was nauseating and Septimus Cole, the butcher, was attacking a huge hunk of meat with a cleaver.

His assistant and delivery boy, Cyril Smith, was busy making sausages. He looked up and a slow grin spread across his face. 'Morning, miss.'

Septimus laid the bloodstained implement on the chopping block. 'Good morning, Miss Lennox. What can I do for you?' His tone was polite but there was no welcoming smile in his eyes.

Daisy's gaze was transfixed by the sight of his hands coated with blood and animal fat. The mere sight of a cut finger had always been enough to make her faint, and now the feeling of nausea was made worse by a choking sensation. She clutched at the counter for support as her knees buckled beneath her and she tumbled headlong into a pit of darkness.

Daisy gasped for breath as the fumes of the smelling salts brought her back to consciousness. She found herself staring up into the chubby face of the post-mistress, Mrs Cobb. 'Are you feeling better, dear?'

Daisy tried to sit up but was pushed back gently onto the horsehair sofa. She could feel the bristles sticking through the thin cotton of her dress and water trickled down her neck from the sponge that Ada Cobb was holding to her forehead. 'I'm all right now,' she murmured. 'Do you think you could stop that, Ada? I'm getting rather wet.'

Mrs Cobb pushed her daughter aside. 'Get back to the shop, silly girl. There'll be customers waiting to be served.'

Ada shook her head. 'No, Mum. They all come with me. They wanted to see what had happened to her.' She stared down at Daisy, her brow puckered in a frown. 'I was at the dance on Saturday night and I saw her canoodling with Barnaby Bowman . . .'

'That's enough, Ada. Go back to the shop this instant and tell them all out there that the show's over. Miss Lennox is all right. It was just a swooning fit.'

Daisy raised herself with difficulty. The parlour behind the shop was small and crammed with huge old-fashioned furniture with hardly enough space to walk between the sofa, chairs and a large tea table covered in a crimson chenille cloth. A sickly-looking aspidistra blocked the light from a small-paned window overlooking the back yard and the slaughterhouse. She could still smell blood and she felt her gorge rise. 'Might I have a glass of water, please?'

Mrs Cobb turned to glare at her daughter who was hovering in the doorway. 'You heard Miss Lennox. Fetch her some water and tell young Cyril to ride his bike to Rainbow's End and get someone to take her home.'

'No, really,' Daisy protested. 'I'll be quite all right to walk, if you'll just give me a moment.'

Mrs Cobb shooed Ada out of the door. 'You stay put, miss. You don't want to go swooning the moment you get outside.' Her gaze wandered to Daisy's flat stomach. 'I used to faint all over the place when I was expecting Ada.'

Horrified, Daisy half rose to her feet but sank down again holding her hand to her head. 'It's not that, Mrs Cobb. How could you think such a thing? It's the heat and the sight and smell of blood.' She raised her handkerchief to her mouth, taking a deep breath. The parlour was stifling and the sofa smelled as though the horse was buried deep inside. She could almost feel the hooves sticking up through the faded velvet upholstery.

'I told you to take it easy.' Mrs Cobb folded her arms across her ample bosom. 'It's none of my business, miss. I daresay it happens in polite circles just the same as it does round here.' She edged her way to the door.

'Rest there and I'll see what's happened to Ada. I'll bet she's forgotten the water and wandered off.' She hurried from the room, leaving Daisy alone in the semi-darkness. Despite her discomfort she lay back on the sofa, closing her eyes. Now it would be all round the village that she was in the family way. It would have been laughable had it not been so embarrassing, and of course she would prove them wrong, but the damage to her reputation would have been done. She could only hope and pray that the gossip did not reach as far as Pendleton Park. She would die if Rupert heard the rumour before she had had time to share the joke with him.

Moments later the sound of footsteps outside the door made her open her eyes. She thought it must be Ada bringing her the water, but when a familiar figure stepped into the room she snapped into a sitting position. 'What are you doing here?'

Bowman knelt down beside her. 'Are you all right?'

'Get up, please. It was just a fainting fit. I can't stand the sight of blood.'

He stood up, a grin spreading across his features. 'Wasn't it a bit foolish to shop here in the circumstances? I should have thought that this was the last place to go if you're squeamish.'

'Go away, Bowman. I don't need you.'

He perched on the edge of an upright chair. 'That's where you're wrong. It's lucky I had to go back to my workshop for some tools. I was just leaving when young Cyril saw me and called me back. I've come to take you home.'

'I'm perfectly capable of finding my own way, thank you.'

'Stand up.'

The abrupt command took her by surprise but as she rose to her feet she found herself swaying dizzily. Bowman caught her in his arms, holding her close. 'This is becoming a habit, Daisy,' he said softly. 'But don't think for a minute that I'm complaining.'

She made a feeble effort to push him away. 'Let me go.'

'Don't be silly. Lean on me and we'll get you outside into the fresh air. My motorcycle is outside and if you're not too proud you can ride on the crossbar.'

'I'll walk. I wouldn't be seen dead perched on that contraption like some common shop girl.'

'Suit yourself, but it's a long walk home.' He hitched her arm across his shoulders and helped her out through the shop into the sunshine. 'Can you stand on your own?'

'I haven't got my basket and my purse is in it, and I haven't done the shopping.' She was close to tears. She had failed miserably in a simple task that most of the women in the village would do every day without blinking an eye.

He twisted her round, looking into her eyes with a wry smile. 'You do need looking after, don't you, Daisy? For all your airs and graces you're just a little girl when it comes to taking care of yourself.'

She felt herself weakening. The tug of physical attraction burned like a fire within her and she was tempted to melt into his embrace, but she had her pride and he was a man with a reputation as a flirt. She was still Miss Lennox of Rainbow's End and he was a common labourer, but she was mesmerised by his unwavering gaze. She could not break away. He held her in his power just as Svengali had captured Trilby in the novel she had read over and over again, never thinking that it could apply to her. She had prided herself on being a strong-minded woman. She was a suffragist and yet she had fallen under the spell of this man.

She dimly heard the sound of an approaching motorcar but it was not until it pulled up that she looked round and found herself face to face with Rupert and Lady Pendleton.

Chapter Eight

Rupert's face was like thunder as he climbed out of the driver's seat and strode towards them, resplendent in the uniform of the Rifle Brigade. 'What's going on?' he demanded, glaring at Bowman who had released Daisy and was regarding him with a cynical curl of his lip.

'What does it look like, Captain?'

'It looks as though you were being rather too familiar.' Rupert turned his attention to Daisy and his eyes flashed with anger. 'Was this fellow bothering you, Daisy?'

'No, Rupert. You've got it all wrong. You know that I can't stand the sight of blood and I'm afraid I passed out in the butcher's shop. Such an embarrassing thing to happen.'

His expression changed to one of concern. 'Are you all right now?' He placed his arm around her shoulders. 'Let me take you home.'

'That's just what I was about to do,' Bowman said, clenching his fists at his sides. 'What's the problem, Captain?'

Rupert shot a scornful look at the motorcycle. 'You're thinking of taking Miss Lennox on that suicidal machine? You must be mad. You'll come with me, Daisy.'

She knew it was useless to argue. Despite his quiet manner, Rupert was not the sort of man to take no for an answer in a situation where he believed that he was protecting her honour. She would have some explanations to make but not now. Her head was aching and her knees felt weak. Whether that was a result of the swoon or the fact that Bowman had held her in his arms, she hardly dared to think. She leaned against Rupert's brass-buttoned tunic with an overwhelming feeling of relief. He was her friend after all, and he was part of the world she knew and trusted. 'Thank you, Rupert. That would be most kind.' She met Bowman's quizzical gaze with an attempt at a smile. 'Thank you for being concerned, but as you can see I'll be quite all right now.' She allowed Rupert to help her into the back seat of the Prince Henry. Leaning against the padded leather squabs she struggled to control her erratic breathing.

'What happened, Rupert?' Lady Pendleton demanded when, having cranked the engine into life, he took his seat beside her. 'Is Daisy ill?'

'Just a touch of the sun, I expect, Mother.' He drove off in a flurry of dust. 'I'm taking her home.'

Lady Pendleton turned to Daisy with a look of concern. 'You do look pale, my dear. Perhaps we should send for the doctor.'

'No, really I am fine now, Lady Pendleton. I have this dreadful tendency to faint at the sight of blood. I thought I'd conquered it enough to shop at the butcher's, but apparently not.'

'You poor dear. We'll get you home quickly and you

must lie down in a darkened room with a cold compress on your forehead.'

'I'm not sure that will be possible. I'm afraid I left my purse and shopping basket in the butcher's shop. I'll have to return to the village later anyway as there are things we need urgently.'

Lady Pendleton frowned. 'You work too hard. I'll have a word with Gwendoline. I doubt if she realises how much you do for that family of yours. You weren't brought up to be a skivvy.'

'Quite right, Mother.' Rupert changed gear as they approached the sharp bend in the road that had claimed the Humberette. 'You've been taking on too much, Daisy—' He broke off and swerved as Bowman shot past them on his motorcycle. 'Damned road hog!'

Bowman lifted his hand in a salute, and as he disappeared from view Daisy noticed that her shopping basket was tied to the parcel carrier on the back of his machine. Rupert took the corner at a much more sedate speed and pulled up outside the stable block. He climbed out of the car. 'Are you coming in, Mother?'

She nodded. 'Of course I am. Gwendoline would take it very much to heart if we were to drive off without passing the time of day at least, and I do want a word with her about Daisy.' She accepted Rupert's hand as he helped her from her seat. 'I think it best if I see her on my own.'

Daisy alighted from the car unaided. 'Please don't say anything to upset Mother,' she said anxiously. 'You must know that her nerves have been in a very delicate state since we were forced to leave the house in Warwick Square.'

Lady Pendleton regarded her with the air of someone who understood only too well. 'I know that, Daisy. I listen to your mother going on about it every week when she comes to tea, and I have to say I'm running out of patience with her. I don't wish to be unkind, but one day I will tell her to stop feeling sorry for herself and take control of her life.' She marched towards the house leaving Rupert and Daisy staring at each other in surprise.

'By golly, I've never heard Mother speak so passionately about anything,' Rupert said, smiling for the first time since they met that day. 'She's quite a force majeure when she's got a bee in one of her couture bonnets, the cost of which would feed the average working man's family for a month at least.'

Daisy returned his smile. She had feared for a moment that she had gone down in his estimation, and that hurt more than she could have imagined. 'I didn't know that you held such egalitarian views, Rupert.'

'I hope I'm a fair man. I've been brought up to believe that with wealth and privilege comes responsibility.'

'Noblesse oblige and all that.'

'You were always making fun of me when we were children. If anyone kept my feet on the ground it was you, Daisy Bell.' He proffered his arm. 'Shall we go for a walk in the garden before you go back to slaving in the kitchen like a modern Cinderella? I've been dying to talk to you and to apologise properly for my uncouth behaviour.'

She took his arm with a sigh. 'Me too, Rupert. I should have expressed myself better, but I do care for you, you know that.'

'Of course I do, and as I've got a week's leave, let's make the most of our time together.'

'Will you let me drive the Prince Henry?'

'Better than that, I'll get you a driving licence tomorrow, and then you'll be a legal road user.'

'That would be absolutely splendid. Thank you.' As they walked towards the side gate a small sound behind them made Daisy look round. Bowman was standing in the doorway of the coach house smoking a cigarette and judging by the look on his face he had heard every word they said. She looked away quickly, fighting down the desire to rush over to him and explain that Rupert was simply an old friend. She tightened her hold on his arm and they strolled through the kitchen garden and out onto the sunny lawn. He stopped, raising his face to the hot summer sun. 'This is glorious, Daisy.' He released her, encompassing their surroundings with an expansive gesture. 'This is what a soldier fights to protect.' He looked suddenly bashful like a schoolboy caught writing a love poem. 'And our wives and sweethearts of course: that goes without saying. I don't believe in killing but if there is a war I'll do my bit, just as my ancestors have done in centuries past.'

'Then let's hope that the Germans are just sabre-rattling. That's what Father thinks anyway.'

He gave her a long look. 'Let's hope so, but if it does come to war I'd like to know that there was someone special praying for my safe return.'

'We would all be praying for that, Rupert.'

'That's not what I meant and you know it.' He took her by the hand, holding it in a firm grasp. 'Have you changed your mind at all?' His lips twisted into a wry smile. 'Is there any hope for us, Daisy?'

She met his earnest gaze with a steadiness that surprised her. It would be so easy to say yes and accept all that he had to offer, but somehow the words stuck in her throat, and it was not only her feelings for Bowman that were holding her back. Somewhere deep in her soul she felt the need to prove herself as a person. Surely there must be more to life than being passed like a chattel from father to husband? Her brief connection with the suffragette movement had given her a taste of freedom of thought if not deeds, but even that was denied her now that she was buried deep in the Essex countryside. Shaking her head, she lifted his hand to her cheek. 'Not now, Rupert. Maybe never, I just don't know, and it's not fair to keep you waiting for an answer.'

He nodded slowly, withdrawing his hand. 'I see. Well I've always admired your honesty, even if it's hard to take at times.'

'If you don't want to see me any more I'll quite understand.'

'Good heavens, I'm not as shallow as that. We're still friends, Daisy, and will always be, I hope.'

'And you're all right about things? Truly?'

'Truly.' He leaned over to kiss her on the forehead. 'But I'm not giving up so easily, my dear.'

'No, Rupert . . .' she began, but he silenced her by laying his finger across her lips.

'I've promised to take you out in the Prince Henry tomorrow and that's what we'll do,' he said with a rueful smile. 'I haven't forgotten that cream tea we promised ourselves on the last fateful occasion when you decided to break my poor heart.'

'Now you're teasing me.'

'Yes, because you look even more delightful when you're pouting. Unfortunately it makes it even harder to resist kissing you, but I'll do my best to remember that I'm a gentleman.' He took her hand and led her back towards the house. 'Let's get you indoors out of this hot sun. I was quite forgetting that you'd had a fainting fit.'

'I did not have a fainting fit,' Daisy said with spirit. 'I swooned at the sight of blood. I know it's silly but I've always been like that. Stop treating me like a piece of porcelain, Rupert. I liked you better when we used to play cricket and climb trees.'

'Those aren't the sorts of games that grown-ups play, Daisy Bell.' His deep chuckle was infectious and Daisy found herself laughing with him.

'Let's go and find out if my mother and yours are still friends,' she said, quickening her pace.

'Or if it's hatpins at dawn. I can see the headlines on the front page of *The Times* now.'

'Don't,' Daisy said with feeling. 'That would be the last straw.'

It appeared that there would be no lurid newspaper scandal involving two ladies fighting to the death with hatpins or any other sharp implements, as the two matrons seemed to be on the best of terms when Daisy and Rupert came upon them in the drawing room. Ruby had managed to put together a tray of tea, although she had set it with odd cups and saucers, and had left the sugar bowl in the kitchen. However, that did not seem to have upset the entente cordiale, and Daisy was more than relieved to see her mother smiling happily.

'Jane tells me that you've been overdoing things, Daisy,' Gwendoline said, wagging a finger at her. 'You are a silly girl. You should make Ruby do more. There really is no need for you to parade our misfortunes by going to the shops in person. Write a list and give it to the girl.'

'Yes, Mother.' It was useless to argue. Daisy shot a covert glance at Rupert and he gave her an encouraging smile.

Beaming at them both, Gwendoline turned her attention to Rupert. 'It's so good to have you home, dear boy.' She sent a meaningful glance in her daughter's direction. 'And I'm sure that Daisy feels the same.'

'Yes, Mother. Of course I do.'

'And we hope to see a lot of you while you're on leave,' Gwendoline added with an arch look. 'Make the most of Daisy's company, because I'm certain that she'll be snapped up before we know it. Don't you think so?'

Daisy could see that Rupert had opted for his customary escape route when it came to his mother and her match-making friends, and he was staring abstractedly out of the window allowing all the pointed remarks to pass over his head. She nudged him in the ribs and he took the cue manfully. 'Er, yes, of course, Mrs Lennox. I agree absolutely.'

Gwendoline's smile would have out-grinned the Cheshire cat. She glowed with satisfaction. 'Well, I daresay you two young people will be seeing a lot of each other this week. You are most welcome here at any time, Rupert.'

Lady Pendleton rose to her feet with a rustle of silk and a fragrant waft of L'Heure Bleue. 'I think it's time we left, Rupert. We won't trespass on your hospitality any longer, Gwendoline. I'll expect you on Wednesday as usual for afternoon tea at Pendleton Park. I'll send Parkin for you if Rupert is otherwise engaged.'

'I rather think I might be, Mother,' Rupert said hastily. 'Daisy and I have a longstanding appointment with a plate of cucumber sandwiches and some fancies at the Cosy Corner tea rooms in Colchester.' He winked at Daisy. 'I'll pick you up tomorrow afternoon at two-thirty.'

She smiled and nodded. 'That will be lovely. I can't wait to be a legal road user.'

'What's that?' Gwendoline demanded. 'You're not going to drive one of those infernal machines, are you, Daisy? If you are then I forbid it.'

'Yes, Mother,' Daisy said dutifully, crossing her fingers behind her back.

For the rest of the week Daisy kept out of Bowman's way, and having returned her shopping basket and purse he made no attempt to see her. She spent all her free time with Rupert who was true to his word and duly purchased a driving licence in her name, allowing her to drive as often as possible in order to become fully proficient behind the wheel. On the last day of his leave they took tea once more in the Cosy Corner café. As they sat chatting amicably Daisy was only too well aware of the curious glances they were receiving from the occupants of the adjacent tables.

'We make a handsome couple,' Rupert said, following her gaze. 'You can't deny it, Daisy Bell, so don't pout.'

'You said that pouting made me prettier,' she countered. 'Have you gone off me already, Captain Pendleton?'

'Are you flirting with me, Miss Lennox?'

The smile died on her lips. 'I'm sorry. It was said in fun. You really shouldn't take things so seriously.'

He sipped his tea, eyeing her over the rim of the cup. 'Sometimes I think you do care for me just a little, and then you drift off somewhere far beyond my reach.'

'Don't spoil things, Rupert. We've had a lovely time these last few days. Nothing has changed between us.'

'No,' he said slowly. 'Nothing has changed, but I damned well wish it would. With all my heart, Daisy Bell, I'll love you until the day I die.'

She was aware of the sudden hush around them and she knew she was blushing, which only made matters worse. There was no doubting Rupert's sincerity but she wished that he had not chosen this moment to declare the extent of his feelings for her. She reached out and laid her hand on his. 'That is so sweet. I wish that . . .'

He grasped her fingers, looking deeply into her eyes. 'You wish what?'

She dropped her gaze. She could hear whispers around them and she felt cornered. Her first instinct was to get up and leave, but she could not do that to Rupert. This past week had been one of the happiest she had known for a long time. They were more than compatible and she knew she would miss him terribly when he returned to his regiment. He loved her and perhaps that was enough. Maybe she would grow to love him too. She raised her eyes and was stunned and shocked to see tears standing out on Rupert's thick and almost ridiculously long eyelashes.

'What do you want, Daisy? Tell me and I'll do anything in my power to make you happy.'

She bit her lip. She knew she should refuse but she could hear her mother's voice telling her that she would soon be on the shelf. Her twenty-second birthday loomed and she was a virtual prisoner dependent on her father for everything. Her feelings for Bowman had awakened longings that she had never imagined, and she did not trust herself to resist him for ever. He had only to crook his finger and she would walk into his arms regardless of the consequences. Rupert was offering her a way of escape: the honourable way out.

'Oh for Gawd's sake put him out of his misery, love.' A large overdressed woman with hennaed hair leaned across the aisle between the tables and patted her on the arm. 'You might never get another chance.'

Rupert gave her a broad smile. 'Thanks, but if you don't mind I'll try and do this myself.'

The woman speared an éclair on a pastry fork and waved it at him. 'Well get on with it, young man. She's teetering. I can always tell.'

Daisy wished that the floor would open up and swallow her. She sent a pleading look at Rupert and he rose to his feet. She thought for a moment that he was going to escort her from the café, but to her intense embarrassment he went down on one knee, holding his hand to his heart. 'Desperate situations call for desperate measures, my darling. Daisy Lennox, will you do me the honour of becoming my wife?'

The silence was tangible. Teaspoons were held suspended over cups, and all eyes were upon them. Daisy struggled to find a reason to refuse him yet again but she felt herself weakening. He had made his feelings perfectly clear and she was desperately fond of him, even if he did not make her pulses race. They would do well together. She would bow to the social mores that required her to become a good wife and mother and subjugate her desires and ambitions. She looked into his handsome face and before she could stop herself she whispered, 'Yes.'

For a brief moment he stared at her in disbelief, and as the realisation dawned that she had not rejected him a slow smile spread across his face and he leapt to his feet, drawing her into his arms and kissing her to a spontaneous round of applause. Everyone from the hennaed lady to the waitresses began clapping enthusiastically.

'Well done, my boy.' A bewhiskered gentleman of military bearing rose to his feet and slapped Rupert on the back. 'Courage under fire. That's what this country needs.'

Daisy straightened her hat, blushing furiously. 'I'd like to go now.'

'Of course, darling.' Rupert summoned the waitress with an imperious gesture and paid the bill, adding a generous tip.

They made their way between the tables to a further round of applause and congratulations. 'I hope that none of Mother's friends were there today,' Daisy said as they emerged into the sunny street.

Rupert stopped to put on his peaked hat. 'Who cares? I don't for one.' He slipped his arm around her waist. 'You are sure now, aren't you, darling? I mean, I know I put you on the spot rather. It wasn't planned, I just acted on impulse. You must tell me if you'd rather have time to think about it.'

'I'm quite sure.'

'Then let's go straight to the jeweller's shop and get a ring. I'd have one made for you but there isn't time, and I want to see you wearing it before I leave.'

Swept along on the tide of his enthusiasm, Daisy made no objections, not even when he chose a ring that was opulent to the point of vulgarity. She had not the heart to tell him that she would have preferred a solitaire and that the ornate claw-set diamond surrounded with emeralds was far too large for her small hand. He was like a child in a toyshop at Christmas time, and his enthusiasm seemed to rub off on the dour shopkeeper and his solemn assistants who all congregated outside the shop to wave them off.

Daisy could only suppose that the ring must have cost an awful lot of money to have created such a feeling of goodwill.

At home it was much the same story. Rupert had insisted on stopping off on the way to purchase a magnum of champagne, and he waited impatiently for everyone to congregate in the drawing room before making the announcement. In an unexpected show of emotion, Gwendoline uttered a small shriek and flung her arms around Daisy. 'My dear girl. I'm so happy for you.'

Teddy slapped Rupert on the back and grabbed the bottle of Bollinger. 'Ring the bell for Ruby, Bea. I wonder if we brought the champagne glasses from the old house,' he said hopefully. 'If not we'll have to drink it out of one of Daisy's slippers.'

'I'd rather drink out of the coal scuttle,' Beatrice said, giving the embroidered bell pull a tug. 'Will we have a proper party to celebrate the engagement, Mother?'

Victor cleared his throat loudly. 'Ahem. Isn't there something you've forgotten, Rupert my boy?'

'I'm sorry, sir. I know that I should have asked your permission first, but this all came about rather quickly, and I'm leaving first thing in the morning to re-join my regiment. I hope you have no objections.'

Victor shook his head and his severe features creased into a smile. 'Not at all. I couldn't be happier. You're a lucky man.'

'I certainly know it, sir.' Rupert gazed fondly at Daisy, squeezing her hand gently. 'I'm the luckiest chap alive.'

A shiver ran down Daisy's spine and for a moment it seemed as though a shadow had blotted out the sun. Perhaps it was the ever-present threat of war and the fact that Rupert was in uniform that was unsettling, but the feeling went as quickly as it had come and she was beginning to relax when Ruby appeared in the doorway. Her reaction was one of ill-concealed astonishment when Beatrice blurted out the reason for the celebration. Daisy met her startled gaze with an attempt at a smile. Ruby of all people ought to be pleased that she was no longer a rival for Bowman's affections. She had placed herself above his reach forever, leaving the field clear. Somehow the thought did not make her feel as happy as it ought. She moved a little closer to Rupert and was rewarded with a hug.

'Fetch the best glasses, Ruby,' Teddy said as he attempted to open the bottle. 'Double quick. We're celebrating.'

'Bring one for yourself,' Daisy said gently. 'You've been through so much with us, Ruby. You're one of the family now.'

'Yes, miss.' Ruby bobbed a curtsey and hurried from the room.

'I say, Daisy, did you have to treat her like one of us?' Teddy protested. 'You'll give her ideas above her station.'

Rupert drew her closer to him. 'This is our celebration, Teddy. I think Daisy is entitled to include anyone she likes.'

'Exactly,' Bea said enthusiastically. 'Rupert isn't a snob. That's one of the things I love about him, and now he's going to be my brother. I'd rather have him than you any day, Teddy.'

'Now, now, children,' Gwendoline said hastily. 'Don't start squabbling or Rupert might change his mind, and that would never do.'

'It would take more than that, Mrs Lennox,' Rupert said gallantly. 'Never having had a brother or a sister I enjoy being part of a larger family.'

Gwendoline puffed out her chest. 'Does your dear mama know about this?'

'Not yet, Mrs Lennox. It all came about quite suddenly.'

Beatrice moved closer to Daisy, seizing her left hand. 'Let me see the ring. Oh, it's a darling. It's absolutely huge. How smashing. I want Jimmy to see this.' She hesitated, flushing to the roots of her hair. 'Not that we're thinking of getting engaged or anything like that . . .' She broke off in a state of confusion.

'I should think not. You're only sixteen, not long out of the schoolroom,' Gwendoline said, bristling. 'I don't want to hear any more of that sort of talk from you, young lady. This is what comes of mixing with the lower orders.'

Daisy opened her mouth to protest but was interrupted by the appearance of Ruby bearing a tray of champagne glasses. She placed them on the table and left the room as silently as a shadow. Daisy had to resist the temptation to follow her and explain her reasons for accepting Rupert's proposal, but she was beginning to realise that it was she herself who had created the barrier that now lay between them. By accepting Rupert's proposal she had elevated herself to a level in society far above the ordinary person in the street. From now on much would be expected of her, and easy friendship with those in a lower social class would be impossible. There must always be a fine line between servant and mistress. She glanced at the happy faces of her parents as they raised their glasses in a toast. Beatrice downed hers in one gulp and held her glass out for a refill. Laughingly Teddy obliged, ignoring his mother's protests.

Rupert slid his arm around Daisy's waist. 'Happy, darling?'

She sipped her champagne. 'Yes, of course.' She twisted her lips into a smile but inside her heart was like ice. She glanced down at the sparkling diamond and emerald ring, feeling as though she had gained the world and lost her soul.

'You make such a lovely couple,' Gwendoline said happily. 'Will you stay for dinner, Rupert? I'm afraid it's only something that Ruby has cooked up for us with Daisy not being here to supervise.'

'I'm sure it would be delicious, but my parents are expecting me. As this is my last night at home I wouldn't want to disappoint them and I really should be going.'

'Of course, my boy,' Victor said hastily. 'We understand entirely.'

'I'll see you out.' Daisy hurried from the room. If she had stayed there for another minute she felt she would have suffocated. She led the way to the front door and opened it, taking deep breaths of the cool evening air.

Rupert had been quick to take the hint and he came up behind her, taking her in his arms. 'I hope I haven't rushed you into accepting me, Daisy Bell. You know I'd never do anything to hurt you.'

'Of course I do.' She raised her face, parting her lips, and responded to his kiss in a desperate attempt to capture the passion that Bowman had kindled in her, and failing miserably. Rupert's kiss was gentle, tender and loving, but for her the vital spark was missing. Not so, it seemed, for him. He released her with a sigh of delight.

'I can't wait until my next leave, sweetheart. It will probably be at Christmas and we'll have a ball at Pendleton Park to celebrate. It will give my mother something to plan in my absence. She'll be overjoyed when I pass on our news. I just wish I had a day or two longer so that we could tell her together.'

'It won't be too long until Christmas.' She gave him a gentle push. 'You'll be late for dinner and you know how much your father hates unpunctuality.'

'You know us all so well. We'll make a wonderful couple, you and I, my darling Daisy Bell.' He blew her a kiss before turning away and walking down the path to where his motor was parked. With a last cheerful wave he started the engine and climbed into the driver's seat.

Daisy watched until the Prince Henry was out of sight. She was about to go indoors when she caught a whiff of cigarette smoke. Turning her head she saw

Bowman standing in the coach house doorway. He raised his cigarette to his lips and drew on it deeply, exhaling a plume of blue smoke into the still air. Their eyes met and she moved towards him, drawn by an invisible silken thread that refused to be broken.

Chapter Nine

Daisy was halfway down the path when she saw another shadowy figure emerge from the coach house. A sudden and painful stab of jealousy brought her to a halt as she realised that it was Ruby, and a feeling of nausea gripped her stomach when she saw her stand on tiptoe to whisper something in Bowman's ear. She clenched her fists at her sides, hating herself for being stupid enough to fall for his charms.

She retreated into the house, closing the door as if to shut out the bittersweet memories that came flooding back to her. She could not help comparing the sensations that had all but consumed her during the moments of passion she had shared with Bowman and those evoked by Rupert's tender kiss, and she was instantly ashamed. She must be very wicked to entertain such thoughts and feelings for a man who had simply been toying with her emotions. She could only hope that Bowman would be more honest in his dealings with Ruby.

She hurried back to the drawing room. 'Oh, it's you, Daisy,' Gwendoline said crossly, apparently forgetting that for a brief moment Daisy had been her favourite daughter. 'I've been ringing and ringing for Ruby. Where is that wretched girl? We're all famished.'

'Yes, it's too damn bad,' Teddy complained. 'Father and I have been working all day and we expect a meal on time even if it doesn't come up to scratch.'

'I was just going to look for her,' Beatrice said with a tipsy smile. 'You were ages saying goodbye to Rupert. I'll bet you two were necking.'

'Don't be vulgar, Beatrice.' Gwendoline sank down on the sofa. 'Go and see what's holding the silly girl up, Daisy. Things haven't been the same this week with you gallivanting about with Rupert. We've barely had a decent meal.'

'I'll go now,' Daisy said hastily. It was fortunate that Bea had been too squiffy to go looking for Ruby, otherwise their maid's secret tryst with Bowman would have been discovered and she would almost certainly have been sacked. Daisy went straight to the kitchen, and discovered a pan of potatoes boiling dry on the hob. The salad was prepared and the cold cuts of meat were laid out on a silver platter, but there was no sign of Ruby. Daisy rescued as many of the potatoes as she could and put them in a serving dish. She was about to take them through to the dining room when Ruby rushed into the kitchen, her frilled white cap awry and her cheeks flushed. She came to a sudden halt and they faced each other like duellists.

Daisy was the first to speak. 'We're ready to eat now, Ruby,' she said, making a huge effort to sound calm and in control of the situation, even though her heart was drumming a tattoo inside her chest. She did not blame Ruby for being smitten by Bowman, but she could not quite control the vicious serpents of jealousy that coiled around her heart. She knew it was ridiculous, but she was gripped by an emotion beyond her control. 'I'll take this in if you bring the rest.' She did not mention Bowman. She would never utter his name in front of Ruby again.

'I'm sorry, miss,' Ruby said, straightening her cap. 'I just went outside to get a breath of fresh air.'

'I know where you were and who you were with.' Daisy could not resist the temptation to let Ruby know that she had been seen. 'It doesn't matter. Let's say no more about it. Just serve the food, please.'

'Of course, miss. Right away.'

There was no need to say more. A truce had been declared. In her heart Daisy knew that they were both victims of Bowman's irresistible charms.

Lady Pendleton arrived next morning just as Daisy came in from the garden with a trug filled with freshly dug vegetables. Ruby rushed into the kitchen to pass on the news that Daisy's future mother-in-law was waiting for her in the drawing room.

'How does she look?' Daisy demanded, dumping the trug on the table and hurrying into the scullery to wash her hands. 'Did she seem pleased?'

'I dunno. It's hard to tell with them toffs. They don't give nothing away, but she didn't appear to be put out, so I suppose that's a good sign.'

Daisy ripped off her apron and patted her windswept hair into place. 'Oh well. Here's hoping she didn't mind being the last to find out.' She made her way slowly to the drawing room, but as she opened the door she realised that she had worried needlessly.

Lady Pendleton rose from the sofa, smiling and holding out her arms. 'My dear girl, I can't tell you how happy I was to hear the wonderful news.'

Daisy approached her tentatively. 'I'm sorry that it was sprung on you like that.'

'That's how the best surprises come about.' Lady Pendleton kissed her on both cheeks. 'I've always wanted a daughter and I couldn't have chosen better myself.'

Gwendoline positively glowed, apparently taking this as a compliment directed at her personally. 'She will make Rupert a splendid wife.' She paused, frowning. 'But just look at the state of you, Daisy Lennox. What on earth have you been doing?'

'Digging up potatoes and picking runner beans, Mother. We have to eat.'

Lady Pendleton took one of Daisy's hands and turned it palm upwards, shaking her head. 'This must stop. You have hands like a navvy and that simply won't do.' She turned a serious face to Gwendoline. 'We must get extra help for you, my dear. Daisy is going to be fully occupied from now on. I mean to take her under my wing and train her for her future role.'

'But Jane, we can't afford to take on more servants. I thought you understood our position.'

'Of course I do, Gwendoline. But it need not be a problem. We are overstaffed as it is and I'm sure I can spare one of my kitchen maids. Iris is a reliable girl, according to my housekeeper. I'll send her along this afternoon and you can decide whether or not she suits you.'

'That is more than kind, but I'm afraid . . .' Gwendoline broke off, biting her lip.

'There's no need to talk about payment. Leave all that to me.'

'Too kind,' Gwendoline murmured, dabbing her eyes with a scrap of lace that served as a handkerchief. 'I hope you're suitably grateful, my girl.'

Daisy was about to protest, but she thought better of it when she saw the stubborn set to her ladyship's jaw. She was beginning to realise that, despite her gentle demeanour, Jane Pendleton was used to getting her own way. 'Thank you, ma'am,' she said, bobbing a curtsey. Suddenly it did not seem appropriate to take Lady Pendleton up on her suggestion that she call her by her Christian name. By accepting Rupert's proposal of marriage, Daisy could see that she had placed herself once again in a subordinate position, only now it was the woman who would become her mother-in-law who must be obeyed without question.

'We will start right away.' Lady Pendleton patted Gwendoline on the shoulder. 'If I might steal your daughter away for a few hours, I want to familiarise her with the duties and responsibilities expected of my son's wife.'

'But surely there's plenty of time for that?' Gwendoline said, a worried frown creasing her brow. 'I mean, they've only just become engaged, and Rupert has re-joined his regiment.'

'And there is much for Daisy to learn; quite apart from the fact that I will introduce her gradually to our set both here and in London. It's unfortunate that she has never had a London season or been presented at Court, but it will give me great pleasure to launch her into society.'

Daisy exchanged glances with her mother and for once she knew that they were thinking along similar lines. She laid her hand on Lady Pendleton's arm. 'Don't think I'm being ungrateful, but all that isn't for me. I'll do my utmost to make Rupert a good wife, but I'm not a debutante. We don't move in those circles and I don't think that Rupert would want me to pretend to be something I am not.'

Lady Pendleton's eyes widened. 'I'm shocked that you think I would push you into anything that was alien to you, Daisy. I merely want to ease your transition from all this into polite society.'

'I'll be an army wife, Lady Pendleton. I'll learn as I go along and Rupert will help me. As to being a viscountess, I hope that won't happen for a very long time.'

'Very well, Daisy. I can see that you've made up your mind, and perhaps I was rushing things, but you must allow me to instruct you in the traditions of a great house like Pendleton Park. It's a responsibility as well as a privilege to inherit such an important piece of English history.' Lady Pendleton picked up her parasol. 'We'll start tomorrow. Your mama will bring you to tea and we will discuss matters further then.' She held her cheek for Daisy to kiss. 'I'm delighted to welcome you into our family, my dear.' She left the room in a flurry of L'Heure Bleue and the rustle of silk.

Daisy followed her to the front door. 'I will try to be a credit to you, but you must understand that I need to make my own way, with Rupert's help, of course.'

'I do understand, Daisy. I know you'll make him a good wife, but you must allow me to do my bit. If it's all right with you we'll travel up to London on Sunday and I'll make an appointment for you to visit my couturier.' She glanced at Daisy's print gown with a sigh. 'You need some style, and the attention of my coiffeuse. You will indulge me in this at least?'

'Of course, and thank you.' Daisy stood on the doorstep watching her self-elected role model glide down the garden path like a swan on a glassy lake. Parkin leapt out of the driver's seat to open the gate for her and assist her into the Rolls. 'What have I done?' Daisy murmured as the regal motorcar disappeared around the bend in the road. She was about to retreat into the house when she heard the clank of metal against metal and she knew that Bowman was in the stables, working on the Humberette. She steeled herself to go into the house and close the door, shutting him out of her life for once and all.

In the weeks that followed Daisy suffered the ministrations of hairdressers, beauticians and fittings at the salon of the fashionable London couturier, Lucille. She was measured for morning and afternoon gowns and evening dresses that she might never wear, but according to Lady Pendleton were an absolute necessity if she were to mix in high society. She had her hair washed and trimmed, crimped and puffed up into luxuriant coils, which meant that her head was heavy with pins which gave her a headache. And even when the consultations and fitting were completed there were the accessories to choose. Beekeeper-style bonnets or tasselled motoring hats for keeping the hair tidy when out driving. For spring and summer there were duster coats made of silk and a beaver fur coat for winter. There were exhaustive trips to various milliners in order to select hats for all occasions, including a creation aptly named the Merry Widow, as worn by Lily Elsie in the eponymous operetta. There were confections decorated with osprey or egret feathers and huge, floppy flowers which made her feel as though she had a whole garden on her head. There were fur hats in the shape of pillboxes, shakos and turbans made of satin for evenings at the opera. Then there was the footwear: boots made of kid, slip-on court shoes, brogues for country wear and evening shoes with Cuban heels. As if all that were not enough there were gloves to go with each outfit, and bags made of beadwork or soft leather, and the latest craze, a Dorothy bag, which hung from the wrist on a cord.

To a girl who had been brought up with an eye to economy, it seemed almost too much to bear. But Lady Pendleton was in her element, choosing fabrics and discussing future fashion trends as if their lives depended on being in the forefront of haute couture. Daisy was overwhelmed by her generosity and horrified by her extravagance. She was exhausted by the seemingly never-ending engagements for luncheon, afternoon tea and trips to the theatre followed by supper at exclusive restaurants. She discovered that Lady Pendleton, who she had always thought was peerless in thought and deed, had one weakness. She was addicted to card games, in particular faro, loo and whist, but try as she might Daisy could not summon up an interest in something she found intrinsically boring, and she was hopeless with numbers. She began to dread card parties and would have preferred to stay at home, even if it meant enduring an evening with Lord Pendleton.

He lived in the London house for a greater part of the year, attending sessions in the House of Lords, and it was only when the House was not sitting that he would retire to Pendleton Park. Daisy was a little in awe of the austere gentleman who seemed to have his mind on other matters, and although she had met him on many occasions he always looked slightly puzzled when he found her seated at the breakfast table or passed her on the staircase. She felt sometimes that she ought to be wearing a badge with her name on it in order to remind him who she was. She was not exactly afraid of him but he seemed very old when compared to her father, and unapproachable. She always waited for him to address her before she opened her mouth in his presence. He was obviously a great many years his wife's senior and they treated each other like polite strangers. It was almost impossible to imagine that theirs had been a love match that had transcended the barriers of class. Daisy could not imagine herself and Rupert ever sinking to that level. Not that she had seen him since he returned to his regiment. She had spoken to him on the telephone at the house in Mayfair, but the line had been crackly and he sounded so far away that it had been impossible to have anything like a normal conversation. He said that he hoped to have leave at Christmas but he could not promise anything.

Daisy anticipated their reunion with some trepidation. She knew that she ought to be counting every minute until they were reunited but as the days went by she became more and more worried. When she thought of Rupert she remembered halcyon days in the countryside when they were carefree children, but try as she might she could not imagine them living as husband and wife. Neither could she envisage herself as mistress of Pendleton Park and the grand house in London. She felt trapped by the rules of etiquette that she struggled to remember, and she longed for the freedom she had enjoyed when living at home in Warwick Square. Every minute of every day was carefully mapped out for her by Lady Pendleton, and at every turn there was a servant to carry out her slightest wish. She missed her family and the peace and quiet of Rainbow's End, but she could see no easy way of escape without hurting people for whom she cared deeply, but perhaps not deeply enough.

As Christmas approached Daisy was becoming desperate, but a chance meeting with a young woman called Grace Ashley-Smith at a charity fundraising dinner changed everything. It had been impossible not to notice Grace and her companion Lillian Franklin, attired as they were in scarlet jackets over white muslin dresses adorned with scarlet sashes. Daisy had no idea what organisation this uniform represented but she was irresistibly drawn to the two oddly dressed women. She would have asked Lady Pendleton about them, but she was giving her full attention to a handsome gentleman with mutton-chop whiskers and a row of medals on his chest. Daisy was already feeling bored and out of her depth. She had been introduced to so many new people that her hand was quite sore from being shaken. She decided that the two women looked equally out of place and alone amongst the illustrious company, and she edged her way through the crowd towards them. She held out her hand, smiling. 'I know it isn't done to introduce oneself, but I'm Daisy Lennox. How do you do?'

The more outgoing of the pair shook her hand vigorously. 'Thank God. A woman who isn't afraid to speak up for herself. I thought that Lillian and I were the only two here who didn't conform. I'm Grace Ashley-Smith and this is my friend, Lillian Franklin.'

Introductions over, Daisy stared curiously at their uniforms. 'Do you mind telling me what you represent? I'm frightfully ignorant of this sort of thing.'

'We're FANYs,' Grace said, chuckling. 'The First Aid Nursing Yeomanry.'

'Really? That sounds exciting. Do tell me about it.'

'Let's have a drink first.' Lillian seized two glasses of champagne from a passing waiter and handed them to Daisy and Grace, taking care to take one for herself before he moved on with his silver tray balanced expertly on one hand. 'These dos make me thirsty. They're so awfully dull.'

'Stop moaning, Lillian,' Grace said, sipping her champagne and pulling a face. 'Actually I prefer beer, but it's deeply infra dig.' She cocked her head on one side, looking Daisy up and down with a critical eye. 'Are you interested in joining, by any chance?'

It was the first time that anyone had suggested anything remotely interesting and suddenly the slight depression that had clouded Daisy's mind dissipated like morning mist. 'I might be,' she said cautiously. 'If I knew exactly what it is you do. For one thing I'm not a nurse and I can't stand the sight of blood.'

'But you're engaged to Lord Pendleton's son unless I'm very much mistaken. You'll be marrying into the aristocracy,' Grace said seriously. 'Surely that means you can ride, and maybe even drive a motor car. We need volunteers to do all sorts of things. D'you think you could load and fire a gun, for instance?'

Taken aback by her forceful nature and obvious enthusiasm, Daisy recoiled slightly. 'I can ride a horse, although I've never ridden to hounds or handled a gun, but I can drive a motorcar. I've got a licence.'

'You sound eminently suitable,' Lillian said, smiling.

They were interrupted by the call to dinner and Daisy could see Lady Pendleton beckoning to her. 'I'm sorry, I have to go. Perhaps we could talk later. I'm desperately keen to learn more.'

'Good egg,' Grace said enthusiastically. 'We'll arrange

a proper interview after dinner. Do you know Lexham Gardens, South Kensington?'

'No, but I'm sure I can find it.'

The interview was quite informal and to her amazement Daisy found herself enrolled in the First Aid Nursing Yeomanry, but there were costs associated with this, which presented a problem as she had no funds of her own. There was the initial joining fee of one guinea, and she would be expected to buy her uniform and first aid outfit. Then there were classes in first aid, home nursing and riding lessons which also cost money. In the face of this unexpected expenditure Daisy had no alternative but to swallow her pride and go cap in hand to Lady Pendleton.

She stood before her in the Chinese drawing room feeling like a small child asking for pocket money. Lady Pendleton listened quietly until Daisy had finished speaking. She folded her hands in her lap, keeping her gaze fixed on Daisy's face. 'Is this what you want? Do you think that my son would approve of his future wife joining such an organisation?'

'I don't know,' Daisy said, shifting nervously from one foot to the other. 'I wish I could talk to him about it, but I don't think he would stop me. After all, he is a soldier dedicated to serving his country and I'd like to do my bit. I'm truly grateful for everything you've done for me, but I feel rather useless.'

'Useless?' Lady Pendleton stared at her in undisguised astonishment. 'You astound me, Daisy. What could a young woman do that was more worthy than learning to be a good wife and hopefully a mother one day? You will have the honour and responsibility of bearing the heir who will carry on the name of Pendleton. Isn't that enough for you?'

Daisy hung her head. 'I'm sorry. I can't help the way I am, and these women are so dedicated and brave. If war comes I would be able to do something practical. Maybe even help save the lives of men like Rupert.'

Lady Pendleton recoiled slightly but Daisy could see that she had gained her interest if not her approval. 'This is beyond my experience,' Lady Pendleton said slowly. 'In my day women were happy to serve silently and keep things going until their men returned from battle. I am obviously out of touch with the modern way of thinking.'

'If I might just try it out,' Daisy urged gently. 'Surely that wouldn't hurt? I promise that I'll discuss it with Rupert when he comes home on leave, and if he is set against it then I'll resign.'

For a moment she thought that Lady Pendleton was going to refuse, but she nodded her head.

'All right, Daisy. I'll pay your expenses and you may go ahead with my blessing, but only because I know that you have an independent spirit and that you find society life not entirely to your taste.' She held up a delicate hand as Daisy was about to argue. 'No, my dear, I'm well aware that you don't enjoy tea parties and soirées, and that isn't a bad thing. I suspect that when Rupert eventually leaves the army and takes over the running of the estate he will want to spend far more time in the country than in London. I think that you two will suit very well, and for that reason I'm prepared to humour you in this. Go ahead and order your uniform and whatever you need. Have the bills sent to me.'

Daisy seized her hand and raised it to her cheek. 'Thank you for being so understanding. Might I go to Gamages now? They supply everything I'll need.'

'Gamages? I don't think I know that store.'

Daisy tried not to smile. 'No, I don't suppose you do, ma'am. It's in High Holborn.'

'I don't know that part of London, but I'll ring for Parkin. He'll take you in the Rolls.'

'If you don't mind, I'd rather go on the tube train. It's probably quicker.'

'Then at least take my maid with you. I don't like the thought of you travelling about on public transport on your own.'

'I'll be joining a military group, Lady Pendleton. I think I can go a few stops on the Central Line without fear of being kidnapped or molested.'

'I suppose so.' Lady Pendleton sighed deeply. 'I do admire your spirit, my dear. I've forgotten what it's like to go somewhere unattended.'

Daisy threw herself into her training with more enthusiasm than she had felt for anything in her life. She signed up for evening classes in first aid at the Regent Street Polytechnic at the cost of three shillings, and she ordered her uniform from Gamages. She felt most strange when trying it on for the first time in the privacy of her bedroom. The khaki tunic and divided skirt worn over breeches and puttees with boots and a pith helmet made her look and feel like a totally different person. She dared not wear it in the house for fear of offending Lady Pendleton's sensibilities, and she packed it in a small valise to change into when she reached the stables where she underwent compulsory riding lessons. She repeated the routine each time she attended classes on handling firearms, which she thoroughly enjoyed. Her instructor was a stocky ex-army sergeant who alternately bullied and cajoled her until she had achieved the required standard.

'You're a natural markswoman, miss,' he said one day when she was cleaning her revolver. 'Some of the ladies couldn't hit the side of a barn with a cannon, but you're a good shot. Well done.'

She left the building feeling that she had achieved something remarkable, but the same could not be said when it came to the riding lessons. She had fallen off more times than she could count, but had suffered nothing worse than severe bruising and agonising embarrassment. She was certain that her mount knew that she was nervous and behaved erratically in order to confuse her, and took equine pleasure in unseating her at every opportunity, but she was determined not to be beaten. After many painful landings on the packed earth surface of the arena she was finally beginning to improve, but still had difficulty mounting. Some of the girls seemed to have springs in their shoes and could leap on without any apparent effort, but for Daisy it was a struggle. She had ridden before, but always side-saddle with the aid of a groom and a mounting block. She hoped that if it came to a war, as all the women seemed to think was inevitable, she would be allowed to drive a motor vehicle.

She acquitted herself well in the first aid classes and when she was with her fellow trainees she enjoyed the feeling of liberation and comradeship, something akin to fighting for the cause with the suffragettes. But when she returned to Grosvenor Square she had to revert to her submissive state and it was far from easy. She had to pack away her comfortable uniform and put aside all talk of war, and become once again the decorous young woman who was engaged to the future Lord Pendleton. She was obliged to suffer in silence while her maid laced her corsets until it was difficult to breathe, and it was not uncommon to have several changes of outfit in one day. Daisy managed to bear it all with good grace, but she had glimpsed a different way of life and made new friends and found it unsettling in the extreme.

It was with mixed feelings that Daisy packed her bags for the return home at Christmas. She had been invited to spend the festive season at Pendleton Park but she declined firmly, saying that she had been absent long enough from her own family and they would be deeply hurt if she did not stay at Rainbow's End. She had genuinely missed them all. In retrospect, even her mother's constant criticism seemed like a mere irritation, and she was eager to return to a simpler way of life without worrying if she made a social gaffe or showed herself up in front of the servants. She wondered how Ruby was getting on with Iris; and then there was Bowman. She had barely given him a thought since she joined the FANY. Perhaps she had recovered from the infatuation which had threatened to consume her whole being. She pinned all her hopes on her forthcoming reunion with Rupert. She knew that he would be supportive of her decision to join the Yeomanry, or at least she hoped that he would think it a good move on her part.

Three days before Christmas she set off for Essex in the back of the Rolls with Lady Pendleton. Lord Pendleton had promised to join them on Christmas Eve, travelling first class on the train from Liverpool Street, and Lady Pendleton had accepted his decision, as always, with a vague smile.

It was dark when Daisy arrived at Rainbow's End. The air was crisp and smelled of frost and woodsmoke. Ice particles glistened on the path leading up to the house and the warm glow of lamplight shone from the windows as if to welcome her home. Parkin carried her bags to the front door and rang the bell. 'Merry Christmas, miss,' he said, saluting smartly as he took his leave of her.

'The compliments of the season to you too, Parkin,' Daisy said, smiling. She waited eagerly for someone to let her in, and after a few moments the door was opened, but to her surprise it was Iris who stepped outside to pick up the suitcases. Daisy entered the house, inhaling the familiar scent of lavender and beeswax tempered with just a hint of dry rot and mildew. 'Hello, Iris. It's good to see you, but where is Ruby?'

Iris closed the front door. 'She's not feeling too good, miss. She went to bed early. Shall I take the cases up to your room?'

Puzzled, Daisy nodded. 'Yes, thank you.' She hurried across the hall to the drawing room without stopping to divest herself of her fur coat and hat. Her father rose to his feet and came towards her with his arms outstretched. Teddy and Bea were quick to follow suit. Only Gwendoline remained seated, but she was smiling and nodding with approval.

'You've come at last,' Bea cried, giving her a bear-like hug. 'We've saved some supper for you. Iris is a super cook.'

Victor kissed Daisy on the cheek. 'Welcome home, my dear.'

Teddy slapped her on the back. 'You put us all in the shade, dressed up to the nines in your fox furs.'

She knew he was teasing, but she slipped off the expensive coat and tossed it onto a chair. 'I love you too, Teddy.' She glanced warily at her mother. 'Hello, Mother.'

Gwendoline patted the empty seat beside her. 'Come and sit down, Daisy. I'm sure we all want to hear about your time in London.'

'Give the poor child time to catch her breath,' Victor said, resuming his seat by the fire.

'I'm dying to hear about it,' Bea said excitedly. 'It's so good to have you home, Daisy. I haven't had anyone to tease since you went away. Teddy's no fun. He's always mooning round after Iris.'

'Shut up, brat.' Teddy tweaked her hair, which she

had attempted to put up in a more sophisticated style, and it tumbled around her shoulders causing her to slap him.

'Beast. Now look what you've done.'

'Children, behave.' Gwendoline frowned. 'Your father is quite right. Give Daisy a moment to settle in. Perhaps she would like to freshen up after her journey and have some supper before you wear her out with your questions.'

Daisy shot her a grateful smile. 'Thank you, Mother. Yes, actually, I'd like to go to my room and tidy up a bit before I eat, and then I'm all yours.'

'I'll come with you then.' Bea rushed to open the door. 'I want to hear absolutely everything. Life here has been so dull without you, and I want to know how the toffs live.'

'Don't be vulgar, Beatrice,' Gwendoline said automatically. 'Go if you must, but don't keep Daisy talking upstairs. It's bitterly cold in the bedrooms as, according to your father, we can't afford to light fires upstairs. Anyway, come down quickly. We all want to hear about your time in London. I do miss it so terribly, you know.'

With Beatrice following her, Daisy made her way upstairs to her room. She paused on the landing as she heard a door open on the top floor where Ruby slept in one of the tiny attic rooms. She looked up and caught sight of a pale face peering over the banisters. Ruby's dark hair hung loose about her shoulders and her face was as pale in the dim light as her white calico nightgown. 'Are you all right, Ruby?' Daisy called up the stairs. 'Iris said you are unwell.'

Ruby turned and fled, slamming her bedroom door.

Daisy turned to her sister in astonishment. 'What on earth is wrong with her, Bea? Why wouldn't she speak to me?'

Chapter Ten

Beatrice opened Daisy's bedroom door, beckoning furiously. 'Come in and I'll tell you.'

Daisy shivered as she entered her old room. She had grown used to the warmth of the house in Grosvenor Square, where servants lit fires in the main rooms first thing in the morning and kept them going until late at night. She had also become accustomed to the luxury of electric light, and having her own bathroom with hot and cold running water. It was quite a shock to return to the primitive living conditions in Rainbow's End. 'What is this all about, Bea? Is Ruby sick?'

'She's in pod, Daisy.'

'What do you mean?'

Beatrice gave her a pitying look. 'You are an innocent, Daisy. She's in the pudding club. About four months gone I should say.'

Daisy's knees gave way beneath her and she slumped down on the bed. 'Whose is it?'

'Use your head. She's been sneaking off to see Bowman at every opportunity. It's his of course, and according to Jimmy she's not the first one he's put in the family way.'

'That's just village gossip,' Daisy said faintly. 'Are you sure she's in pod as you so elegantly put it?'

'Jimmy's elder sister is expecting too, although her boyfriend is going to marry her next week so she won't have a little bastard like Ruby. Anyway, I'm not so naïve that I don't know the signs.'

A wave of nausea left a bitter taste in Daisy's mouth. She swallowed convulsively. 'I think I've heard enough, Bea.' She forced herself to rise to her feet and hurried to the washstand, filling the flower-patterned bowl from the jug. She splashed her face with ice-cold water. 'Go downstairs, there's a dear. I'll just do my hair and I'll be down in five minutes.'

Bea stood with her hands clasped behind her back, angling her head. 'You aren't upset, are you? I wouldn't have blurted it out like that if you hadn't asked.'

'I worry for Ruby if what you say is true, but I prefer to hear it from her lips. There might be some other explanation.'

'I'm right, you'll see. And Iris will be the next one if Teddy isn't careful. That's if he lives long enough to become a father. Jed Smith has threatened to put out his lights if he doesn't leave Iris alone. Not that she needs any encouragement. She's a wonderful cook, but in my opinion she's a fast cat.'

Torn between laughter and disapproval, Daisy made an effort to keep a straight face. 'Mother would die if she heard you talking like that.'

'I don't care. I'm only telling you what's been going on while you've been living the high life in London. I'd be green with envy if it didn't sound so deadly dull.' Beatrice hesitated in the doorway. 'You won't tell anyone what I said, will you, Daisy?'

'Of course not. And don't worry. I'll sort it all out in the morning.'

Daisy slept from sheer exhaustion that night but she awakened early. It was still pitch dark and for a moment she thought she was back in her splendid bedroom in Grosvenor Square, but as she reached for the switch her fingers touched the old-fashioned oil lamp on her bedside table, and everything came flooding back to her. She struck a match but she was shivering so much that it took several attempts to light the wick. As she slipped her silk peignoir around her shoulders she could see that there was ice on the inside of her bedroom windows and her breath curled around her head like smoke. She rose from her bed and braced herself to wash her face and clean her teeth in water that had been standing all night and had a faint skim of ice on the surface. She only now realised how spoilt she had become in a very short time. The family had lived in relative comfort in Warwick Square, but it was as nothing compared to the pampered existence of the Pendletons in their London home. She felt slightly ashamed even making the comparison and dressed quickly in her warmest wool merino morning gown. She wrapped a cashmere shawl around her shoulders, hugging it around her in an attempt to keep warm as she went downstairs to the kitchen. She found Ruby whey-faced and shaky having been sick in the scullery sink. 'So it's true,' Daisy said calmly. 'Beatrice told me that you're expecting, but I wanted to hear it from you.' She glanced down at the swell of Ruby's belly just visible beneath her serge skirt. 'Does anyone else know?'

Ruby's eyes filled with tears and she shook her head. 'No.'

'What about the father?'

'I told him.'

Taking her by the shoulders, Daisy pressed her gently down on a chair. 'It's Bowman, of course.'

'Yes.' Ruby bent her head and tears fell unchecked onto her clasped hands. Her whole body shook and she rocked backwards and forwards. 'I love him, miss. And I thought he loved me.'

'Is he going to marry you?'

Ruby raised a tear-stained face. 'He can't. He's got a wife already.'

'Married?' Daisy pulled up a chair and sat down. 'But that's impossible. Everyone in the village would know about it.'

'She don't come from round here.' A sob racked Ruby's thin frame and she buried her face in her hands. 'I dunno what I'll do. It'll be the workhouse for me and the baby.'

'Nonsense,' Daisy said with more certainty than she was feeling. 'Bowman must be made to look after you both. And you have a family in London. If the worst came to the worst, wouldn't they take you in?'

'Me dad would kill me. I daresn't show me face there again. Your mum will sack me as soon as she discovers that I'm in the family way, and I'll be out on the street.'

'You most certainly won't. Not while I've got a breath

in my body.' Daisy rose somewhat shakily to her feet, but she was motivated by anger now; cold hard implacable rage against the man who had lied and cheated his way into their hearts. She moved swiftly to the range and riddled the ashes until the embers glowed into life. She built up the fire and filled the kettle at the tap in the scullery, placing it on the hob. 'Where is Iris? I take it that she doesn't live in.'

Ruby wiped her eyes on her sleeve and sniffed. 'No. She still has her old room in the servants' quarters at the big house, but she'll be here in time to cook breakfast.' She glanced at the wall clock. 'In about half an hour.'

'She doesn't know about . . .' Daisy gazed pointedly at Ruby's stomach.

'No one does, except your sister. I think she's guessed, but she's a good kid. She won't say nothing.'

'She told me and it's only a matter of time before it's obvious to everyone. We'll have a cup of tea and then I'm going out. You must act normally. We don't want Iris to get suspicious.'

'I don't trust her. She's a sly one on the quiet and she's got her eye on Mr Teddy.'

'So Beatrice said. I'll have words with my brother, but first I'm going to sort out Mr Barnaby Bowman.'

'No, miss. Please don't say nothing to him. He won't like it.'

'He most certainly will not. That's my whole aim. I'm going to tell him exactly what I think of him. I may not wield any authority in the village but my future father-in-law does, and I think he could make life very difficult for Bowman. Barnaby won't be so cocky if he can't get work.'

'He'll just move on. He's done it before.'

'We'll see about that. Has he finished working on the motorcar?'

'Not quite, miss. He's waiting for a part to come from the manufacturers, but I'll say this for him, he's done a really good job on it.'

Daisy warmed the teapot. 'Has he now? That may be to his advantage.' She made the tea and filled two cups, passing one to Ruby. 'Drink up and cheer up. We're still sister suffragists at heart, Ruby.'

Ruby answered with a watery smile as she sipped the hot, strong tea. Daisy drank hers quickly, regardless of the fact that she had burnt her tongue. She was furious and she wanted to keep the anger going until she saw Bowman.

Leaving Ruby to do her morning chores, Daisy put on her old coat and felt hat and set off for Bowman's cottage. It was just getting light as she hammered on his door. He opened it moments later, tousle-haired and with his shirt unbuttoned. His eyes widened with surprise when he saw her. 'Miss Lennox.'

Pushing past him, she marched into the living room. A candle flickered in the middle of a deal table littered with used crockery, newspapers and what looked like small pieces of a car engine. Bowman shoved his feet into his shoes, running his hand through his sleep-tangled hair in a vain attempt to tame it into shape. 'I'd ask you to come in, but you've already done so. Is there a problem?'

'I'd say you're the one who has a problem, Mr Bowman.' Daisy faced him, holding on to her anger. In his sleepy dishevelled state he looked suddenly much younger and defenceless. He was watching her warily and she had to quell a surge of sympathy for him. Instead of wanting to pummel him with her fists, she longed to put her arms around him and hold his head to her breast. But that was ridiculous. She remembered Ruby's condition and her admission that Bowman was already married. She hardened her heart with difficulty. 'You know why I'm here, of course.'

'To collect the spare part for the Humberette?' His lips twitched and the old familiar twinkle in his eyes teased and tormented her.

'Don't try to be funny,' she said angrily. 'Ruby is expecting your child. What are you going to do about it?'

He pulled out a chair, dusting it off with his shirt sleeve. 'Won't you sit down, Miss Lennox? How about a cup of tea, or would you like something stronger? It's a bitter cold morning to be out and about so early.'

She shook her head. 'I don't want to sit down, nor do I want anything from you other than your promise to stand by Ruby and her baby.'

He shrugged his shoulders. 'I can't marry Ruby, as I'm sure she told you. I'll do my best to support her and the child, but I'm not a rich man.'

'You told her that you're married. Is that true?'

'Unfortunately, yes. She was in the family way, although I wasn't sure if the kid was mine. I suppose I felt sorry for her and we got married but it went wrong from the start. She told me that I wasn't the father and she'd only married me to save face. She left me soon after the wedding and went back to live with her family. That was five years ago and I've hardly seen her since.'

'Being married didn't prevent you from ruining Ruby's life. How many children have you fathered in that way, Mr Bowman?'

He grinned. 'Can't say I've ever kept count, miss.'

'You're a bounder and a cad.'

'You didn't seem to think so back in the summer. As I remember it you and me were good together, Daisy.'

'How dare you bring that up? You're not a gentleman.'

'I never pretended to be anything of the sort. And you forgot you was a lady sometimes, as I recall with great pleasure.'

He took a step closer and his eyes burned into hers causing her pulses to race and her knees to tremble. She moved backwards but the kitchen table was in the way and she was trapped. 'Don't come any nearer, Bowman.'

'I might not,' he said slowly, 'but on the other hand I might.' He seized her round the waist and pulled her into his arms. His mouth found hers, hard and demanding. She fought and struggled but it was a losing battle. The whole intoxicating scent of him filled her nostrils and all her good intentions flew out of the window. In those few mindless moments she felt nothing but the primeval urge to give herself to the dominant male. Their physical beings seemed to melt into one seething mass of uncontrollable passion, but in the end the need to catch her breath brought her abruptly back to reality. She pushed him away.

'That was an unspeakable thing to do.'

He nodded, a lazy smile curving his lips. 'But thoroughly enjoyable, and don't try to deny it, Miss High and Mighty.'

Daisy waved her left hand in front of his face. 'I'm engaged to be married. You've no right to take advantage of me in this way.'

He threw back his head and laughed. 'Excuse me, ma'am, but you're the one who marched into my house at daybreak, catching me half dressed and in my stockinged feet. If that wasn't an invitation to a tumble, I'd like to know what is.'

Daisy was shaking from head to foot and she knew she was blushing furiously, which only made matters worse. What rankled even more was the fact that he was right in one respect. She should never have come here at all, let alone under the cover of darkness, and if she were to be completely honest she knew in her heart that it was the sudden desire to see him again that led her to undertake such a reckless course. She edged away, moving towards the door. 'You're mistaken,' she said icily. 'I am very much in love with my fiancé, but I can see that you might have misunderstood my reasons for coming here.'

Bowman sprawled on a chair, eyeing her with some amusement. 'You disappoint me, Daisy. I thought you were lusting after my manly body.'

'You are quite disgusting.'

His expression darkened and he leaned forward,

holding her gaze with a straight look. 'So why did you come exactly? You knew that I couldn't make an honest woman of Ruby even if I wanted to.'

'So you were just amusing yourself with her. Is that it?'

'I've never forced a woman to do anything she didn't want to. Ruby was a willing partner.' He stood up, pushing the chair aside. 'I've told you that I'll do my bit, so why don't you go back to your posh soldier-boy and stop interfering.'

His harsh words swamped her like a shower of iced water and she gasped, staring at him in disbelief. 'Do you dislike me so much?'

He was at her side before she had a chance to open the door and he placed his hands on her shoulders, looking deeply into her eyes. 'You won't stop until you force it out of me, will you, Daisy? You know and I know that we were made for each other.' He laid his finger on her lips as she opened her mouth to protest. 'That's why you keep coming back for more, even though you'd never give yourself to a man like me. I bedded Ruby because I knew I couldn't have you.' A rueful smile lit his dark eyes. 'Don't look so shocked, girl. What I'm trying to tell you is that I love you. I fell in love with you the moment I first saw you, and I think you felt the same.'

She shook her head, attempting to twist free from his grasp and failing. 'You're just saying that,' she whispered. 'You don't mean it.'

He opened the door and thrust her outside into the bitter cold of a winter dawn. 'I meant every word of it, and that's why you've got to go now before anyone sees you.' He slammed the door in her face and she heard him groan loudly and beat his fists on the wooden panels. She stood as if frozen to the spot, but the sound of footsteps approaching along the street galvanised her into action. She fled in the direction of home, running as fast as her legs would carry her. She did not stop until she reached the coach house. Gasping for breath she went inside and collapsed on the front seat of the Humberette, clutching the wheel and sobbing as if her heart would break.

Everything he said had been true. She had gone to Bowman's cottage telling herself it was for Ruby's benefit when all along she had secretly been yearning to see him again. He was like a drug that once taken had become an addiction. He thrilled her and sent her senses spiralling out of control. She ached for him physically, even though she had no experience and only a vague notion of what passed between man and wife in the intimacy of the marriage bed. She knew that she was no better than Ruby. If Lady Pendleton had not spirited her off to London for four months she might well have ended up in the same dire predicament.

She leaned her head against the wheel, breathing deeply until the storm of grief and shame eased and she regained her self-control, but she felt his presence even though he was nowhere near. The smell of the workshop was in the air she breathed just as it had clung to Bowman's hair and clothes. Sitting in the machine on which he had worked for so many hours brought him closer than she could have imagined. She felt in her pocket for a hanky and blew her nose. It was Christmas Eve and Rupert was due home later in the day. There was much to do and she must put all thoughts of Bowman from her head, if not her heart.

She slid off the seat and made her way out of the coach house and round the side of the house to the back door. Pausing only to pat her hair in place, she opened the door and went inside. Ruby pounced on her as she entered the kitchen. 'You've been ages. What happened?' She recoiled, staring at Daisy's face. 'What's the matter, miss? You've been crying. Has that brute upset you?'

Daisy glanced round anxiously. 'Is Iris here?'

'No, she's very late. Tell me what happened. If he's done anything to make you cry I'll go down there right away and give him a piece of my mind.'

'Don't get excited, Ruby. It's bad for the baby. I made a mistake going to see Bowman but he was quite reasonable, for him.'

'Then what's wrong?'

'I don't know. Everything, I suppose. It's just not fair. None of it is fair.' Daisy stiffened as she heard the click of the latch on the outside door. 'That must be Iris. I don't want her to find me in the kitchen. We'll talk later.' She hurried from the kitchen without giving Ruby a chance to argue. She raced upstairs to her room and shut the door, leaning against it and covering her face with her hands to muffle a sob. What had she done? Her cheeks burned and her heart pounded against her ribs like a wild animal trying to escape. At best she had made a complete fool of herself. At the very worst she had been forced to face the fact that far from being over, her affair with Bowman had barely begun.

She paced the floor, wringing her hands. Life had been so much easier in London, especially since she had joined the FANY. While she was training she had felt part of something great and important, but returning home had brought her face to face with feelings that she had strenuously denied in the past. Even so she could not quite believe that she had fallen in love with a man who was so far beneath her in every way. She had agreed to marry Rupert, her childhood sweetheart, for that was what he was in essence. Rupert was everything she could ever want in a husband, but her pulses did not race whenever she saw him. Her body did not cry out to be possessed by him, and his kisses did not send her into paroxysms of delight.

Her heart felt as though it would explode and she could not breathe. She went to the window and flung the casement open, leaning out to take deep breaths of the frosty morning air. A sulky dawn had split the dark sky open to reveal heavy clouds that threatened snow. There was a smoky taste to the air and as the sharp east wind fanned her hot cheeks she began to feel calmer. Rupert would arrive some time later in the day and she must greet him as if nothing had changed. He deserved better than a wife whose heart belonged to another, but she would take care that he never discovered the truth. She closed the window and went to her dressing table to tidy her windblown hair. She stared at her reflection and was amazed to see the face of innocence gazing back at her. None of her inner turmoil was apparent and for that she could only be thankful. She hoped that Rupert would not look into her eyes and see her troubled soul. Only she herself and Bowman knew her dark secret, but she was not sure whether she could trust him to keep it to himself. Perhaps she ought to confess everything to Rupert and start married life with a clear conscience.

Daisy was standing on a stepladder decorating the Christmas tree that Jimmy Gurney had felled from the woods and delivered to Rainbow's End earlier that morning. As she reached up to put the star on the topmost branch she heard the sound of a motorcar engine.

'I'll bet that's Rupert,' Bea said, running to the window. 'Yes, it is. How handsome he looks. I wish Jimmy would enlist in the army so that I could see him in uniform.'

'I'm sure you don't really,' Daisy said, standing back to admire her efforts. 'You wouldn't want him to be sent into battle.'

'There won't be a war. Father says so.' Beatrice hurried from the room, calling over her shoulder. 'I'll let him in. You've got pine needles in your hair, Daisy. Look in the mirror and you'll see.'

Daisy raised her hand to her forehead and grimaced as she felt the tiny green spikes sticking out of her hair. She was halfway across the room when Rupert appeared in the doorway. He held out his arms. 'Daisy Bell. How wonderful you look.' He rushed forward to give her a hug and brushed her lips with a kiss. 'I've missed you so much, my dear girl. Have you missed me?'

'Of course she has,' Beatrice said, grinning broadly. 'Kiss her properly, you idiot. Don't mind me.'

He chuckled. 'Thanks, Bea. I don't need permission to kiss my fiancée.' He threw his peaked cap onto a chair and claimed Daisy's mouth in a tender kiss.

She struggled free, laughing. 'Not in front of the child. She's much too young to see such things.'

Bea stuck her tongue out. 'I'm nearly seventeen I'll have you know, and quite grown up for my age. I've been kissed.'

'I wouldn't let Mother hear you say that or she'll never allow you out of the house again.' Daisy met Rupert's enquiring look with an attempt at a smile. 'It's wonderful to have you home again. Won't you take a seat? I'm sure that Bea would love to fetch something for you from the kitchen.'

He sat on the sofa, pulling Daisy down beside him. 'No, I'm fine, thanks. Parkin picked me up at the station so I went home first, said hello to Mother and then I came here to see my beloved.' He raised her hand to his lips. 'How are you, darling? You look a bit pale.'

'She's healthy as a horse,' Bea said dispassionately. 'Daisy has never had a day's sickness in her life.'

Torn between annoyance and laughter, Daisy pointed at the door. 'Kitchen, Bea. Go and see if lunch is ready. We might persuade Rupert to stay and eat with us after all.'

'Oh, all right. Spoilsport.' Bea flounced off, stamping

her feet on the polished oak floorboards as she crossed the hallway.

Rupert wrapped his arms around Daisy. 'How have you been, darling? Did you miss me?'

She lowered her gaze, unable to look him in the eyes. 'Of course I did, but I have a confession to make. I wanted to tell you before anyone else did.' She felt him tense and unwillingly she raised her head. His ingenuous look of concern, bereft of suspicion and totally trusting, speared her heart like a knife thrust. To tell him about Bowman would be like kicking a puppy.

'What is it you have to tell me, sweetheart? It can't be anything too terrible, I'm sure.'

'I – I . . .' She gulped and swallowed. 'I've joined the First Aid Nursing Yeomanry, Rupert.'

He let out a long sigh. 'Is that all?'

'You don't mind?'

'Why should I? I think they're a brave bunch of women, although I wouldn't want to think that you were risking life and limb.'

'I'm not,' she said hastily. 'It's all terribly well organised.' She put her head on one side, studying his face in an attempt to read his thoughts. 'Most men disapprove heartily, and the army refuse to recognise us. I was afraid you might want me to give it up.'

'Absolutely not, my love. If it makes you happy and gives you something to do that you feel is worthwhile then I'm all for it. To be honest I'd rather you were affiliated to the FANY than to the suffragists. It's probably a lot safer, just so long as there isn't a war, but I can't imagine that the authorities would allow women to risk their lives on the front line.'

'No,' Daisy said doubtfully. 'I suppose not.'

He placed his arm around her shoulders and drew her closer. 'Anyway, I'm home now even if it is only for a short while. We'll make the most of it, and Mother has invited your family for Christmas luncheon. You will come, won't you?'

'Of course we'd be delighted to accept.' Gwendoline breezed into the room, holding her arms outstretched. 'My dear boy, how lovely to see you again.'

He rose hastily to his feet and suffered her embrace with a stoicism that Daisy could only admire. Really, she thought, Mother can be so embarrassing at times. She stood up. 'Rupert and I were just going for a spin in the motorcar, Mother.'

'Really?' Gwendoline stared at her blankly. 'I thought that Beatrice said he was staying for lunch.'

Taking his cue from Daisy, Rupert nodded his head. 'It's terribly kind of you, Mrs Lennox, but perhaps another time. I was rather hoping that Daisy would come home with me. It's the Pendleton Park servants' Christmas luncheon today. It's a long established custom. The family waits on the staff and I thought Daisy might like to help this year.'

'Of course I would,' Daisy said enthusiastically. 'Lady Pendleton has done so much for me, Mother. It's the least I can do.'

Gwendoline sank down on a chair. 'Oh, well, if it's for dear Jane, then of course you must go, Daisy.' She brightened up a little. 'But we'll all be there tomorrow,

Rupert. Do tell your mother that we're looking forward to it immensely.'

Daisy grabbed Rupert's hat and thrust it into his hand. 'Come along then. Am I dressed for the occasion, or should I change?'

He took her by the hand. 'My darling, you would look perfect wearing a potato sack, but what you've got on is absolutely fine. Good day, Mrs Lennox. Please give my regards to your husband and Teddy.'

Leaving Rupert in the hall, Daisy went upstairs to her room and slipped on the fur motoring coat and tasselled turban that Lady Pendleton had insisted on buying for her, and for once she was glad she had accepted such a generous gift. She took a pair of fur mittens from her dressing table drawer and a long scarf which she wound round her neck. It was going to be cold driving in an open car but she did not mind. It would be wonderful to escape from reality even for a short while. She went downstairs to join Rupert, and as soon as they were outside and safely out of earshot she gave him a questioning look. 'Did you make that up about the servants' Christmas lunch?'

'Of course not. It is perfectly true, but all my ghastly relations have descended upon us for the festive season, and as no one was expecting me to arrive this early they were prepared to go ahead without me, so if you would rather do something else . . .'

Daisy climbed into the passenger seat of the Prince Henry. 'Actually, if you don't mind, I think I'd rather go for a drive and perhaps have lunch somewhere quite a long way from here.'

He closed the door and went round the front of the car to crank the starting handle. As soon as the engine kicked into life he vaulted into the driver's seat. 'What a splendid idea. I know a delightful riverside pub where they serve the best trout I've ever tasted and treacle tart that makes my mouth water just thinking about it.'

'That sounds wonderful, Rupert.'

'And I want to have you all to myself for a couple of hours at least. I don't want to share you with anyone, Daisy Bell.' He patted her hand as it lay in her lap. 'Have I told you recently that I love you, darling?'

They enjoyed lunch in an ancient hostelry decorated with boughs of holly and hung with mistletoe. A log fire roared up the chimney in the ingle nook and as they sat and talked over their meal of warming vegetable soup followed by grilled trout, it seemed as though they had never been apart. Daisy had almost forgotten what a charming and amusing companion Rupert could be and she relaxed in his company, putting the morning's events out of her mind. He even allowed her to drive home. It felt as though they were an old married couple, content in each other's company with few surprises to come as they parted with an affectionate kiss at the front door of Rainbow's End. Daisy waved goodbye as he drove off, but she could not help comparing their comfortable relationship with the passion she had experienced in Bowman's embrace. She rattled the door knocker but when no one answered she walked briskly round to the back of the house. It was late afternoon but already dusk and tiny flakes of snow fluttered about her head like confetti. She entered through the scullery door and found the kitchen in darkness. Iris must still be up at the big house, but where was Ruby? She lit a lamp with a spill from the range and went through to the drawing room, but that too was deserted. As she ascended the stairs she could hear gentle snores emanating from her parents' room. She smiled, deciding that Mother must be taking her afternoon nap, although she would soon be demanding a cup of tea and there was no one in the kitchen to answer her bell. Of Bea there was no sign.

Daisy went to her own room and divested herself of her outer garments. Perhaps Ruby was also taking advantage of the quiet afternoon, putting her feet up. Daisy had no idea how a pregnant woman would feel, but she knew they needed rest. She went up the final flight of stairs to the attic rooms and was about to knock on Ruby's door when she heard a faint moan. 'Ruby, are you all right?' She opened the door and stepped inside.

Chapter Eleven

'Ruby?' Holding the lamp high, Daisy stepped into the room. The shadows flickered and shifted beneath the eaves but she could make out a figure lying on the narrow iron bedstead.

'Help me,' Ruby groaned, clutching her belly. 'It's the baby, miss. I think it's coming before its time.'

Daisy placed the lamp on the pine chest of drawers. 'It can't be, Ruby. It's much too early.' She leaned over the bed and was horrified to see Ruby's face contorted with pain. Beads of sweat stood out on her forehead even though it was bitterly cold in the attic room, and an icy wind whistled through the gaps in the tiled roof.

'I'm losing it. I seen it happen to me sister.' Ruby pointed to a dark stain on the coverlet. 'I'm bleeding to death.'

Recalling her home nursing lessons with difficulty, Daisy adopted a brisk tone. 'No, you're not. I'm here now, and I've been trained to cope with this sort of thing. You'll be fine. I'm not going to let you die.' She spoke with more confidence than she was feeling, and her knowledge of childbirth was limited to having read a few pages devoted to it in the nursing manual. 'Perhaps I'd better go for the doctor.'

Ruby reached out and grasped her hand, squeezing it with surprising strength. 'No, don't do that. No one must know about this. I'll lose me job if your ma gets wind of what I've done.'

'But I don't see how I can keep this a secret. You need proper medical attention.'

'It'll be over soon. I told you I seen this before. Stay with me, please.' Another violent contraction robbed Ruby of speech and she stuffed her hand into her mouth to stifle a cry of pain.

Daisy waited until the spasm had passed. 'All right, I understand, but I must leave you for a few moments. We'll need clean towels and warm water, and we don't want Iris coming upstairs to look for you.' She patted Ruby's limp hand. 'I'll be as quick as I can. Don't be afraid, Ruby dear. I'll take care of you.'

It was easy to say but Daisy was inwardly terrified. This was the first real test of her nerve and her ability to deal with a difficult and potentially life-threatening situation. The sight and smell of blood was already making her feel faint and nauseous. She escaped from the attic room to lean over the banisters, taking deep breaths. This was not the time to give in to a phobia that had plagued her since childhood and she made her way downstairs, stopping outside her mother's bedroom door. She knocked gently and receiving a faint reply she went inside.

Gwendoline raised herself on her elbow, blinking at her in the lamplight. 'What's wrong, Daisy? Where's Ruby with my cup of tea?'

'That's what I came to tell you, Mother. Ruby is unwell.

She must have eaten something that disagreed with her and she isn't in a fit state to do anything.'

'Oh dear, I hope none of us ate the same thing. I do feel a little nauseous.'

Daisy backed towards the door. 'I'll send Iris up with your tea, and I'll look after Ruby.'

'Do you think we ought to send for the doctor?'

'I think she just needs rest and quiet, Mother. I'll see to everything.'

Gwendoline lay back on her pillows. 'You're a good girl, but you mustn't get sick. What would Rupert say if he knew that you were nursing a servant?'

'He'd say well done, Daisy. He's a soldier, Mother. He's seen far worse things than someone with an upset tummy.' She left her mother to think about this and hurried downstairs to the kitchen. She found Iris riddling the coal in the range in an irate manner that did not bode well.

'I've just come to tell you that Ruby is quite poorly,' Daisy said firmly. 'I'm afraid you won't have any help this evening, Iris.'

'There's nothing prepared, miss,' Iris said sulkily. 'I'll have to start dinner from scratch and it's Christmas Eve. We're all supposed to go to midnight mass.'

'And I'm sure you'll be finished well before then. Keep it simple and you can go as soon as you've served dessert.'

'What about the washing up, miss?'

Daisy smiled. 'It won't be the first time that my sister and I have had to do such a chore, Iris. After all it is very nearly Christmas and I wouldn't want to make you late for church. The family will be guests at Pendleton Park tomorrow so you may have the day off.'

Iris bobbed a curtsey. 'Thank you, miss.'

'I'll need a jug of hot water. Ruby's been very sick and I'm looking after her, so there's no need for anyone to venture to her room, just in case it's something catching.'

'Oh, I won't go anywhere near her, miss.'

'Quite right. I won't be dining with the family either, so if you'll leave something cold for me that would be quite sufficient.'

'Yes, miss.'

Daisy filled a jug with water from the kettle and was making her way upstairs when Beatrice called to her from the hallway. 'What's up with Ruby? Iris made it sound as though she's got the plague.'

'It's probably just a bilious attack or something she ate. It's nothing to worry about.' Daisy hesitated with one foot on the next step. 'Where have you been? You shouldn't be out alone in the dark.'

'I wasn't alone. I was with Jimmy. We're stepping out together if you must know, Daisy. And don't say I'm too young to know my own mind, because I do, and I'm going to marry Jimmy whether Mother and Father like it or not.'

'Are you indeed? Well, good luck with that, Bea.' Too tired to argue, Daisy went on upstairs, collecting a pile of old towels from the linen cupboard before continuing on to the top floor. Her sister's romance seemed unimportant compared to the struggle between life and death in the cold attic room.

It was all over by late evening. Daisy was with Ruby every minute of her premature labour, holding her hand, mopping her brow with a damp cloth and attempting to keep her mind off things with small talk. She wrapped the tiny foetus, no bigger than her own hand, in a cloth and laid it reverently in the gaudy cardboard trinket box in which Ruby normally kept her small treasures. She saw to Ruby's needs and stripped the bed, making it up with fresh linen and dressing Ruby in one of her own nightgowns before tucking her up like a small obedient child. 'You can cry if you want to,' Daisy said gently. 'I'll understand.'

Ruby turned her face to the wall. 'I got no tears left. I sobbed me heart out when I realised that I was expecting, especially when I found out that Barnaby already had a wife and kid. Now I just feel numb. I don't think I'll ever feel nothing again.'

Daisy scooped up the bloodied sheets and towels, concealing the tiny makeshift coffin in their midst. 'I'll make you a nice hot cup of tea, and bring you something to eat.'

Ruby shook her head. 'A cup of tea would be lovely, but I ain't hungry, ta.'

'I won't be long.' Daisy left the room and tiptoed downstairs clutching her bundle and praying silently that the rest of the family were happily ensconced in the drawing room. If anyone saw her now the cat would be out of the bag, but as luck would have it she made it to the kitchen without being seen, and Iris had taken her at her word and left early. Braving the cold, Daisy took the soiled sheets and towels to the wash house and put them in the copper. She filled it with water from the pump and left them to soak overnight. Satisfied that she had done all she could in the circumstances, she hid the cardboard box under the mangle, intending to come out later and bury it somewhere in the garden. She did not think that Ruby was in a fit state to be involved in a sad farewell to a life that had ended before it had begun. She went back indoors and made a pot of tea, but she was trembling violently and she had to sit down for a while and rest before she felt able to take a cup to Ruby.

She found her sleeping soundly, looking very small and almost child-like with her pale face and mouse-brown hair spilling over the white pillowcase. Daisy leaned over to tuck her in. Ruby was tough, but Daisy could only imagine what it must be like to suffer a miscarriage, and it wrung her heart to even contemplate such a terrible loss. 'Sleep tight, Ruby.' She left the room, closing the door softly behind her.

In the kitchen the detritus left after the preparation and consumption of dinner was still waiting for her. Beatrice obviously had no intention of helping out and for that Daisy was grateful. She put her pinafore on and set about clearing up the kitchen and washing the dishes in the scullery. She found the dull routine oddly comforting and it took her almost an hour to have everything sparkling clean and the crockery stowed in its place. She rewarded herself with another cup of hot sweet tea, but she had no appetite for the plate of food that Iris had left for her, and she tipped it into the bin reserved for scraps which would eventually be fed to the Gurneys' pigs. She took a seat at the table and sipped her tea, but a quick glance at the clock revealed that it was almost half past eleven. She knew that she would not be able to sleep until she had committed the sad little cardboard box to the ground. She was trying to gather the courage to get up and go out into the darkness when the door opened and Teddy breezed into the kitchen. He stopped short when he saw her, his jaw dropping comically. He gaped at her apron and her reddened hands. 'What on earth are you doing in here this late at night?'

'I might ask the same of you,' Daisy said sharply.

'I – er – I was looking for Iris.'

'Were you now? Why doesn't that surprise me?'

'Don't take that tone with me, Daisy. I'm your elder brother, and don't you forget it.'

'As if I could. You've reminded me of it enough times in the past. Anyway, I told Iris she could leave early as it's Christmas Eve. She wanted to go to midnight mass . . .' She broke off, staring at him. 'That wasn't true, was it? She was going to meet you.'

'That's my business.' Teddy's face flushed dark red and he scowled at her. 'It's between me and Iris. I can see her if I want to. There's no law against it.'

Daisy rose to her feet. 'But Jed Smith will think differently. You had a narrow escape on the night of the village dance, Teddy. Surely you don't want to end up with your good looks spoilt by a black eye or worse. She's his lady friend after all.'

'She likes me and I like her. He doesn't own her.'

Daisy was too tired to argue. 'Suit yourself, Teddy. But don't say I didn't warn you.'

'I'm going out.' He turned on his heel and was about to leave the room when he paused, glancing over his shoulder. 'You'll keep quiet about this, won't you, old thing?'

'Of course I will,' Daisy said with a reluctant smile. 'But please be careful, and don't let her run away with the idea that this is anything other than a bit of fun.'

His face fell. 'Oh Lord, you don't think she hears wedding bells, do you?'

'I don't know, but it's not fair to lead her on.'

'You certainly know how to make a fellow feel like a toe-rag. Perhaps I'll give it a miss tonight after all.'

'And leave her waiting for you out in the cold? Don't be a coward, Teddy. You have to let her down easily.'

'Women,' Teddy said with feeling. He left without another word, closing the door behind him with unnecessary violence.

Daisy sighed, shaking her head. She could foresee Teddy's affair with Iris ending badly and even if Jed did not beat him to a pulp, he would have to answer to their father for his misdeeds. She took her old coat from its peg in the scullery and shrugged it on. The threat of snow had abated but there was a bitter chill in the air when she stepped outside into the yard, but she had one last duty to perform before she could go to bed.

With only the sound of the wind soughing sadly in the tree tops and the occasional shriek of a barn owl hunting its prey, she buried the tiny cardboard coffin deep in the rose bed and said a prayer before filling in the grave. 'Sleep well, little one,' she murmured and her hot tears fell on the cold earth.

A hard frost during the night had turned the grounds of Pendleton Park into a fairytale landscape, sparkling in the feeble rays of a wintry sun. Parkin drove slowly, allowing the family time to absorb the grandeur of the scene, and even Beatrice was silent during the short drive to the great house. Daisy could appreciate the view but she was still shaken by the events of the past evening.

She had risen early in order to check on Ruby, and had found her attempting to dress herself but with little success. Having persuaded her to go back to bed, Daisy went downstairs. She had given Iris the day off and with Ruby unfit for work it fell to her to get the fire going and prepare breakfast for the family. She attended to Ruby first, filling a hot water bottle and carrying a tray of tea and toast up to the top of the house. Ruby was propped up against the pillows, pale and subdued but resolute in her determination to carry on as normal when she had recovered her strength. Daisy could only admire her bravery. She doubted whether she would be able to behave with such fortitude in similar circumstances. Although Ruby assured her that she would rather be left alone to rest, Daisy was unhappy about leaving her for any length of time, but she had no choice. Even now she wondered if she had done the right thing.

She turned with a start as Beatrice nudged her in the ribs. 'You haven't been listening to a thing I said, Daisy.'

'Sorry, I was miles away.'

'That's obvious. I was just saying that I wish all this was going to be mine one day. You're a lucky cat.'

Gwendoline tut-tutted. 'That's enough, girls. We're here, so don't you dare disgrace me by squabbling.' She turned her head to peer out of the rear window. 'Your father and Teddy have just pulled up behind us. Thank goodness the motorcar is working properly again.'

'Thanks to Ruby's boyfriend,' Beatrice murmured, winking at her sister.

'Shut up, Bea. That's not funny.' Daisy climbed out of the Rolls and stood on the gravelled carriage sweep waiting for her mother and Beatrice to join her. The Humberette drew up and Victor proffered his arm to his wife, leading the family up to the imposing front entrance.

'It always reminds me of Dracula's castle,' Bea whispered, giggling.

'Be quiet, Beatrice.' Gwendoline shot her an angry glance as Victor tugged on the bell.

Almost immediately, the door opened and they were greeted by Warrington who ushered them into the great hall where Rupert was waiting to receive them. He had abandoned his uniform for a more casual tweed suit but he still looked dashing and almost too handsome for a mere mortal. His beaming smile encompassed the whole family as he welcomed them to his home, and his blue eyes darkened with pleasure when he saw Daisy. She handed her fur coat to a waiting maidservant.

'You look absolutely splendid, my darling,' Rupert said softly. 'Merry Christmas, Daisy.' He tucked her hand into the crook of his arm. 'If you would all like to follow us, we'll go to the long gallery and I'll introduce you to the members of my family who quite regularly descend upon us like one of the plagues of Egypt.' He smiled at Daisy, adding in a whisper, 'God help you all. It's like the Chamber of Horrors in Madame Tussaud's.'

She stifled a giggle. 'Don't be mean, Rupert. I'm sure they're perfectly nice, ordinary people.'

'I'd reserve judgement if I were you, Daisy Bell.'

They ascended the grand staircase to the first floor with its wide corridors hung with old masters and furnished with heavily carved Jacobean chests and monks' benches. She could hear Beatrice chattering to Teddy as they followed them up a second flight of stairs to the top floor of the house, most of which was occupied by the long gallery. They were met by a buzz of conversation and the resinous aroma of pine logs blazing up the chimneys in the fireplaces at each end of the oak-panelled room. The floorboards shone with the patina of centuries of wear and the application of beeswax and elbow grease by a succession of dedicated housemaids.

Heads turned to look at the new arrivals and Daisy could feel herself being closely scrutinised by young and old alike. Lady Pendleton rose from a throne-like seat and glided across the floor to greet them. Lord Pendleton broke away from a group of gentlemen and joined her to exchange the compliments of the season, after which he wandered back to continue the conversation with his contemporaries. It was left to Rupert to introduce the Lennox family to the gathering.

Daisy had met some of the aunts, uncles and cousins in London, but as Rupert said when they snatched a few moments of relative privacy at the far end of the gallery, relations crawled out of the woodwork at this time of the year, eager to partake of free food and drink, and then disappeared again until the next festive season, family wedding or christening. As far as Daisy could see there did appear to be a hard core of portly gentlemen and their ladies who imbibed as much as they could before luncheon but contributed little to the general atmosphere of goodwill, and were less than effusive in their congratulations when she was introduced to them as Rupert's fiancée. His explanation for their reticence centred on the fact that these distant relatives were in line of succession to the title and estate, but their chances of inheriting anything would diminish significantly when he married and produced a son or sons. Rupert seemed to find it amusing but Daisy thought it somewhat sinister. She saw them darkly, like carrion crows hovering and waiting for something dire to befall Rupert in order to bring them closer to inheriting something they had done nothing to earn or even deserve.

It was a relief when at last luncheon was announced and everyone trooped downstairs to the dining room.

Daisy was surprised to see that Iris was on duty but it was not her business to ask why, although she was quick to notice that Teddy made a point of speaking to her whenever the opportunity arose. She could tell by the looks that Lady Pendleton was giving him that she disapproved of the familiarity between the two of them, and she made up her mind to warn her brother yet again that such conduct was unacceptable. She could only hope that their mother had not seen anything untoward, but Gwendoline seemed to be conversing happily with Rupert's Uncle Joshua, who quite obviously had an eye for the ladies. He was leaning unnecessarily close to her, twirling his mustachios like a villain from the silent screen, and her mother seemed to be revelling in his attentions.

Daisy was relieved to note that her father did not appear to have noticed. He was chatting amicably to the Dowager Lady Pendleton, who was eighty-nine and affected to be slightly deaf but somehow managed to hear the softest whisper if it happened to relate to herself or any of her close family. Daisy was a little afraid of the redoubtable old lady, but Rupert assured her that his grandmother was a darling despite her caustic tongue and acerbic wit.

After luncheon the party seemed to fragment. The elder family members opted to sit in the library and drink port or nap by the fire, and Lady Pendleton invited Gwendoline and some of the other ladies to retire to the crimson and gold saloon for a game of whist. Rupert marshalled the younger family members together and suggested a brisk walk in the grounds to brush away the cobwebs. Warrington sent a maid for the guests' outer garments and soon they were strolling across the deer park, breathing in the ice-cold air and enjoying the soft kiss of the winter sunshine. Rupert and Daisy walked on ahead of the others, and he held her hand in a firm grasp. He stopped beneath an ancient oak tree, gazing up into the gnarled bare branches. 'Do you remember this, Daisy Bell?'

'Of course I do. You leapt upon us from a great height and frightened me half to death.'

'I was a little beast then. I apologise.'

She squeezed his fingers. 'No you weren't. You were a high-spirited boy and we were just children. Although Bea had nightmares about it for weeks afterwards.'

He glanced over his shoulder. 'She seems to have recovered now.'

Following his gaze, Daisy saw her sister flirting outrageously with one of Rupert's younger cousins. 'She does seem to have taken a shine to Sebastian. Jimmy Gurney would be furious if he could see them now.'

'The farmer's son from Long Wheatley?'

'That's right. Bea told me only yesterday that they were stepping out together. Her words, not mine.' She tightened her hold on his arm and they walked on, distancing themselves from the rest of the noisy party. 'She's much too young to think of such things.'

'But we're not, darling.' Rupert drew her to a halt as they reached the edge of the spinney. 'Why don't we name the day? Who knows what's going to happen in the next few months. If there's a war I'll be the first to be sent into active service. I want to go away safe in the knowledge that you'll be looked after should anything happen to me.'

She shivered as icy fingers clutched at her heart. 'Don't say things like that. You make it sound as though war is inevitable.'

'I'm afraid it is, although of course I hope I'm wrong, but we can all see it coming. What do you say, Daisy? Why wait? Let's get married as soon as possible.'

It would be so easy to fall in with his wishes, but she was taken off guard. 'This is a bit sudden, Rupert. You can't expect me to give you an answer right away.'

He frowned. 'Why not? We're engaged. You've said you love me and want to be my wife. Why wait?'

'Because there are other people involved. There are your parents and mine. Getting married is a huge step and it needs planning.'

'Then we'll elope to Gretna Green.' He chuckled and bent down to place a kiss on the tip of her nose. 'I'm joking, of course. But seriously, darling, I want to name the day, even if it's in the middle of next summer or early autumn. You'll want a wedding dress and trousseau designed in Paris, and all the things that girls love to have before they tie the knot, but all I want is you. If and when I go to war I want to have someone waiting for me on my return. Is that too much to ask, darling Daisy?'

She could not argue with the passion he put into his words, or the beseeching look in his eyes that was for her alone. She could not go back on her promise to marry him now, especially with the threat of war looming over them like a great black cloud. She met his intense gaze with a tremulous smile. 'All right, Rupert, but only if you allow me to continue with the FANYs. It's even more important should there be a war, which I pray to God there won't. But I can't sit back and do nothing.'

'You may do anything you want if it makes you happy.' He took her in his arms, confirming his answer with a kiss that ought to have swept her off her feet and taken her to heaven, but left her feeling sadly disappointed. She could only hope that passion on her part would come later. With time and familiarity she would learn to give him her whole heart and body, if not her soul. He released her with a triumphant whoop of joy. 'We'll go and tell them now.' He waved his arms to the stragglers some way behind them. 'Come here. We've got something wonderful to tell you.'

'Don't,' Daisy said urgently, tugging at his sleeve. 'We ought to speak to our parents first.'

'We'll do that next. I want the whole world to know that we'll be married as soon as humanly possible, and I'm not giving you the chance to back out, Daisy. This is real and it's going to happen. You'll be a June bride, or sooner if it can be arranged. I want you now and always, my love.'

Despite Daisy's protests Rupert called everyone together and announced their intention to name the day. The news was received enthusiastically and with much merriment and good-natured banter.

It was a noisy party that invaded the sanctity of the great hall, to Warrington's obvious displeasure, which he conveyed with the twitch of a shaggy grey eyebrow and a thin-lipped stare. Rupert grasped Daisy by the hand, meeting his butler's rigid stance with a happy smile. 'Warrington, you've known me since I was born, and you got me out of many a scrape when I was a naughty little boy. I want you to be one of the first to know that Miss Lennox and I are about to set the date for our marriage.'

Warrington's lined face crumpled into a semblance of a smile. 'Congratulations, sir.' He bowed stiffly to Daisy. 'May I offer you my very best wishes, miss?'

'Thank you, Warrington.' Daisy felt a sudden surge of relief. She was slightly more in awe of Warrington than she was of Lord Pendleton, and she was certain that the entire staff of Pendleton Park felt the same.

Rupert gave her hand a gentle squeeze of approval. 'I think this announcement calls for champagne, Warrington. I hope that everyone in the servants' hall will join in the toast to our future happiness.'

'Indeed, sir.' Warrington stood aside as Rupert led Daisy inexorably towards the grand staircase and the inevitable meeting with both sets of parents. Behind them Bea and the noisy Pendleton younger generation were chattering like a flock of parakeets, but as Daisy glanced over her shoulder there was no sign of Teddy. Her heart sank. She had sensed his edginess throughout the day, which was unlike her normally easy-going brother. She could only guess that the cause of his anxiety was the lovely Iris, with her willowy figure and lustrous hazel eyes set in an almost perfect oval face. It was little wonder that Jed

Smith was besotted with her and that she had Teddy in her thrall.

'Come along, darling,' Rupert said as they stood outside the crimson and gold saloon. 'Let's tell the mothers first, as they're the ones most likely to take over the whole event.'

Daisy nodded mutely, but her heart was pounding as they entered the magnificent room to interrupt the game of whist.

Gwendoline was hysterically happy and Lady Pendleton serenely overjoyed. The two fathers were summoned and Daisy realised that the matter had been taken out of her hands. June, Gwendoline suggested tentatively, was always a good time for weddings, but Lord Pendleton said he preferred to wait until July or August when the House was in recess. There could be no gainsaying him and it was then a matter of choosing the exact date. Lord Pendleton and Victor wandered off in the direction of the billiard room, and the female family members gathered together to exchange views and reminisce about past weddings, christenings and even funerals.

Daisy and Rupert found themselves redundant and they crept away to join the young people who had assembled in the great hall. Champagne corks were popping like cannon fire, but there was still no sign of Teddy. It was only when the sound of voices raised in anger drowned out the general hum of conversation that anyone in the hall realised there was a fracas in progress. Rupert hurried into the corridor which led to the servants' wing, and the younger men followed close on his heels, hallooing as though they were joining the hunt. The girls crowded after them, chattering excitedly. Daisy had just managed to push her way to Rupert's side when the baize door flew open and Teddy was pitched onto the flagstone floor with an irate Jed Smith at his throat.

Chapter Twelve

All hell broke loose. Warrington made an ineffectual attempt to separate the brawling men, but was pushed unceremoniously aside by Rupert and his cousin Giles. The rest of the young male guests joined in with whoops of glee. Jed was dragged off Teddy but he still struggled, and it took both Rupert and Giles to keep him from renewing the attack. 'I'll get you, Lennox,' Jed shouted as they frog-marched him through the great hall. 'Keep your hands off my girl or it'll be the worse for you, you bastard.' His voice died away and the resounding slam of the front door put an abrupt end to his threats.

Daisy helped her brother to his feet, taking his handkerchief from his pocket and staunching his bleeding nose. She turned her head away as the all too familiar reaction at the sight of blood threatened to overwhelm her. 'What did I tell you,' she said in a low voice. 'I was afraid that something like this would happen.'

He shrugged her off with an irritated twitch of his shoulders. 'Don't lecture me, Daisy. I'm not in the mood. I'd have sorted the so-and-so out if they hadn't stopped me.'

'Of course you would,' she whispered. 'But this isn't the time or place, and she was his girl before you came on the scene. You can see his point.' She glanced nervously over her shoulder but the others had drifted away now that the excitement was over, and sounds of merriment from the great hall suggested that the party was getting into full swing.

'I'm going home,' Teddy said thickly. 'I don't want Iris to see me like this.'

'Where is she? And what were you doing when Jed found you?'

'I wasn't doing anything as it happens. She collared me.'

'But it must have been more than that to make Jed so angry.'

'It's nothing. Don't trouble your head about it, Daisy.'

She looked up and was relieved to see Rupert coming towards them. 'You speak to him,' she said urgently. 'Can you make him see sense?'

Rupert put his arm around Teddy's shoulders. 'What was that all about? He looked as if he wanted to kill you.'

'He's been seeing Iris,' Daisy said when Teddy remained obstinately silent. 'She was keeping company with Jed before we came to Rainbow's End.'

Frown lines puckered Rupert's brow. 'I'd say there's more in it than that. I've known Jed Smith almost as long as I've known you, Teddy, and he's a stable sort of chap, not given to physical violence as a rule.'

Teddy shot an anxious glance at Daisy. 'I can't say,' he muttered into the folds of the hanky. 'Not in front of my sister.'

Horrified, Daisy stared at him. Not again, she thought

miserably. Surely it can't have happened to Iris as well as Ruby. 'She's not – I mean, it's not yours, is it?'

'Well, is she?' Rupert demanded angrily. 'You can't have been such an idiot.'

Teddy nodded. 'She says it's mine but she's lying. She thinks that we're rich and that I'll have to marry her or give her money that I simply haven't got.'

'Oh, Teddy.' Daisy shook her head. 'How could you?'

'Don't rub it in, Daisy. My head's splitting and I think my nose is broken. I'm going home.' He blundered towards the doorway but Rupert stopped him.

'Not that way, Teddy. I'll drive you, and we'll go out through the servants' quarters.'

Teddy shook his restraining hand off. 'No. You stay here with Daisy. This is your night, and I've ruined it.' He gave Daisy a sheepish smile. 'I'm sorry.'

She laid her hand on his arm. 'Let Rupert drive and I'll come with you. I'll patch you up. It'll be good practice.'

Teddy bowed his head. 'All right. I do feel a bit queasy. Thanks, Daisy.'

'I'll bring the car round,' Rupert said, making for the baize door. 'Wrap up warm, Daisy. We don't want you catching your death of cold just because of this silly ass. Wait for me by the front door. I won't be long.'

She watched him go with a feeling of gratitude mixed with guilt. She did not deserve a man like Rupert, and if he knew the truth he might revise his opinion of her. She felt tarnished by her brief relationship with Bowman. It was over, but she could not forget the way he made her feel and probably never would. She helped

Teddy to a chair. 'I'll fetch our coats and I'll let Mother know that we're going home.'

He raised his head. 'You won't tell her about Iris and me?'

'Of course not. I just hope that Giles and the others don't mention what went on between you and Jed, but I'll see if I can find him and warn him not to say anything.' She left Teddy clutching his hanky to his sore nose.

She found Giles drinking champagne and flirting shamelessly with a distant cousin. He seemed to have forgotten the incident already, and promised not to breathe a word of it to the rest of the family. His companion, who appeared to be more than a little tipsy, showed no interest in the conversation. 'Do stop being a bore and dance with me, Giles,' she said, tapping her foot in time to the music being played on a shiny new gramophone.

Daisy recognised Scott Joplin's catchy 'Maple Leaf Rag', to which couples were performing an energetic rendition of the Bunny Hug. At any other time she would have loved to join in, but she had more important matters on her mind and she rang the bell to summon a servant.

Warrington appeared, looking like a grumpy genie of the lamp. 'You rang, miss?'

'Yes, Warrington. I wonder if you would be so kind as to tell my parents that I'm leaving early. I have rather a bad headache and my brother is going to see me safely home.'

He bowed solemnly. 'I'll attend to it immediately,

and I'll send someone for your outer garments if you would like to wait in the vestibule.' He walked off with a measured gait, and only a slight twitch of his shoulders betrayed his disapproval of the goings-on in the ancient great hall.

When they reached Rainbow's End Rupert handed Daisy from the Prince Henry before turning his attention to Teddy. 'Come on, old chap. Let's get you indoors.' He helped him down the path and Daisy went on ahead to unlock the front door. The house was in darkness and she set about lighting lamps, but as there was no fire in the drawing room they opted for the kitchen where the range emitted a welcoming glow and the kettle simmered on the hob.

'Ruby must have kept the fire going,' Daisy said, setting the oil lamp down on the table and lighting a few candles. 'I hope she's feeling better.'

'It's lucky she was the only one to get sick,' Teddy murmured as he sank down on a chair. 'If it was food poisoning we'd all have been clutching our bellies and groaning.'

'How's the nose feeling?' Rupert regarded him with a worried frown. 'Perhaps we ought to send for Dr Grimshaw. He's not a bad chap and very discreet.'

Teddy raised his hand to his face. 'It's sore, but I don't think it's broken and the bleeding's stopped.'

'It serves you right,' Daisy said unsympathetically. 'Have a cup of tea and you'll feel better.'

Rupert grinned. 'I think something stronger might be more to the point, Daisy Bell. Where does Mr Lennox keep the brandy?'

'In the drawing room on the wine table by the window,' Teddy said eagerly. 'Fetch a couple of glasses while you're about it, old man.'

Daisy folded her arms across her chest, waiting until Rupert was out of earshot before she spoke. 'You're impossible, Teddy. Now it's all a big joke and you'll be boasting about this forever more, but aren't you forgetting something, or somebody?'

He gave her a puzzled look. 'I don't think so.'

'Iris,' she said pointedly. 'Iris and her unborn child. Are you the father or are you not?'

'I don't know, Daisy, and that's the honest truth. I suppose it's possible, but . . .' He broke off, flushing and looking away. 'It's not the sort of thing one discusses with one's younger sister.'

'Well then, could it be Jed's? Has she been intimate with him as well as you?'

'Maybe. I didn't ask her.' He shot her an anguished look. 'Please, Daisy, this is terribly embarrassing. You shouldn't talk about this sort of thing.'

'So she can claim that you are the father and you can't or won't do anything about it.'

He shrugged his shoulders with a sigh of resignation. 'What can I do? As I said, it's possible, but it's her word against mine. All I know is that Jed promised to have my liver and lights if I saw her again, and I don't fancy my chances if he caught me unawares.'

Rupert entered the room carrying a tray laden with a decanter and three glasses. 'I agree. If this gets round the village you might end up at the bottom of the river and no one would point a finger at Jed Smith.'

'You don't really think so, do you?' Daisy stared at him aghast. 'Surely that can't happen in a civilised society?'

Rupert and Teddy exchanged wry glances. Rupert set the tray down and poured three tots of brandy. He pressed one into Teddy's hand and offered another to Daisy. 'Here, my love. I think you need this as much as we do.'

She shook her head. 'No, thank you. I can't stand the smell of the stuff. I'd rather have a cup of tea, and I'm going to take one up to Ruby. I need to see how she is.'

'You shouldn't mollycoddle the servants,' Teddy said, tossing back the brandy in one gulp. He held the empty glass out to Rupert. 'I'll drink Daisy's if she doesn't want it.'

'That's rich coming from you, Teddy.' Daisy poured the tea. 'You've just got one of the servants in the family way, and you think you can lecture me on how to treat Ruby, who is more a friend than an employee.' She lit a lamp and placed it on a tray with the tea. She paused in the doorway, turning her head to give Rupert a steady look. 'You sort him out. He might listen to you.' She left the room without giving either of them the chance to respond, and she was suddenly angry. Her fear for her brother's wellbeing was suddenly overcome by her concern for Iris, who was probably suffering as much as Ruby had done when she had discovered her condition. It was all very well for men to have their fun, but it was always the girls who paid the price. She had never had much sympathy for fallen women in the past, indoctrinated as she had been by her mother's teachings that purity was the most important virtue for an unmarried girl, but her emotional and physical response to Bowman had turned her world upside down. She could understand what led young women to risk everything for love, and how commonsense could fly out of the window when passions were aroused. She went upstairs to Ruby's room and knocked on the door.

'Come in.'

She entered and found Ruby curled up in bed with a hot water bottle. The only candle in the draughty attic had burned down to a mere stub and was guttering. Daisy placed the tray on the chest, and the glow of the paraffin lamp made a warm circle around the bed. 'How are you feeling?'

'Better, thanks.' Ruby raised herself on her elbow. 'You was a brick last night, miss. I dunno how to thank you for what you done.'

Daisy perched on the edge of the bed, covering Ruby's hand with hers. 'Don't mention it. You'd have done the same for me if I needed help.'

'I can't imagine you getting yourself into that sort of trouble.' A slow smile lit Ruby's pale face. 'You're a lady and I'm not.'

'We're sisters under our skins, as Rudyard Kipling so rightly put it. Have you eaten anything today?'

'I made meself a sandwich and had several cups of tea. I'll be up and about as usual tomorrow. You needn't worry about me.' Ruby eyed her curiously. 'But you ain't had such a merry time by the looks of you.'

'You've an uncanny way of reading my mind,' Daisy said ruefully. She hesitated, not wanting to burden Ruby with her personal problems, but somehow it all came spilling out. She had not meant to breathe a word of what had passed that day, but suddenly she had to confide in someone. She told Ruby everything, from Rupert's request to set the date to Teddy's fight with Jed and the cause for their enmity.

Ruby listened in silence, sipping her tea. 'Well, there's a to-do, I must say. It'll take that snooty Iris down a peg or two, but I wouldn't wish what's happened to me on anybody. I know exactly how she must be feeling now, and if neither of the blokes want to make an honest woman of her then she's in trouble.'

Daisy rose to her feet. 'You're right, and my brother must take responsibility for what he's done. Even if Jed is the baby's father, we'll never know for certain and one of them must stand up to be counted.' She leaned over to pat Ruby on the shoulder. 'I'm glad to see you looking so much better, but I do sympathise with your loss as well. I can't imagine what you must have been going through, but I'm glad you're on the mend.'

'Ta. That means a lot to me.' Ruby snuggled down below the coverlet. 'I'll be down at the usual time tomorrow.'

'I'm sure you will.' Picking up the lamp, Daisy left her in darkness and went downstairs to the kitchen where she found Teddy and Rupert sitting opposite each other at the kitchen table, drinking brandy. 'I suppose you've decided to let matters drop,' she said icily. 'Never mind what happens to the girl.'

Rupert rose to his feet. 'Actually, that's not quite true, darling. Teddy and I have talked it over and I'm going to have a few words with Jed first thing in the morning. I know he'll do the right thing by Iris, with a little financial encouragement.'

'So you're going to pay him to marry her?'

'Call it a wedding gift,' Rupert said easily. 'And Teddy has decided to join my regiment, haven't you, old boy?'

Slightly bleary-eyed and with bruises beginning to show after his bout of fisticuffs, Teddy managed a crooked grin. 'It's something we talked about at school, Daisy. I always said I'd join the military and now seems as good a time as any. If there's a war we'll be called upon to do our duty anyway, so I might as well get a head start and enlist now.'

'So as usual, you men have arranged everything,' Daisy said, frowning. 'What if the child is yours, Teddy? Don't you care that your flesh and blood will be raised by another man?'

He shook his head. 'Frankly, no. It's not real to me, and if Jed Smith don't mind then that suits me. I rather fancy myself in uniform.'

'It's the best way all round, sweetheart,' Rupert said gently. 'Jed is a good sort beneath the rough exterior, and he's obviously frightfully keen on Iris, or he wouldn't have come to the house as he did. Leave it to us, and don't worry about Iris. She's no vestal virgin.'

Daisy said nothing but she was horrified by their callous indifference to the girl's feelings, and their casual assumption that she was no better than she should be. She sat down at the table and drank her tea, listening to their eager talk about army life. Teddy seemed to have forgotten his painful nose and blackened eye, and was hanging on Rupert's every word. In the end she put down her cup and saucer and rose to her feet. 'I'm very tired. If you'll excuse me, Rupert, I'm going to bed.'

He jumped up with a guilty smile. 'I'm so sorry, darling. We've been neglecting you.'

'Not at all. You talk sense to Teddy. If the army is what he wants, then that's what he must do, although I wouldn't want to be there when he tells Mother.' She kissed him on the cheek. 'Goodnight.'

He caught her by the hand, holding it as if unwilling to let her go. 'I'll see you tomorrow. We've lots to talk about.'

She smiled. 'Yes, of course, Rupert.' She withdrew her hand gently. 'Goodnight, Teddy. And if I were you I'd think up a good reason for that black eye and bloodied nose.'

'Oh, Lord,' Teddy murmured. 'That's a point. What the hell do I say, Rupert?'

'That's up to you, old man. I think a slip on the icy cobblestones might do it, or we could say we were larking around and you bumped into my fist.'

Their laughter followed Daisy as she went upstairs to her room. She loved them both dearly but they were just boys at heart, not ready for the responsibilities that came with marriage and fatherhood. She felt genuinely sorry for Iris.

* * *

Teddy got away with it somehow, but then he always had. Both parents accepted his explanation of the injuries he had suffered without question. Daisy had realised long ago that he could twist their mother round his little finger, and their father was almost as soft-hearted when it came to his son and heir. She had never resented Teddy's claim to their parents' affections, and Beatrice was too much immersed in her own life to care one way or the other. Daisy could only wonder what would happen when Teddy announced that he intended to join the army. She did not have long to wait.

On the penultimate day of Rupert's leave he told her that he was meeting Teddy in Colchester at the recruiting office. Teddy could not afford to buy a commission and there was no question of his attending Sandhurst, therefore he would join as an ordinary soldier. Daisy did not think that would go down well with her parents but there was nothing she could do to prevent it happening. She could only wait until he came home either a civilian still or an enlisted man.

'Why do you keep looking out of the window?' Beatrice demanded. 'Are you expecting Rupert?'

Daisy returned to the task of taking the decorations off the Christmas tree. 'Yes, of course. He's going back to his regiment tomorrow. This will be his last evening.'

'Are you doing anything special?'

'Not really. We're having dinner at Pendleton Park and listening to his mother going on about the wedding, even though it's months and months away.'

Beatrice continued her task of unclipping the tiny

candle holders, grimacing as she pricked her fingers on the sharp pine needles. 'You don't seem very excited about it. If it was me I'd be thrilled to bits.'

'They're deciding everything for me. Mother and Lady Pendleton have got their heads together and they're arranging every last detail from the date in August to the wedding gown itself. I feel like a puppet with someone else pulling the strings.'

'Well, you're going up to town in January, aren't you? You'll have more say in things when you're away from Mother.'

Daisy glanced anxiously over her shoulder. 'Don't speak so loudly. She might come in at any moment and she'll hear you.'

'I don't care. I only speak the truth. You should stand up for yourself more, Daisy. Tell them that you want a quiet wedding and that you don't want to wait until August.'

'It's not that,' Daisy said slowly. 'I mean I would like to get married without all the fuss, but . . .' She hesitated. It was almost impossible to put her feelings into words. She should be overjoyed at the prospect of marrying so well, but she was still tormented by doubts. She wished that she was as certain that they were doing the right thing as Rupert, who had no qualms whatsoever. She knew that he was desperately in love with her and she ought to be able to return the feeling, but something was stopping her and she was afraid to speak his name even in her thoughts. She had not seen Bowman since their brief meeting in his cottage. He had completed the work on the Humberette and now there was no reason for him to call at the house. He seemed to have abandoned Ruby completely and that alone was evidence of his perfidy, but somehow she could not believe that he was a bad man at heart.

'They're here,' Beatrice said, breaking into Daisy's thoughts. 'Teddy is with Rupert and he looks frightfully smug. What do you think they've been doing?' She dropped the box of candle holders on the floor and ran from the room.

Daisy stood motionless by the tree, waiting to learn the worst, or maybe the best. She was in two minds as to whether it was a good or a bad thing for her brother to join the army. Moments later Rupert breezed into the drawing room and crossed the floor to take her into his arms. His lips found hers in a warm embrace. 'Have you missed me, Daisy Bell?'

She extricated herself from his grasp. 'Of course I have. What a silly question.' She glanced over his shoulder. 'Where's Teddy? Did he . . .' She broke off as her brother strode into the room followed by an excited Beatrice.

'Guess what?' Beatrice cried before anyone had a chance to speak. 'Teddy's only gone and joined up. What a lark.'

Daisy managed a tight little smile. 'So you did it?'

He saluted, grinning. 'Absolutely. Private Edward Lennox reporting for duty, ma'am.'

Rupert took her hand in his. 'Don't worry, darling. I'll look after the boy.'

'Less of that,' Teddy said, chuckling. 'I'll be looking after you, old chap.'

'And less of the old chap,' Rupert said with mock severity. 'It's sir from now on, Private.'

Beatrice flopped down on the sofa. 'Well I think it's terribly exciting. Teddy's going to be a hero.'

'Teddy's going to be a what?'

Everyone turned to look at Gwendoline as she stood in the doorway with her hand pressed to her bosom. 'What have you done, Edward?'

He pulled up a chair. 'Sit down, Mother. I wanted to tell you myself, but Beatrice can never keep her mouth shut.'

'Never mind what Beatrice does or doesn't do.' Gwendoline sank down on the seat, gazing up at him with an anxious frown. 'You haven't done anything silly, have you, Teddy?'

He knelt at her side, taking her hand and chafing it. 'Not silly, Mother. I've enlisted in the Rifle Brigade, just like Rupert. I'll be off to serve king and country and I'll make you proud of me.'

Gwendoline snatched her hand away. 'Proud? You stupid boy! Of course I'm proud of you already. I don't need to see my son in uniform to be proud of him.'

Daisy made a move towards the door. 'We'll leave you two to talk it over,' she said softly. 'Come along, Rupert.'

'I'm staying,' Beatrice said, curling her legs beneath her on the sofa. 'I wouldn't miss this for the world. Are you going to give him a good dressing down, Mother?'

Daisy hurried from the room without giving Rupert the chance to argue. She went into the dining room. It was getting dark and Ruby had not yet lit the fire. She wrapped her arms around herself, shivering. 'How long has he got before he leaves us, Rupert?'

He took her in his arms and held her so close that she could feel his heart beating. 'I'm sorry if you're upset, Daisy Bell, but it's what he wanted, and it does get Teddy out of a damned awkward scrape.'

She tilted her head to look him in the eyes. 'Is that all the poor girl means to you men? She and her unborn child are just a scrape to be avoided at all costs.'

He frowned. 'I didn't mean to sound uncaring, but Iris is Jed Smith's responsibility now. The man is madly in love with her and who knows whether he is the father or if it's Teddy. The main thing is that the girl will be looked after. Mother will see that she's paid off handsomely and that will be an added incentive for Smith to make an honest woman of her.'

'And so that it goes smoothly and without a fuss my brother is putting himself in harm's way.'

'Teddy always wanted to join the army, darling. He wanted to go to Sandhurst but your father wouldn't allow it. Now he's done an even braver thing if you ask me. Having been to public school makes him different from the ordinary enlisted man. Teddy will have to earn his stripes in more ways than one. It takes courage to do what he's just done, so be kind to him, Daisy.'

She laid her head on his shoulder. 'I will, of course, but I can't help wishing that he'd found another way.'

Rupert held her close and they were silent for a while in the darkening room. He was the first to speak, holding her a little way from him and smiling into her eyes. 'I'm leaving first thing in the morning, Daisy. Kiss me and wish me well.'

She slid her arms around his neck and raised her face, closing her eyes. 'Come back to me soon,' she whispered and to her surprise she realised that she meant it.

She shed a few tears next day when she waved goodbye to Rupert and Teddy, and was surprised to receive a comforting hug from Beatrice. 'Never mind, Daisy,' she said sympathetically. 'I'm sure they'll look after each other.'

Daisy wiped her eyes on her crumpled hanky and stuffed it back in her pocket. 'You're right, of course, Bea. I'm just being silly.'

'No, you're not. I'd cry buckets if it was Jimmy going off like that. Let's go indoors and have a cup of cocoa with lots of sugar and cream. Who cares about getting fat?' Beatrice took a few steps towards the front door, paused and beckoned to her. 'Come on. You won't bring them back any quicker by staying there and catching cold.'

Reluctantly, Daisy followed her into the house. It seemed odd to think that her little sister had grown up seemingly overnight. She herself had been too immersed in her own affairs to notice that Bea had left childhood behind and was now a capable young woman. Perhaps Bea really was serious about her farmer. It was a sobering thought. Daisy shivered as she entered the relative warmth of the house. She had not realised how chilled she was until she came indoors, and the entrance hall was certainly not what anyone would describe as being overheated. She followed Beatrice to the kitchen which was the only warm place in the house, and they heated milk to make cocoa and sweetened it with the last of the sugar.

'I'll have to go to the village with the grocery list,' Daisy said as she helped herself to a spoonful of the cream skimmed from the top of the milk and poured it into her cup.

Ruby stopped kneading the bread dough. 'I'll go if you like, miss.'

'No, Ruby. It's too soon after your illness.' Daisy said firmly. 'I feel like a walk.'

'I'll come too.' Beatrice gulped the last of the cocoa. 'I heard that they've got a telephone in the post office. I want to see if it works.'

'But who will you ring, miss?' Ruby stared at her in surprise.

A dull flush suffused Beatrice's round face. 'The Gurneys had one installed last week and I've been waiting for a chance to ring Jimmy. I haven't seen him for two days, and I want to know if he's missed me.'

'I'd let him wait if I was you, miss,' Ruby said, shaking her head. 'Blokes don't like to be chased. They want to think they're the hunters not the hunted.' She tapped the side of her nose, leaving a dusting of flour on it. 'Mark my words.'

'Words of wisdom, Bea. Take note.' Daisy rose to her feet. 'I'm going anyway. I've been cooped up indoors for days and I need the exercise.'

Ruby put the dough to prove, covering it with a

damp tea towel. 'When are you off to London with Lady Pendleton, miss? Is it this week, or next?'

'Next week. So I'll have to rely on you and Bea to take over the housekeeping while I'm away.'

'We managed without you before,' Beatrice said with confidence. 'We can do it again. Come on then, Daisy. Let's get our coats and hats on if we're going to the village.'

Minutes later they were muffled up in their winter coats with hats pulled down over their ears to fend off the bitter east wind that had skimmed the North Sea and blundered across the salt marshes. When they reached the village, Daisy left Beatrice in the post office attempting to get a telephone connection to the Gurneys' farm while she went to deliver the order to the butcher's shop. She was met with a grim-faced Cyril Smith. He took the shopping list from her with a grunt, making his feelings obvious, but not daring to be overtly rude when his employer was present. Daisy left the shop and was studying the list of groceries she was about to hand in to Mrs Cobb when she almost bumped into a man who was carrying what appeared to be a large wooden cupboard. Although she side-stepped, so did he, making a collision inevitable. 'Look where you're going.' She caught her breath in a gasp as he lowered the piece of furniture and she found herself face to face with Bowman.

Chapter Thirteen

'I didn't see you,' Bowman said slowly. 'But now I do, you're a sight for sore eyes, Miss Lennox.'

His appreciative glance made her dizzy with delight but her heart was pounding and she was finding it hard to breathe. She wanted to return his smile but she was afraid to give way to the feelings that threatened to engulf her. 'Good day to you, Mr Bowman.' She attempted to walk past him but he put the cupboard down, blocking the pavement. She stepped into the road but his hand shot out and he caught her by the sleeve.

'Don't run away, Daisy.'

She stared straight ahead, not daring to look him in the eye. 'Please let me go.'

He released her immediately but for some reason she could not move.

'Go on then,' he said harshly. 'Walk off. Pretend that you don't give a damn about me. Don't listen to what I have to say.'

She raised her head. 'You can't have anything to say that would interest me. We've been through all this before and nothing has changed.'

'Only that you've named the day. You're throwing yourself away on a toff with more money than sense, who'll probably get killed by the first German bullet that's fired.'

'That's a horrible thing to say, even for you, Bowman.'

'But it's true. You belong to me, Daisy Lennox. Heart and soul. Don't deny it.'

Their eyes locked as if in mortal combat and she knew that part of what he said was true, but it was not meant to be. Their story could never have a happy ending. 'You're married,' she said abruptly. 'And even if you were a free man it wouldn't make any difference. You're a womaniser, Bowman. You take what you want and then you tire of the poor soul who's fallen in love with you.'

'I'd never tire of you, Daisy. I love you truly and deeply. I can't sleep for wanting you, but we're worlds apart and I don't intend to drag you down to my level.'

Her whole body felt as though a flame had passed through it. The scent of him filled her nostrils and her heart beat all the faster. Whatever it was that drew her to him was stronger than thought alone. No matter how hard she fought against it, she knew it was a basic animal instinct that made her want him as much as he wanted her. Those hypnotic brown eyes held her gaze, drawing her towards him, robbing her of the will to simply walk away. His lips invited hers to open and taste his kisses . . .

'Daisy.' Beatrice's voice made Daisy come back to earth with a jolt that was physical in its intensity. 'I've been looking for you everywhere.' Beatrice raced up to them, stopping dead when she saw Bowman. 'Oh, hello. Sorry, I didn't mean to interrupt, but I must speak to my sister.' She grabbed Daisy by the arm and drew her aside. 'Jimmy's going to pick me up in the dog cart. I'm to wait here for him. That is all right, isn't it, Daisy? You won't tell Mother where I've gone?'

Dazed and disorientated, Daisy took a moment to gather her thoughts. 'Why ever not?'

'Because we're going into town for lunch and maybe we'll go to the picture house or something. Mother doesn't mind when I'm at the farm with Jimmy's family, but she wouldn't approve of us being seen together in public. You won't say anything, will you, darling Daisy?' Steepling her fingers as if in prayer, she gave Daisy her most appealing smile. 'Please promise me this one little thing.'

Daisy sighed. 'I suppose nothing I can say will stop you.'

'Oh, thank you.' Beatrice hugged her and raced back towards the post office.

'I must go,' Daisy said unnecessarily. 'This conversation never happened, Bowman.'

He bowed his head, saying nothing, and she walked on slowly, forcing herself to put one foot in front of the other. This time she believed him. She knew for certain that his love for her was as real as hers was for him, but that did not make it right. They had met at the wrong time and in the wrong place. There was no beginning and there would be no end. She made her way to the post office and general store to hand in the grocery list.

Life went on much as usual in Rainbow's End, despite the fact that Teddy had left home filled with enthusiasm for his new career in the Rifle Brigade. Gwendoline openly mourned for him, but, as usual, Victor kept his feelings to himself. The only comment he made was that it was dashed inconvenient businesswise, but very soon he had hired someone to take Teddy's place at work.

Arley Meadows was a quiet young man who lived with his widowed mother on the outskirts of Colchester. Daisy had only met him once when she called in at the office to beg a lift home with her father, but she had been less than impressed by Arley's subservient demeanour. There was nothing she could put her finger on but she knew from the first moment she saw him that he was not as meek and mild as he pretended to be. In his cheap but immaculate black cut-away jacket, starched wing collar, pinstripe trousers and white spats worn over his highly polished shoes, he was patently trying to be something that he was not. Daisy had no patience with humbugs and mountebanks. She hoped that her father would not put as much trust in Arley Meadows as he had in his former partner, who had let him down so badly.

Despite her low spirits after Teddy's departure Gwendoline rallied enough to compile guest lists for the coming nuptials, and she visited the great house twice a week to discuss the arrangements with Lady Pendleton. Daisy tried to keep a low profile. She realised that she had little or no say in the matter anyway, and she was eager to return to London to continue her training with the FANY. By dint of acquiescing to all Lady Pendleton's plans for the wedding, Daisy found herself in an ideal position to suggest that it might be a good idea to leave her mother in charge of the arrangements in Nutley Green, and for herself and Lady Pendleton to continue what was turning out to be a military-style campaign from the house in Grosvenor Square.

The details were finally agreed and at the end of January Daisy returned to London with Lady Pendleton, but despite her desire to spend most of her time at evening classes or weekend camps with the FANY she found herself caught up in a succession of social engagements and even more wedding plans. There was the design of the wedding dress to be discussed, and once chosen there were visits to the fashion house for fittings. There was the trousseau to be selected, and accessories, hats, gloves, bags and shoes must be purchased to complement the gowns suitable for every occasion. It seemed to Daisy that they had done all this only a few short months previously during her first visit to Grosvenor Square. Her tentative suggestion that the garments and accessories already purchased would do very nicely for the honeymoon was immediately dismissed by Lady Pendleton, who seemed totally oblivious to the true cost of her extravagant purchases. Daisy could not help feeling guilty and embarrassed by this display of unwarranted largesse. She had been brought up to a considerable degree of comfort but she had experienced what it was like to be relatively poor, and spending this amount of money on luxuries seemed almost wicked when there were many families living on or below the breadline.

As to the round of parties and entertainments, if the truth were told, Daisy was rapidly becoming bored with the interminable afternoon teas, dinner parties and charity events that she was forced to endure in London. Even trips to the theatre had begun to pall, although in April she had enjoyed the first night of *Pygmalion* with Mrs Patrick Campbell playing the part of Eliza Doolittle, and Sir Herbert Beerbohm Tree as Professor Higgins. Daisy had seen a little of herself in the character of Eliza, although she knew that her mother would be horrified at such a thought. Even so, Daisy could relate to Eliza, who was flung into a life that was so different from the one to which she had been born and raised. She just hoped that she would not make quite as many faux pas as the cockney flower girl. She had laughed out loud when Eliza forgot herself and uttered a really bad swear word, although there had been gasps of horror from some of the more elderly people in the audience. She had enjoyed *Pygmalion* unreservedly, but the more intellectual theatrical productions so beloved of Lady Pendleton went over her head, occasionally sending her to sleep. She found symphony concerts boring, and grand opera even worse. She had actually dropped off during a piano recital in the Bechstein Hall in Wigmore Street, and had been rudely awakened by a sharp dig in the ribs from her ladyship when the programme came to an end.

Daisy was beginning to realise that she was far more at home in the country than she was in the social whirl of London, and she had come to the conclusion that she might do very well living quietly in Pendleton Park. She resolutely put all thoughts of Barnaby Bowman out of her mind. She did follow the activities of the suffragettes in the newspapers, although she had been shocked when Mary Richardson had slashed the Rokeby Venus with a meat chopper at the National Gallery. She could not condone such vandalism, and she found herself for once in complete accord with her future mother-in-law, but she still held true to the idea of the WSPU, even though their meetings were now out of bounds to her.

The months went by and the wedding drew ever nearer, and it was only her connection with the FANYs that kept Daisy from going completely mad. Surprisingly Lady Pendleton had no objection to Daisy attending their training sessions, and the occasional weekend camp where the volunteers had the opportunity to undergo training by the military. Daisy even managed to persuade Lady Pendleton to allow her to attend the summer camp at Pirbright in Surrey, where the FANYs were instructed in cavalry drill by the 19th Hussars.

Despite her initial dislike of riding Daisy was beginning to look forward to the lessons. She had been very nervous at the start of her training, but after a while she managed to overcome her fears and found it quite exhilarating to gallop and even to take fences. She learned how to drive a horse-drawn field ambulance and how to cater for a large number of hungry military personnel in the cookhouse. Life at camp was far removed from the palatial surroundings of Pendleton Park or the house in Grosvenor Square, but even the discomforts of living under canvas did not dull Daisy's spirits. She felt free for the first time in her life, and more than that she felt useful. She was doing something that if war came, and it seemed inevitable after the assassination of the archduke and his duchess at Sarajevo, she would be able to do her bit for her country.

She returned to London after the summer camp with a feeling of confidence in her own capabilities and renewed optimism. The wedding was now only three weeks away and they were to travel to Essex the next day. Lady Pendleton was eager to get home in order to supervise the final arrangements for the wedding reception at Pendleton Park. She had left Gwendoline to liaise with the vicar, having given her a list of instructions as to the readings and the hymns, the anthems and the seating of the guests. Now the real work was to begin as the last minute checks were put in place.

The journey to Nutley Green began early in the morning. Lady Pendleton and Daisy travelled in the Rolls, and the second car, an Austin Grenville landaulet which was kept for just such an occasion, followed on behind. Their considerable amount of baggage was piled on the roof, and Lady Pendleton's maid, Worley, was entrusted with the onerous task of taking care of the wedding gown, which was wrapped in tissue paper and draped over her lap for the entire journey. For practical purposes, Rainbow's End being too small to store the precious garment in the required manner, the gown was to be taken to Pendleton Park where it would have a whole room to itself and the constant attention of Worley, who treated it with the reverence that a designer creation in pure silk and Brussels lace deserved. The rest of Daisy's trousseau would be aired, ironed and repacked by Worley and her acolytes in Louis Vuitton luggage as befitted the bride of the future Viscount Pendleton. Matters had been taken from Daisy's hands and she was powerless to do anything other than to acquiesce gracefully.

It was only now, when they drew nearer to their destination, that Daisy realised how much she was looking forward to a brief respite with her family. She had missed them all during the long months in London, and her mother's constant carping and criticisms seemed like a small price to pay for being reunited with those she loved most. Perhaps when she was a married woman her relationship with her mother would improve; she hoped so anyway.

It was approaching midday when the Rolls pulled up outside Rainbow's End and Daisy climbed out of the motorcar, eager to stretch her legs. Taking her leather valise from Parkin, she hesitated, resting her hand on the front gate as she gazed at the old house, savouring the moment of homecoming. The hot July sunshine reflected off the lattice windows and she spotted a bird's nest stuck on top of one of the tip-tilted chimneypots. She made a mental note to have it taken down before the weather changed in the autumn and it became necessary to light fires. She lifted the latch and walked up the path, noting with a frown that the flowerbeds were overgrown with weeds and the grass needed cutting. The paintwork was peeling off the front door and the brass lion's head knocker was in need of a good polish. She must do something about that, she thought as she knocked and waited. She was expecting to see Ruby's perky face smiling at her as the door opened with a groan of rusty hinges. But to her astonishment it was her mother who stood there, and even more surprising, she was wearing a pinafore.

'Mother, it's good to see you.' Daisy stepped over the threshold and embraced her, but the response was unexpectedly cool.

Gwendoline pushed her firmly away. 'You're early. I didn't think you would arrive until later.'

Daisy put the valise down, looking about her with a worried frown. The smell of dust and soot lingered in the air and there was a vague hint of burning, as if a pan had boiled dry on the hob. 'Where's Ruby, Mother? Why didn't she answer the door?'

Gwendoline sniffed and tossed her head. 'Don't mention that woman's name in my presence.' She stalked off in the direction of the kitchen and Daisy ran after her.

'But what has she done? Where is she, and why are you going to the kitchen?' She hesitated in the doorway, gazing in horror at the sight that met her eyes. Obvious attempts at pastry making had seemingly met with disaster. There was a veil of flour misting the furniture and the floor, with pieces of dough sticking to the walls. The fire in the range was a mere glow of embers and as she looked around in dismay the source of the smell became obvious. A blackened saucepan had been set on the windowsill and the charred remnants inside might have once been potatoes. The air was thick with smoke and Daisy flung a window open. 'What's going on, Mother?'

Gwendoline's face crumpled and she sank down on the nearest chair. 'I can't cook, Daisy. Heaven knows I used to once, at the very beginning when your father and I were first married, but I've forgotten everything I knew. It's been ghastly. Absolutely ghastly.'

Daisy peeled off her gloves and divested herself of her duster coat and hat. She plucked a clean apron from a drawer and tied it around her waist. 'I'll put the kettle on and we'll have a nice hot cup of tea and you can tell me what's been going on.'

Gwendoline fished in her apron pocket and produced a hanky. She blew her nose, shaking her head. 'It's been positively awful since Teddy joined the army, and then you deserted us. Beatrice spends all her time at that dreadful farm and she seems intent on marrying a farmer. Can you believe that?'

Daisy riddled the ashes and shovelled more coal onto the fire. 'Jimmy seems a nice enough chap, and Bea is very fond of him. She could do worse.'

'Worse?' Gwendoline's voice rose to a shriek. 'My eldest daughter is marrying a lord and my youngest wants to tie herself to a peasant. I don't think she could stoop much lower than that.'

'It's a changing world, Mother,' Daisy said gently. 'And Jimmy is a nice young man. I believe that he loves Bea and she adores him. Why shouldn't they be happy together?'

'Your father will never permit it,' Gwendoline said

resolutely. 'I know Victor. He'll put his foot down when he knows what's going on.'

'You haven't told him?' Daisy filled the kettle and put it on the hob.

'I daren't. You know what a temper your father has when he's roused.'

Daisy had never heard her father so much as raise his voice, but she did not bother to challenge this statement. She pulled up a chair and sat down beside her mother, taking her hand in a firm hold. 'Tell me what's been going on. Where is Ruby? And why are you slaving away in the kitchen?'

Gwendoline mopped her eyes on the crumpled hanky. 'I caught that person consorting with a workman. They were outside in the garden. I saw them from my bedroom window.'

Daisy held her breath. Her heart felt as though it was trying to escape through her mouth. 'What man?'

'Does it matter? I can't remember his name, but it was the wretched fellow who fixed the Humberette. Your father asked him to come and do some odd jobs around the house and garden, and that was how he repaid us.'

The kitchen seemed to be spinning in concentric circles around her head. Daisy had to exert all her willpower to remain in control of her wildly fluctuating emotions. Bowman was up to his old tricks again, and Ruby was fool enough to be taken in by him. He had betrayed them both, professing undying love for her and then taking advantage of poor Ruby, who had already suffered pain and loss at his hands. She rose to her feet, and her hands were shaking as she selected china from the dresser.

'Well? Aren't you going to say anything?' Gwendoline demanded angrily. 'I'm telling you, Daisy. That girl was consorting in our garden, and it wasn't quite dark. I could see everything.'

'A kiss and a cuddle is hardly a crime, Mother. Ruby is young and attractive. She was bound to have a boyfriend sooner or later.'

'It had obviously gone much further than that, Daisy. The harlot is in the family way. Of course I sent her packing the moment I discovered the truth. I won't have such loose morals in my house.'

'Are you certain?'

Gwendoline stared at her in astonishment. 'Why would I make up a story like that? Of course I'm sure. She was being sick and fainting all over the place. I recognised the symptoms, and when I charged her with it she said it was true. What's worse the man is already married. He has a wife and a child and she knew it. She is a fallen woman and I won't have anyone like that near my innocent daughters.'

Daisy made the tea. Concern for Ruby was overriding her anger and disgust for Bowman. She should have warned her parents that they were harbouring a cheat and a liar. He was a man who seduced women without any thought or care for the consequences and poor, besotted Ruby was the one to suffer. She had lost one baby and now she was pregnant again and probably alone. Daisy poured the tea, forcing herself to remain calm and objective. 'When did all this happen, Mother? Do you know where Ruby went?'

'Why would I care what happens to her? I assume that she's got family. She's their problem, not mine.' Gwendoline lifted the cup to her lips. 'Where's the sugar? You know that I take one lump in my tea. Anyway, now you're home you can take over the cooking. I'm quite worn out with it all, and we haven't had a decent meal since Ruby left three weeks ago.'

'She's been gone three weeks?'

'I don't know why you are making such a fuss about a slut like her. I've tried to get other help but that Iris is no better than she should be. She left us in the lurch months ago, but at least the man married her.'

Daisy smothered a sigh of relief. 'So Jed married her after all.'

'I believe you knew about it all along,' Gwendoline said, frowning. 'You might have warned me, Daisy. It was all round the village that Teddy was involved but of course that was just idle gossip. Anyway we've lost our cook and we can't afford to hire anyone else, or so your father says, although I think he enjoys making me suffer. He said that business is flagging since Teddy left, but he has that nice fellow, Arley, helping him. I think he's just being mean.'

Daisy patted her on the shoulder. 'You're exhausted, Mother. You should never have attempted to take on this sort of work. Go upstairs and rest and I'll have everything sorted in no time.'

Gwendoline stared at her with tear-filled eyes.

'You're a good girl, Daisy. I don't know what I'll do without you when you're married.'

'I'll only be half a mile away, Mother, and I'm going to ensure that you have adequate help in the house. If Lady Pendleton had known, she would never have allowed this state of affairs to exist. Now, please do as I ask and leave things to me.'

Gwendoline rose unsteadily to her feet. 'I feel so much better now that you're here.' She made her way slowly from the room.

Daisy had been keeping a tight rein on her temper, but now anger roiled in her belly. She picked up the last lump of sticky grey pastry and hurled it at the wall. It stuck there for a moment before plopping onto the tiles below.

She set about tackling the mess with a will but her mind was racing. Where would Ruby have gone? She might have returned home, but as her relationship with her father was strained at the best of times it seemed unlikely that she would throw herself on his mercy. She had a sister living somewhere south of the river, but where exactly Daisy did not know. She worked frantically, cursing herself for being so wrapped up in her own affairs that she had neglected those who were left at home. For all she knew Ruby might have lost this baby too. She might have died in childbirth or be starving on the streets of London. At this moment, Daisy did not know who she hated most in the world, Bowman or herself.

When she had finished tidying the kitchen she put on her hat and gloves and set off for the village. It was still only mid-afternoon and the sun was high in the sky. Heat haze shimmered off the road surface and bees droned lazily in the hedgerows. The scent of honeysuckle and dog roses filled the air and above her head a skylark warbled its sweet song, but she was too intent on her purpose to appreciate the peace and tranquillity of her surroundings.

She found Bowman in his workshop tinkering with the engine of a Model T Ford. The mere sight of his dark head bent over his work was enough to make her heart lurch against her ribs, but she held on to her anger, forcing herself to think of Ruby's sorry plight. 'Bowman, I want words with you.'

He straightened up but his initial smile faded as he met her furious gaze. 'Daisy?'

'Where is she?' Daisy had to curb the instinct to fly at him and pummel him with her fists. If she had a pistol in her hand she might well have shot him through his black heart. 'Where is Ruby?'

'I dunno, and that's the truth.'

'I don't believe you. She's expecting your child, but of course you know that, don't you?'

He shrugged his shoulders, eyeing her warily. 'She told me, but there wasn't much I could do about it.'

'You are the lowest of the low, Bowman.'

He grinned with a spark of his old humour. 'So I've been told.'

'I'm not interested in you or what you think, but I do want to find Ruby. You must have some idea of where she's gone.'

His cocky attitude changed subtly and was replaced

by a look of seemingly genuine concern. 'I gave her all the cash I had. It wasn't much but I said I'd give her more for the kid. I would tell you if I knew where she was, but I don't and that's God's honest truth.'

She clenched her fists at her sides. 'You are quite despicable.'

'That's not what you thought just a little while ago, my lady. I suppose things are different now that you're about to marry into the aristocracy.'

'I'm going to find Ruby if it's the last thing I do, and you're going to help me.'

'Oh, yes? How's that, ma'am? Are you going to get Sherlock Holmes on the case?'

'That's not funny.' Daisy glared at him in silence for a moment and then it came to her. She turned her attention to the motor car. 'Who does this belong to?'

'Major Henderson. It's going back to the Manor House tomorrow.'

'No it damn well isn't,' Daisy said firmly. 'You're going to make sure it's roadworthy and tomorrow morning, first thing, you'll deliver it to Rainbow's End. I'm driving up to London to look for Ruby and bring her home.'

His eyes widened and his skin paled beneath his tan. 'I can't do that. The major would have me shot.'

'If he doesn't then I will,' Daisy said calmly. 'Believe me, Bowman, I can handle a firearm. I've been trained to shoot and I'm a good marksman. It would give me enormous satisfaction to put a bullet between your eyes, and I could do it. You'd better believe me.'

He held his hands up in a gesture of submission.

'Has anyone told you that you look even more beautiful when you've got murder in mind?'

'I think justice would be a better way to describe it. I don't think a court in the land would convict me of murder.' She backed towards the doorway. 'I'll expect you with the car at seven sharp tomorrow morning.'

'And what if I say no?'

'If you've got a shred of decency in you, Bowman, you'll do this for Ruby. You owe her that at least.'

He made a move towards her, his eyes darkening with desire. 'You are the only woman I've ever really loved, Daisy Lennox. I was crazy about you before but now I'd give anything to take you in my arms and never let you go.'

The old familiar tug of physical attraction threatened to overwhelm her, but she forced herself to meet his ardent gaze with a stony stare. 'Seven o'clock tomorrow morning and I want a full petrol tank. If you let me down I'll make your life hell and that's a promise.'

Chapter Fourteen

Daisy barely remembered the walk home, but she had had the satisfaction of seeing Bowman at a loss for words. She knew that she had won that particular battle, but in spite of everything he had done she was finding it impossible to hate him. His faults were legion but she did not believe that in his heart he was a bad man. Perhaps she had seen a flicker of concern in his eyes when he had spoken of Ruby, or maybe it was wishful thinking, but she was certain that he would deliver the car next morning as she had demanded.

She arrived at Rainbow's End to find the house slumbering peacefully, and she set about the mundane task of cooking the evening meal. The simple act of preparing meat and vegetables for the pot calmed her nerves, and by the time Beatrice arrived home Daisy was able to act as though nothing untoward had happened. She did not take her sister into her confidence about her plans to drive to London next day, and she certainly did not mention it to her parents when the family sat round the dinner table that evening. She was, however, concerned to see her father looking thinner than normal, and the lines on his face seemed to have deepened over the past few months, or maybe that was simply her over-active imagination.

He was patently delighted to see her again, and she basked in the approval of both parents.

Victor congratulated her on making a delicious meal and Gwendoline graciously echoed his sentiments, although Daisy could see that it cost her mother a good deal of swallowed pride to admit that her own culinary efforts had been less than successful. Beatrice, as usual, was oblivious to any undercurrents or tensions in the family and she chattered on about the forthcoming harvest supper as if it were far more important than her sister's wedding. Daisy was content to sit back and allow the conversation to flow over her head. Her mind was filled with plans for the following day. She did not bring up the subject until everyone was saying goodnight and preparing to go upstairs to bed. 'Oh, by the way,' she said casually. 'I've got to go up to town tomorrow. I'm afraid I forgot to pick up my going away outfit from the fashion house.'

Gwendoline's mouth formed a small circle of surprise. 'But, darling, surely one of the servants from Grosvenor Square could do that for you and send it down by road or rail.'

'No, Mother. I'll have to try it on to make certain that the alterations are to my satisfaction. I have to go in person.'

Victor frowned. 'But how will you travel, Daisy? Surely you don't mean to go on the train?'

'No, Father. I intend to drive myself. I've arranged to hire a motorcar for the purpose.'

'A hired car?' Gwendoline shook her head. 'I don't

like the sound of that, and you shouldn't go alone. Beatrice must accompany you.'

Beatrice opened her mouth as if to protest and then closed it again, looking thoughtful. 'That might be fun, although I was supposed to be helping Mother Gurney prepare pies for the harvest supper.'

'Then you mustn't let her down,' Daisy said hastily. 'I'm sure that's far more important than my going away gown.'

Beatrice gave her a calculating look. 'On the other hand it would be nice to see London again. I'm getting to be such a country bumpkin. Actually, Daisy, I'd love to come with you. If that's all right with you, of course.'

There was a challenge in Bea's eyes and Daisy knew that she suspected something. She managed a smile. 'Of course, Bea. We'll go together, but the motor is being delivered early. You must be ready by seven or I'll go without you.'

'Don't worry, dear sister. I'm used to getting up at crack of dawn. That's what farmers' wives do, you know.'

Bowman pulled up outside the house at seven o'clock on the dot. Daisy was waiting for him at the front door and Beatrice was adjusting her hat in the hall mirror. 'Hurry up, Bea,' Daisy said impatiently. She was eager to be off before either of her parents realised that it was Bowman who had delivered the motorcar. She hurried down the garden path, acknowledging him briefly as he opened the gate for her. 'I'll return the car this evening.'

He nodded. 'I hope you find her.' He put his hand in his pocket and produced a crumpled pound note. 'Give her this from me. It's all I've got to spare but if you give me her address tell her I'll send her as much as I can afford. My wife bleeds me dry.'

Daisy climbed into the driver's seat. 'Don't expect me to feel sorry for you.' She beckoned frantically to Beatrice, who was ambling down the path at a snail's pace. 'Bea. If you don't get into this car now I'm driving off without you.'

Beatrice broke into a run and leapt in beside her. 'What's the rush?'

'It's going to take at least four hours to get to London if I keep to the speed limit all the way.'

'Drive carefully,' Bowman said seriously. 'And good luck.' He cranked the handle to restart the engine and Daisy drove off without a backward glance.

'What was all that about?' Beatrice demanded, holding on to her hat. 'Why did he wish you good luck? What's going on?'

Daisy explained the situation during the long and tedious drive. Their journey was punctuated with frequent stops when the engine boiled over. They had to allow it to cool down before refilling the radiator with water drawn from village pumps or begged from cottagers on the way. Eventually they reached London and Daisy had to concentrate hard, using all her driving skills to negotiate the chaotic traffic conditions. It was past midday when they finally crossed Vauxhall Bridge and entered what to them was foreign territory, south of the river.

'I don't know how you expect to find her,' Beatrice said, wrinkling her nose as they reached the vinegar works in South Lambeth Road. 'You don't have a proper address.'

Daisy pulled into the main entrance. 'I know that her father was employed here and so was Ruby. The chances are that she'd come back to the place she knew, or if she was truly desperate she might have contacted her father. Wait here while I go into the office and enquire.' She alighted from the vehicle without giving her sister a chance to argue, and made her way to an outbuilding with a corrugated iron roof. She entered through the door marked *Office* and found herself in a small room smelling strongly of ink, vinegar and tobacco smoke. A man sat behind a counter with a pipe stuck in the corner of his mouth. He was writing something in a ledger, but he paused briefly to glance at her through a wreath of smoke. 'Yes? What d'you want?'

It was not the most encouraging beginning but Daisy explained that she was trying to trace a family friend, and to her relief he responded to the name.

'Flagg,' he said, taking the pipe from his mouth. 'I knows Ernie Flagg all right. You don't want to get on the wrong side of him.'

'And his daughter, Ruby? Does she work for you now?'

He shook his head. 'Left here some time ago. Got mixed up with them blue-stocking suffragettes. Bad business.'

In the end she managed to glean the information

that Ernie Flagg no longer worked there but the clerk somewhat unwillingly gave her his address, adding a warning to hold on to her purse if she was going to venture into Balaclava Villa. She thanked him and hurried out to re-join Beatrice who was looking decidedly nervous.

'Thank goodness you've come,' she said, clutching her dolly bag as if she were afraid someone might snatch it from her. 'There are some rough-looking types wandering round here. I thought you were never coming out of that shack.'

'Balaclava Villa,' Daisy said, cranking the engine and jumping into the driver's seat. 'It's not far from here, according to the man behind the desk. It's where Ruby's father lives.'

'I'm starving,' Beatrice moaned. 'Can't we stop for lunch somewhere first?'

Daisy drove out through the gates into the main street. 'Oh, yes, and where do you suggest we try to buy lunch in this neighbourhood? No wonder Ruby wanted to get away from all this.'

Beatrice subsided into a sulky silence while Daisy negotiated the narrow streets, avoiding the piles of horse dung which were covered in seething masses of blowflies and bluebottles. The stench from the streets and outside privies was making Daisy feel nauseous, but they had come this far and she had no intention of giving up now. After driving round for a while she found Balaclava Villa and discovered that it was a tenement building which had seen better days. Barefoot children, who ought to have been in school, loitered in the doorways. Some of the older boys were smoking roll-ups, while the ragged girls minded the babies and toddlers.

Daisy's enquiries came to nothing. Ernie Flagg, she was told, rented two rooms on the top floor but he was never at home during the day. She might find him in any one of a number of public houses, but she would be lucky to discover him sober. No one had seen Ruby, although one heavily pregnant woman with a baby at her breast did volunteer the information that Nellie, Ruby's older sister, lived in Doris Street, Kennington, not far from the workhouse. The very mention of the dreaded place made the woman pale alarmingly and she slammed the door in Daisy's face.

Dispirited but determined not to give up, Daisy returned to the motorcar to find the bonnet crawling with small boys, and Beatrice making futile attempts to swat them off like wasps around a picnic table. One turn of the cranking handle was enough to scatter them and Daisy climbed back into her seat. 'Doris Street,' she said tersely. 'If we don't have any luck there I think we'll have to give up.'

Beatrice fanned herself with her hanky. 'Oh, Lord. Another five minutes and I think they'd have taken the motor to pieces. Let's go home, Daisy.'

'I'm not leaving London until I find someone who knows Ruby's whereabouts, or can give me some information about her.'

Doris Street was lined with two-up, two-down terraced cottages, and if the exteriors were anything to go by they were all in a similar state of dereliction. Daisy pulled in at the kerb and asked the first person she saw if he knew Nellie Flagg. The old man spat in the gutter and walked on.

Beatrice leapt out of the car. 'I'm sick of this. I'm hungry and I want to go home. I don't care if I never see London again.' She marched up to the nearest house and hammered on the doorknocker.

After a few seconds it opened a crack and a child of about six peered out at her. 'Who are you?'

'I'm looking for a lady called Nellie Flagg,' Beatrice said patiently. 'Do you know her, little girl?'

'I'm a boy. Clear off.' The door slammed in her face.

'Don't you dare laugh,' Beatrice said, turning to Daisy with a scowl. 'I'm not giving up. Follow me.' She marched to the next house and the next, receiving very little encouragement.

On her fifth attempt a young woman answered her knock, and she actually smiled. 'She ain't Nellie Flagg no more. She's Nellie Toms and she lives next door. I think she's at home.'

On hearing this, Daisy got out of the car and hurried to her sister's side. 'We need to speak to Mrs Toms urgently.'

'Do you now?' The woman eyed her curiously as she reached over and tapped on the door. 'She's got four little 'uns, so give her a minute, ducks.' She leaned against the jamb, regarding Beatrice and Daisy with unconcealed interest. 'That's a nice motor. We don't see many of them round here.' She straightened up as her neighbour's front door opened and a woman of a similar age appeared on the threshold. 'You got visitors, Nellie. Proper posh they are too.'

Daisy held out her hand. 'How do you do, Mrs Toms? You don't know us but we're friends of Ruby's.'

Nellie recoiled slightly. 'I don't recall that she had no friends of your sort, miss.'

Daisy felt the blood rise to her cheeks. 'Well, what I meant to say was that she worked for my family in Warwick Square, and when we moved to the country she came with us.'

'Lucky bitch,' the neighbour murmured. 'Ain't you going to ask the ladies in, Nellie? Where's your manners?'

'Shut up, Gladys. It's got nothing to do with you.' Nellie folded her arms across her chest. 'What do you want? I ain't got all day.' As if to confirm her statement a baby started crying and another child began wailing miserably. Nellie turned her head, leaning into the house. 'Be quiet or I'll give you something to cry for.' The wailing ceased but the baby cried even louder.

'We're just looking for Ruby,' Daisy said in desperation. 'She left without giving us a forwarding address. I have some money for her.'

A calculating look brightened Nellie's face for a second and then was gone, leaving her sulky and suspicious. 'I dunno where she is. We had a falling out years ago. We don't talk, and you won't get nothing out of me dad, neither. He won't have her name mentioned in our house. So I'll bid you good day. I got things to do.' She retreated into the house, closing the door but leaving a waft of something very disagreeable in the air.

Gladys shrugged her thin shoulders. 'So be told. She don't know nothing and neither do I. That Ruby was always trouble. She thought she was a cut above the rest of us, the snooty bitch.' She went inside and slammed the door.

'Nice neighbourhood,' Beatrice said, glancing about nervously. 'Let's go before things turn really nasty.'

They hurried back to the motor but it refused to start on the first few cranks of the handle. Daisy was beginning to sweat copiously. The sky had darkened and the air had turned a sulphurous yellow. She could hear thunder rumbling round in the distance and at any moment the heavens might open. In desperation she cranked the handle again and this time the engine fired on all cylinders. Regardless of dignity she almost threw herself into the driver's seat and gunned the engine so that the Model T roared off down the street, backfiring and causing people to rush out of their houses to find out what was causing the hullabaloo. When they were far enough away from Doris Street, Daisy stopped the car and with Beatrice's help she put the hood up to protect them from the worst of the rain that had started to fall in sheets.

Despite Beatrice's constant complaints that she was dying of starvation, Daisy drove on until they were at a safe distance from London before stopping at a respectable-looking tea shop on the outskirts of Brentwood, where Beatrice demolished ham sandwiches, scones and cakes as if she had not eaten for a month. Daisy sipped a cup of tea and nibbled at a slice of fruitcake, but she had no real appetite. Their journey had been wasted and she had no more idea where to find Ruby than she had at the start of the day. She was tired and dispirited but she was not going to give up. 'I'm going to put advertisements in the newspapers,' she said suddenly, causing Beatrice to jump and spill some of her tea on the tablecloth.

'What on earth are you talking about, Daisy?'

'I'm going to write an advertisement asking Ruby to contact me, even if it's just to let me know that she's all right. I won't rest until I find her, Bea.'

Licking her fingers one by one, Beatrice gave her a calculating look. 'There's more to this story than you've told me, isn't there?'

Assuming what she hoped was an innocent expression, Daisy shrugged her shoulders. 'I don't know what you're talking about.'

'Ruby was just a servant when all is said and done.'

'She's a friend too, and as far as we know she's on her own. It's impossible for a woman in her condition to get work.'

'She's Bowman's problem, not yours.' Beatrice leaned across the table. 'It's him, isn't it, Daisy? Bowman is the reason you disappeared off to London for months on end.' She shook her head, chuckling. 'Who would have believed that my big sister, the pure-minded suffragist, has fallen into the deadly trap?'

Daisy lifted her hand to signal to the waitress. 'May I have the bill, please?'

'Yes, miss. Right away.' The girl took a pad from her

pocket and began to write laboriously with the tip of her tongue held between her teeth.

Beatrice dabbed her lips with a napkin. 'You won't get away with it that easily, Daisy. We've got three hours or more stuck in that rattletrap. I'll get the truth out of you before we arrive back at Rainbow's End.'

'There's nothing to tell,' Daisy said, recovering gallantly. She loved her sister but she did not trust her to keep such a dire secret to herself. She placed some coins on the bill proffered on a plate by the young waitress, adding a generous tip, and she rose from her seat. 'Come along, Bea. The storm's passed over and I want to get home before dark.'

Bowman had not been there when she delivered the car to his workshop after her fruitless trip to London, and she had parked it at the kerb and walked home. He had not made any attempt to see her, and although she was relieved she was angry that he had not bothered to enquire about Ruby. He truly was a heartless wretch. She held grimly on to that thought and spent the next couple of days writing advertisements asking Ruby or anyone who knew her current whereabouts to contact her. She posted them off to both the national and local newspapers, although with little hope of receiving a reply.

With the wedding almost upon them she had little time to herself, although her mother and Lady Pendleton were confident that they had thought of everything. Even so, there were last minute crises and causes for panic when two of the smallest bridesmaids went down with chickenpox, and the Scottish salmon which had been sent down by train arrived in a less than fresh state. Another order was placed, but if it did not arrive on time the guests would be eating chicken instead of galantine of salmon.

On a more personal level, Victor's morning suit had not yet arrived from Moss Bros in Covent Garden and he was considering whether or not to take a day off work and travel up to London to collect it, and Gwendoline was not happy with the hat she had ordered from the milliner in Colchester. When she was not panicking about trivial matters she was bemoaning the fact that she could no longer afford to shop in Bond Street. Daisy kept as low a profile as possible, but she rushed to get the post every day in the hope that there might be something from Ruby, and each time she was disappointed.

Despite the desperate situation in Europe and the ever present threat of war, Rupert and Teddy had been granted two days' leave and were due to arrive home on Friday. Gwendoline was in a high state of excitement at the thought of seeing her son, and had hired a girl from the village to clean the house from top to bottom, paying special attention to Teddy's room. The bed was aired and made up with freshly laundered sheets and pillowcases. A small nosegay of clove-scented pinks from the garden had been lovingly placed on the dressing table by his mother, and one of the under-cooks from Pendleton Park had been delegated to Rainbow's End to cater for the family up to and for a short time after the wedding.

Daisy herself was becoming increasingly nervous. She had not seen Rupert since Christmas and she was beginning to realise how difficult life must be for an army wife, with the inevitable long separations and the reunions which might at best be blissful or at worst slightly awkward.

It was late on Thursday evening when the telegram boy arrived at Rainbow's End. The maid had gone home and it was Daisy who answered the door. She took the envelope with trembling fingers.

'Any answer, miss?' The boy, whom she recognised as Percy Bourne, the miller's son, shuffled his feet.

She held the lamp high enough to read the brief message. *Leave cancelled. Will telephone. All my love, Rupert.*

'Any answer, miss?' Percy's freckled face looked pale and pixie-like in the shadows.

She shook her head. 'No. Thank you, Percy.' She took a few pennies from her pocket and thrust them into his outstretched hand. 'Goodnight.'

He saluted and ran down the path to vault onto his bicycle.

'Who is it, dear?'

She turned to see her father standing behind her and she flung her arms around his neck, allowing the telegram to flutter to the ground.

Next day Daisy left the house soon after breakfast to walk the half-mile or so to Pendleton Park. She found Lady Pendleton in the morning room. She was still wearing her flimsy silk peignoir and the swirling, semi-translucent material flowed around her as she paced the floor, giving her the appearance of an agitated butterfly. She came to a halt as Daisy entered the room and rushed over to hug her, enveloping her in a cloud of L'Heure Bleue. 'Daisy, my dear girl. This is terrible news. Henry has been on the telephone to the War Office since last evening when we received the telegram.'

'I don't understand,' Daisy said dully. 'Why has Rupert's leave been cancelled?'

'I can't say for certain, my dear. I believe it's the wretched political situation, but one can never be sure of these things. Everything is shrouded in secrecy. Even my husband is finding it difficult to get an answer.'

'Rupert said he would telephone. May I wait here until he does?'

Lady Pendleton released her and sank down on a chair at the table, which was set for breakfast. 'Of course, Daisy. Ring for the maid and I'll have fresh coffee and toast brought to us. I couldn't manage anything more substantial, unless you, of course . . .' She broke off, leaving the question suspended in thin air.

'I couldn't eat a thing,' Daisy murmured, pressing the bell push. 'But coffee would be lovely.' She went to sit at the table, folding her hands on her lap. 'Does this mean that the wedding is off, ma'am?'

Jane Pendleton's eyes filled with tears of sympathy as she patted Daisy's hand. 'I don't know, my dear. I really have no idea whether Henry can pull enough strings to grant Rupert and your brother a few hours' compassionate leave. It depends on the situation in Europe, but I'm afraid that it's getting very serious.'

'You don't think we're going to war, do you?'

Lady Pendleton bowed her head. 'That's exactly what I think, but we will have to wait and see.'

It was the longest morning of Daisy's life. She drank copious cups of coffee but she had no appetite for food. Lady Pendleton retired to her bedroom to get dressed but when she came downstairs an hour later, looking pale but elegant in a dove-grey silk morning gown, there had been no change. Lord Pendleton remained in his study, appearing occasionally to tell them that he was unable to get any sense out of the War Office, and had demanded to speak to the minister for war in person. The waiting seemed endless.

Gwendoline arrived at the house shortly before lunch time but was in such a state of nerves that Lady Pendleton sent her home again in the Rolls with Worley in attendance, having given her strict instructions to settle Mrs Lennox in bed and remain with her until she was feeling able to cope. Victor was sent for and also Beatrice, who as usual had gone to the Gurneys' farm.

Daisy paced the floor in the crimson and gold saloon. Suddenly everything seemed totally unreal. She felt nothing other than a state of confusion. She did not know whether she was sorry or even slightly relieved that Rupert's leave had been cancelled at the last moment. It was almost impossible to believe that tomorrow was supposed to have been her wedding day. She was left very much to her own devices as

Lady Pendleton was fully occupied dealing with the wedding guests who were already at the house, including the distant relations whom Rupert so disliked, and those who were still arriving.

Daisy was shielded from this but in truth she would have appreciated having something to do. Time hung heavy on her hands, and when everyone took their places in the dining room at lunch time she had to suffer sympathetic looks and whispers, although quite obviously Lady Pendleton had forbidden anyone to raise the subject that was uppermost in their minds.

In the afternoon everyone drifted off to walk in the grounds or to play cards in the library. Some retired to the billiard room while others elected to take a nap so that they were fresh for the evening. Despite the slightly subdued atmosphere it was impossible to pretend that they had not gathered together for a wedding celebration. The only problem was that the bridegroom was missing and, unless Lord Pendleton managed to exert his considerable influence, likely to remain so. Sitting at the window and gazing onto the parkland, Daisy wondered vaguely what they would do with all the food that was still being prepared in the kitchens, and the crates of champagne that were cooling in the cellars. She had not seen the floral decorations in the church, but she could imagine the mixed fragrances of roses, lilies, freesias and orange blossom that scented the cool interior of the ancient building, and hopefully smothered the smell of must from aged hymnals and the hint of dry rot and damp that welled up from the crypt.

She jumped as someone tapped her on the shoulder, and she rose quickly when she realised that it was Lord Pendleton himself. 'Sir?'

'Rupert is on the blower in my study, Daisy. He wants a word.'

Chapter Fifteen

Daisy sat down, still clutching the telephone receiver in her hand long after they had said goodbye. It seemed so final. Rupert was not allowed out of the barracks even for the shortest possible period of time, despite the fact that it was so close to home. There was little he could tell her other than the fact that all leave had been cancelled as they were under orders, and it appeared that the wedding must be postponed indefinitely. His voice had cracked with emotion but she had remained quite calm. She knew that she ought to have been desolated by the news but if truth were told she felt as if a great weight had been lifted from her shoulders. All the wealth and grandeur of Pendleton Park meant very little to her, especially when her country's safety was at risk. If she had been a man she would have wanted to be at the forefront, even though the thought of violence and bloodshed terrified her. She looked up as the door opened and Lady Pendleton billowed into the room with her arms outstretched.

'My darling girl. I am so desperately sorry.' She enveloped Daisy in a hug. 'Rupert must be utterly devastated, as I'm sure you are too.' She took the receiver from Daisy's hand and hung it back on the hook. 'Would you like to lie down? You may use my room and I'll send a maid with tea and smelling salts, or perhaps a little brandy might help?'

Daisy rose to her feet. She could hardly breathe and she felt that she would suffocate if she stayed in this house one moment longer. 'Would you mind awfully if I went home? I'd like to tell Mother in person and I think it might embarrass all your house guests if I stayed. They wouldn't know what to say to me.'

Lady Pendleton kissed her on the cheek. 'You are a sweet, thoughtful girl, Daisy. I am truly sorry that this has happened. Henry has done his uttermost to overturn the army's decision, but they remained adamant that all leave is cancelled and that goes for everyone, including Rupert. But this present crisis must surely come to a swift end, and the wedding will take place at the first possible opportunity.'

Daisy felt a twinge of conscience. 'But all that expense. The wedding breakfast alone must have cost a fortune.'

'My dear girl, it's vulgar to talk about money. We will entertain our guests and your family will be most welcome to join us. After all, I can't condone waste and the salmon won't keep.'

'But the church, and all those beautiful flower arrangements . . .'

'The congregation will enjoy them, and perhaps they will lift their spirits a little.' Lady Pendleton regarded her with a frown puckering her brow. 'I shouldn't tell you this, Daisy, and you must promise to keep it secret, but Henry thinks we will be at war with Germany within the week. It's not official so don't breathe a word to anyone. That is the only explanation for the way that our darling boy has been treated, and you young people are the first to suffer.'

War. Daisy had heard rumours in the camps but it had always seemed such a distant threat, and now it was becoming a reality. 'Lady Pendleton, might I ask for your support? There's something I desperately want to do?'

'Of course, my dear. But what is it?'

'If what you say is true then I want to do something for my country. You know that I've been training for the First Aid Nursing Yeomanry.'

'Yes, and I applaud your patriotism.'

'I want to do more than that. I want to volunteer for active service.'

Lady Pendleton sank down on the nearest chair. 'But Daisy, I don't think that's a very good idea. What would Rupert say?'

'I think he would encourage me, and I'm certain he wouldn't try to stop me.'

'But your parents would be terribly upset.'

'I'm almost twenty-three, Lady Pendleton. I'm a free woman and I'm of age. I can make up my own mind.'

'Oh, dear.' Lady Pendleton held her hand to her brow. 'Now I think I could do with a tot of brandy. Ring the bell for Warrington, Daisy.'

War was declared on the fourth of August, and Rupert's battalion left for France. He had the Prince Henry delivered back to Pendleton Park with a note giving Daisy permission to use it until his return. Lady

Pendleton had made no objections and furthermore she had insisted that Daisy make full use of the house in Grosvenor Square. She herself would be remaining in the country for a few weeks yet, but then she would be travelling up to London and it would be nice to know that Daisy was there, waiting for her. Daisy was grateful, and although it seemed like cheating to take such an easy option it was a much better proposition than living in a rented room in a poorer part of town as did some of her friends in the Nursing Yeomanry. She said goodbye to her family amidst tears from both her mother and Beatrice, and a stern lecture on keeping safe from her father. She drove off in the Prince Henry with her luggage piled high in the back seat, and headed for London.

It seemed strange at first, living in the echoing mansion alone except for the servants, the number of whom was declining as the younger male members of staff were enlisting in the army at an alarming rate. Daisy did not fancy sitting in solitary state in the enormous dining room at a table intended to seat twenty to thirty guests; neither did she want gargantuan meals. She sent instructions to the kitchen to serve her the same food as they ate in the servants' hall when she dined alone in the morning room. Lord Pendleton also took up residence, in order to fulfil a senior position in the War Office, but Daisy saw him infrequently and only on the rare occasions when he dined at home. Otherwise she was very much alone in the house, but she did not mind as it gave her time to concentrate on her search for Ruby. She continued to put advertisements in the newspapers in the hope that she might see them and get in touch, but without success.

She worked tirelessly to raise funds for the FANY. It was frustrating that they were barred from taking part in the war effort, and in desperation many of them had taken jobs with the VAD, but Daisy threw herself into organising sewing parties and collecting equipment in the hope of being able to utilise it should the authorities undergo a change of heart. Not only had they come up against a brick wall of prejudice from the War Office, but there was also considerable public opposition to women risking their lives and morals in the male-dominated theatre of war. The French and Belgian authorities were similarly inclined but Belgium had been invaded and was now in desperate need of medical assistance.

In a heroic attempt to prove them all wrong, Grace Ashley-Smith decided to go it alone and travelled to Belgium in September, where she was stationed in a field hospital in Antwerp. Accounts of her valiant struggle against filth, disease and the dire conditions in which she attempted to help nurse the wounded and dying men filtered back to London, making Daisy and her colleagues even more eager to take an active part in the war.

Their chance came at the end of October. Organised by Grace, working on behalf of the Belgians, the first FANY unit left Folkestone for a wet and windy Calais, and Daisy was proud to be amongst them. Within two days they had taken charge of Lamarck, an old convent school next to the cathedral in the rue de la Rivière. Although she had taken classes in nursing, Daisy had never been in a hospital before, let alone worked in one, but she tackled the tasks assigned to her with a will. The old buildings were in a desperate state and Daisy and her colleagues, most of whom had never done housework of any sort, found themselves faced with conditions which would have daunted the most experienced skivvy. The stench from the row of latrines was overpowering and only faintly masked by the copious amounts of disinfectant that they used to scrub the floors and wash down the walls.

Daisy's hands were raw by the end of the first day and her back ached miserably but she was determined to carry on without complaining. Some of the other young women found it even harder to cope with heavy physical work that would normally have been done by their servants. Daisy endeavoured to raise their flagging spirits, but it was difficult to remain positive and cheerful under such trying conditions. Each day was a battle against filth and lack of the most basic amenities. With just one stove and a small kettle to heat water it was almost impossible to achieve and maintain the minimum standard of cleanliness. They were short of the most fundamental needs for setting up a hospital, and had to cut sheets in half in order to make the beds ready to receive their first patients. Food was also in short supply and their staple diet of bread and jam washed down by cocoa was monotonous, but after a heavy day's work Daisy was glad of anything.

At first the girls were billeted in private homes, but

after a few days Grace found an abandoned shop which she managed to acquire for their use. Making it habitable was easier said than done but it provided a welcome relief from the back-breaking work at the hospital. They scrubbed floors and cleaned windows, and in a desperate attempt to make their austere surroundings a little more homely they cut pictures from magazines and stuck them on the walls. They slept on camp beds or straw-filled palliasses but even then there was still a shortage of beds. In the morning when the day shift got up, the night nurses would climb in between their still warm blankets and settle down to get some well-earned rest.

Despite their constant attention to hygiene, many of the women succumbed to debilitating attacks of dysentery. This meant that those who did not fall ill were compelled to do double shifts, and during the first few weeks at Lamarck Daisy lived in a constant haze of exhaustion. She was fortunate enough to avoid contracting the illness, but she collapsed onto her narrow cot at night fully clothed and did not wake until first light.

Despite the battle raging at Ypres, the first patients at the hospital were mainly suffering from typhoid. When they were brought in from the trenches the soldier's bodies were invariably flea-ridden and running with lice, added to which they were covered in filthy mud and their own excrement. They had to be stripped of their uniforms, washed and deloused before they could be put into clean nightshirts and admitted to the wards. Performing such intimate tasks on strangers was shocking to someone like Daisy, who had never seen a naked man before, but she realised that it was just as embarrassing for the men who had no alternative but to endure her ministrations.

Even though she had never intended to become a nurse it was a position thrust upon her by necessity, and she tried hard to develop a professional approach to her work, but she had to steel herself not to pass out at the sight of blood. She had fainted several times in the first week, but it was surprising how quickly she became accustomed to dreadful sights. Apart from the dreaded typhoid, gas gangrene, trench foot and shell shock, there were the terrible injuries inflicted by shrapnel from exploding shells. For some there was little that Daisy could do other than hold their hands and comfort them as they passed away. Sometimes she sat and wrote a letter at the dictation of a dying soldier, sending his last words to his wife or mother, and she could barely see the paper as tears welled up in her eyes. Her schoolgirl French had improved rapidly and she was able to converse reasonably well with the Belgian nurses and doctor as well as the patients.

No matter how hard they struggled to save lives, the coffin man was the most regular visitor at Lamarck, and Daisy dreaded hearing the rumble of the cart-wheels as it entered the courtyard. She managed to cope by simply not thinking of anything other than the task in hand. She did not look back at the life she had left in England, nor did she allow herself to dwell on thoughts of her family at Rainbow's End. All that seemed like another world. She had been a different person then, and she could hardly recognise herself as the young woman whose main problem each day had been what gown to wear and the choice of accessories. Now her first thoughts on waking were for Rupert and Teddy. She hoped against hope that they were not suffering in the trenches like the men who were brought daily to the hospital.

She was homesick, of course, like all the other young women who had given up comfort and safety in order to help others, but they supported each other and one thing they all had in common was waiting anxiously for news from home. Letters arrived infrequently and were tucked in Daisy's pocket to be brought out at night when she was either on duty in the hospital or lying down to sleep on the narrow camp bed in the shop window. Even in the darkness she could hear the muffled sobs of some of the other girls, but Daisy had built a protective shell around her heart and she did not cry as she struggled to decipher Bea's spidery scrawl, or studied the perfect copperplate written by her mother. As the weeks went by it began to feel as though she was reading about strangers. Their lives were so far distant from her own that they might have been living on the moon. When she had finished the letters she added the precious links to a life once lived to a bundle tied together with a scrap of ribbon she had found on the floor of the shop.

Despite the fact that she was doing a worthwhile and necessary job, Daisy longed to do something more active, and just before Christmas, when one of the drivers took sick with typhoid, she was given the task of driving one of the two motorised Ford ambulances. Her job was to collect the wounded from trains arriving from the Front and transport them to hospital or to the docks for repatriation. It was often heavy work as she had of necessity to assist the stretcher bearers and load the injured men into the vehicle. Some of the soldiers were barely alive, and all of them were in desperate need of medical attention. She became adept in dealing with delirious patients who attempted to escape or lashed out at her thinking she was the enemy. She learned how to soothe the fears of the younger soldiers who thought, sometimes rightly, that they were going to die, and she often found herself in the role of surrogate mother, sister or confidante. Despite her active role she was still required to help out on the wards when they were short-staffed, and she did so with a willing heart. She found it deeply touching and rewarding to be able to help the men who had survived the carnage on the Front, and it was good to know that at least some of them would eventually be considered fit enough for repatriation.

Every time she met a train she searched the soldiers' faces in case one of them turned out to be Rupert or Teddy. She had long forgiven her elder brother for all the taunts and teasing of their childhood days, and now she remembered only his good points, but she was still confused as to her feelings for Rupert. She wore her engagement ring on a gold chain hung around her neck, but she could not imagine how she might have felt had they been able to take their marriage vows. Sometimes she wondered if she had ever loved him, or if she had merely been dazzled by his looks and social standing. He seemed distant, like a hero from a novel who was real only in her imagination, and if she ever allowed Bowman to sneak into her thoughts it was also with mixed emotions. Love and hate were there in equal parts, or perhaps her feelings for him were simply a fatal attraction to someone wholly unsuited to her. She did not allow herself to dwell on those unbidden thoughts. All she knew was the intense flood of relief when none of the tired, unshaven men, damaged mentally and physically who filed past her at the station was her brother or Rupert. Again and again she pushed such dire thoughts to the back of her mind.

With Christmas close at hand, Daisy volunteered with several others to take comforts to the troops in the trenches. These consisted of knitted articles sent from England, including socks and Balaclava helmets, cigarettes and tobacco. The scenes that she witnessed had a nightmare-like quality. The mud, the desolation, the stench and the squalid conditions in which the soldiers lived and died were too terrible to contemplate. Despite the brief ceasefire on Christmas Day, when the Germans and the British exchanged cigars and cigarettes and sang carols, the carnage continued on into the New Year. Daisy was beginning to feel that the war would never end. The constant boom of the guns echoed in her head night and day, and the cries and groans of the injured soldiers haunted her dreams. Despite this, when the ambulance driver was well enough to return to work, Daisy volunteered to drive the mobile kitchen to take soup and sustenance to the troops.

She had just driven back from such a mission one cold and windy night in the middle of March when she came across a scene of devastation at Lamarck. A Zeppelin raid on Calais had dropped bombs on the surrounding buildings, damaging the cathedral chapel and smashing windows in the hospital building. The railway station had been hit and there appeared to be many casualties. She alighted from the vehicle and ran to aid a soldier who, although wounded, was struggling to get an even more badly injured man to safety. 'Let me help,' she said, taking the unconscious soldier's arm and looping it around her shoulders. 'We must get him under cover quickly.'

'Yes, miss.'

The voice was achingly familiar, although his face was unrecognisable in the semi-darkness and with mud and blood caking his features.

'Bowman?'

His rictus grin exposed a row of white teeth, which contrasted oddly with his smoke-blackened face. 'Yes, miss.' His eyes rolled upwards, revealing the whites, and he slumped to the ground, almost taking her and the wounded soldier with him.

'Help needed here.' Daisy's voice broke as she shouted loud enough to make herself heard through the background noise of gunfire and the screams of the injured.

One of the Belgian orderlies rushed forward to pick up Bowman and throw him unceremoniously over his shoulder. 'Can you manage, mademoiselle?'

'Yes,' Daisy said stoutly, although the man was a

dead weight and of a big build. Somehow she managed to half carry half drag him into the hospital, where she found Bowman struggling back to consciousness and attempting to stand. 'Sit down,' she said firmly. 'You'll be seen to as soon as possible. Where are you hurt?'

With his right hand covered in a bloodied dressing he pointed to his left shoulder. 'Shrapnel got me.'

She felt his brow and frowned. He was feverish, but a cursory examination of his shoulder revealed a wound that was undoubtedly painful, and would need the doctor to probe for fragments of metal, but was nowhere near fatal. She took a gauze dressing from the trolley and covered the area. 'Hold that in place,' she said firmly. 'The doctor will see you as soon as he can.' She frowned, eyeing his bandaged hand. 'What happened there?'

He pulled a face. 'You don't want to know.'

'Don't be silly. I can't assess how urgent your case is unless I know what's wrong.' She glanced anxiously at the wounded soldier, who cried out in agony as the orderly laid him on one of the trestle tables which were being utilised as makeshift beds. 'That man is in more urgent need of attention than you, Bowman.'

He raised his right hand to hold the pad in place. 'You want the truth, Daisy? Then I'll tell you. I shot my trigger finger off. Men are doing it all the time. It's a free passage home, or in my case I did it because I wanted to find you.'

'What?'

'Don't look so shocked. You know it happens.'

She did know all about the extremes that some of

the soldiers went to in order to be repatriated as unfit for active duty, but she could not believe that Bowman had mutilated himself for her sake. 'You're delirious,' she said warily. 'You wouldn't talk such nonsense if you were in your right mind.' She was about to walk away but he reached out with his good hand and caught her by the wrist.

'It's the truth. When I found out where you'd gone I volunteered for the London Regiment. I'd read what the newspapers said about you and the other crazy women who want to be at the forefront of war and so I joined up too. It didn't take a genius to work out that we'd be sent to the Front, and I knew that's where I'd find you. I attached myself to the Belgians as a stretcher bearer, but I was unlucky and took a hit.'

She snatched her hand away, staring at him in disbelief. 'You're a deserter. You must be out of your mind.'

He nodded dully. 'That's what you've done to me, Daisy Lennox. I can't get you out of my head.'

The orderly coughed politely. 'Do you want me to shift this one, mademoiselle? He's a case of shell shock if ever I saw one. Shall I put him somewhere quieter?'

Daisy shook her head. 'I'll deal with it, thank you. I can manage.'

He saluted and hurried away.

'I'm not crazy,' Bowman said with a sigh. 'But at least I've found you. It's taken me six months, but I've done it.' He closed his eyes and his head drooped forward onto his chest.

'Sit there and don't move.' Daisy adopted the tone she might have used to a small child. 'The doctor will get to you as soon as he can.' She left him and moved on to the soldier, who was groaning loudly.

It was a long night, and as the grey dawn broke a sudden sense of calm descended upon the previously frantic wards and the courtyard, which during the hours of darkness had been a desperate place where the medics had done their best to save lives. Daisy did the rounds of the men she had cared for during their emergency treatment, and found Bowman lying across two chairs with a blanket thrown over him. Sound asleep despite the dressing on his shoulder where the wound had been probed without the advantage of anaesthetic, he looked pale but peaceful and somehow much younger and defenceless. Daisy stood for a moment gazing at him, oddly bereft of emotion. She felt neither love nor hate, but she was curious. She wondered how much of the improbable tale he had related was true, or whether his rambling story was the result of shell shock or a fevered brain.

He stirred, as if sensing her presence, and opened one eye and then the other. He struggled to a sitting position but she laid a hand on his shoulder. 'Don't get up. You must rest.'

'You didn't seem surprised to see me last night,' he said with an attempt at a grin.

'Nothing surprises me any more,' Daisy said dully as a wave of exhaustion threatened to overcome her.

His brow darkened. 'You should be lying down, not me.'

'I'm going off duty. Someone will take you to the ward when they have a bed free.'

'Do you want to know another reason why I volunteered for the London Regiment?'

She met his intense gaze coolly. 'Not really.'

'I was running away.'

'From what?'

'Myself mainly. I'm not proud of what I did to young Ruby. She's a great girl and she didn't deserve the way I treated her, but as I couldn't have you she seemed like the next best thing.' He held up his hand as Daisy opened her mouth to protest. 'I know, I was a real bastard, and if I could turn the clock back I would. I'm truly sorry for the way I treated both of you, but what I told you before was God's honest truth. I was desperate to find you and let you see that I'm not a bad fellow at heart. I'd do anything for you, Daisy.'

She shrugged her shoulders. 'Don't expect me to feel sorry for you, Bowman.' She walked off without giving him a second glance.

She slept, but her dreams were violent and disturbing although she could only vaguely remember them when she awakened at midday. Someone was shaking her by the shoulder and she looked up to see Clarice Edmonds, a distant cousin of the Pendletons, whom she had taken under her wing when she found her sobbing with exhaustion and homesickness on Christmas Eve. Clarice looked pale and tired but her dark eyes were alive with excitement. 'Wake up, sleepyhead.'

Daisy raised herself on one elbow. 'What's happened? Is it another Zeppelin raid?'

'No, nothing like that, but we've got to take the soup kitchen today. Rosemary and Enid have been up all night tending to the casualties and they're exhausted.'

'All right. Give me a few minutes to get dressed.'

Clarice chuckled, pointing to Daisy's crumpled uniform. 'You didn't take it off last night. Poor thing, you must have been fagged out.'

Daisy struggled to her feet with a wry smile. 'My mother would have a fit if she could see me now.'

'So would mine.' Clarice handed her a tin mug filled with tea. 'Here, drink this. There's no milk but I managed to pinch a spoonful of sugar.'

Daisy sipped it gratefully. 'You're a brick, Clarice.' She drained the lukewarm, weak but sweet tea, and put the mug on the windowsill. 'I'll just wash my hands and face and then I'm ready. I'll meet you in the yard.'

'I'll go and help them finish loading the truck,' Clarice said eagerly. She bounced off like an excited puppy anticipating a long walk.

Daisy sighed, hoping that nothing would happen to dull Clarice's optimism and enthusiasm for life and the work she had set out to do with such determination. Clarice had Rupert's niceness and genuine concern for others, and getting to know her had made Daisy feel even guiltier for not loving Rupert as she knew she should. Putting such thoughts aside, she had a quick wash, but instead of going directly to the courtyard where the mobile kitchen was parked she went to the ward where she expected to find Bowman. She made her way between the packed beds but he was not there. She found the young Belgian doctor who had been attending to the wounded all night. He was pale-faced and in desperate need of a wash and a shave. He looked at her dully when she enquired about Bowman.

'Can't place him,' he said in perfect English. He picked up a sheaf of papers and scrutinised them carefully. 'What's his name again?'

'Private Bowman, doctor.'

He ran his hand through his already tousled mouse-brown hair. 'Trigger finger. Yes, Englishman. I remember him now. Shrapnel successfully excised from his left shoulder. Possible shell shock. I put him down for repatriation. Not much chance of a cowardly chap like him being much use to the army, or anyone else for that matter. He'll probably end up in prison when he gets back to England.'

Daisy stared at him aghast. 'But surely he wasn't fit to travel?'

'If he was fool enough to cripple himself he'll survive the journey home. Let the authorities deal with him. We've got genuine cases to look after here.'

Daisy did not wait for him to continue. She ran from the ward. Whatever Bowman had done she could not stand by and allow him to travel on a troopship so soon after a painful operation undertaken without the benefit of anaesthetic. He should be resting in bed until he was fully recovered. She had to find him.

Chapter Sixteen

Daisy raced past Clarice. 'I'll be back in two ticks.' She did not wait for a response but ran on, slipping and sliding on the wet cobblestones, determined to reach the docks before the troopship sailed. Regardless of the steady drizzle she pushed her way through the crowds of civilians and soldiers, arriving at the quay only to find that the ship had already left. Disheartened and soaked to the skin, she turned on her heel and hurried back to Lamarck. Feelings for Bowman that she had thought were dead had come back to haunt her.

'Where have you been?' Clarice cried anxiously. 'I've been getting black looks from everyone and I was afraid I'd have to go on my own. I don't know the way and I'd be really scared.'

Tucking her wet hair under her cap, Daisy climbed into the driver's seat. 'Well, I'm here now. Let's get going.'

Clarice leapt in beside her. 'Where did you go? What got into you, Daisy? I've never seen you so upset. You're usually so calm.'

Concentrating on manoeuvring the large vehicle out onto the street, Daisy did not answer immediately. She hesitated as the need to confide in someone almost overcame her natural reticence. Her feelings for Bowman were a guilty secret that she had endeavoured to suppress but had suddenly come rushing to the surface. Even so, she could not bring herself to speak his name. She shot a sideways glance at Clarice, whose face was agog with interest, and Daisy knew that she would not be satisfied until she had at least a small part of the true story. 'I knew one of the injured men,' she said, attempting to sound casual, but her voice broke and she swallowed hard.

'You know a Belgian soldier?'

'Not very well. It's a long story.'

'He seems to have made quite an impression on you,' Clarice said seriously. 'I mean, you must have thought a lot of him to go haring off like that. You could have been in real trouble if I hadn't covered for you. I told Boss that you'd had a sudden case of the runs and had to rush to the latrine. It's lucky she believed me.'

'Thanks. I know I shouldn't have done it but I was concerned for his welfare. He should have been kept on a ward, but the doctor thought he was malingering. I think he was suffering from shell shock.'

'I'm sure he'll be better off at home. They'll treat him sympathetically in a military hospital.'

'I don't know about that,' Daisy said, turning the wheel to avoid running into a donkey cart loaded with potatoes. 'He could end up in prison or even in front of a firing squad.'

Clarice whistled through her teeth. 'No. Surely not? What had he done?'

'He tried to get himself repatriated illegally, but he might have been better off taking his chances here.' Daisy honked the horn as a man on an ageing bicycle wobbled into the centre of the muddy road ahead of them. 'Let's not talk about it any more. There's nothing to be done except take this contraption as near to the Front as we can and start serving hot soup and bread to the poor devils in the trenches.'

Clarice shivered and wrapped her arms around herself. 'It's bad enough in the truck; I can't imagine what it's like being up to one's knees in cold water for any length of time. I wish this war would end.'

'Amen to that,' Daisy said with feeling. 'But until then we've got a job to do, Clarice. I hope you've brought your waders, because it's going to be very muddy where we're going.'

Daisy drove on, knowing that their efforts could only bring comfort to just a few of the thousands of troops on the front line which stretched from the North Sea towards the Swiss border at Alsace. When they arrived at their destination they found a scene of total devastation, houses riddled with shell holes standing out like skeletons in a sea of mud. Half deafened by the reverberating boom of guns, they handed out food, cigarettes and garments knitted by loving hands at home. It seemed little enough to give the battle-weary soldiers who were barely recognisable as men, with gaunt, unshaven faces and eyes reflecting the full horrors of war. But despite their suffering they still managed to smile and thank the young women for their bravery and kindness. Daisy found herself fighting back tears on many an occasion, especially when the soldier who clutched her hand and thanked her so sincerely for a bowl of lukewarm soup was little more than a boy. She wondered what his mother would say if she could see him now, but she knew it would break the poor woman's heart.

They returned to Lamarck as dusk fell, exhausted and silent. Daisy was painfully aware that the small amount of comfort they had brought to the trenches would be short-lived when the shells rained down again. Men were dying in their tens of thousands and existing in the most terrible conditions; she could only hope and pray that Teddy and Rupert were not amongst them.

Having parked the vehicle in the courtyard, Daisy and Clarice spent a good hour or more cleaning it and making it ready for the next day. It was late by the time they finished restocking the shelves and filling the petrol tank so that everything was prepared for an early start. Having missed supper, they sat in the tiny kitchen huddled over a paraffin stove on which Daisy had boiled water to make cocoa. By the light of a single candle they ate bread smeared with a little blackcurrant jam and washed it down with cocoa sweetened with a few grains of sugar. Daisy could see that Clarice was falling asleep even as she sat on the hard wooden chair, and she took the empty mug from her hand. 'Go to bed. I'll clear up here.'

With a grateful smile Clarice rose somewhat shakily to her feet. 'Thanks, Daisy. Sorry to leave the washing up. I'll do it tomorrow.'

'Night, night,' Daisy said, as Clarice stumbled out of the kitchen, half asleep already. She began clearing away, but as she listened to the rain lashing down on the roof her thoughts turned to Bowman, and she could not help wondering what had become of him. Almost certainly he would face a firing squad when he arrived back in England. He might be there already if he had boarded the troopship that morning. Perhaps he was languishing in prison. She could not find it in her heart to blame him for his apparently cowardly act. He had told her that he had gone to such extremes in order to be near her and somehow she believed him. He was not the sort of man who would behave in such a quixotic manner unless driven by strong emotions. She wiped the mugs and hung them back on their hooks with a heavy sigh. War made men behave in extraordinary ways.

She was about to extinguish the candle when a soft tapping on the window made her spin round. Her hand flew to her mouth as she saw a pale face pressed against the glass. It disappeared into the darkness only to be replaced by a beckoning finger. She snuffed the candle and opened the door leading into a narrow passageway which opened out into the courtyard. She gasped with fright as someone grabbed her by the arm and drew her deeper into the shadows. A hand clamped over her mouth.

'Don't scream. It's me.' Bowman released her and she turned on him in a sudden fury.

'What on earth d'you think you're doing? Why weren't you on the boat for England?'

He laid his finger on his lips. 'Hush, you'll have the orderlies rushing to your aid. I don't mean you any harm, you know that.'

'Answer my question. Why did you come here?' In the half-light she could not make out his features but she could tell from the way he was standing that he was tense and nervous. 'What do you want from me?'

He shrugged his shoulders. 'A bite to eat and a place to sleep.' He staggered and leaned against the wall. 'I don't feel so good.'

Forgetting everything other than the need to tend to a human being in distress, she felt his brow. 'You're feverish. I told the doctor that you shouldn't have been discharged in this state.' She thought quickly. There was a small room kept for special cases where the patient was either disruptive or exhibiting the symptoms of cholera or dysentery. At present it was vacant and it was unlikely that anyone would think to check it at this time of the evening. She knew she was taking a risk but she could not send him out into the teeming rain. 'Come with me and don't say a word.' She led him through the kitchen and down a long corridor at the side of the main ward. She made him wait outside while she checked the room, and to her relief it was unoccupied. 'Come in and close the door.'

She helped him out of his sodden greatcoat and top clothes, and made him comfortable in the narrow iron bed. 'Don't make a sound,' she said, tucking him in. 'I'll get you something to help you sleep, but you'll have to leave again first thing in the morning.'

'I'm thirsty,' he mumbled. 'Water, please.'

'Of course. Just lie quietly and I'll be back in a minute.' She hurried off to fetch water and laudanum.

He was lying quietly staring up at the ceiling when she returned and he took his medicine without a murmur. There was little else she could do other than to ensure he had a good night's sleep and did not give himself away. He would be clapped in irons and put on the first boat for England if anyone discovered his whereabouts. She waited until the drug began to take effect before returning to the kitchen. She locked the laudanum in the medicine chest, put on her coat and hat, and went outside to brave the rain as she made her way back to the billet.

She climbed into bed and fell into a deep sleep, awakening with a start as the first cold grey light of dawn filtered through the ill-fitting curtains. She was up and about before anyone stirred. The night staff were still on duty when she arrived back at Lamarck, but all was quiet apart from the muted moans and groans of the patients. She found Bowman sleeping fitfully and obviously in the grip of a high fever. She frowned, gazing down at him. They would both be in trouble if his presence was discovered, but he was obviously too ill to leave. She went to the kitchen to fetch fresh water and another dose of laudanum from the medicine chest, but to her dismay she found one of the newer recruits sitting at the table with her head bowed and her shoulders shaking.

Daisy put her arm around her. 'What's the matter, Mary?'

'He died holding my hand and calling for his mother.'

With tear-filled eyes Mary gazed up at her. 'I'm supposed to lay him out but I just can't do it, Daisy. I got to know Soldat Smets when I was nursing him and I can't bear to look as his poor dead face. He wasn't much older than my brother and he was so scared of dying. D'you think I'm a frightful coward?'

'No, of course not. It's perfectly natural to feel like that, and you've been on duty all night. You're just overwrought and exhausted.'

Mary sniffed and twisted her mouth into a feeble attempt at a smile. 'You're always so kind, Daisy. I don't think the others will be so sympathetic.'

'Of course they will. We were all new to this six months ago, and we've had to learn to cope.' Daisy stared at her thoughtfully as an idea came to her. It was bold and shocking in its simplicity. 'Where is the poor fellow?'

'The last bed on the left. I pulled the screens round him but the thought of going back there and doing the necessary makes me feel sick, and then there's the paperwork to do. I'm so tired I can hardly keep my eyes open.'

The plan was maturing in Daisy's mind. It was risky, but these were desperate times. 'Go to bed, Mary. I'll see to everything. It's time you went off duty anyway.'

'D'you mean it?' Mary stood up, gazing at her in astonishment and awe. 'You are a brick, Daisy.'

'Just go and don't mention a word of this to anyone.'

'I won't. Cross my heart and hope to die.' Mary's eyes widened. 'I'm sorry. I didn't mean to say that. It was silly of me.'

Daisy patted her hand. 'Go and get some sleep.' She waited until Mary had left the building before unlocking the medicine chest, and taking the bottle of laudanum she slipped it into her pocket.

The night staff were in the process of writing up their notes and making ready to hand over to those coming on duty and no one noticed her as she walked into the ward. Despite her encouraging words to Mary, she felt that she would never get used to the sight of a dead body, and she had to steel herself to take over where Mary had left off. She made the unfortunate Soldat Smets ready and called for an orderly to take his remains to the mortuary, but she took the identity disc from the soldier's neck and tucked it into her pocket. Leaving his hospital notes on the foot of the bed, she closed the curtains and she hurried from the ward.

Bowman was awake but still drowsy as the effects of the laudanum were beginning to wear off and he was able to cooperate to some extent. With a superhuman effort Daisy managed to get him into a wheelchair. The changeover from night to day staff had begun and she thought it unlikely that any of the hard-pressed and overworked nurses or doctors would spot the difference between the two young men. Soldat Smets had suffered similar injuries to Bowman's, although in the end he had succumbed to pneumonia. She eased Bowman's identity disc from around his neck and replaced it with that of the dead soldier. She wrote up a fresh set of notes describing Bowman's treatment and hung them at the foot of the bed. The only flaw in her plan was if someone realised that there was one Soldat Smets in the mortuary and another lying in the ward, but it was a common enough name and it was a risk she would have to take. Having given Bowman another dose of laudanum potent enough to make him sleep for several hours, she had no alternative but to leave him in the hands of the day staff. With a degree of reluctance she went to find Clarice and made ready to leave once again for the Front.

It seemed that the angels were on their side. It was early evening when Daisy visited the ward and found Bowman semiconscious but improving. She read his chart and notes with grim satisfaction. She was harbouring a war criminal but she did not care. Everything was topsy-turvy in this war-torn land, and the normal rules that people lived by seemed to be of little importance when it was a matter of life and death. She laid her hand on his brow and he opened his eyes. Despite the fever she knew that he recognised her and she smiled. 'Go back to sleep. You're safe here as long as you keep your mouth shut. Try to remember that you're a Belgian, Soldat Smets, and for God's sake please don't tell anyone your real name or you'll get us both shot.' She patted his hand and tucked it beneath the thick grey blanket. 'I'll be back first thing in the morning.'

Bowman remained in a critical condition for several days but, to Daisy's intense relief, no one questioned his identity. He was accepted as Soldat Smets, and as soon as he was capable of grasping the situation he had little alternative other than to play his part.

Daisy and Clarice were relieved of their job operating the mobile kitchen when the original driver and her helper returned from a brief home leave. Those who had remained on duty clustered around them eager for news of home and the small treats they had brought with them. There was real coffee, chocolate and best of all a dozen eggs, which were almost unheard of luxuries in the war-ravaged French and Belgian countryside.

Daisy ate her boiled egg slowly, savouring each mouthful. She tried not to hark back to the days in Warwick Square when the sideboard had groaned with silver breakfast dishes filled with steaming hot bacon, kidneys and buttered eggs, or kedgeree and her father's favourite, a grilled kipper. She, like all the other women, had lost weight and her clothes hung about her like a flour sack. She had to fasten her leather belt several notches tighter in order to keep her skirt from falling down, but there was little time to fret or indulge in vanity; the work at Lamarck was never-ending. The casualties and sick men arrived daily.

It was several days before Bowman was genuinely well enough to be considered for discharge, and Daisy had been racking her brains for a solution. When the time finally arrived she had been out all day, transporting injured soldiers from the station to the port to await the next sailing for England. It was late at night when she arrived back at Lamarck and she went straight to the ward, but to her horror Bowman's bed had been stripped and there was no sign of him. She felt suddenly faint and weak at the knees. She sat down on the edge of the bed hoping that none of the nursing staff would notice, and it took her a few moments to recover her composure. Not knowing what had happened to him was the worst thing. Had he been sent for repatriation or had he decided to make a run for it? She took several deep breaths and rose to her feet. Steadying herself, she went to find the nurse on duty.

'Soldat Smets discharged himself this morning. He said he wanted to return to his unit even though the doctor refused to pass him as fit for active service.'

'Do you know where he might have gone?' Daisy asked tentatively.

'I don't think that should concern you, Miss Lennox.' The nurse eyed her suspiciously. 'Fraternisation with the patients is forbidden, as you well know.'

'Yes, of course. I only knew him slightly, but he asked me to write to his mother in Bruges. I was concerned for her sake.'

'I see.' The nurse raised an eyebrow, making it quite clear that she understood only too well. She gave Daisy a searching look and her expression softened slightly. 'I'm sorry, Miss Lennox. I have to get on.'

'I'm sorry, nurse. I didn't mean to take up your valuable time.' Daisy walked off in a daze. She should not concern herself about Bowman. He was, after all, a deserter and he would never be able to return home to England without the risk of court martial and the inevitable death penalty. He was not her responsibility, but somehow it felt as though he was.

She could do nothing more that night, and next

morning she was still no closer to finding a solution to his predicament. She could only hope that he had found some way to get back to England. It would be useless to make enquiries around the town as he would simply merge into the shifting mass of servicemen who crowded the streets.

There was nothing Daisy could do other than to concentrate on her work, and she threw herself into it with even more gusto than before. She drove the ambulance all day and spent hours cleaning and maintaining it. She learned how to change a tyre, and to do minor repairs, ending up covered in mud and engine oil, but exhausted enough to fall asleep as soon as she climbed into bed. Days merged into weeks and the fighting around Ypres intensified. As she was seen to be a competent driver Daisy spent most of her time doing just that. Occasionally it was taking the mobile kitchen to the Front, but more often than not she and Clarice worked together ferrying the wounded to and from hospital. The two of them became close friends and it was not simply Clarice's distant relationship to the Pendletons that made her a good companion.

Clarice was young enough to think that life was still a great adventure and Daisy admired her spirit. She also felt very protective towards her. Clarice was easily frightened although she tried very hard to be brave. They often came under shell fire when driving the mobile kitchen and occasionally came upon scenes of such appalling annihilation that they were physically sick. But somehow they carried on, and gradually Daisy began to put Bowman's plight out of her mind.

He was, after all, a grown man and in charge of his own destiny. Where that had led him remained a mystery, but she was not eager to learn his fate. She set her sights on doing the best job she could and helping to bring a little solace to men whose daily lives were a living hell.

Despite the fact that they were far from home there was no shortage of news, most of it bad. The allied forces' landing in Gallipoli with vast numbers of casualties was bad enough, but at the beginning of May the sinking of the Cunard liner the *Lusitania*, with its appalling loss of life, cast a shadow over everyone at Lamarck. Somehow their spirits revived as the miserable spring gave way to warmer summer weather. The fighting around Ypres had virtually come to an end and Daisy had been away from home for almost nine months. She had the occasional letter to keep her up to date with family matters and everything seemed to be going along as usual, until the fateful day when a telegram arrived.

She had been about to drive to the station to transport wounded soldiers to the waiting troopship when a messenger pedalled into the courtyard on a rusty old bicycle. She stared at the telegram for several seconds before gathering up enough courage to open it. Her fingers trembled as she tore the envelope and the words danced before her eyes. Clarice took it gently from her. 'Oh, Daisy, I'm so sorry. You've talked so often and so fondly of your brother. I am terribly, terribly sorry.'

Daisy gulped and swallowed, but she was too stunned to cry. For months she had been expecting the worst but she had been lulled into a false sense of security when no news was good news. Now she must face what women all over Britain and the Empire had been facing for almost a year. She had lost someone very close to her.

'You must go home,' Clarice said gently. 'You're due for some leave anyway, Daisy. You must tell Boss and she'll let you go on compassionate grounds.'

'Yes,' Daisy said, dully. 'Yes, of course. I must go home.'

Rainbow's End was in deep mourning. The curtains were closed and it was a sad-faced Beatrice who opened the door. After a fond and tearful greeting, Daisy took off her hat and gloves and sat down at the kitchen table. It had been a long journey, starting the previous day when she boarded a troopship after a heated argument with the officer in charge who, despite her uniform, was adamant that women were not allowed to travel on a vessel commandeered by the army. In the end she was allowed on board but only if she promised to stay in the captain's cabin and not venture out on deck until they docked in Dover. There had been a long wait at the station and then the train journey to Victoria. She took a taxi to Liverpool Street, but even so it had taken all day to get to Nutley Green and she was overwrought and exhausted.

Beatrice eyed her warily. 'Are you all right, Daisy?'

'I'm just tired. I'd love a cup of tea.'

Beatrice went into the larder and came out with a

bottle of brandy. 'Purely medicinal,' she said with a wry smile as she poured two tots into tumblers. 'Sip this while I make the tea.' She busied herself at the range. 'You don't have to talk if you don't want to. I'll understand.'

Daisy took a sip of the brandy and felt its heat strike her stomach like a bolt from a crossbow. 'That's Father's Armagnac unless I'm very much mistaken.'

'You're absolutely correct,' Beatrice said with a rueful smile. 'Mrs Aitken from the village has a weakness for a drop of tiddley, so we don't put temptation in her way. She's a good cleaner, when she's sober. But I do miss Ruby, and her cooking. It's a pity that she had to go.'

Daisy choked on the brandy. 'Do you ever hear from her?'

Beatrice put the teapot on the table and sat down. 'Not a word. I'm sorry, Daisy. I know you were fond of her, but she hasn't been in contact.'

'She never answered any of my advertisements. I suppose the poor girl thinks we treated her very badly.' Daisy put the glass down. Drinking brandy on an empty stomach was making her feel light-headed, and she needed to keep her wits about her. 'You said that Mother has taken to her room. Doesn't she come downstairs at all?'

'Not since we received the telegram four days ago. We've had the doctor to her but he just advises rest and gives her something to make her sleep. He says he's seen it dozens of times and he expects that she'll rally. Maybe she will when she sees you.'

'I doubt it. I was never her favourite. It was always Teddy and then you. I always came a poor third.'

Beatrice reached out across the table to hold her hand. 'She doesn't mean half the things she says. It's just her way.' She smiled and set about pouring the tea. 'It's Father I'm worried about. He's taken Teddy's death very much to heart and he practically lives at the office these days.'

'But what about his assistant? Surely he could take over and give Father some time at home with Mother.'

Beatrice shook her head. 'I don't like Arley Meadows. I don't trust the blighter.'

'That doesn't sound like you, Bea.' Daisy stared at her in surprise. It seemed that in the relatively short time she had been away from home her sister had suddenly matured beyond her years. 'What's wrong with him?'

'He's a Uriah Heep,' Beatrice said, pulling a face. 'He pretends to be so nice and humble but I think he's cheating Father out of money, although I can't prove a thing.'

'What makes you say that?'

'I can't base it on anything other than the fact that money is so tight. I know that Father works really hard and has rebuilt the business, but he's always worried. He won't tell me anything, of course, because I'm just a girl and the baby of the family. Or that's what he thinks.'

'I can see that you're completely grown up,' Daisy said, smiling. 'You'll be getting married next. I can see it coming.'

Beatrice's fresh face flushed to the roots of her hair. 'I am, actually. Jimmy and I plan to be married before Christmas, but I daren't tell anyone. Not yet, anyway. It would seem heartless in the circumstances. Although, of course, I know I'm under age and will need Father's consent, but I'm sure he'll be sympathetic.' She paused with her cup halfway to her lips. 'And what about you and Rupert? Have you heard from him?'

'He writes occasionally, although they're just little notes really. I would hardly call them love letters. But then I've seen what it's like at the Front. It's terrible, Bea. Just too awful to describe. I can only hope and pray for him.'

Beatrice put her cup down and fumbled in her pocket for her hanky. 'It's the same for so many people, Daisy. Jed Smith was killed three months ago, and Iris is left alone to bring up her little boy. We don't know if it's Teddy's, but I'd like to think that there's something of him left to carry on. He's a beautiful baby. I quite often visit Iris and she lets me hold him. He has blue eyes just like Teddy's.'

Daisy could take no more. She rose to her feet. 'I'd better go upstairs and see Mother. Perhaps I can persuade her to come down for dinner.'

'Good luck with that,' Beatrice said grimly. 'Father promised to come home early, so let's hope he gets away from Arley's clutches.'

Daisy frowned. She only had a short home leave but she would put Arley on her list of things to do. Tomorrow she would walk to Pendleton Park and call upon Lady Pendleton, but perhaps she could borrow the Prince Henry and drive into Colchester afterwards. Maybe a surprise visit to her father's office would reveal exactly what Mr Meadows was up to.

'You look dreadful, Daisy,' Gwendoline said when Daisy walked into her bedroom. 'You're thin as a lath and your face is tanned like a farm labourer's. You obviously haven't been looking after yourself properly.'

Daisy would have laughed if she had not been so close to tears. She perched on the edge of the bed. 'I can see you're feeling a bit better, Mother.'

'My heart is broken, and I don't think I'll ever feel anything again after losing my dear boy. I hate this war and everything about it. I want it to end, and you must come home and look after us again. Your father is a shadow of his former self, and Beatrice spends most of her time at the farm. I'm afraid she'll make a dreadful mistake and marry that Jimmy Gurney. I'll never hold my head up again at one of dear Jane's soirees, if I have a daughter living in a hovel.'

'The Gurneys are a very respectable family, Mother. And I'd hardly describe the farmhouse as a hovel. It's twice the size of Rainbow's End.'

'Stop, you're giving me a headache.' Gwendoline clutched her forehead in a dramatic gesture. 'It's all too much for me.'

'We all need you, Mother. You're the one who keeps everything together.'

'Do you really think so?'

Daisy smiled. 'I know so, Mother. Now please, get up and get dressed so that we can have dinner as a family, and raise a glass to Teddy. That's what he would want, wouldn't he? He'd hate to see you laid so low.'

Gwendoline raised herself on her elbow. 'He would. Teddy always liked to see me dressed in my best with my hair done nicely, and just a touch of lip rouge. Not too much, of course.'

'Of course not.' Daisy rose to her feet and went to the wardrobe. She opened the door and riffled through the elegant gowns hanging inside. She selected her mother's favourite lilac tussore afternoon gown and laid it across the foot of the bed. 'No black for any of us, Mother. Teddy hated to see women wearing black. He said it made them look like crows.' She backed towards the door. 'I'll leave you now, but if you need any help just give me a call.'

Gwendoline sat up and swung her legs over the side of the bed. 'I really miss having my own maid. It's terrible being poor, Daisy. I do so hope that Rupert doesn't get killed before you have a chance to marry him. I don't want you ending up a sad old spinster living off the pittance that your father will be able to leave you.'

'I'm a modern woman, Mother,' Daisy said, trying desperately to be patient. 'If I don't marry I'll earn my own living. Anyway, we won't worry about that now. I'll see you downstairs.' She left the room before she said something that would burst the bubble in which her mother obviously still lived. Untouched by the real world, Gwendoline Lennox inhabited a dream-like place rooted in the last century when the old queen ruled a huge empire and no one questioned their position in the class structure. Daisy suspected that things would be quite different when the war finally came to an end.

She went downstairs to help Beatrice in the kitchen. She found her deep in conversation with Donovan, the head groom from Pendleton Park. They stopped talking when she entered the room and Beatrice rushed over to her waving a piece of paper. 'Darling Daisy. There's a note from Lady Pendleton. She's got the most marvellous surprise for you.'

Chapter Seventeen

Daisy opened the envelope. It was hard to imagine what Lady Pendleton could have to say that would make any difference to the terrible sense of loss that hung in a dark cloud over Rainbow's End. Nothing, other than time itself, could ease the suffering caused by Teddy's death. She unfolded the sheet of expensive hand-crafted writing paper with its embossed family crest, and scanned its contents.

'Well, what does it say?' Beatrice tugged at her sleeve. 'We could do with some good news.'

'Rupert is in London,' Daisy said dully. 'Lady Pendleton wants me to travel up to town with her tomorrow morning. But it's impossible.'

Beatrice shooed Donovan out of the kitchen with a murmured excuse. She came flying back and grasped Daisy by the shoulders, giving her a good shake. 'Stop behaving like an idiot. Moping around here won't bring Teddy back; nothing will. He's gone, bless him, and he's hopefully in a better place, but life has to go on. He loved Rupert. They were best friends all through school and university, so you must go with Lady Pendleton tomorrow. You simply must.'

Daisy stared at her in astonishment. Where was scatterbrained, spoilt Beatrice who lived for the moment?

This forceful young woman with flashing eyes and a determined tilt of her chin was a virtual stranger. 'You think so?'

'I do indeed.' Beatrice gave her a hug. 'Things have changed, Daisy. Nothing is the same as it was before the war, and we can all take care of ourselves, even Mother. Although of course she pretends to be helpless and a victim of circumstances, but beneath the silk and lace there beats a heart of pure steel.' She kissed Daisy's cheek. 'Now sit down and write a note to Lady Pendleton saying that you'll be delighted to go up to London to see your fiancé.' She moved swiftly to the dresser and took a pen and a bottle of ink from the drawer. 'Write it on the bottom of her letter; she won't mind. After all, there is a war on and we must save paper.'

Daisy sat down at the table and penned a few lines.

'That's right,' Beatrice said, nodding with approval. 'But where's your engagement ring? I've only just noticed that you're not wearing it.'

Daisy tweaked the gold chain which hung round her neck and pulled it so that the ring dangled between her fingers. 'I've worn it round my neck for safe keeping.'

Beatrice frowned. 'Your hands are in a worse state than Mother Gurney's, but you'd better wear the ring tomorrow or Rupert will think you don't love him any more.'

'Of course,' Daisy murmured. 'I wouldn't want to upset him.' She unhooked the chain and slipped the ring on her finger. 'Are you satisfied now, miss?'

'It's not me you have to please, Daisy Lennox.' Beatrice seized the letter and blew on the ink until it dried. She folded it and slipped it back into the envelope. 'I'll give this to Donovan, and you can help me by peeling a few potatoes for dinner.' She hurried off without giving Daisy a chance to argue.

Lady Pendleton was in a high state of excitement as they sat in the back of the Rolls with Parkin in the driver's seat.

'It's such a wonderful coincidence that Rupert has leave at the same time as you, Daisy dear.'

'Yes, ma'am. It's quite amazing.'

Lady Pendleton turned her head to give Daisy a quizzical look. 'You do look very thin and pale. Are you quite well? You must have endured so much in France.'

'I'm fine,' Daisy said stoutly. 'Just a bit tired after the journey, but otherwise I'm quite well.'

'You must tell me all about it. I lead such a sheltered existence that sometimes I feel quite guilty, although I suppose we all have our part to play in the grand scheme of things. I myself am on several fundraising committees.'

'I'm sure that's a great help,' Daisy said dutifully.

'I hope so indeed.' Lady Pendleton relaxed against the soft leather upholstery, folding her gloved hands in her lap. 'We send knitted garments to the troops and organise raffles. I also assist as much as I am able in encouraging young, able-bodied men to enlist in the army, but Henry fears that conscription might become law if there aren't enough volunteers.' She frowned, shaking her head. 'I abhor the practice of sending white feathers to men who for reasons of their own do not enlist, or have not yet plucked up the courage to do so. In my opinion it's a cruel and rather cowardly act. It inflicts pain and humiliation without giving the person concerned the opportunity to explain why they don't choose to defend their country.'

'I agree,' Daisy said earnestly. 'No one can have any idea what it's like in Flanders unless they've seen the battlefields and the utter destruction of farms and villages for themselves.' She stared out at the green hedgerows in their full summer glory and the ripening corn studded with poppies, cornflowers and moon daisies. The flat Essex countryside looked so peaceful and serene that the war seemed a million miles away. She shot a sideways glance at Lady Pendleton's calm countenance and wondered what her future mother-in-law would say if she knew about her feelings for Bowman. Not for the first time Daisy suffered the agony of guilt. She was not worthy of Rupert. He deserved better.

They arrived in Grosvenor Square at midday and found Rupert waiting for them, but the young army officer who came to greet them was a shadow of the man whom Daisy had known for most of her life. Thin, gaunt and deeply tanned, Rupert said all the right things, but his manner although welcoming was slightly aloof, and there were deep lines radiating from the corners of his mouth. He seemed tense, and although he was obviously trying hard to be sociable Daisy could tell that his thoughts were elsewhere. Pain was etched in his eyes, as though he had witnessed more suffering than was good for any man, and his haunted expression hinted at ghastly sights that he could not put from his mind.

He kissed his mother and then Daisy, but his lips were cold and he might as well have been greeting a maiden aunt for all the passion there was in his embrace. Daisy was at a loss to know how to treat him. She had been genuinely pleased to see him, but now she felt as though she was speaking to a stranger. A glance at his mother's face revealed that Lady Pendleton felt similarly baffled by her son's detached manner.

Luncheon was served in the grand dining room but conversation was stilted, and Lady Pendleton's attempts to coax Rupert to open up failed miserably. Daisy ate very little although the chef had excelled himself and there was little sign of food shortages in the Pendleton household. Rupert consumed everything on his plate but Daisy could see that he was hardly aware of the delicious morsels created to tempt a jaded appetite. He answered his mother's questions with monosyllables and drank rather too much wine with each course. Daisy was relieved when at last the meal was over and Lady Pendleton suggested that they might like to take coffee in the Japanese saloon.

Rupert rose to his feet. 'If you'll excuse me, Mother, I would really like to get some fresh air. I find it quite stifling in London. It's never been my favourite place in the summer.'

Lady Pendleton managed a tight little smile, nodding her head. 'Of course, I understand. Perhaps Daisy would like to accompany you. Green Park is quite lovely at this time of the year.'

'A turn around the gardens in the square will suit me well enough, Mother.' Rupert glanced at Daisy. 'Would you?'

She knew that she must face him alone at some stage, and she stood up. 'Yes, that would be lovely. I'll just get my hat and gloves.'

In the quiet of her bedroom, the one she had always occupied when staying in Grosvenor Square, Daisy checked her appearance in the cheval mirror, adjusting her hat so that it perched on top of her hair, which Beatrice had put up for her earlier that morning. She felt slightly uncomfortable in a silk gown that was at least a size too large for her and had to be cinched in at the waist with a cummerbund, and her tanned face looked oddly out of place beneath a wide-brimmed hat trimmed with flowers and ostrich feathers. Perhaps Rupert found her too much changed now, and unattractive. The war had altered both of them. Rupert's boyish charm was gone, perhaps forever, and he seemed like a stranger. She left the sanctity of her room to join him in the vestibule.

He proffered his arm. 'I won't keep you out too long, Daisy. I expect you're still rather tired after all the travelling you've done.'

She was inexplicably touched by this sudden show of consideration, and she felt tears stinging the backs of her eyes. She swallowed hard, forcing herself to smile. 'I'm tougher than I look, Rupert.'

Sedgwick, the Pendletons' butler in Grosvenor Square, hobbled forward to open the heavy double doors and Rupert thanked him with a warmth that had been lacking when addressing his mother or Daisy. 'How are the rheumatics, Sedgwick? Not troubling you too much, I hope.'

'Not too bad, sir. I'm always better in the warm weather.' Sedgwick returned his smile with the indulgence of a much older man speaking to a favoured child. 'It's good to have you home again, sir.'

'It's good to be home, Sedgwick.' Rupert put on his peaked cap and stepped out into the sunshine with Daisy on his arm. They descended the steps and crossed the road to enter the gated garden, which seemed to slumber in the hazy afternoon heat. There were a few nannies pushing their charges in their coach-built prams, and some more elderly residents seated on benches in the shade of the London plane trees. It was cool and green and peaceful with the smell of newly mown grass filling the warm air and birdsong wafting on a gentle breeze. They walked in silence for a while. There was so much that Daisy wanted to say, but she could not find the words to express her feelings.

'I'm afraid I'm not much company,' Rupert said at length. 'Can't quite get used to being back in London where nothing much seems to have changed.'

'I know what you mean,' Daisy said softly. 'I feel the same.'

He stopped and for the first time he looked her in the eyes. 'Do you really?'

'Yes, I do. No one here can imagine what life is like across the Channel, or the true suffering of the men in the trenches.'

He dashed his hand across his eyes. 'It's hell. Sometimes I think I'm a coward because I can't stand the mindless carnage and loss of life. It all seems so bloody pointless.'

She squeezed his hand. 'I know, and you're not a coward. I won't let you say that about yourself.'

He snatched his hand away and she noticed that it shook as he took a silver cigarette case from his pocket. 'Do you mind if I smoke?'

'Of course not, but that's something you never did before.'

'Almost everyone does over there. It helps to calm the nerves, or so I'm told.' He took a cigarette and held it between his lips while he attempted to strike a match, but his hands trembled so much that it went out and he threw it down with an exclamation of annoyance. Daisy peeled off her gloves and tucked them into her pocket, and taking the matches from him she struck one and lit his cigarette. He inhaled deeply before exhaling a stream of blue smoke into the foliage above them. 'Thanks.'

She dropped the dead match onto the dried earth beneath the tree. 'You're the one who needs to rest, Rupert. I've never seen you like this.'

He sucked smoke into his lungs, shaking his head. 'I'm not fit company for anyone just now. I think I'd like to go on alone, if you don't mind.'

'But I do mind. Why won't you talk to me? I've seen something of what you must have endured in the trenches. I understand how you must be feeling.'

He turned his head to give her a stony stare. 'No you don't. Nobody does, least of all a woman. I don't want to hurt you, Daisy, but I'm not the man I was. I don't think I'll ever be that person again. Leave me before I ruin your life.' He walked off, leaving a trail of smoke in his wake.

Daisy stood still, hardly daring to breathe. This was not how she had imagined their meeting, and she could not simply allow him to walk away. She experienced the sudden need to bring everything out into the open, including her own fall from grace. She ran after him, clutching at his sleeve. 'Wait a moment. What are you saying, Rupert?'

He came to a halt, staring straight ahead and avoiding her gaze. 'Isn't it obvious? I've changed, Daisy. You don't want to tie yourself for life to a man who can't hold a cup without spilling it down himself; a man who cries in his sleep like a baby.'

She touched his cheek with the tips of her fingers and her eyes filled with tears. 'I'm so sorry, Rupert. I don't know what to say.'

He removed her hand gently, staring down at the diamond ring as it sparkled in the sunlight. 'Release me from our engagement, Daisy. I doubt if I'll survive much longer anyway, and you'd be a widow almost before you were a wife. The chances are that very soon I'll be joining Teddy in heaven or hell, wherever the poor chap is now.'

'Don't say things like that,' Daisy cried, choking on a sob.

'I'll instruct my solicitor to settle an annuity on you so that you'll be independent for the rest of your life, but let me go with as good a heart as you can, and forgive me.'

Blinded by tears, she tugged at the ring and thrust it into his palm, closing his fingers around it. 'I do release you from your promise if that's what you want, but please allow me to help you. I've seen men suffering as you are now, and you shouldn't go back to the Front. There are places . . .'

'You mean a convalescent home or a mental institution. They're for cowards who want to get away from the fighting. I've risen to the rank of major and I'm not going to disgrace my family name by taking the easy way out.' He strode off and she ran after him, causing heads to turn but she did not care. She could not bear to see him in such a distressed state.

'Wait, please. Don't walk away from me. You would never be called a coward, Rupert.'

He quickened his pace. 'Go away, Daisy. Leave me in peace.'

She caught up with him at the gate, barring his way. 'Where are you going?'

'To my club and I'll dine there this evening. I'm leaving for Dover tomorrow, and I don't want a lot of fuss.' A fleeting smile softened his harsh features and he bent over to brush her lips with a kiss. 'This is goodbye, Daisy Bell.' He lifted her aside bodily and let himself out of the garden.

She stood for a moment frozen to the spot. Nothing had prepared her for this. Despite the summer heat she was chilled to the bone and shivering. She watched him until he was out of sight, heading for his club in Pall Mall. She felt bereft and desperately sad. Perhaps he had sensed that she had reservations about their marriage? If so she was sending him off to war in the cruellest possible way, and it shocked her to realise how much he really meant to her. She had lost someone who was more than a lover: he was her lifelong friend.

She stood very still, as if frozen to the spot, but she could not face returning to the house and the inevitable interrogation by Lady Pendleton. She had no notion what she would say, or how she would explain Rupert's behaviour to his mother. She spotted an empty seat on the far side of the garden and eventually gathered enough energy to make her way there. She sat down, staring into space, barely noticing the gradual disappearance of the nannies with their young charges, followed eventually by the elderly ladies and gentlemen, who were no doubt returning to their comfortable homes for afternoon tea or to take a nap before changing for dinner.

Sparrows pecked in the dust around her feet and pigeons waddled about on the grass seeking out the odd worm and insect. Eventually, when a robin landed on the bench at her side, cocking its head and staring at her as if silently asking her why she was still here, she came to her senses and rose to her feet. The small bird flew up into a tree to perch on an overhanging branch and it seemed to wink at her. Its cheeky stance brought a reluctant smile to her face. She was shocked and saddened, but life would go on. Her heart ached for Rupert and she wished that there was something she could do to help him, but she knew him only too well. The Pendletons had a stubborn streak and once he had made up his mind there was only a slim chance that he might have a change of heart.

She made her way slowly back to Pendleton House. Sedgwick opened the door and she could tell by the expression on his lined face that he had already guessed the truth. He had known Rupert since the day he was born and had watched him grow to manhood. There was little or nothing that happened in the Pendleton household that escaped Sedgwick's shrewd eye, and Daisy felt that here at least she had an ally. 'Mr Rupert will be dining at his club this evening, Sedgwick,' she said softly.

His gaze never wavered from her face, but he inclined his head slightly. 'Exactly so, Miss Lennox. Lady Pendleton is in the drawing room if you would care to join her. I'll instruct Betsy to bring a fresh pot of tea.'

'Thank you, Sedgwick. I'll go to my room first, but I'll be down shortly.'

Dinner that evening was a sombre affair. Lady Pendleton was visibly upset by her son's absence and she confessed to being worried about him. Daisy tried to reassure her but even to her own ears her words sounded hollow. They took coffee in the drawing room but it was obvious that Lady Pendleton's thoughts were elsewhere and she excused herself early, saying that she had some letters to write. Daisy was left in solitary state amongst the priceless antiques and elegant furnishings, but she felt uncomfortable and out of place. This was not a home, it was a mausoleum filled with precious artefacts but it had no soul. It was little wonder that Rupert felt more at ease in a gentlemen's club than in his parents' town house. She found herself wishing that she was back in Rainbow's End. The old building might be in danger of tumbling down and it boasted none of the modern amenities, but its welcoming atmosphere always wrapped itself around her like a warm hug. Daisy felt suddenly homesick. The only possible course open to her was to return to Nutley Green on the first available train next morning. She went to bed early but sleep evaded her. She could only think of Rupert and worry about him. He was in desperate need of help, but there was nothing she could do to heal wounds that were mental rather than physical. She fell asleep just as dawn was breaking and was awakened some time later by Betsy, who brought her a cup of tea and offered to run her bath.

At breakfast, when Daisy asked if Parkin might drive her to Liverpool Street station, Lady Pendleton begged her to stay for another day at least. 'It's bad enough that Rupert has such a short leave. I've no idea why he stayed away last night,' she said, giving Daisy a searching glance. 'There's nothing wrong between you, is there, my dear?' Her gaze alighted on Daisy's left hand and her eyes widened with concern. 'Where is your ring?'

Daisy's hand went automatically to the gold chain which she still wore around her neck. 'I've grown used to wearing it close to my heart. I can't wear jewellery of any sort when I'm on duty.'

Lady Pendleton breathed a sigh of relief. 'I thought for one dreadful moment that you had broken off your engagement. You wouldn't desert Rupert now, would you, Daisy?'

'Of course not, ma'am.' Daisy prayed that she would be forgiven for the lie, but she did not want to add to Lady Pendleton's worries for her son's wellbeing.

'I just can't understand why Rupert dined at his club on his last evening at home.' Lady Pendleton buttered a slice of toast, leaving it on her plate untasted. 'It's so unlike him. He seemed so preoccupied, and I don't think he looked in the best of health. I thought he would have a few days with us at least, but it was almost as if he couldn't wait to go back to his unit. What do you think, Daisy?'

'I think he's a very brave man,' Daisy said truthfully. 'He has to do what he thinks best.'

Lady Pendleton's lips curved in a smile. 'You're right, of course. It's just that one never ceases to be concerned for one's children, even if they are grown up.' She picked up the slice of toast and nibbled at a corner before putting it down again. 'But you will stay on for a day or so, won't you?'

'I'd like to of course, but I really ought to go home and see my family.'

'Yes, I understand, but I do so enjoy young company. Why don't you go shopping this morning? You can purchase anything you like and charge it to my account. I want to spoil my future daughter-in-law.'

'That's very kind of you,' Daisy murmured. She was trapped and she knew it. She longed to make a clean breast of things but she knew that the truth would hurt Lady Pendleton, and she could not bear to see her suffer. It was cowardly, but Daisy was in full retreat and she made her escape as soon as possible.

Despite her pressing need to return home, Daisy spent a surprisingly pleasant morning exploring the department stores in Oxford Street. She had almost forgotten what it was like to see shops filled with luxury items and to see people who were well dressed and well nourished. It was like being in another world, and putting the past resolutely behind her, for a morning at least, she decided to enjoy her brief taste of freedom.

She bought a pair of kid gloves and a small bottle of her mother's favourite perfume, but she paid with her own money. She had no intention of taking up Lady Pendleton's generous offer; it would seem like stealing. By lunch time she was footsore and hungry, and as she had spent most of her money she made her way to the relatively new and reasonably priced Lyons Corner House in Coventry Street. She had often visited it with Beatrice when it first opened and had been impressed by the grandeur of the building and the different types of restaurants, all with their own unique style. She chose the brasserie and was shown to a table by the window. It was a relief to sit down and she was studying the menu, trying to decide between a ham salad and a dish of macaroni cheese, when a uniformed waitress approached her table. 'May I help you, miss?'

The menu fell from Daisy's nerveless fingers. She leapt to her feet and threw her arms around the young woman, causing the other diners to gasp in amazement.

'Ruby, I can't believe it's really you.' Laughing and crying at the same time, Daisy hugged her as if she would never let her go. 'I've been searching for you ever since you left us.'

Ruby pushed her away gently. 'Please don't. Everyone's looking and I'll get the sack if the restaurant manager spots me hobnobbing with the customers.'

Daisy released her instantly and sat down. 'I'm sorry. I was just so surprised and pleased to see you.'

Ruby glanced nervously over her shoulder. 'Would you like to order now, miss?'

'We must talk,' Daisy said firmly. 'When do you finish your shift?'

'Three o'clock. Now for God's sake give me your order. I can feel the manager's eyes boring into my back.'

Daisy felt a bubble of hysterical laughter rising in her chest but she managed to suppress it somehow. 'I'll have a ham salad, please, and a roll and butter.'

'Would you like anything to drink, miss?'

'Water, please.' Daisy handed her the menu. 'You look awfully tired, Ruby. I hope they're not working you too hard.'

'Your lunch will be with you in a jiffy, miss.' Ruby scuttled off towards the service door, leaving Daisy in a state of confusion and exhilaration. She drummed her fingers on the starched white tablecloth as she waited for Ruby to return with her order. It was not that she was hungry, her appetite had quite deserted her, but she was determined to pin Ruby down to a meeting.

She waited outside the staff entrance for more than an hour, pacing the pavement in a state of nervous anticipation. It had been impossible to have a conversation with Ruby in the restaurant but now Daisy was hoping for an answer to the riddle of Ruby's disappearance which had been bothering her for over a year. Her patience was rewarded at last when Ruby emerged into the street. This time the hugging was mutual and Ruby's eyes were wet with tears as they drew apart. 'I was sorry to leave without seeing you, miss.'

Daisy shook her finger at her. 'If you call me miss once again I'll throttle you, Ruby Flagg.'

Ruby's small features creased into a wide grin. 'You and whose army?'

They collapsed against each other, giggling like schoolgirls. Daisy was the first to recover. 'I want to know everything. Why didn't you answer my advertisements in the newspapers?'

'I had my reasons.'

'But you were in the family way. I know that's why Mother sacked you, which was terribly wrong of her. Bea and I came up to London looking for you. We couldn't find your father and we went to see your sister but she wasn't very helpful.'

'Don't tell me,' Ruby said, pulling a face. 'Our Nellie didn't want to know either.'

'That's right. Where did you go and how did you manage?'

'Look, Daisy, it's not that I don't want to chat about old times, but I've got a bus to catch. I got to get home.'

'Then I'm coming with you. You won't run away from me this time.'

'All right, but where I live isn't the sort of place that you'd normally go to.'

A vivid memory of the mud and filth of the Ypres battlefield and the appalling conditions when they first entered Lamarck flashed through Daisy's mind. 'You'd be surprised,' she said mildly. 'Come on then. Let's go.'

Chapter Eighteen

The bus journey to Liverpool Street station took longer than Daisy had expected, but it was a relatively short walk past the railway sidings to Skinner Street, a narrow road lined with run-down tenements and warehouses. Daisy refrained from comment, but conversation would have been almost impossible against a background of noise from shunting engines, train whistles and great gusts of steam billowing from the iron monsters on the tracks. The smell of hot cinders and coal dust mixed oddly with the aroma of roasting coffee beans from a factory nearby. Ruby stopped outside a tall building. Its broken windows were stuffed with newspaper and the blistered paint was peeling off the front door, which did not appear to be locked. Ruby opened it and stepped inside.

'I warned you,' she said darkly. 'This ain't the sort of place you're used to.'

'Are you going to let me in, or aren't you?' Stepping over the threshold Daisy felt her gorge rise at the mix of noxious smells. The odour of rancid cooking fat was mixed with the stench wafting from an overflowing outdoor lavatory and a faint hint of rodent droppings. The floorboards were bare of any form of covering and the banisters had supports missing. With some misgivings she followed Ruby up to the third floor. Most of the doors leading off the landing were closed, but those that were open revealed scenes of such squalor that Daisy was tempted to retreat downstairs and hail the first taxi that came her way. She steeled herself for what was to come.

Ruby opened a door at the end of the passage and they were met by the loud wailing of a baby. Ruby crossed the floor in giant strides to snatch her child from the arms of an unkempt woman, who was slouched in a chair by the window with a cigarette dangling from the corner of her mouth.

'Why is he crying?' Ruby demanded fiercely. 'What have you done to him, Gert?'

'He's a bad-tempered little bugger, that's what he is,' Gert said, rising to her feet. 'I dunno what's wrong with him, but he's been a misery all day. Driven me crazy, he has. I've had enough.'

Ruby held her son tightly, rocking him and rubbing her cheek against his dark hair. 'If I find as much as the smallest bruise on him I'll have your guts for garters.'

Gert spat the soggy cigarette end onto the floor. She pushed her face close to Ruby's. 'Ungrateful cow. That's the last time I look after his nibs. You can find some other juggins to look after the brat from now on.' She stomped out of the room, her large bulk swaying as she walked. She slammed the door behind her causing the sash windows to rattle, and the baby to howl even louder.

Daisy looked round the room with a sinking heart.

So this was where Ruby had come to hide the shame of giving birth to an illegitimate child. A single bed occupied one wall and a china chamber pot was stowed beneath a rickety table with a broken leg propped up on a brick. From the overpowering smell of urine Daisy could only suppose that Gert had availed herself of the facilities. A small pine table was placed beneath the window with two mismatched wooden chairs, and the only other piece of furniture was a chest of drawers on top of which was a gas ring, a kettle, and an enamel wash bowl.

The baby had quietened as Ruby continued to soothe him gently. 'It's not much of a place,' she said defensively. 'But it's clean and it's cheap.'

Daisy swallowed hard. 'I can see that you've kept it nice, Ruby.' She moved towards the window, looking out through the grimy panes at the shunting yard below. 'Why didn't you get in touch? I could have helped you.'

'I was carrying his baby. You fancied him too, whether you care to admit it or not.'

It was no use pretending otherwise. Daisy could not look her in the eyes and deny the emotions that had caused her so much heartache and soul-searching, and still did if she were to be completely honest. 'You're right, of course,' she murmured. 'I'm not proud of myself, but like you I suppose I just can't help it.'

'Can't?' Ruby said suspiciously. 'You sound as though it's still going on. Are you seeing him again?'

Daisy turned slowly to face her. 'Not exactly. I'll tell you about it, but first see to your baby. Poor little fellow, he seems to have had a bad day.' She moved closer, drawn by the instinctive need to look at Bowman's son. 'How old is he, and what's his name?'

'His name is Martin,' Ruby said, glaring at her. 'What's the matter? Do you think that's too grand a name for a little bastard, or did you think I'd name him after Barnaby? Well, I wouldn't saddle my kid with the sins of his father. My boy is Martin Flagg and he's seven months old. As far as I'm concerned Bowman is dead.'

'But you loved him, didn't you?'

'I dunno. I wouldn't call it love exactly and he never pretended that he loved me, but he made me feel special and I couldn't say no. Does that make me a tart? Maybe it does, but I've paid for my mistake.'

'I am so sorry, Ruby. But you have a beautiful baby boy. May I hold him?'

Ruby's grim expression melted into a smile. 'Of course, but he whiffs a bit. Maybe you'd best wait until I've changed him.'

'I'm sure I've smelt worse than that,' Daisy said, chuckling. 'I've looked after soldiers with dysentery and typhoid. I don't think that Martin's number twos would bother me.'

'Why don't you put the kettle on?' Ruby said, laying Martin on the bed as she prepared to change him. 'I could do with a cup of tea. There should be water in the jug, but if not I'm afraid you'll have to go downstairs. There's a cold water tap in the back kitchen.'

Luckily the kettle was full which saved Daisy a trip to the nether regions of the building. She lit the gas and put the kettle on the ring. 'You can't stay here,' she said firmly. 'This is a dreadful place and you're obviously working yourself to the bone.'

Ruby kept her head down, concentrating on the task in hand. 'I don't mind being a Gladys. The pay isn't marvellous but I get quite a lot of tips.'

'A Gladys?' Daisy stared at her in amazement. 'I thought you were a waitress.'

'I am. A Gladys is what they call us girls who wait on table at Lyons Corner House. I don't know where it came from, but there it is.'

'Well, you can't keep this up, and that foul woman shouldn't be left in charge of a dog let alone a baby.'

'I know, and I agree with you. I'm not letting her near Martin again.'

'So how will you manage?'

Ruby fastened the scraps of towelling with a safety pin, and lifted Martin to a sitting position. 'I'll be glad when I don't have to do this any more,' she said, pulling a face. 'It'll be so much easier when he can use the lavvy.'

'It must be so difficult for you to manage on your own,' Daisy said sympathetically.

'I can't imagine what my life would be like without him now.' Ruby dropped a kiss on Martin's head. 'I love him so much, Daisy. I'd do anything for my boy.'

'Then you must put him first. Forget everything that went on before and come home with me.'

Ruby's eyes widened in surprise. 'What? Go back to Rainbow's End? Your mother wouldn't like that.'

'Things are different now,' Daisy said, choking back a sob. 'Teddy was killed at Ypres.'

'I'm so sorry.' Ruby's eyes filled with tears. 'I had a lot of time for Mr Teddy. He used to pull my leg about being a skivvy, but I knew he didn't really mean it. Why do the good 'uns have to die and the bastards live on? I suppose you'll tell me next that Bowman is alive and well.' The baby had begun to grizzle and she undid the buttons of her blouse, putting him to her breast.

Daisy was saved from answering as the kettle had started to bubble and she set about making the tea. There was no milk but she poured the brew into two cups and added a little sugar. She set one down on a stool beside Ruby. 'I'll tell you about it sometime, but not now. We've got more important things to discuss.' She gazed round the sparsely furnished room. 'This isn't for you, Ruby. Come home with me tomorrow and I can guarantee that Mother will welcome you with open arms.'

Ruby reached for her cup and took a sip of tea. 'And what if she don't? It's one thing for me to turn up on me own, but I've got Martin to think of. Mrs Lennox wouldn't have him in the house and I'm not being separated from my baby.'

'I think you're underestimating the situation at Rainbow's End,' Daisy said gently. 'Beatrice is going to marry Jimmy Gurney and I'm only on compassionate leave. I've got to return to France very soon. Mother doesn't know one end of a saucepan from another, and it's hard to get staff these days. The village girls can earn good money working in factories, and they simply don't want to go into service. Lady

Pendleton told me that herself. They're even having difficulty with hiring servants at the big house. So you see, Ruby, we really do need you.'

'Are you sure of that?'

'I'm absolutely certain. Please come with me, Ruby. I'm leaving early tomorrow morning. Just say the word and I'll meet you on the station platform.'

Ruby put her head on one side, frowning thoughtfully. 'I suppose it would be better for my boy to be brought up in the country. But everyone in the village would know he was Barnaby's kid.'

'Not necessarily, and I don't think any of us will see Bowman again.'

'You mean he might not come back from the war?'

'I think I'd better tell you everything, and then you can decide for yourself.'

Exhausted both emotionally and physically, Daisy took a taxi back to Grosvenor Square. It was extravagant and took almost all the money she had left, but she could not face travelling on public transport, and she needed to see Rupert before she returned to the country. There were things that had been left unsaid and she did not want to send him back to the Front thinking that she cared so little for him. Her talk with Ruby had put everything into perspective. They had both been snared by similar emotions and allowed themselves to be charmed by a man who thought only of himself. She had to find Rupert and tell him that she refused to break off their engagement, and that she would wait for him no matter how long the wretched war went on.

She paid the cabby and ran up the steps to the front entrance, hammering on the knocker as if her life depended upon it. Sedgwick answered her urgent summons at his own measured pace. She brushed past him. 'Is Mr Rupert at home?'

He closed the door. 'I'm sorry, Miss Lennox. Mr Rupert left for the station over an hour ago.'

She had been rehearsing what she would say to Rupert during the taxi ride from Liverpool Street, and now the force of Sedgwick's casual pronouncement hit her like a shower of ice-cold water. It was all her fault. She had allowed Rupert to walk away without putting up a fight. She had been so caught up in her own self-centred world that she had failed to give him comfort when he needed it most. She had seen many men suffering from shell shock, but she had not recognised the signs in the man she had promised to marry. It was only now that she fully comprehended the desperation he must have been feeling, and now he was on his way back to the hell of the battlefield.

She realised dimly that Sedgwick was speaking to her but she had not understood a word that he said. She met his gaze and was both shocked and surprised to see sympathy in his pale grey eyes. 'I'm sorry, Sedgwick. What did you say?'

'Her ladyship is in the drawing room, Miss Lennox. She said that she would like you to join her there as soon as you returned.'

'Yes, of course. Thank you, Sedgwick.' Daisy made her way upstairs to her room. She tossed her packages onto the bed and peeled off her gloves before taking a seat at her dressing table and unpinning her hat. She studied her reflection, shaking her head. The thin-faced woman with dark shadows beneath her eyes was almost a stranger to her. No wonder Rupert had been so aloof and had found it easy to break off their engagement. 'You're a fool,' she told herself severely. 'You didn't appreciate what you had until you lost it. You deserve to end up a withered old spinster with no one to love you.' She put a dab of powder on her nose and added a touch of rouge to her cheeks. She must present a positive face to the world, and she must not upset Lady Pendleton by blurting out the true account of what had passed between her and Rupert. She must keep up the pretence that all was well in order to save the feelings of those left at home. Soon she too would be returning to war-torn France and then she would be nearer Rupert in spirit if not in body. Her heart ached for his suffering and she knew that she would never forgive herself if he were to die thinking that she cared nothing for him. She changed into the afternoon gown that Betsy had laid out for her and made her way downstairs to face Rupert's mother.

Next morning Daisy was up early and had just finished breakfast when Lady Pendleton joined her in the dining room. She looked pale and strained but she managed a weary smile. 'I simply couldn't let you go without saying goodbye, my dear. I'll be staying in London for a while longer, and I might not see you before you have to return to France. You know my feelings on that score, I think.'

Daisy swallowed a mouthful of coffee, nodding her head. 'Yes, indeed, but I have to do my duty, just as Rupert has to do his.'

'And what if you are killed? You are to be the mother of my grandchildren, and I can never approve of you risking your life in this way. No wonder Rupert was upset. I can't help blaming you a little for his behaviour while he was at home, and to tell the truth I think you let him down. The poor boy obviously needed a shoulder to cry on, and it was not his mother he wanted.'

'You can't blame me any more than I blame myself,' Daisy said sadly. 'I know I let him down, but this war does dreadful things to people. I was at a loss too.'

Lady Pendleton plucked a handkerchief from the dolly bag hanging from her wrist and dabbed her eyes. 'Yes, I know. I'm probably being unfair to you.' She replaced the hanky and took out a purse, handing it to Daisy. 'This will cover your fare home, although I would be much happier if you allowed Parkin to drive you there in the Rolls. I don't like to think of you travelling unchaperoned.'

'I'll be quite all right, Lady Pendleton. You mustn't worry.' Daisy held the purse in her hand. She could tell by its weight that it was a generous amount and she would have liked to refuse, but she had the added expense of buying a ticket for Ruby as well as herself. 'Thank you. You're very generous.'

Lady Pendleton poured coffee into her cup. 'Not at all. God willing, you'll soon be part of the family. What train are you proposing to catch?'

* * *

The taxi seemed to take an interminable time to reach Liverpool Street station. The mixture of horse-drawn and motorised traffic caused chaos on the roads. Drays, costermongers' barrows, hansom cabs, motorbuses and cars all vied for precedence in the narrow city streets. Daisy fretted and fumed at the delays, but her main worry was that Ruby might think she was not coming. Perhaps she had had second thoughts and had decided to go back to work as a Gladys, leaving her son with some other totally unsuitable person. Daisy's palms were damp with sweat by the time they drew up outside the station. She paid the cabby, adding a generous tip as he leapt out and hailed a porter to carry her suitcases, and she hurried to the ticket office to buy two first class singles to Colchester.

The porter carried her luggage to the platform and found her an empty compartment. He climbed inside and hefted the bags onto the luggage rack. She pressed a tip into his hand and he saluted her with a cheery grin before heading off to assist another traveller with her baggage. Daisy stood by the open door, praying silently that Ruby had not had a change of heart. Passengers were boarding and carriage doors slammed along the length of the train. The guard stood poised with his whistle and his green flag and Daisy was about to give up when she saw Ruby racing along the platform with her son clutched in her arms. The same porter who had helped Daisy was hurrying along at her side with a carpet bag in his hand. Daisy thrust Ruby into the compartment and leapt in after her. The train had started to glide along the track and the porter tossed Ruby's baggage and slammed the door.

'I thought you weren't coming,' Daisy gasped. 'Let me hold Martin while you see to your luggage.' She sat down carefully, hugging the sleepy child.

'I almost didn't,' Ruby said, breathing hard as she hefted her carpet bag onto the rack. 'Then I had a bit of a to-do with my landlord who thought I was running off without paying the rent. He took me last penny, the old devil. Now I'm stony broke.' She held her arms out for her son, who had fallen asleep with his head on Daisy's shoulder.

'I'll see that Mother pays you a week in advance,' Daisy said, leaning back in the seat with a sigh of relief. 'Don't worry about a thing, Ruby. You're coming home and everything will be all right.'

'No, no, no!' Gwendoline cried, clapping her hand to her forehead. 'Daisy, I won't have that slut and her illegitimate offspring in my house.'

Daisy closed the drawing room door hastily. She had left Ruby and Martin in the kitchen with Beatrice and she could only hope that her mother's shriek of horror had not penetrated that far. 'Mother, this is Ruby we're talking about. She's had a bit of bad luck, that's all, and she needs a home and you need help in the house and someone who can cook. Ruby does all those things, and you won't notice the baby.'

'That's not the point and you know it. I can't be seen to condone her immoral behaviour. What would the vicar say?'

'Isn't that a bit unfair, considering that Teddy might well be the father of Iris's child?'

Gwendoline clasped her hands to her bosom. 'That's another matter, and it might be untrue.'

'But Teddy was having a relationship with Iris, Mother. We all knew and I suspect that you did too, and yet you did nothing to put an end to it.'

'There's one rule for men and another for women. Iris was a slut too and I don't want anything to do with her.'

'But it's unfair to blame the children for the sins of their fathers; surely that's what the vicar would say?'

'Perhaps, but that doesn't mean that I have to put a roof over the head of the girl who slept with our handyman and bore his illegitimate offspring. Send them packing, Daisy.'

'No, I won't. You need her as much as she needs you. I've only got a few days' leave left and then I'll be gone. Bea is going to marry Jimmy whether you like it or not, and there simply aren't the girls wanting to go into service nowadays. The world is changing, Mother.'

'Not for the better in my opinion.'

Daisy was quick to note a change in her mother's tone. 'At least give her a chance to make up for her mistake. A month's trial would be reasonable and if it doesn't work out she'll understand that she has to find another place.' Daisy went to the wine table and poured a stiff sherry. She placed it in her mother's outstretched hand. 'I'm sure that Lady Pendleton would be only too pleased to take her on.' She had played her master card, and she waited for her mother's reaction.

Gwendoline sipped her drink, nodding slowly. 'You always had a way with words. You take after your father in that respect.' She downed the rest of the sherry in one gulp. 'All right. She can have a month's trial, but she must keep the child out of my way.'

'Thank you, Mother. You won't regret it, I'm sure.'

'She can have her old room back, and I think Beatrice's cot is stowed away in one of the attic rooms. I didn't have the heart to throw it out.'

Daisy wrapped her arms around her mother and kissed her lined cheek. 'You are an angel.'

'And no doubt I'll get my reward in heaven,' Gwendoline said with a touch of wry humour. 'Don't soft soap me, Daisy Lennox. Go and give the girl orders for dinner. She can start by cooking the ghastly pair of rabbits that Mrs Gurney sent over.'

'I'll see to it,' Daisy said, refilling her mother's glass. 'Don't worry about a thing.' She left the room and hurried to the kitchen to pass on the good news.

Beatrice hugged Ruby. 'I'm so glad you're going to stay. Welcome home.' She sat down with Martin on her knee. 'He's adorable. You must be so proud of him, Ruby.'

Ruby puffed out her chest. 'He's a good little chap. Mrs Lennox won't know he's in the house. Thank you, Daisy. You must have worked hard to bring your mother round.'

'Not really. She has a soft heart beneath her rather frosty manner.'

'I'll take your word for it.' Ruby took off her hat and jacket and hung them on the peg in the scullery. She emerged wrapping a large apron around her waist. 'Where shall I start?'

'Mother said something about rabbits,' Daisy said tentatively.

Beatrice pulled a face. 'Mother Gurney sent them over and I haven't had the stomach for it. That's one thing that Jimmy will have to do if he wants me to cook game for him.'

Ruby took a knife from the rack. 'Leave it to me. I'm not squeamish. I grew up south of the river. Remember?' She disappeared into the scullery, calling over her shoulder. 'Keep an eye on Martin, please, Miss Bea. I'll put him in my bed for a nap when I've seen to the bunnies.'

Beatrice pulled a face. 'I suppose it's good practice for when Jimmy and I start a family.' She chuckled. 'Don't look so worried, Daisy. I'm not that way and don't intend to be for some time. I want to enjoy married life before we hear the patter of tiny feet.'

'I hardly recognise you these days,' Daisy said, suppressing a sigh. 'When I left home you were just a kid, and now look at you.'

Beatrice rubbed her cheek on Martin's soft curls. 'It happens,' she said, grinning. 'You've been gone for almost a year.'

'And I've only got three days' leave left,' Daisy said gently. 'You will look after Ruby, won't you? I feel so responsible for her now, and I'm afraid that Mother might be influenced by some of the self-righteous old biddies in the village and take it into her head to turn Ruby and Martin out onto the street.'

'Don't worry. If the worst came to the worst I'm sure that the Gurneys would help out. They're a smashing couple, Daisy. I love them dearly, and I can't wait to marry Jimmy.' Martin had begun to wriggle and she set him down on the floor. 'I wonder if they've got any old toys in their attic. I'm sure they'd let me bring some over for this little chap.' She shot a sideways glance at Daisy. 'What about you and Rupert? Are you going to wait until this wretched war is over before you get married?'

'We'll see,' Daisy said cautiously. 'It's almost impossible to plan anything these days.'

'But you were together in London,' Beatrice said, angling her head. 'You must have talked things over.'

'He's changed, Bea. War does terrible things to people. He broke off our engagement.'

'Oh, Daisy, that's rotten. I'm so sorry.'

'Don't be. I expect it will work out in time, but I don't want anyone else to know. Not yet, anyway.'

'I won't say a word.'

Daisy could see that Beatrice would not be satisfied until she knew the full story but she was not ready to confide in anyone just yet. 'That's enough about me. Tell me everything that's been going on here since I went away.'

Beatrice frowned. 'Father's business is going downhill again, but I told you that.'

'Yes, you said you didn't trust Mr Meadows.'

'I don't.'

'What has he done to make you feel that way?'

'He's too nice, for once thing. Too eager to please

and so respectful that it makes my flesh creep. You must pay a visit to Father's office and judge for yourself. I'm afraid that history is going to repeat itself and Father will lose this business as well, if he isn't careful.'

'Perhaps we ought to go into town tomorrow morning. I'll see if I can borrow the Prince Henry.'

Arley Meadows was in the outer office, his balding head bent over a ledger. They could see him through the window and Beatrice nudged her sister. 'He looks like Bob Cratchit, only Father isn't Scrooge.'

'First he was Uriah Heep and now he's Bob Cratchit. I thought you hated Dickens?'

'Not really, I just didn't like our English teacher. Anyway, let's go inside and I'll look around while you keep him talking.'

'You've been reading too many Sherlock Holmes books.'

Beatrice gave her a shove towards the door. 'Shut up and do it. At least you can judge for yourself, but I think he's up to no good.'

Meadows looked up and saw them. Daisy had no alternative but to open the door and step inside.

Chapter Nineteen

'Miss Lennox.' Meadows rose from his seat behind the desk. 'And Miss Beatrice Lennox. This is a pleasure, ladies.'

Daisy held out her hand. 'We met briefly some time ago when I came to the office to ask Father for a lift home.'

His grin almost split his pale face in two as he took her hand in a limp grasp, releasing it almost immediately. 'I remember the day well, Miss Lennox. What may I do for you?'

'Is my father in?'

'I'm sorry, no. He had an appointment to see a client, but he should be back quite soon.'

Beatrice pushed past Daisy. 'We'll wait in Father's office.'

Meadows moved swiftly to bar her way. 'Perhaps you have some shopping to do? You might have quite a long wait.'

'No,' Beatrice said firmly. 'We'd rather stay here.' She turned to Daisy with a meaningful nod and a wink. 'My sister is very interested in butterflies, Mr Meadows. I believe that's your hobby?' She turned away and her shoulders shook with suppressed laughter.

Daisy could see that her sister was about to give

way to a fit of the giggles and she stepped forward. It did seem ridiculous that a man with the name of Meadows was obsessed with butterflies, but it was one of the small details that Beatrice had told her about Arley and his widowed mother. It was not much but it was a start. 'I'm surprised that you have time for hobbies, Mr Meadows,' Daisy said hastily. 'You obviously have a lot of work to get through.'

'I do my best, Miss Lennox.'

'You two can have a nice little chat,' Beatrice said, smiling innocently as she opened the inner office door. 'I'll wait in here.' She closed it behind her.

Daisy pulled up a chair and sat down. 'I apologise for my sister, Mr Meadows. I'm afraid she's rather used to having her own way, but please don't let me interrupt your work. I can see that you're busy.'

He chewed his lip, a habit which Daisy was already finding slightly irritating, and he glanced at the closed door as if uncertain of his next move. With an exaggerated twitch of his shoulders he went to sit in his chair and picked up a pen. 'I do have rather a lot to do, Miss Lennox.'

'I understand. I won't interrupt you.' Daisy sat quietly, gazing round the office. The desk took up most of the space, and placed directly behind it a breakfront bookcase was crammed with files and ledgers. Unimaginative brown linoleum covered the floor and the walls below the dado were painted a similar colour, and above it a murky cream reminiscent of curdled milk.

Silence stretched between them like a piece of taut elastic. Daisy could see that he suspected something and she smiled, attempting to put him at his ease. 'Please tell me about your butterfly collection, Mr Meadows.' She had to dig her fingernails into her palms to prevent herself from laughing. 'Do you go out into the countryside to collect them? Or do you sketch them in situ?'

A flicker of interest lit his eyes for a brief moment and then he averted his gaze, staring out of the window as if hoping that his employer would return and rescue him. 'I catch them wherever I can by using a special net, Miss Lennox. Sometimes it's in our garden, although it is rather small, but more often I go for long country walks and that's where I get my best specimens. I have two cabinets filled with them in our box room.'

'Utterly fascinating,' Daisy said politely. 'But I don't suppose you have much free time. I know my father works long hours, and I assume that you do too.'

'Quite so, Miss Lennox. And I have to look after my aged mother. She's a martyr to her rheumatics.' He rose to his feet. 'Would you like a cup of tea? We have a small kitchen at the back of the premises.'

'No, thank you. My sister and I stopped at a tea shop on our way here.' She rose to her feet. 'Perhaps I ought to leave you to get on with your work in peace. I'll join my sister and wait for Father in his office. I'm sure that he'll be here soon.' She moved swiftly, entering the inner office and closing the door before he had a chance to stop her. She leaned against it, staring in dismay at the chaotic jumble of files and ledgers scattered all over their father's desk. 'Bea, what on earth are you doing?'

Beatrice clutched her chest, breathing heavily. 'You

gave me a fright. I though it was Awful Arley coming in to catch me going through Father's papers.'

'What do you hope to find? This is crazy.'

Beatrice shook her head, her lips curving in a triumphant smile. 'Not at all. Look.' She thrust an open ledger under Daisy's nose. 'I'm no mathematician but even I can see that these accounts have been doctored. It's been done very carefully but someone has written the original figures in pencil and then gone over them in pen. I think Father's eyesight must be failing if he can't see something so obvious.'

'Surely not? How could Meadows hope to get away with something like this? Father must have an accountant to go over the books.'

'I don't know, but it would explain why he's losing money hand over fist. I only wish I'd had the courage to come here on my own.' She jumped visibly as the door opened and Meadows entered the room. His proptotic eyes opened even wider. 'May I ask what you are doing, Miss Beatrice?'

She stabbed her finger on the columns of figures. 'Do you deny that these have been altered?'

He shook his head. 'I don't know what you're talking about. This really is outrageous behaviour and I will have to report your conduct to Mr Lennox.'

'This was written first in pencil and then overwritten in ink,' Beatrice said angrily. 'It's quite clear.'

'That is what I do, so that Mr Lennox can check the figures. Then I go over the whole thing in ink.'

'Oh.' Beatrice turned an agonised face to her sister. 'What do you think, Daisy? Is he telling the truth?'

'Miss Beatrice, I am not in the habit of telling lies,' Arley said angrily. 'I demand an apology.'

Daisy stepped forward, taking the ledger from Beatrice, and closing it with a snap she replaced it on her father's desk. 'Mr Meadows, it seems that my father's business is losing money. I'm sure you know about the shocking events that almost bankrupted him in London, and now the same thing seems to be happening once again.'

'It's not fair to blame me, Miss Lennox.' His expression of aggrieved innocence was almost believable, and Daisy found herself at a disadvantage. She was beginning to wonder if Beatrice had imagined the whole thing, but she noticed that his fingers twitched nervously at his sides and beads of sweat stood out on his forehead. Her sympathy evaporated and she faced him with a new determination to set matters straight. 'We can't prove anything, Mr Meadows. It's your word against ours and if Father's accountant hasn't spotted any discrepancies in the books then I must assume that either you are quite innocent or that you are much cleverer than you look.'

His neck appeared to lengthen above his stiff white collar, like a tortoise sticking its head out of its shell. 'I am deeply insulted, Miss Lennox.'

'If you are truly innocent, I apologise,' Daisy said calmly. 'But if my father's business continues to run at a loss, when to all intents and purposes it should be making a profit, I promise you there will be a full inquiry and an official audit of the books. Do I make myself clear?'

Meadows stiffened, his face flushing a deep red. 'Perfectly clear, but I can assure you . . .'

Daisy held up her hand. 'I don't want to hear any more. My sister and I are leaving and I suggest that you tidy up this mess.'

'I hope this is the last time we have this sort of conversation, Mr Meadows,' Beatrice said as she opened the door. 'It will be the police who call on you should there be cause for concern in the future.' She stepped into the outer office. 'Let's go, Daisy.'

'I'm coming.' Daisy hesitated in the doorway, glaring at Meadows. 'My father is a good man. He deserves loyalty from his staff.'

'I'm deeply distressed that you should think so little of me, Miss Lennox,' he said, wringing his hands. 'I am the most trustworthy of employees.'

She smiled. 'Then you have nothing to worry about, have you?' She followed Beatrice out into the dusty street. 'That was very unpleasant. I'd almost rather be back at the Front than have to do anything like that again.'

'Do you think he was telling the truth?' Beatrice asked anxiously. 'I don't know much about it but those figures did look as though they'd been altered to show a loss.'

'We'll probably never know, but he's had fair warning. If things don't improve you must tell Father and allow him to handle the matter.'

'Meadows might continue to swindle Father but do it more carefully in the future.'

Daisy tucked her hand in the crook of Beatrice's arm. 'I think that Meadows has had a bad fright, and he's not stupid enough to make the same mistake again. If he loses his job he'll have difficulty finding another one, and if Lord Kitchener brings in conscription Arley Meadows might find himself looking in vain for butterflies on Flanders fields. Let's go home, Bea. I want to enjoy my last couple of days of freedom.'

Two days later, on Daisy's last evening before returning to France, Victor arrived home with a huge bunch of roses for his wife. Gwendoline gazed at him open-mouthed as he presented her with the bouquet. 'What's this for, Victor? It's not my birthday or our wedding anniversary.'

He leaned over to kiss her on the cheek. 'It's a small token of my appreciation, Gwendoline. You've had to put up with so much over the past year or two. I don't know of many women who would have borne things with so little complaint.'

Gwendoline had the grace to blush and Daisy exchanged wry glances with Beatrice. Considering the fact that Mother had done nothing but complain since they moved to Rainbow's End, Daisy thought it very generous of him to give her such an accolade.

Beatrice flung her arms around her father's neck. 'You're looking very chipper, Father. Has something good happened?'

Daisy sent her a warning look. 'Weren't you going to give Ruby a hand in the kitchen?'

Ignoring her, Beatrice gave him a hug and kissed him on the cheek. 'Do tell, Daddy darling. Why the big smile?'

'You're strangling me,' Victor protested, but he was

obviously delighted by this outward demonstration of affection. 'Actually I have some good news at last. Meadows has been through the books and found several errors in accounting. By his reckoning we are actually in the black.'

Gwendoline frowned. 'What does that mean, Victor? Tell us in layman's terms.'

'My dear, we're solvent for the first time since we moved to rural Essex. I must confess that I've been lax, especially since we lost Teddy. I'm afraid I let matters slide.' He gulped and swallowed, visibly upset as he uttered his dead son's name, but he rallied quickly, taking a deep breath. 'For a while I simply didn't care and I thought I might have to give up the business, but now I can see a way forward. If Meadows had not been so conscientious an employee we might have been struggling for years, or at worst been faced yet again with bankruptcy.'

'I think this calls for a toast.' Daisy could see that Beatrice was beaming with satisfaction and might at any moment give the game away, and she gave her a warning frown. Moving swiftly to the wine table she poured sherry into three glasses and was about to fill the fourth when her father held up his hand.

'No, thank you, Daisy; I need a proper drink. Beatrice, my dear, run to the kitchen and fetch the cooking brandy. Ask Ruby to join us too.'

'What on earth for, Victor?' Gwendoline demanded suspiciously. 'Ruby's place is in the kitchen.'

He shook his head. 'That young woman looks after us well. She should hear the good news.'

Gwendoline choked on her sherry. 'Victor, do you have to be so egalitarian? Ruby is a servant. We must draw the line somewhere.'

'The old order is changing, my dear,' he said solemnly. 'Things will never be quite the same again when this dreadful war ends, and I for one am glad. Ruby has been through a hard time and we let her down in her hour of need. What's more we'll probably have to depend upon her to look after us in our old age.'

Beatrice had been about to leave the room but she hesitated, frowning. 'Don't say that, Father. You've still got Daisy and me.'

'I know, my dear. But you'll be married before long and then it will be Daisy's turn.'

She stared at him in disbelief. 'You don't object to Jimmy and me getting married?'

'I bow to the inevitable,' he said, smiling. 'Now where's my brandy?'

'You're the best father in the whole word,' Beatrice cried delightedly. 'I'll be back in two shakes of a lamb's tail.' She ran from the room, leaving the door to swing on its hinges.

'Have you gone mad?' Gwendoline said angrily. 'Are you really going to allow her to marry a farmer?'

'They're very well-to-do farmers,' Daisy said gently. 'And Jimmy's a good man.'

Victor nodded his head. 'I agree, Daisy. And then it will be your turn.'

'Unless Rupert gets himself killed in this dreadful war,' Gwendoline said darkly. She glanced at Daisy beneath her lashes. 'I'm sorry, but you know how many young men have already gone to their deaths. It's a great pity that you didn't get a wedding ring on your finger while you had the chance.'

'Gwendoline,' Victor said severely. 'That's enough of defeatist talk.' He turned to Daisy with a tender smile. 'You're a brave young woman, my dear. I doubt if I've ever told you this, but I'm very proud of you, and I hope and pray that Rupert will be spared and that you will marry and have a long and happy life together.'

Daisy grasped his hand and gave it an affectionate squeeze. 'Thank you, Father. I do love you both, even if it's not the done thing to say so in this family.'

Victor returned the pressure on her fingers and his eyes were moist. 'Perhaps that's the one good thing to come out of the horrors of war. Maybe we appreciate each other a little more and are not afraid to show our true feelings.'

'You're getting maudlin, Victor,' Gwendoline said crossly. 'Sit down and stop embarrassing me.'

Daisy was to remember her mother's acerbic response as she endured a rough Channel crossing in a troopship, but it brought a smile to her lips. The family were accustomed to Gwendoline's adverse reaction to any outward display of affection or emotion. Mother, Daisy thought, had been born with a stiff upper lip, and perhaps she herself had inherited a small part of that stoicism. Maybe that had been the real reason why Rupert had been unable to share his deepest thoughts and fears with her. Perhaps if she had shown more sympathy for his obvious distress he might have behaved in a different manner. The bleak expression in his eyes haunted her and she was finding it increasingly difficult to forgive herself for allowing him to suffer his private demons alone. It was in a sombre mood that she arrived in Calais and made her way to Lamarck through streets pockmarked with bomb sites, and buildings reduced to skeletons of charred brick and stone.

It was midday and quiet in the old convent. The motorised vehicles were all out, leaving the courtyard empty. The cobblestones gleamed with patches of oil and puddles of soapy water were evaporating in the feeble rays of the September sun. Daisy checked in with her superior and was greeted warmly but wearily and almost immediately put to work. Very soon her brief sojourn in England was a faded sepia tint of a memory and she was pitched once again into the shocking reality of war. The daily hardships, the constant battle to save lives and the terrible suffering of the sick and wounded were eased only by the companionship and mutual support that the women gave unstintingly to each other.

Once again, Daisy and Clarice worked as a team, driving the old Ford ambulance. Each morning their first task was to clean and disinfect the inside of their vehicle. Their eyes stung from the fumes of strong disinfectant and the smell of carbolic clung to their hair and clothes. It was a relief afterwards to be out in the fresh air while completing the routine maintenance checks on the engine before setting off for their first pick-up that day. Daisy sometimes joked that she could always get a job in a garage when the war was over, and she tried to ignore her broken fingernails and oil-ingrained, calloused hands.

The days shortened as winter approached and at Christmas there was a festive atmosphere at Lamarck. Food parcels from home were shared around and the Belgian doctors brought wine to add to the jollity of the occasion. Thus far in the war the FANYs had been working only with the Belgians, but after the disastrous offensive at Aubers Ridge earlier in the year the British authorities had had second thoughts about making use of their skills. Grace Ashley-Smith, who was now Mrs Ronald McDougall, having married an officer in the King's Own, had worked tirelessly to persuade the authorities to recognise the FANY and allow them to work with the British army. There remained many in the establishment who disapproved of women in a men's world, but in December, after a long, hard battle with the powers that be, Grace announced that at last their work was being recognised. They would be allowed to provide transport for sick and wounded British soldiers, and in January 1916 Unit Three was formed.

Daisy and Clarice were amongst the first to be sent to the new camp where tents had been pitched on the sand dunes overlooking the Channel. They endured the winter living in the draughty tents, which had been intended for the Indian army and were not well suited to the chilly northern climate. They slept in army-issue sleeping bags on flimsy camp beds, but some of the more fortunate women commandeered bathing machines and converted these into sleeping quarters. All through the long winter more permanent accommodation was being built, and when it was completed they had the luxury of a cook house and a bath house. Living in a camp also meant sharing the day to day duties of gathering and chopping wood to feed the furnace, and cooking. Then there was the general maintenance of the site, which included keeping the latrines as sanitary as possible, which was not the most popular task, but everyone pitched in without too much grumbling.

When winter melted into spring Clarice discovered a liking for gardening. She dug a small plot in which, as the seasons progressed, she grew vegetables to supplement their diet. In their lighter moments they decided that when the war finally ended Daisy was to become a mechanic and maintain Lord Pendleton's motor cars, and Clarice would become head gardener at Pendleton Park. She declared herself eager and willing to take orders from the future Lady Pendleton, but Daisy said nothing to this. She had not told anyone except Bea that Rupert had ended their engagement. It was a secret she hugged to herself, buried deep with the feelings she had once had for Bowman. She wrote letters to Rupert, receiving the occasional brief note in reply, telling her very little other than that he was still alive.

As to Bowman, she had no idea what had happened to him. He might be dead for all she knew, or clapped in irons in a military prison, awaiting his sentence for desertion. She tried not to think about things that might have been. Life was much simpler now. It was merely a question of getting through each day as it came, and she knew that worse was to come.

It started in July when the casualties came pouring in from the battlefields of the Somme, and life became even more dangerous with Zeppelin raids on Calais. The sounds of gunfire and exploding shells reverberated in the clear summer skies with shrapnel falling like deadly rain. There was little respite for anyone and Daisy worked shifts covering the night hours as well as daytime. Sometimes she went for several days with little or no sleep as the injured men arrived in their thousands.

She enjoyed a brief home leave in September but was back in France within a week. Her one regret was the fact that she had not been able to go home for her sister's wedding, but she was at least able to attend the christening of Beatrice and Jimmy's daughter, and was godmother to little Joyce Daisy Gurney. This time her memories of home had been happy ones. Her father's business was doing well and he could not speak highly enough of Arley Meadows. At least, Daisy thought, she could take some credit for that turn of events, even though it had been Beatrice who had found the discrepancies in the books.

On a different level she was pleased to see that her mother had fully accepted Ruby as a key member of the household, if not one of the family. Young Martin, now a playful toddler, was thriving and to Daisy's surprise he was quite a favourite with her mother. But then Teddy had always been their mother's pet, and perhaps having a small boy in the house was a small consolation to Gwendoline after the loss of her beloved son. Whatever the reason, she doted on Martin and he responded with uninhibited displays of affection. He was an attractive little fellow with thick, dark curls and huge brown eyes, and was a miniature version of his father. Daisy had felt a tug at her heartstrings when she saw him on her first night at home, but he was a genuinely lovable child and it was impossible to hold his parentage against him.

Ruby was every inch the proud mother. She had put on weight and was patently thriving on the fresh country air and the security of living and working at Rainbow's End. Daisy couldn't have been happier for all of them, but in some ways she was beginning to feel excluded. Her wartime experiences were so different from the placid life in rural Essex, and so horrific, that she could not even begin to make them understand the suffering she had witnessed daily.

Perhaps the only person with whom she felt quite comfortable now was Lady Pendleton, and her most relaxing moments during her brief sojourn in Nutley Green had been spent at Pendleton Park. There was a bond between herself and Lady Pendleton and a mutual understanding that was hard to explain, but Daisy had felt inexplicably a part of the lovely old house and its peaceful grounds, even though it would never be her home. It saddened her to think that she had allowed her infatuation for Bowman to influence her to such an extent that she had rebuffed the man who had genuinely loved her. She knew that she had lost Rupert forever, and it hurt more than she could have imagined. She had thrown away her chance of real happiness, and she would have to live with the knowledge for the rest of her life. It was no more than she deserved and it was the price she must pay for her folly.

She set to work back at Unit Three, making a huge effort to put everything out of her mind apart from the day to day duties that were put upon her, and there were many and all of them distressing and painful. She comforted the dying and endeavoured to keep up the spirits of the seriously wounded men she transported to hospital or to the docks for repatriation. Some of them were mere boys and many of them reminded her painfully of Teddy. She could only hope that someone kind had eased his last moments as he left this world on his journey into the unknown. She had seen so much suffering that she was beginning to think that miracles never happened.

As the year drew towards its end the fighting intensified and there were more and more casualties. The weather closed in and everyone agreed that it was the coldest winter in living memory. Daisy drove her ambulance wearing the fur coat that Lady Pendleton had given her before the war. Driving at night was even more hazardous than in daytime. The use of headlights had been banned as they increased the danger of being picked off by enemy snipers, and windscreens were taken out in order to prevent injuries from flying glass. Adding to the perils of night driving, the roads were rutted with shell holes and covered in freezing snow.

One bitterly cold night just before Christmas Daisy was huddled round the Primus stove in the cookhouse waiting for the inevitable call for an ambulance. There had been intense fighting that day and all the other vehicles were already out. It was unlikely that she would be able to spend the night in the comparative warmth of the hut, and sure enough the call came at midnight. She donned her fur coat and went out into a snowstorm. It took several attempts to crank the engine into life and she leapt into the cab, clenching her teeth in an attempt to stop them chattering.

She had been given instructions to pick up the wounded soldiers from one of the canal barges and take them to the hospital in Calais. The casualties who travelled this way were always the most seriously wounded who could not stand being jolted about for long hours in the field ambulances, and she knew that it was going to be a difficult task. She set off muffled in her coat, squinting as the driving snow half blinded her and stung her face.

She arrived at the landing stage in time to see the last ambulance drive slowly into the darkness, and she climbed down onto the hard-packed snow. Already she was stiff with cold and her hands and feet were numb despite her fur-lined gloves and boots. The feather-like flakes swirled around her, thick as fog, as she tied back the canvas flaps at the back of the vehicle. The stretcher bearers made their way carefully over the frozen ground and Daisy stood aside as they lifted their charges gently into the ambulance. It was just a matter of handing over the paperwork and Daisy was about to climb into the driver's seat when a shout from the barge made her stop and look over her shoulder.

'Got another passenger for you, love. Walking wounded so he don't need no special treatment.' The private who had been supervising the disembarkation of the injured soldiers came towards her, half dragging a man in a ragged uniform who was limping badly. He thrust him unceremoniously into the back of the ambulance. 'He's one of them Belgians, miss. Don't speak much English, but he won't give you no trouble. I think he got separated from his unit, or else he could be on the run. Anyway, that's not our problem. Just deliver him to the hospital and let them work it out.' He saluted with a cheery grin and walked away, swallowed up almost immediately by the blizzard.

Daisy shrugged her shoulders. Her job was simply to obey orders, and the sooner she delivered her charges and returned to camp the better. This was not the sort of night when anyone ought to be out and about. She started the engine with even more difficulty this time and climbed into the driver's seat. She wished that Clarice was with her but she had been called out earlier and, at this moment, was probably drinking hot cocoa in the hospital canteen. She drove off slowly, not wanting to skid and cause more pain than necessary to the wounded men, but after a while she began to realise that she must have missed the road into town. She could see only a few yards ahead and the countryside was blanketed in snow which obliterated any landmarks that she might have recognised. Driving in total darkness it was difficult to keep to the road and she dared not stop for fear that the engine would cut out and they would be stuck here until morning. With a sinking heart she realised that she had lost all sense of direction. She was totally disorientated. It was eerily quiet as though the guns had been silenced by the snowfall, and there was no sign of habitation.

There was little that she could do other than keep going straight ahead. There must be a village or a farmhouse along the way soon. She was chilled to the bone and exhausted. She could not see the petrol gauge but she knew that it must be getting low. She was beginning to panic when she thought she saw a glimmer of light ahead, and she headed for it in the hope that she might find shelter for herself and the injured men until morning.

As she drew closer she could see that it was a rather grand house, its outline emphasised by the snow clinging to the stonework giving it the appearance of a huge, glistening iced cake. She braked and came to a halt at the foot of the stone steps leading up to the front door. She slid to the ground, flexing her cramped muscles. She had one foot on the bottom step when the door opened and a ghostlike figure stood on the threshold brandishing a gun.

For a terrifying moment Daisy thought it something other-worldly, but then she realised that the woman was a nun. She raised her hands above her head. 'Don't shoot.' She pointed to the red cross on the ambulance although it was only partially visible through the dancing snowflakes. 'I have wounded men in the ambulance,' she said, hoping the woman understood her schoolgirl French.

The nun stood there, motionless as if frozen with fear, and when Daisy attempted to approach her she backed into the building, waving the weapon. Daisy came to a halt, realising that she needed help. The wounded soldiers inside the ambulance depended upon her and they would all freeze to death if they could not find shelter. It was then that she remembered the walking wounded. He was probably a Belgian deserter, but he would almost certainly understand French even if he spoke Flemish. He would be able to interpret for her. She ran down the steps and pulled back the flap.

The ragged man toppled out, knocking her to the ground. She scrambled to her feet and helped him to stand. His face was partially covered with a filthy woollen scarf and his eyebrows and lashes were frosted with snowflakes, but she would have known him anywhere.

Chapter Twenty

'Is it you?' Daisy said slowly. 'It can't be.'

Bowman pulled the scarf from his face, twisting his lips into a semblance of a grin. 'By God, it's Daisy. I hardly recognised you.'

Standing in the snow outside what appeared to be a French convent with a nun pointing a rifle at them, Daisy felt as though she was in the middle of a bizarre nightmare, and at any moment she would wake up in her sleeping bag back at camp. 'They said you were a Belgian,' she said slowly. 'I thought you were dead.'

Bowman's crack of laughter echoed off the cold stones. 'I will be if I have to stand in the bloody snow for a moment longer.' He shuffled towards the steps holding his hands above his head. 'We need sanctuary, sister,' he said in fluent French that Daisy was able to interpret because of his English pronunciation.

The nun lowered the weapon, turning her head and saying something in a low voice to the woman who had come to join her. There was a murmur of conversation and then Bowman beckoned to Daisy. 'They say we can come in.'

'I have badly injured men in the ambulance.' Daisy made expansive gestures with her arms. 'I need help to carry the stretchers.'

Bowman made a move towards her but his knees buckled and he crumpled to the ground. Daisy sprang forward to help him. 'Are you all right?'

He allowed her to help him to his feet but he shook off her restraining hand. 'I can manage. I just slipped on the snow.'

'Ask them if someone can help me carry the men inside.'

Bowman translated the request and after a moment's discussion the younger of the two nuns handed the rifle to her superior and came running down the steps. 'I help,' she said in English.

She did not look very robust but Daisy had little choice. Between them, with a bit of help from Bowman, they hefted the first stretcher into the building, but when they went back for the second man, Bowman shook his head. 'He's a goner. Best leave him here for the night.'

The young nun crossed herself. 'Take to chapel,' she said firmly. 'We pray for his soul.'

There was no point in arguing and Daisy covered the young man's head with the blanket before they slid the stretcher from the ambulance, and with some difficulty manhandled it up the steps and into a small room off the main entrance hall which had been turned into a makeshift chapel. The stretcher was laid across three wooden chairs set in front of the candlelit altar. The smell of incense and hot wax filled the air and suddenly Daisy felt quite faint.

'Come,' the nun said gently. She beckoned to them as she glided from the room.

Bowman took Daisy's hand and tucked it into the crook of his arm. 'I know you don't need help,' he murmured, 'but I do. Shrapnel in my left thigh. Very painful.'

She allowed him to help her into the chilly entrance hall with its echoing stone floor and a vast staircase, which led to several galleried landings. 'Where have you been?' she whispered. 'What have you been doing all this time?'

'I hardly think that matters at the moment, love,' Bowman said with a wry smile. 'I think we'd best explain our presence to the Mother Superior.' He jerked his head in the direction of the nun who was advancing on them with a purposeful step. He opened his mouth to speak but she held up her hand.

'I speak English,' she said coolly. Her eyes flicked over Bowman with a dispassionate stare and then she turned her attention to Daisy. 'You are attached to the British army?'

'Yes, Mother. My name is Daisy Lennox and I am from Number Three Unit of the First Aid Nursing Yeomanry stationed at Calais. I'm afraid I lost my way in the snowstorm. I was trying to get the wounded soldiers to hospital.'

'You are some miles distant from your destination, my child. But you are welcome to shelter here until it is safe for you to travel on.'

'The ambulance is very low on petrol, Mother. And the surviving soldier needs urgent medical attention.'

'We are a nursing order. This is a convalescent home for Belgian soldiers, but we will do our best for the

Englishman. You do not need to worry.' She glanced at Bowman. 'You are not a soldier.'

He shook his head. 'I was one once, Mother. I fell from grace but I have been doing my best to atone.' He held up his mutilated right hand. 'I am not proud of what I did, but I could not return to my regiment, so I became a stretcher bearer. I am English, and I stole the identity of a dead Belgian soldier, Soldat Smets, but I have done nothing to dishonour his name.'

Daisy stared at him in astonishment. 'I can't believe you got away with it.'

The Mother Superior made a tut-tutting sound. 'Come now. None of this matters at this moment. Let Sister Benedict show you where to go.'

'Thank you, Mother,' Daisy said softly. 'We will not trespass on your hospitality any longer than necessary.'

Mother Superior raised an eyebrow. 'That will rest with God, my child. I'm afraid the snow has set in and will last for days, if not weeks. But perhaps we can get a message through to your unit so that they know you are safe.'

'Thank you.' Daisy sent a silent message to Bowman, hoping that he understood.

He bowed awkwardly. 'Thank you, Mother Superior. I am grateful that you do not judge me too harshly.'

She gave him a cool appraising look. 'It is up to a higher authority than me to judge your actions.' She laid her hand on his sleeve as he was about to follow Daisy and Sister Benedict. 'No, my son. You need medical attention. You will come with me.'

'Yes, of course. Thank you, Mother.' With his limp

even more pronounced than before, Bowman gave Daisy a knowing wink as he followed Mother Superior from the room.

She had not been fooled for an instant by his submissive attitude, and she knew that beneath the contrite and humble exterior he was the same cocksure, arrogant Barnaby Bowman who had charmed and beguiled her. Perhaps it was the hallowed atmosphere that the nuns had created in the once palatial chateau, or maybe she herself had changed and matured, but the magic had gone. She saw him now for what he was: shallow and selfish with nothing to recommend him other than his dogged determination to survive. She thought of all the young men whose lives had been tragically cut short, including her own brother, and by comparison Bowman emerged a lesser man.

'Come,' Sister Benedict said, holding out her hand.

Daisy's room was in the attic and had undoubtedly been part of the servants' quarters in days gone by. It was small and its only furnishings were a single bed and a washstand. There were no curtains at the dormer window and the floorboards were bare of any covering. It was more like a prison cell than a bedroom and it was bitterly cold. The window fitted badly and the glass panes were iced up on the inside. Daisy sat on the bed and took off her puttees and boots. The leather was sodden despite the energetic application of wax polish, and her thick woollen socks were soaked. She slipped off her skirt and tunic and went to bed in her underwear. The thin coverlet afforded little protection against the cold and with chattering teeth Daisy piled her outer garments on top of the bed, including her fur coat. She slid back beneath the covers and immediately fell into a deep and dreamless sleep.

Next morning the snow was still falling. Daisy dressed hastily and made her way down the narrow stone stairs to the basement kitchen where Sister Benedict had taken her the previous evening and had given her a cup of bitter ersatz coffee. All heads turned as Daisy entered the room and the nuns stared openly at her khaki uniform. There was a subdued murmur of conversation and then, just as she was beginning to feel that she was trespassing, Sister Benedict came hurrying forward and motioned her to take a seat at one of the long refectory tables. She filled Daisy's cup with coffee and passed her a slice of dark rye bread. No one spoke to her and she ate quickly, sipping her drink and burning her tongue on the hot liquid, but even before her cup was empty Sister Benedict reappeared at her side. 'Come,' she said with a gentle smile. 'Please.'

Daisy drank the last of the coffee and rose to her feet. Sister Benedict appeared to glide over the rough flagstones and Daisy had little option but to follow in her wake. They navigated a series of draughty corridors, finally arriving at a flight of stone steps which took them back to the main entrance hall. The chateau must, Daisy thought, have been very grand at one time but it was now an echoing shell, bare of furnishings and carpets that might have brought an elegance and softness to the harsh stone walls and bare floorboards.

Sister Benedict stopped outside a door close to the chapel, knocked and waited before opening it to usher Daisy inside.

Seated in a throne-like chair behind an ornately carved table, Mother Superior sat with a pen poised in her hand. She replaced it on a glass inkstand. 'Good morning, Miss Lennox. I trust you slept well.'

'Thank you, yes.' Daisy glanced at the mullioned window but her view of the outside was obscured by a lacy pattern created by ice and snow. 'You have been most hospitable, but we must leave as soon as possible.'

Mother Superior's lips twitched. 'That will depend upon the will of God. As you can see the snow is still falling and the roads will be all but impassable.'

Daisy was at a loss. They would think the worst back at camp. 'Is there any way I can get a message to my unit, Mother?'

'I've already notified them, Miss Lennox.'

'You have?'

The faded blue eyes twinkled. 'Not perhaps in the way you're thinking, my child.' She indicated a candlestick telephone on the desk behind her. 'The lines have been recently restored and I was able to put a call through to the hospital in Calais last night.'

Daisy breathed a sigh of relief. Somehow she had not imagined that the holy women would have anything as modern as a telephone. 'Thank you. I was so worried.'

'Naturally, but put your mind at rest. They will contact your unit and as soon as the roads are passable no doubt someone will bring the fuel you need to fill your petrol tank, and you will be able to leave. Until then, perhaps you would like to help us here? We are very short-staffed and our wards are makeshift and overflowing with poor souls who have received terrible injuries both physical and mental.'

'I'll be glad to do anything I can to help, Mother.' Daisy glanced nervously at Sister Benedict who was standing a few feet away from her. She did not want to say anything that might be misconstrued. She turned back to Mother Superior. 'The English soldier, what will happen to him?'

'You are well acquainted with that young man, I believe?'

'I knew him before the war, Mother. But that is not what I meant.'

Mother Superior nodded her head. 'I understand. We may live reclusive lives but I am well aware what happens to deserters and the men who mutilate themselves in order to get out of military service. It seems that Private Bowman, or should I say Soldat Smets, might come into that category.'

Daisy nodded. 'Yes, Mother.'

'He will be treated just the same here as any other wounded soldier. This is neither a military establishment nor a prison. It is not up to me to judge another human being.'

'Thank you.' Daisy met the Mother Superior's intense gaze and she felt in some mysterious way that the older woman had understood the emotions which had tormented her for such a long time, and that by a minor miracle she had been absolved of all guilt. For someone who had never been particularly religious or spiritual, this was a strange and slightly eerie feeling. Perhaps it was the unusual situation in which she found herself, or maybe it was the isolation of the old chateau and the pious nature of the women who had devoted their lives to God and good works, which had deeply affected her. She realised that the ageing nun was watching her closely and she made a conscious effort to steer the conversation to safer ground. 'The young soldier who died, Mother? What will happen to his remains?'

'We will make the necessary arrangements and I will leave it to you to return his papers and personal effects to the British army.'

'And the other man, Mother? The wounded soldier?'

'Alas, my child. He did not survive the night. The same applies.'

Daisy lowered her gaze. It would not do to cry in front of this stoical holy woman, and she did not even know the names of the dead men, but she had never become hardened to the terrible loss of life inflicted by the war. She said nothing and was relieved when Mother Superior continued in her cool, calm way. 'Sister Benedict will give you instructions. Now you must excuse me, Miss Lennox. I have several letters to write to parents of young men in our care who did not survive their injuries.'

It was as if Daisy had been up before the headmistress at school, and had been summarily dismissed. There was nothing left to do other than put herself in the hands of Sister Benedict, and offer up a prayer for a break in the weather so that someone would arrive with a can of petrol and she could return to her unit.

The blizzard continued for three days without any signs of abating and then the freeze set in. Daisy was gradually absorbed into the routine of the convalescent home. She discovered that there were French, Belgian and even a few British soldiers who were being cared for by the nuns. None of the surviving men had life-threatening conditions, although some of their injuries had been horrific and there were several amputees amongst their number. The British soldiers were pathetically eager for news from home, and were keen to show her the photographs of loved ones that they had carried with them throughout their horrific time in the trenches.

When it came to looking after the French and Belgians, Daisy was allowed to use Bowman as an interpreter. Bathed and clean-shaven he seemed like a different person from the ragged, foul-smelling individual who had been foisted upon her as walking wounded. The nuns had procured a clean uniform for him, even if it was more suitable for Soldat Smets than Private Bowman, and he was once again the irrepressible character that Daisy had fallen for in the old days, although now she was immune to his wiles and watched with some amusement as he tried to charm the nuns, young and old.

It was three weeks before the thaw set in and each day Daisy walked to the gates at the end of the drive in the hope of discovering that the roads might be passable with care, but she was told to await orders from her unit and she was growing impatient. Then, one evening after supper, Mother Superior called Daisy into her office to tell her that arrangements had been made for a despatch rider to deliver a can of petrol first thing in the morning. Relieved but suddenly anxious about what would happen to Bowman, Daisy went in search of him. She found him outside in the yard, leaning against the kitchen wall and smoking a cigarette. He stood to attention as she opened the door, but he relaxed visibly when he saw her. 'I thought it was one of the sisters,' he said, taking a drag on his cigarette and exhaling into the frosty air.

'I'm leaving in the morning,' Daisy said abruptly. 'What will you do?'

He tossed the cigarette butt onto the snow-covered yard. 'I can't go back. They'll clap me in irons if I give myself up.'

'So do you intend to stay here?'

He grinned. 'I don't think the Mother Superior would have me. I might come with you as far as the outskirts of town and work it out from there.'

'They'll catch you sooner or later.'

'I've got away with being Soldat Smets for all this time. I think I can be him for a while longer. Stretcher bearers are needed everywhere and they don't ask too many questions.'

'And when the war ends?'

'I take each day as it comes, love.'

'But I told you about Ruby's baby. You have a son and he's a fine boy. Don't you want to see him?'

Bowman turned his head away. 'No. I'm not cut out to be a dad or a husband, come to that. My old man used to set about me with a strap when he staggered back from the pub. I hated his guts and I wouldn't know how to treat a kid of my own.' He shot her a mischievous glance. 'Unless it was a girl. I'm good with women.'

'But you don't really care about them, do you?' The words crystallised in the ice-cold air and hung between them, reverberating like the strings of a harp.

He met her gaze with a rueful grin. 'No. I suppose not.' He thumped his chest. 'I haven't got a heart, Daisy. It was ripped out when Mum walked away and left me with the old devil. I was four years old and she went off with her fancy man. I never saw her again.'

Touched by his bleak expression and then realising that he was simply tugging at her heartstrings, Daisy shook her head. 'Oh, no. You won't get me that way. In another moment you'd have had me sobbing on your shoulder if I didn't know you so well.'

He threw back his head and laughed. 'It was worth a try. But you will give me a lift into town tomorrow, won't you? I know I can trust you, Daisy.'

'You're a rogue, Bowman.'

'But you love me really.'

She angled her head, giving him a steady look. 'I did, once, but not now. Goodnight, Barnaby.'

'That's the first time you've ever called me by my Christian name.'

It was her turn to laugh. 'And the last. I'll see you in the morning.'

* * *

The lanes were still hazardous but driving with care Daisy was able to get to the main road and found the going there much easier. But with the slight rise in temperature fog had crept in, devouring the trees and fields like a hungry predator. She slowed the engine so that they were barely moving and Bowman stuck his head out of the window in an attempt to navigate and keep them from going off the road. It was exhausting and Daisy was in two minds as to whether or not to turn round and go back to the chateau. She could hear the distant thunder of howitzers and lighter artillery fire, and then suddenly the sounds changed to the steady tramp of marching feet and the clattering of horses' hooves on metalled roads.

As they rounded a bend in the road they were met by a column of marching men led by officers on horseback. Daisy slammed down hard on the brake. She breathed a sigh of relief. 'They're ours.'

'Bugger.' Bowman drew his head into the vehicle. 'I'm Soldat Smets, remember.'

Daisy leaned out of the window, catching the eye of the young officer at the head of the column. 'Where are you headed for?'

He regarded her with battle-weary eyes. 'To the coast, ma'am.'

'The coast,' Daisy repeated, gazing at the gaunt grey faces of the men on foot, marching like automatons, their uniforms and boots caked with mud. They looked exhausted and in need of food and a hot drink, and she wished that she had the mobile kitchen instead of an empty ambulance. She watched helplessly as they moved past her, dragging their feet. She looked round for Bowman but he was nowhere to be seen, and she could only guess that he was hiding somewhere within the vehicle. She knew that it was her duty to give him up, but although he was a deserter and a coward she could not bring herself to betray him. She was about to climb back into the ambulance when out of the thick morass of fog she saw a familiar figure riding towards her. Regardless of her own safety she pushed between the marching men.

'Rupert! Rupert, it's me.' She waved her arms frantically and his horse reared in fright, almost unseating him. His ashen face resembled a death mask rather than a living breathing human being, but his expression lightened when he saw her.

He drew his mount to a halt. 'Daisy Bell. It can't be you.'

She moved as close as she could without getting trampled. 'I can't believe I've found you on this desolate road and in the middle of a peasouper.'

He leaned down so that his face was close to hers. 'You shouldn't be here, Daisy. We're sitting ducks if the Germans realise that we're heading for the coast.'

'Are you going home? Is the war ended at last?'

His cracked lips stretched into an attempt at a smile. 'Far from it. I can't tell you more but get away from here as quickly as you can.'

'We must move on, Major.' One of his fellow officers saluted smartly, pointing towards the coast. 'Any moment now—' He broke off abruptly as a barrage of shots rang out over their heads. 'Take cover,' he shouted, but his words were lost as all hell broke loose around them.

The blast of a powerful gun almost deafened Daisy and it was followed by volley after volley. Men scattered and some fell in bloody pools on the melting snow. Rupert leapt off his horse, pushing Daisy roughly towards the ambulance. 'Keep your head down and get inside.'

His fellow officers were too busy directing their men to pay any attention to her and Daisy had witnessed too much carnage in the trenches to want to argue. She made for the ambulance and was about to dive for shelter when a shell exploded in the middle of the road. In the swirling fog and steady rain of shrapnel she saw Rupert struck down even as he tried to save his men. 'No.' The word was ripped from her throat as she saw him crumple to the ground amidst the wounded and dying. She was about to run to his aid when someone grabbed her bodily and she was dragged into the ambulance.

'Are you trying to get yourself killed?' Bowman hissed.

'Let me go. They need help,' Daisy cried, struggling to free herself from his grasp.

He pushed her down on the seat. 'You won't be able to help anyone if you're dead, sweetheart.' He flung himself out of the vehicle and crouching down he hefted an unconscious man over his shoulder and made for the rear of the ambulance. 'Loosen the bloody ties,' he shouted, staggering beneath the dead weight of the injured man.

Moving like an automaton, Daisy obeyed without question. She threw back the heavy canvas and reached out to drag the wounded man to safety. Without a word, Bowman scuttled off and even as she was attempting to make the young boy comfortable he returned with another casualty.

'Where's Rupert?' she cried anxiously. 'I saw him fall. Get him now, or I'll do it myself.' She leaned out, peering into the murk of fog and smoke. The smell of cordite, blood and burning flesh filled the air, making her retch, but she could see Rupert lying inert while those who had escaped the blast sought any cover they could find and fired round after round at the invisible enemy. Bowman was limping badly and she could see fresh blood on his tunic, but as he reached Rupert a shell exploded close enough to send him flying. They lay side by side, their tunics cut to ribbons and stained with blood. Daisy leapt from the ambulance and falling to her knees she crawled towards them. A young corporal came to her aid and helped her to raise Rupert, who was unconscious but still breathing. 'He's alive,' she murmured, choking back a sob. 'We must get him into the ambulance.'

'This one's badly hurt too, miss.' The corporal lifted Bowman's head. 'Hang on, mate, you'll be okay. We'll soon get you fixed up.'

Bowman opened his eyes. 'Daisy.' His voice was ragged and so faint that she had to lean closer to hear what he was trying to say. He raised his hand to touch her face. 'I love you.' His eyelids fluttered and closed.

Too fraught even to panic, Daisy struggled to her

feet. 'We must get these men back to Calais,' she cried, grabbing the corporal by the sleeve. 'You must help me—' She heard the explosion and felt a sudden sharp pain – and then nothing.

Chapter Twenty-One

Daisy opened her eyes and found herself staring into Clarice's familiar face. 'What happened?' she murmured, wincing as she attempted even the smallest movement. 'Where am I?'

'You're in the casino,' Clarice said, smiling. 'They found you a private room or you'd have been on the ward with all the soldier boys. They might have enjoyed your company but I doubt if the feeling would have been mutual.'

'In the casino,' Daisy said dully. 'How did I get to Calais?'

'They brought you back in your ambulance, and you're lucky to be alive,' Clarice said to her severely. 'You were caught in the crossfire and if it hadn't been for a Tommy with knowledge of first aid, you might have bled to death and you certainly wouldn't be here now.'

It was all coming back to her. Daisy closed her eyes. She could hear the whinnying of horses and the nightmare percussive booming of heavy artillery and small arms fire. She could smell blood and smoke and then everything had turned to darkness, but just before that she had been cradling Rupert's head on her lap and Bowman had told her that he loved her. Tears trickled down her cheeks to soak the pillow beneath her head. 'Rupert – is he?' She could not bring herself to say the word.

'He's alive, but he's still in a critical condition.' Clarice took her hand and held it. 'But I'm afraid the other one didn't make it, Daisy.'

'Do you mean Bowman?'

'They said that the man who tried to help you was a Belgian by the name of Smets.'

'He was badly wounded . . .' Daisy choked on a sob as fresh memories of that terrible scene came flooding back to her.

'Don't distress yourself, dear.' Clarice squeezed her fingers and her blue eyes were moist with unshed tears. 'He didn't make it, I'm afraid. He gave his life to save yours, Daisy. He was a brave chap. A real hero.'

For a wild moment Daisy wanted to laugh. Bowman – a hero? That would have amused him no end. But he was dead and that was even harder to believe. She had seen him fall and had heard what must have been his last words, but it was almost impossible to think of his lust for life quenched in an instant of selfless bravery.

Clarice passed her a hanky. 'You're still very weak, Daisy. You really mustn't upset yourself.'

'Don't take any notice of me. I'm still a bit groggy.'

'That's only natural. You had several pieces of shrapnel removed from your shoulder and the nurse told me that a bullet had shattered your collar bone. The surgeon who operated on you said that it would heal in time.'

'I'm more concerned about Rupert than myself.'

Daisy dashed the tears from her eyes with her good hand.

'You mustn't worry about him,' Clarice said softly. 'Just concentrate on getting your strength back. I've missed you terribly and they've given me a new girl to work with who's never been away from home before. She tries her hardest but she's not you.'

'You mean she doesn't boss you around?' Daisy forced her lips into a smile. She knew that Clarice was trying to cheer her up, but at this moment all she wanted was to be left alone. She needed time to think and time to grieve for Bowman, who for all his many faults had occupied a special place in her heart no matter how hard she had tried to forget him.

Clarice patted her hand. 'I can see that you're tired, Daisy. I'll go now but I'll come back and see you whenever I get the opportunity.'

'Please do,' Daisy said weakly. 'I'm not used to being laid up like this.'

'Well, darling, you'd better get used to it because you're going to be here for a while yet.' Clarice rose to her feet and leaned over to kiss Daisy on the forehead. 'Take care of yourself and don't worry about Rupert. He's on a ward here and he's in the best of hands.'

A feeling of panic seized her and Daisy caught Clarice by the sleeve. 'Please don't go. Stay a bit longer.'

'I can't, Daisy. I've got to get back to the unit, but I promise I'll come again very soon.'

Daisy was too weak to do anything other than release her hand, and she watched her go with a sinking heart.

She felt helpless and alone, and what was worse even the smallest movement caused her excruciating pain. She knew that this was the end of her time in France. Her collar bone would heal but it was unlikely that any medical board would pass her as fit to work alongside the women she had come to think of as her sisters. She closed her eyes and drifted back to sleep.

The nurses were kind but overworked and had little time to spend chatting. They did what was necessary to make Daisy comfortable but after that she was left to her own devices. On the third day she had had enough of being bedridden and she was desperate to see Rupert. No one would tell her anything apart from the fact that he was doing as well as could be expected, and she was determined to find out for herself. She waited until the relative quiet of evening before rising from her bed. She was weak and her legs felt like jelly, but somehow she managed to slip a dressing gown around her shoulders, and drag a comb through her hair. Following the example of many of the women she had taken scissors to her long tresses soon after she joined Unit Three. It had cost her dear but now she was glad that she had short hair. It curled around her head, giving her the appearance of a street urchin rather than a well-brought up young lady, and it would be some time before she would be able to put it up or have it coiffed into the elaborate styles that had been fashionable at home. Vanity had never been one of her vices, but she clung to the vague hope that short hair would become the latest thing when she returned to civilian life. She opened the door, checking both ways to make sure that no one was coming. The night nurse was not due on her rounds for a good hour and hopefully that would give her time to find Rupert.

She crept along the corridor, peering into the side wards which had once been the offices of the staff who ran the casino, and eventually she came across him in a small room at the head of the stairs. She went in and stood at his bedside, gazing down at his sleeping face. Fine golden stubble covered his chin and his cheeks were ashen and sunken. His hair had been shaved off on one side and a livid scar puckered his scalp. His bare chest was bandaged from shoulder to waist and his right leg was in a plaster cast. Her heart swelled with pity as she gazed down at his inert figure, and she felt suddenly protective and responsible for him as though he were her child, and not the grown man she had promised to marry.

She pulled the sheet up to his chin and tucked it around him. 'Sleep well, Rupert,' she whispered, dropping a breath of a kiss on his forehead. 'I'll come again tomorrow.'

Next morning she was up before the nurse came to bring her a cup of tea, which caused raised eyebrows, but Daisy was unrepentant. 'I'm getting better now,' she said when she was told to get back to bed in no uncertain terms. 'I don't want to lie around all day. Perhaps I can help around the wards and make myself useful.'

The nurse stared at her in amazement. 'I heard that

you lot were tough, but you're under my orders now, Miss Lennox. You'll do as I say.'

Daisy sipped her tea, hoping that her rebellious spirit would go unnoticed. 'Of course,' she said meekly. 'You're the boss.' She put the mug down on the bedside cabinet. 'But, if I promise to be very good, will you give me some information about another patient?'

The nurse allowed herself to smile. 'Bribery won't wash with me, miss.'

'Please, I wouldn't ask but Major Pendleton is my fiancé. I'm almost his next of kin so I have a right to know how he is doing.'

'Really?' A glimmer of interest shone in the woman's dark eyes. 'Well, I don't suppose it will hurt if I tell you that he had a piece of shrapnel lodged in his brain and it had to be removed. It's too early to tell if he's suffered lasting damage, although the surgeon hopes that he will make a full recovery.'

'And his other injuries?'

'Have you been wandering around the wards, Miss Lennox?'

'I just wanted to see him and reassure myself that he was still alive.'

'He's very much alive, but you mustn't roam about the hospital. It's not the done thing, as you must know.'

'I am his fiancée.'

'But you're not engaged to the rest of the soldiers in my care. Need I say more? You've been here long enough to understand the rules, Miss Lennox.'

'Of course, and I'm sorry. But please tell me about Major Pendleton's other injuries. His chest wound, for instance, and his leg is in plaster. Is this the extent of his injuries?'

The nurse frowned and hesitated for a moment, but as her eyes met Daisy's she gave a reluctant smile. 'I know you'll find out one way or another, but for heaven's sake don't tell anyone that I told you this.'

'I won't. I promise.'

'A bullet passed within inches of the major's heart, but luckily it went straight through and out the other side. Another one fractured his femur, which of course will heal in time, but a piece of shrapnel lodged in his spine, and although it's been removed the doctors fear he might never walk again.' She stopped to take a breath. 'But it's the head injury which is giving them the most concern. Major Pendleton is, to put it plainly, in a coma. I wouldn't tell you this but I think you might be of help to him. If you promise to rest your arm, I'll let you sit with him in the daytime. Perhaps if you talk to him he might hear your voice and recognise it. Who knows?'

'I'll go now.'

'Not like that you won't. Put some clothes on, young lady. I don't want a riot on the wards. Your khaki tunic should put most of them off. It's not the most flattering garment I've ever seen.'

Daisy laughed. 'Sister Newman, I do believe you've got a sense of humour beneath that stern exterior.'

'Don't talk nonsense, Miss Lennox. Now get dressed, or do you need me to help you?'

'I think I can just about manage. I don't want to keep you from your really sick patients.'

It was easier said than done, but somehow Daisy managed to get her skirt on and one arm through the tunic sleeve, hitching the rest of it around her shoulders and fastening it with her belt. She grinned as she caught sight of her reflection in the glass door panel. Sister Newman had a point. It was not the most attractive uniform, but it had served its purpose and now she was on another mission. She was not going to let Rupert slip away. He had a life back in England and a family who loved him. She loved him. It came as a surprise to her, but seeing him on that snowy road near the chateau had crystallised her feelings for him. She had felt passion for Bowman and overwhelming physical attraction, but that was not a recipe for a life-long commitment. Despite the fact that he had declared his love for her, she knew only too well that he was not a one-woman man. Heartache and heartbreak would have ended their relationship as it had with his wife and with Ruby. But Rupert was a part of her. She had only truly come to realise it when she had seen him cut down by enemy fire. He had known it all along, but she had rebelled against the unavoidable fact that fate had intended them for each other. She knew now that he was her future, and even if he were to be a permanent invalid she wanted nothing more than to spend the rest of her life caring for him.

She made her way to his room and sat all day at his bedside. She talked until her throat ached, relating stories of the day to day running of Lamarck, which was now closed and missed by all the women who had worked there. She told him about the draughty tents they had occupied at Unit Three, where in that first bitter winter they had been lulled to sleep by the sound of waves pounding on the shore. She described the camaraderie she had enjoyed with Clarice and the other women who toiled in unspeakable conditions with cheerfulness and dedication, carrying out duties that would challenge the hardiest of souls. She talked about the old times when they were children and spent long hot summers running wild in the grounds of Pendleton Park with Teddy and Bea. She told him that Bea had married Jimmy Gurney and that they had a baby daughter. She went into details of how she had found Ruby working as a Gladys in Lyons Corner House, and that she had a little boy, although she did not mention the fact that Bowman was the child's father.

During the following few days she poured her heart out to Rupert, but she did not tell him that it was Bowman who had saved her life. That was part of the past which was dead and buried with him in a foreign land. Ruby was the only person who understood the feelings he had aroused, and Daisy spent hours composing a letter to her, in which she broke the news of his death.

Clarice visited as often as possible, but one day she told Daisy sadly that she was being posted to Unit Five, working with the Belgians, and her duties would take her further afield, transporting their wounded to hospitals in an even wider area than before. They clung to each other for a long while, promising to keep in touch if at all possible and to meet up again as soon as hostilities came to an end. 'It must come soon,' Clarice said, sniffing and wiping her eyes on the sleeve of her khaki tunic. 'We'll be cousins when you marry Rupert and I'll dance at your wedding.'

Daisy hugged her. 'Of course you will. And I'm to be sent home. I'd much rather stay and see out the rest of the war with all my dear friends, but I'd be no use with this injured shoulder.'

'What about Rupert?'

'He's still in a coma. They say they daren't move him until he comes round.'

'And he will. I know he will.'

'I hope so, Clarice. But even if he remains like this for the rest of his life, I'll stay at his side. I'll fight for him even if he cannot battle for his own survival. I won't allow him to die.'

'Good luck, darling.' Clarice broke away with a muffled sob. 'Got to go now. See you soon back in old Blighty.' She hurried from the room, leaving the door to swing shut.

The muffled thud brought Daisy back to reality: she rose to her feet and made her way to Rupert's room. Something had drawn her to him, she could not say what it was, but she had half expected to find him sitting up in bed. Her disappointment was acute when she saw that he remained exactly as she had left him a couple of hours previously. She sat on the chair beside him and took his hand in hers. 'Rupert, it's me, Daisy. They want to send me home next week but I won't go without you. I promise never to leave you and I'll stay by your side no matter what.' She lapsed into silence, still holding his hand, and her mind was made up. She would stay on as an auxiliary nurse or a ward maid. She would speak to Boss and persuade her that even if she could not work with the FANYs now, she could still do something for the war effort. She was so busy planning her speech that she almost ignored the slight pressure on her hand. She stared down at their entwined fingers, watching closely and hardly daring to breathe. She almost shouted for joy when she felt it again and this time it was stronger. She clutched his hand to her breast, leaning over and kissing him softly on the lips. 'Rupert, come back to me.'

His eyes opened slowly and she held her breath. He turned his head to stare at her and his lips moved silently. She squeezed his fingers. 'Darling Rupert. You're safe, my love. I'm going to take you home.'

When all the formalities were completed, Daisy was allowed to accompany Rupert on the troopship returning to England. He was sent at first to the London General Hospital at Denmark Hill for assessment of his condition. Daisy, now permanently retired from the FANY due to her injuries, stayed at Pendleton House in Grosvenor Square and visited him daily. She would have volunteered as a VAD but it would be months before her collar bone healed properly. It was difficult to do the simplest things with one arm, but with the help of Betsy, the parlour maid, she was able to make herself presentable. For the first time in almost three years, apart from her brief home leaves, she was able to dress in elegant clothes and her perfume was

Jicky instead of carbolic. Her hair, it seemed, was fashionably short and skirts were raised above the ankles. Looking at the well-dressed ladies in London who were outwardly untouched by the horrors of the war, it was hard to equate their lifestyles with the suffering that Daisy had witnessed during her time in Flanders. She knew that whatever her future role in life, she would not become one of the idle rich.

She put all her energies into caring for Rupert. She visited the hospital each morning and stayed there all day. Sometimes Lady Pendleton joined her. She had travelled to town immediately on hearing that her son was in hospital, and eventually Lord Pendleton arrived, but he seemed to find it hard to cope with Rupert's injuries. He left at the first opportunity having made gruff noises to the effect that Rupert must get well before the glorious twelfth and the start of the grouse shooting season, which seemed utterly tactless to Daisy, although Lady Pendleton merely smiled.

'Don't take any notice of my husband. He finds it hard to express his innermost feelings.' She rose from her chair at Rupert's bedside and leaned over to pat him gently on the hand. 'I have to fly now, darling. I have an appointment with my dressmaker, but I'll see you again very soon.' She beckoned to Daisy as she left the private ward. 'My dear girl, we must have Rupert sent home as soon as possible. For one thing it's terribly inconvenient having him here, and I do so hate the hospital smell, it clings to one's clothes and hair for simply hours after one leaves.'

'And the other thing, Lady Pendleton?' Daisy tried to keep the acid tone from her voice.

'The other thing?' Lady Pendleton frowned thoughtfully. 'Yes, of course. We can look after him at home. You're a nurse, aren't you? You looked after all those poor devils in France.'

Daisy lifted her arm in the sling just a little, and even then the pain stabbed like a knifepoint. 'I'm afraid I can't do much until my shoulder heals.'

'No, quite. Well, there's a military hospital at Colchester barracks, and once Rupert's case has been fully assessed I'm sure they will transfer him there.' She closed the door to Rupert's room. 'I don't want the poor boy to hear this, but his speech is still quite slurred and he often forgets what he's saying. Do they think that the damage is permanent?'

Daisy shook her head. 'I don't think that the neurologists have the complete answer, but he's making progress every day. His memory is returning gradually and his other wounds are healing well, although they still don't know if he will ever be able to walk again. We must just wait and hope.'

Lady Pendleton enveloped her in a perfumed embrace, kissing her on both cheeks. 'You are such a treasure, my dear Daisy. Your loyalty to my son is touching.'

'I love him, Lady Pendleton,' Daisy said simply, and she knew that it was true. She would stay with him every step of his gradual recovery, and even if he was never quite as handsome or as dashing as before it would not make the slightest bit of difference.

'You are a dear girl,' Lady Pendleton said, smiling. 'Now I really must go. I'll see you at dinner.'

'Yes, of course.'

Lady Pendleton hesitated for a moment. 'You really ought to have a break from all this hospital business, Daisy. Perhaps a weekend at Pendleton Park or even Rainbow's End? I'm sure your parents would be overjoyed to see you again.'

'There's plenty of time for that,' Daisy said calmly. 'When Rupert is well enough to go to a convalescent home, then I'll feel able to see my family, but until then he is my chief concern.'

On a cold, bleak day in February, Rupert was transported by ambulance to the Sobraon Barracks Military Hospital at Colchester, and Daisy returned home to Rainbow's End, politely but firmly declining Lady Pendleton's invitation to stay at Pendleton Park. Her parents welcomed her with open arms but neither of them made any attempt to hide their relief on hearing that she had been deemed unfit to return to Flanders.

Ruby burst into tears at the sight of her but young Martin had obviously forgotten her and clung to his mother's skirts with his thumb plugged firmly into his mouth, eyeing her warily. At the age of two he was a sturdy little fellow with a mind of his own and temper to match, but he had inherited his father's charm and he had only to smile and gurgle with laughter in order to wrap Daisy's parents and his own mother round his tiny little finger. Martin, Daisy thought after the first few days at home, was verging on becoming a very spoilt little boy. However, even she was not immune to his winning ways and very soon they were the best of friends.

'He's so like his dad,' Ruby said, watching him playing with a puppy that Victor had given him for his second birthday in January. 'He's Barnaby all over again.'

Daisy pulled a face. 'I hope not.' She laid her hand on Ruby's shoulder. 'At least I hope he takes more after you than his father.'

'But you was soft on Barnaby, wasn't you?' Ruby's dark eyes scanned her face as if desperate to seek an honest answer. 'You loved him too. I know you did.'

'I was infatuated, Ruby. He could charm the birds from the trees if he so chose, but he died a hero, and that's what you must tell Martin when he's old enough to understand.'

Ruby glanced fondly at her son as he rolled about the kitchen floor with the puppy. 'I will, and hope to God that this is the war to end all wars like they say it is.'

Daisy picked up her reticule. 'Amen to that. Anyway, I'd love to stay and chat with you, but I promised Bea that I'd drive over to the farm and see her before I go to the hospital. It's been a great help having the Prince Henry so that I can visit Rupert whenever I like.'

'Tell her to bring Joyce to see us soon. It won't be long before she's big enough to play with Martin. That's if Miss Beatrice doesn't mind her daughter hobnobbing with the servant's kid.'

'Don't be silly. Bea isn't like that and well you know

it. I'm sure that Martin and Joyce will be the best of friends.'

'I hope so.' Ruby stopped kneading the bread dough, wiping her forehead with the back of her hand. 'Before you go, is it all right if I have tonight off instead of Saturday?'

Daisy paused in the doorway. 'Yes, of course. I'll be here as well as Mother and Father. Are you going somewhere special?'

Ruby's face flushed so that her cheeks were bright pink. 'Arley and me are going to the music hall.'

'You and Arley Meadows?'

'I know you didn't like him much at the start, but he's a nice, kind man, and once you get him off the subject of blooming butterflies he can he really interesting.'

Daisy stared at her in amazement. 'You're stepping out with him?'

'We're keeping company.' Ruby covered the dough with a damp cloth and placed it closer to the range. 'There's nothing wrong in that, is there?'

'Absolutely not. I'm really pleased that you're getting out and about. I'd hate to think of you spending the rest of your life grieving for what might have been.'

'I know that Barnaby would never have married me. Apart from the fact that he already had a wife and child, he didn't feel the same about me as I did about him. But he gave me Martin and he's the best thing that ever happened to me.'

'And does Arley get on well with your boy?'

'He's amazing with him, and that awful mother of

his quite dotes on my Martin. She's not a bad old stick if you know how to handle her, but Arley don't stand up to her enough.'

'I imagine that you will, though,' Daisy said, chuckling.

'I put her in her place from the start. I had plenty of practice with my old man and me sister.'

'Well, good for you, Ruby.' Daisy rushed over to give her a hug. 'You're a very special lady, and if you should decide that your future's with Arley, then he's a very lucky fellow.'

Daisy related this conversation to her sister later that morning, sitting in Beatrice's comfortable living room with its chintz-covered squashy armchairs and large sofa on which a yellow Labrador sprawled, snoring gently.

'I had no idea she was seeing Meadows,' Beatrice said in amazement. 'To think we almost shopped him to the police for embezzling Father's money.'

'It was probably the best thing that we never did,' Daisy said, smiling. 'At least we brought him up short and now he's the model employee. Father can't speak highly enough of him. He's even talking about making him a partner in the firm. Can you believe that?'

Beatrice's eyes widened. 'Never! Well I'm blowed.' She rose from the sofa and went to look out of the window. 'Just checking on Jojo. She's asleep in her pram, but she'll be waking soon for a feed.' She gazed down at her full breasts with a resigned sigh. 'I feel like one of our best dairy cows.'

'You look wonderful, Bea. A picture of health and happiness.'

Beatrice smiled dreamily. 'They say you can't get pregnant while you're breast feeding, but I'm living proof that that is an old wives' tale.'

Daisy leapt to her feet. 'You're not – are you?'

'I just said I was. Jojo will have a little brother or sister in six or seven months. I never thought I was the maternal type, but I was wrong. I'm thrilled and so is Jimmy. He says he'd like a big family and we've made a good start.'

Daisy enveloped her in a warm embrace. 'I'm so happy for you, Bea. Who'd have thought my wayward little sister would have a husband and children before I did.'

'I'm so sorry, Daisy.' Beatrice's bottom lip trembled. 'I didn't mean to be so tactless. How is Rupert?'

'You weren't, and he's making progress.' Daisy frowned. 'At least, the doctors say he is, but I'm not happy with the way he's being treated in hospital. His wounds are healing but his speech is still very slurred and they leave him to lie in bed all day. I think he should be encouraged to do more, and it's the same with the other men on his ward.'

Beatrice put her head on one side, regarding her sister with a knowing smile. 'It's not like you to let the grass grow under your feet. Why don't you do something about it?'

Daisy seized her hand and shook it. 'You're absolutely right. I don't know what I've been thinking of these past weeks while I've stood by and watched the man I love dwindle into a shadow of his former self.'

'What are you going to do?'

'I'm going to call at Pendleton Park on the way home. I've got an idea, thanks to you, Bea. I'll let you know if I can pull it off after I've spoken to Rupert's mother.'

Chapter Twenty-Two

'I don't know, Daisy,' Lady Pendleton said, pacing the Aubusson carpet in the crimson and gold saloon. 'It would mean a terrific amount of upheaval.'

'Not necessarily, ma'am. I'm not proposing to turn the whole of the house into a convalescent home, only a part of it. You could keep your own wing absolutely private, but just think of the benefit it would bring Rupert and some of the other men who've suffered similar injuries on the battlefield.'

'I'd have to discuss it with Henry, of course. The estate belongs to him and will go to Rupert on his demise, which I hope won't be for many years to come, but one never knows. Lady Osborne's husband dropped dead at the card table just last week and he was three years Henry's junior.'

'But you will consider it, won't you?' Daisy clasped her hands in front of her, praying silently that Lady Pendleton would agree to champion her cause. 'Think of Rupert. He needs specialist care and all the advances in modern medicine to bring him back to full health and fitness. Do you want him to end up in a wheel-chair, barely able to put a sentence together and having difficulty in recalling your name?'

'That's cruel, Daisy.'

'It's the truth, ma'am. It's the plain, honest truth. I've visited him every day and his progress is pitifully slow. I'm terrified that he will just give up, and I simply won't allow that to happen.'

Lady Pendleton came to a halt in front of her, gazing into Daisy's face as if seeing her for the first time. 'You really do love my son, don't you?'

'I do, ma'am. I'm begging you to allow me to do this for him, as well as other men in similar circumstances.'

'Could we not just bring Rupert here and employ specialists to treat him at home?'

'It would be hideously expensive, Lady Pendleton. Besides which, I doubt if they would want to spread their expertise so thinly. Whereas if we turn Pendleton Park into a convalescent home and specialised treatment centre, we would be doing something for the men and boys who have given so much for their country. Of course, we would have to get the backing of the medical establishment and the military, but that's where you and Lord Pendleton come in. You both have so much influence; I'm begging you to bring it to bear.'

'I'll have to think about it, Daisy. It's becoming hard enough to run the house with so many of the servants either away fighting or doing war work, but I'm not sure how we would cope with having our home turned into a hospital.'

'It would be for Rupert's sake.'

'Yes,' Lady Pendleton said thoughtfully. 'It would be wonderful if he could make a full recovery.'

* * *

With Lord Pendleton's blessing, Daisy drove up to London and made her base in Grosvenor Square while she lobbied every influential person who might be of some help in establishing the convalescent home. She used her experience with the FANYs to her advantage, citing her experience in Lamarck and Unit Three as evidence of her capability to run such an establishment. She had heard that the WSPU had abandoned their militant actions and put all their energies into the war effort, and taking advantage of this change of heart Daisy was quick to contact Christabel Pankhurst in order to seek her support. As former sisters in adversity they had something in common, and Christabel was a person to be reckoned with.

Eventually, after several months of petitioning, writing letters and generally making a nuisance of herself in high places, Daisy was granted permission from the military to go ahead with her scheme. Funding the project was her next priority and she organised charity concerts, dinners and a grand ball at the Hotel Cecil. She enlisted Lady Pendleton's help in contacting wealthy benefactors and pleaded for their assistance in raising the required sum of money with one proviso: she made it perfectly clear that all ranks were to be catered for. She could do nothing to repay Bowman for the heroic gesture that had saved her life, but she hoped that she might be able to help other enlisted men to return to their families and live as normal a life as was possible. She worked tirelessly, often staying up half the night as she went through piles of correspondence and made plans for her campaign like any good general. By the middle of summer she was exhausted but triumphant: the target had been achieved and the alterations to Pendleton Park were given the go-ahead.

Daisy returned home to Rainbow's End and received a rapturous welcome from her family, although Ruby scolded her soundly for not looking after herself. 'You need feeding up, my girl,' she said, eyeing her critically. 'I seen more meat on a skinned rabbit than you've got on your bones.'

Gwendoline was equally frank. 'You look as though you haven't slept for a week, Daisy. You'd better get some rest before you go and see Rupert. You look terrible.'

Beatrice had come over for the day with Joyce. She laid her sleeping baby on the sofa cushions before enveloping Daisy in a fond hug. She drew back, holding her at arm's length and eyeing her critically. 'Mother's right. I don't know what you've been doing to yourself in London, but it's a good thing you're home now. I've brought butter, eggs and cheese from the farm and Ruby is going to make sure you eat, even if she has to stand over you at table.'

Halfway between laughter and tears, Daisy picked up Martin who had been clinging to her skirt and dropped a kiss on his curly head. 'I'm perfectly well. Just a little tired, but I promise to be good and do as I'm told from now on.'

'Hmm.' Gwendoline pursed her lips. 'That will be a first, Daisy Lennox.'

Martin began to wriggle and Daisy handed him to his mother. 'He's grown so much in the last few months.'

Ruby gave him a kiss and set him down on the floor. 'He's into everything, aren't you, my pet?'

Martin toddled from the room, chuckling mischievously.

'He leads me a merry dance,' Ruby said as she hurried after him. 'I'll put the kettle on and there's a batch of scones in the oven. We'll have some tea.' She raced off in pursuit of her son.

'How is everything?' Daisy asked warily. 'I'm afraid I've neglected everyone.'

Gwendoline patted her on the cheek. 'We're managing, but it's good to have you home, Daisy. Now I hope everything will get back to as near normal as possible, although nothing will ever be quite the same without Teddy.'

Joyce chose that moment to open her eyes and whimper. Beatrice snatched her up and gave her a cuddle. 'We'll never forget him, but when you see Iris's little boy you'll realise that Teddy hasn't completely left us.'

Daisy shot an anxious glance at her mother, but Gwendoline merely smiled. 'It's all right,' she said calmly. 'Your father and I have got over the shock and he's a dear child. So like Teddy at that age. Life has to go on, Daisy. I've learned that the hard way.'

Next day, after an uninterrupted night's sleep, Daisy visited Rupert in hospital. She had not seen him for several weeks and was agreeably surprised by his slight but significant progress. His delight on seeing her made her heart sing with happiness and she knew that she had truly come home. She sat with him for more than an hour, but when he began to look tired she said a reluctant goodbye, kissed him tenderly on the forehead and promised to return again the next day. He clung briefly to her hand, his eyes fixed on her face. 'Daisy Bell.' He curved his lips into a twisted smile.

She drove home in the Prince Henry feeling much more optimistic about Rupert's prospects for a complete recovery. The sun was shining and the countryside was lush and green. For the first time since the beginning of the war she felt confident about the future.

Pendleton Park Convalescent Home was ready to take in its first patients by the late autumn of 1917. Daisy could have wished it had been sooner, but there were alterations that had to be made to the ground floor. In accordance with Lady Pendleton's wishes, these were kept to a minimum, but extra bathing and toilet facilities had to be installed as well as ramps for wheelchairs, hoists and the general paraphernalia needed to care for the severely disabled. Then there were other necessities to order, such as beds, linen, medical supplies, and so many other items that Daisy spent most of her time at her desk in the old still room which she now used as her office.

The grand opening was conducted with due ceremony in the presence of many dignitaries who had travelled down from London for the occasion. Every able-bodied person in the village had turned out, although Daisy suspected that they were motivated more by curiosity and the offer of a free tea than anything else. Beatrice and Jimmy were there, together with Gwendoline and Victor, and for once Daisy received her mother's unstinting praise for her achievements. Ruby had come with Arley and he in turn had brought his stern-faced mother, who seemed to view life with a permanent look of disapproval, but Ruby herself was brimming over with happiness. She watched with a fond smile as Martin toddled off to play with Iris's son, who bore such a strong resemblance to Teddy that it made Daisy feel quite weak at the knees every time she looked at him.

Iris, looking trim in her widow's weeds, gave her an appraising glance. 'You done well, Miss Lennox.'

Daisy held out her hand. 'Times have changed, Iris. It's just Daisy from now on. By the way, if you're looking for work we're in desperate need of more ward maids, and you have the advantage of knowing the house.'

'You're offering me a job?'

'It can't be easy bringing up a child on your own.'

'It isn't, but I've got the kid to look after. Me mum works full time at the munitions factory and me sister-in-law Flossie's a lazy cow. I wouldn't leave a kitten in her care let alone me only son. So you see there's no one to have Ted.'

'He's very like his father,' Daisy said, meeting her cold stare with a smile. 'I'm sure we could come to some arrangement, Iris. Perhaps Ruby would look after your boy in the daytime while you went to work. She loves children.'

Iris curled her lip. 'I'm sure your mum and dad wouldn't want their son's little bastard running round the house.'

'They loved my brother and they're not as stuck up as you seem to think. Ted is their grandson after all, and Mother thinks the world of him.'

'Now she's got over the shock,' Iris said with a touch of dry humour.

'Absolutely. Will you give it a try?'

'You'd have to make it right with her.' Iris jerked her head in Ruby's direction. 'I'm not begging for favours.'

Daisy nodded, smiling. 'Let me speak to her first. I'll let you know how things stand first thing tomorrow morning.'

Iris shrugged her shoulders and walked away to join her heavily pregnant sister-in-law and Cyril, who had been declared medically unfit to enlist, even though rumour had it in the village that he was malingering. Daisy stood for a moment watching the villagers rubbing shoulders with the dignitaries as well as some of the more mobile patients. The men who were too incapacitated to get up lay in their beds placed for the special occasion in the open doors of the conservatory, while others sat in wheelchairs with blankets wrapped around their knees. Despite the late autumn sunshine there was a cool breeze and leaves fell in bronze and copper showers over the lawns, forming heaps like pirate gold around the trees.

It was all such a far cry from the horror of the battlefields that it brought a lump to her throat. She realised just how much she loved the historic old house and its quintessentially English setting, and she had come to realise that this was where she wanted to be for the rest of her life, but not as the privileged lady of the manor. She knew now that women could do almost anything once they had set their minds to it, and if she could not serve her country at the Front, then she could help to rehabilitate the gallant soldiers who had already given so much, and give them hope for a brighter future.

She returned to the present with a jolt as the clink of china cups and saucers indicated that tea was being served on the terrace. Cucumber sandwiches, seed cake and jam tarts had been specially prepared by Cook and were disappearing at an astonishing rate. Altogether there was a festive atmosphere, almost like a village fete in the old days before war had torn their world apart. Daisy made her way to the sunny spot on the terrace where Lady Pendleton was sitting on a wrought-iron bench, talking to Rupert who looked much fitter and happier now, even allowing for the fact that he was still confined largely to a wheelchair.

Lady Pendleton rose to her feet as Daisy approached. 'This has all gone stunningly well thanks to your superb efforts, my dear.' She glanced down at her son with a fond smile. 'Don't you think she's a wonderful girl, Rupert?'

He nodded his head. 'Yes, Mother.'

'You mustn't tire yourself, darling,' she said, frowning.

'Perhaps he ought to go indoors, Daisy? Too much excitement might set him back.'

'I'm fine,' Rupert said wearily. 'Fine, really.'

'Oh, well, dear. You know best.' Lady Pendleton picked up her parasol and walked sedately to join a group of military men with a dazzling array of gold braid on their uniforms.

'Mother fusses,' Rupert said, patting the empty space beside him. 'Sit with me, please.'

She sat down. 'I can take you indoors if all this is too much for you, Rupert.'

'I'm home,' he said simply. 'I'm happy.'

'And you'll soon be back on your feet again,' Daisy said, curling her fingers around his. 'Some of the most eminent specialists in the country have agreed to visit on a regular basis, and there are women trained in physical therapy who will help you to become fully mobile again.'

He smiled weakly. 'I feel like a baby – learning to walk and talk.'

'You just need time to rest and recuperate, and I'm sure that being in your old room will speed your recovery.'

'You did all this for me. I can never repay you, Daisy.'

'Of course,' she said, squeezing his fingers gently. 'That's what old friends do for one another.'

A shadow crossed his face. 'Old friends?'

She leaned across to kiss him on the cheek. 'The best of friends forever.'

His mouth worked soundlessly and she patted his hand. 'It will come in time. Don't tire yourself, darling.'

The term of endearment slipped out unintentionally and she withdrew her hand hastily. He was the one who had broken their engagement and she must not distress him by reminding him of what had gone before. If she had lost him she must bear the blame. She had taken his love for granted, giving him very little in return. She had allowed her infatuation with Bowman to control her thoughts and deeds, and she had treated Rupert with callous indifference. Now, too late, she realised that Rupert was the real love of her life, only she had been too besotted to see it. She rose to her feet. 'I'll fetch you a cup of tea and a slice of cake.' She hurried off without giving him a chance to respond.

In the ensuing months Daisy found herself fully occupied with the day to day running of the home. Somehow she seemed to have taken full responsibility for organising everything from the hiring of staff to supervising the patients' menus. She used all the skills she had learned at Lamarck to run the wards and no detail was too small to escape her attention. She worked all day every day, including Sundays, and often late into the evening. But to her it was more than a job; it was the vocation that had been calling to her since she was a young girl. She was at last doing something useful and doing it well. Her parents worried that she was working too hard, but when she did visit them at Rainbow's End they had to admit that she had never looked better or been in such high spirits.

Ruby had taken to Ted without any reservations and

both Victor and Gwendoline patently adored him. He could never replace Teddy in their hearts, but they took a deep interest in the child's wellbeing, even planning to send him to a private prep school when he was old enough. Daisy did not think that Iris would approve of this idea, but she wisely said nothing.

At Christmas Ruby and Arley announced their engagement and Victor confirmed his intention of making Arley his partner in the firm. It was time, he said, to take things easy, especially as he now had a man in whom he could place complete trust to run the business to his high standards and to continue making a very nice profit. Beatrice was a picture of burgeoning motherhood and it was obvious to all that Jimmy was totally devoted to her and to their daughter. Joyce was now toddling and she followed Martin everywhere. He suffered her attentions for a time but after a while he became bored and ended up playing with his dog or with Ted. When all of three children were together it took all the adults to keep an eye on them for fear of what they might get up to next.

Rainbow's End rang with the laughter of children, the barking of the dog and the general hubbub of a growing family. The old house had been spruced up and had lost the sad, neglected look of previous years. The roof no longer leaked and the gardens front and rear were well tended. Someone had even taken the trouble to oil the front gate so that it no longer groaned a protest whenever it was opened, and the interior of the house had been polished so that the floorboards glowed like conkers freshly plucked from their shells.

The scent of lavender and beeswax mingled with the delicious aroma of freshly baked bread, which Ruby had mastered to perfection.

Daisy loved to visit, but at the end of the day she was glad to return to the relative peace and quiet of Pendleton Park. Lord and Lady Pendleton spent much of their time in London, but when they returned home they seemed content enough in their private wing of the house. Daisy had her old room, which was just across the landing from Rupert's, and she slept with the door ajar just in case he were to call out in the night. At first he had suffered from terrible nightmares, and she had had to rush into his room and stay with him until he drifted back to sleep. But after several months of intensive treatment from the specialists and therapists, these gradually lessened. Daisy had very little to do with this side of things, but she was delighted and relieved to see a definite improvement in both his speech and his movement.

There was a steady influx of soldiers in need of rest and recuperation as well as the specialist services that Pendleton Park was now able to offer. In the winter they used the long gallery for exercise and they gathered in the great hall around huge log fires in the evening after dinner to play cards, read books and magazines or even to cluster round the piano and sing the songs that had kept them going in the trenches.

With the coming of finer weather in the spring they were able to exercise in the grounds, and with the onset of summer and lighter evenings the pleasure gardens were filled with ambulant men in various stages of recovery, some of them on crutches and others pushing their more disabled comrades in wheelchairs. There were, of course, budding romances between the young nurses and their patients. Daisy did nothing to discourage these relationships unless they threatened to subvert the clearly laid out rules of conduct. She was no martinet, unlike some of the nursing sisters whom she had come across in Flanders, but this was England, and some of the men were going to need devoted wives who understood their condition and could cope with a husband with missing limbs, or suffering from shell shock, or deafened by bomb blasts, blinded by shrapnel or poisoned by chlorine gas.

Although the war seemed far distant from the peaceful English countryside, Daisy read the newspapers daily and she received short but telling letters from Clarice and some of her other friends who had remained in Flanders. Sometimes she wished that she could join them, but then she comforted herself with the fact that her work was just as vital as theirs. They were in the business of saving lives, and hers was the task of rebuilding those that had been shattered by the mindless violence of war.

She was concerned for all the men in her care, but it was hard to remain detached and professional when Rupert's progress was involved. He had responded well to treatment and gradually regained the use of his legs. She watched him critically day by day, month by month. In the summer she walked with him in the gardens, delighting in the way he managed now without crutches and the fact that his speech was improving, even though occasionally he was stuck for a word and had to stop and struggle to find the one that had slipped his mind. The temptation to prompt him was almost overwhelming, but she learned to wait until he asked for help, although this was not often. He was doggedly determined to conquer the impediment that at times caused him to stammer, and to master the language that he had had to relearn like a baby enunciating his first words. Daisy could only admire his courage and the cheerfulness with which he sought to make a full recovery.

Even though her heart was with Rupert every step of the way, she did not neglect the other patients in the home. She knew them all by name and gave each one her individual attention. She spent hours talking to those who were physically able but scarred mentally by their wartime experience, and took time to find out about their lives before the war. The men who liked working with their hands were encouraged to take up woodwork and given jobs around the estate in which they could practise their skills. Others who showed an interest in gardening were allocated plots in the walled garden where they could grow flowers or vegetables. There were jobs to be done in the stables and the motor vehicles were always in need of attention.

Those who were more academic had free run of the library and Daisy was always glad of help in the office. The patients' records were confidential but there was a seemingly insurmountable pile of correspondence to be dealt with as well as bills to be paid. Daisy was quick to spot a talent, even a latent one, and to treat the men as individuals and not pigeonhole them by their disabilities. Her understanding of what it was really like in the thick of battle and her first hand knowledge of the conditions under which the men had lived helped to lower the previously insurmountable barriers of class and sex. No matter whether the man was an officer or a private, she could talk to them on their own level, and by the end of the first year she was seeing astounding and satisfying results.

Rupert, she felt with pride, was her most outstanding success. Her heart swelled with love at the mere sight of him and she was finding it increasingly difficult to keep control of her emotions. Sometimes she was within an ace of blurting out her feelings, but then she reminded herself that it would be taking an unfair advantage. He was deeply grateful for all that she had done for him, but she did not want him to marry her out of gratitude. Sometimes she despaired, convinced that they would live for the rest of their lives merely as devoted but platonic friends.

One September evening, after dinner, Rupert suggested a walk in the pleasure gardens. Purple shadows were consuming the herbaceous borders and the last roses of summer drooped from the pergolas. The air was still warm with a touch of coolness in the light breeze that heralded the approach of autumn. Rupert linked her hand through his arm. 'Daisy, my dear girl, you know I can never repay you for what you've done for me.'

She smiled and her heartbeats quickened a little. 'What brought this on?'

He stopped beside the stone fountain, taking both her hands in his. 'There's something I have to tell you, and I'm afraid you won't like it.'

Her breath caught in her throat. 'What is it? For God's sake, Rupert, tell me.'

'I thought you might have guessed. You know me so well.'

'I'm not a mind reader.'

His eyes were troubled as he gazed into hers. 'You know Parkin drove me into Colchester yesterday.'

'Yes, of course. You said that you had business there.'

'I went to the barracks.'

She knew then what it was that he had to say. 'You've re-enlisted.'

'How would you feel if I said that I had? Would you send me off with a good heart?'

'How could I send you off with a smile, knowing what I know of war? I think you're mad, and a bit selfish.' She tore her hands free and turned away from him to hide the angry tears that threatened to spill from her eyes.

'I survived, thanks largely to you. I owe you a huge debt of gratitude.'

'A debt of gratitude.' She spun round to face him, anger replacing sorrow. 'We were going to be married. You told me that you loved me.'

'And I do,' he said softly. 'I was a stupid idiot to break off our engagement and I regretted it bitterly afterwards but it was too late to do anything about it. I love you with all my heart and soul, but I'd only be half a man if I took the easy way out. You, of all people, should understand that.'

'I don't believe you have any real feeling for me. I think you're in love with love, and I come a poor second.'

'That's just not true.' He pulled her into his arms and claimed her mouth with a kiss that was almost brutal in its intensity. 'Never say that I don't love you,' he said angrily as he released her lips, only to claim them again with a passion that both shocked and thrilled her.

She laced her fingers at the back of his neck, inhaling the scent and taste of him. She was light-headed with the release of feelings long suppressed. 'Then don't go. Stay here with me.' She leaned against him, painfully aware that his heart was beating as fast as hers. She could feel the tension in his muscles as he held her, but she knew that if she loved him she must let him go. 'You're right,' she whispered. 'I've no right to keep you here. Actually I feel the same about the FANYs but they wouldn't pass me as fit.'

He rubbed his cheek against her hair. 'Thank you, Daisy Bell, but you needn't worry. They turned me down.'

She drew away from him. 'That was cruel and unkind. Why did you let me think that you were going back to France?'

'I had to find out if your feelings for me were as deep as the ones I have for you.' He put his hand in his breast pocket and took out her engagement ring, holding it so that the diamond twinkled in the light of the huge harvest moon that hung suspended in the darkening sky. 'I'm not much of a catch, I'm afraid, but I love you more than life itself. Will you marry me, my dearest Daisy Bell?'

She held out her hand so that he could slide the ring onto her finger. 'Yes, with all my heart.' She stared at it, hardly daring to believe that she was not in the middle of a dream. 'But there's one thing we must get straight, Rupert.'

His smile enveloped her in its warmth. 'Anything. I'd give you the moon and stars if I had it in my power.'

She laid her hand on his chest, marvelling at the fire in the diamond which matched the flame in her heart. 'I can't just be a good little woman who sits at home doing nothing.'

'I realise that, my darling girl. I wouldn't have you any other way.'

'I would want to keep the convalescent home going, even after the war is ended, which according to the papers might come quite soon. I want to found a charity for the returning heroes. There's so much I have to do, Rupert.'

His lips twitched and his eyes shone with amusement. 'You drive a hard bargain, Miss Lennox. But I'm with you all the way.'

'But do you accept?'

He threw back his head and laughed. 'I thought that was my line. Yes, darling, with all my heart, I do.'